# THE OIL PRINCE

Another Karl May translation featured by the WSU Press:

*Winnetou*
Translated and abridged by David Koblick

# THE OIL
# PRINCE

**Karl May**

Translated by
Herbert Windolf

Foreword by
Albert W. Bork

WSU
PRESS

Washington State University Press
Pullman, Washington

Washington State University Press
PO Box 645910
Pullman, Washington 99164-5910
Phone: 800-354-7360
Fax: 509-335-8568
E-mail: wsupress@wsu.edu
Web site: www.wsu.edu/wsupress

©2003 by the Board of Regents of Washington State University
Translated from Karl May, *Der Ölprinz,* Karl May's Collected Works,
as published by the Karl-May-Verlag, Bamberg, Germany
First printing 2003

*Der Ölprinz* was initially published in Germany in 1877–78 in serial form. It
appeared first in book form in the German language in 1897.

*Library of Congress Cataloging-in-Publication Data*

May, Karl Friedrich, 1842-1912.
  [Der Ölprinz. English]
  The oil prince / Karl May ; translated by Herbert Windolf ; foreword by
Albert W. Bork.
    p. cm.
  ISBN 0-87422-262-1 (alk. paper)
  I. Windolf, Herbert, 1936- II. Title.
PT2625.A848O313 2003
833'.8—dc21                                                    2002155412

Illustrations by Caryn Lawton

# TABLE OF CONTENTS

Map of Old Arizona, setting of the
action described in *The Oil Prince*

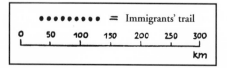

•••••••• = Immigrants' trail

0    50   100   150   200   250   300

km

# FOREWORD

ARL MAY, A POOR WEAVER'S SON, was born in Ernstthal, in the then-kingdom of Saxony, Germany, on February 25, 1842. He died on March 31, 1912, in Radebeul, Germany.

A prolific writer (with nearly 80 works to his credit) of mostly travel and adventure novels, May wrote essentially, but not exclusively, for young people. For the most part, his stories play in the American West and the Arab world. Although he visited the *eastern* United States only toward the end of his life, after he had written most of his adventure tales, his narrative was generally well researched. At times, though, he took artistic license and gently shifted historical fact and geographical detail to suit his story line. For example, although this story takes place in the late 1860s, his principal villain, the Oil Prince, encounters a never-so-named Pony Express rider in northern Arizona, even though this mail system flourished only from 1860 to 1861 and never crossed Arizona.

Because May wrote first and foremost for the German public, his western protagonists, *Westmänner*—i.e., western frontiersmen, trappers, and adventurers—were largely of German descent, particularly from his home state of Saxony. Into the frontiersman, Old Shatterhand, May projected his own fantasized self-image. Because of Old Shatterhand's ability to "shatter" an enemy with a quick blow against the brow and because he possessed two magnificent weapons—a rare repeating rifle and the large-bore "Bear Killer"—this hero accomplished great feats. In the persona of Winnetou, the author created the noble Indian, a legendary Apache chief and doer of colossal good deeds.

Millions of May's books have been sold in the German-speaking world. *The Oil Prince* alone, since first published in book form over a century ago, has seen over two million copies published and is still in print. Many generations of German youngsters have received their first introduction to the American West by reading Karl May. For many in Germany, the lure of May's *Wilder Westen* (Wild West) followed them into adulthood, as evidenced by the many annual festivities and gatherings in which men and women dress up in authentic western and Native American garb and act out events, imagined and real, that supposedly took place over a century ago in a foreign land. It is probably safe to say that Germany, like no other country outside the United States, is fascinated with America's West. The boom of German tourists who still swarm the western states is likely due in no small part to imaginations stirred by the pen of Karl May.

On a historical note, Karl May was working on this novel about the time the territorial government of Arizona was engaged in warfare with the native inhabitants of the area. The tribe identified by May as the Nijora was known by that name to the Spanish explorers in the latter years of the sixteenth century and into the seventeenth. According to the *Handbook of the American Indian* (New York and Washington, 1904), "Nijora," or "Nixora," means "slaves or enslaved" to the Pima, their neighbors to the south in Arizona. Earlier Spanish sources place the Nijora as inhabitants of the Gila River Valley to the east of present-day San Carlos. In the confusion of identities that arose during the last three decades of American warfare with the Yavapai and others in the Arizona Territory (1853–1886), the old name was apparently lost; thus May's "Nijora" Indians were probably the people anthropologists and other English-language writers now distinguish as Mohave Apache or Tonto Apache.

Albert W. Bork

# 1

## THE WAGERS

F, IN 1868, you traveled the old route from El Paso del Norte across the Colorado River to California, you would likely pass the ancient mission of San Xavier del Bac before reaching Tucson. It was located approximately nine miles south of the then-capital of the Arizona Territory in the valley of the Santa Cruz River. It was established in 1668 by the Jesuits, and, because it was such a beautiful building, such a shining witness to civilization in the midst of the Arizona wilderness would have surprised the traveler.

At each corner of the building rose a high bell tower, its front displaying rich sculptural ornamentation. The main chapel supported a large dome, and on the walls were heavy cornices and tasteful decorations. The structure would be an adornment to any large city.

This mission was partly surrounded by a village where, at the time of our story, there lived about 300 Papago Indians. The Papago, who call themselves Tohono O'odam, have always been a peaceable and industrious tribe who have made their area marvelously productive through their artificial irrigation systems. They diligently plant wheat, corn, pomegranates, squash, and other produce.

Unfortunately, these Indians suffered greatly at the hands of the white outlaws who had chosen Arizona as their playground. This territory, completely surrounded by mountains and deserts, in effect existed without government. The arm of the law could reach across the borders only with difficulty or not at all; thus many of those who disdained justice and law flooded in from Mexico and the United States to lead a life of violent brutality.

Although an army garrison was stationed in the capital and entrusted with the maintenance of public safety, there were only two companies, far too few to cover a territory of approximately 115,000 square miles. In addition, circumstances were such that these worthies were happy to be left in peace by the riffraff; help could hardly be expected from them.

This was known only too well to the bands of unprecedentedly impudent outlaws. They even approached the immediate vicinity of Tucson. No one felt secure unless he was carrying a weapon, and no one dared venture more than a quarter hour outside the town limits. An American traveler described conditions in the area in the following way: "The most desperate scoundrels from Mexico, Texas, California, and other states found a safe haven from the prosecutor. Murderers and thieves, cutthroats and gamblers formed the bulk of the population. Everybody had to be armed, and bloody scenes occurred daily. No one talked about a government, much less about protection by the law or the military. The Tucson garrison occupied itself by getting drunk and letting everything happen as it would. Thus Arizona was perhaps the only part of the country under the protective aegis of a civilized government where everyone handled justice in his own interest."

Thus it was that in San Francisco, across the mountains, honest-thinking, courageous men gathered to form a "Public Safety Committee," which was to be active throughout California, although it eventually made its strength felt in neighboring Arizona as well. Bold men appeared, now here and now there, sometimes alone, at other times in groups, to cleanse the territory of the rabble, and never did they disappear without leaving the clearest signs of having meted out judgment.

At San Xavier del Bac, an Irishman who most likely had not come to Arizona for the most honorable reasons settled among the Papago. He opened a store and offered, he said, a full line of merchandise. In truth, however, he offered for sale nothing other than a type of hard liquor that served to give him the title of "concocter of poisons." His reputation was such that honorable people did not associate with him.

On a very beautiful day in April, he sat at one of the rough-hewn tables in front of his adobe brick cabin. He seemed to be in a bad mood, for he banged the tabletop with his empty glass. When no one appeared immediately, he called angrily, turning toward the open door, "Hey, you old witch! Don't you have any ears? I want brandy. Brandy! Hurry up, or I'll show you how to get a move on!"

An old Negro woman with a bottle in hand stepped from the cabin to fill his glass. Emptying it in one gulp, he had her refill it as he remarked, "All day not a single customer has shown up! The red rascals don't want to learn how to drink. Without even a stranger showing up, I can just sit here and burn holes in my stomach!"

"No sit alone," soothed the old one. "Customers come."

"How do you know?" he asked.

"Did see."

"Where?"

"On way here from Tubac."

"Oh, really, who is it?"

"Don't know. Old eyes not recognize. It be horsemen, many horsemen."

At these words, the Irishman got up and rushed around the corner of the cabin, from where he could see along the trail to Tubac. Then he quickly returned, shouting at the old woman, "It's the Finders, do you understand, the Finders, and, not only that, but all twelve of them! They know how to drink. That'll help us out. Get inside quickly; we have to fill the bottles!"

Both disappeared into the cabin. A few minutes later, twelve horsemen entered the village, stopped in front of the shack and, after dismounting, let their horses roam freely. They were wild-looking characters, daredevils, and very well armed. Some wore Mexican garb; others hailed from the States. One could see that clearly. One thing they all had in common, though: not a single one would inspire trust by his looks.

They shouted and cursed noisily. One of them stepped to the open door, pulled his pistol, and, firing a shot into the cabin, yelled, "Hello, Paddy! Are you at home, you old poisoner? Come on out with your sulfuric acid! We're thirsty!"

As is generally known, "Paddy" is a nickname for an Irishman. The innkeeper appeared with a full bottle under each arm and holding twelve glasses. While setting the glasses out on two tables and filling them, he responded, "Here I am, sirs. You have been announced already. My Negro woman saw you coming. Drink, and receive the blessings of my house!"

"Keep the blessings to yourself, you old rascal, unless they're meant as preparation for death! Whoever drinks your stuff commits suicide!"

"Go ahead, Mr. Buttler! I'll revive you with the next bottle. Haven't seen each other for weeks. How's it been? Have you made any good deals?"

"Good deals?" answered Buttler with a disparaging wave of the hand while he downed his glass's contents, his comrades following suit. "It's been terrible, miserable as never before. Haven't made a single deal worth speaking of."

"But why? You're known as the Finders; that's what you call yourselves. Haven't you kept your eyes peeled? I'd hoped to do well by you today."

"Meaning you wanted to buy the spoils of our robberies and cheat us again, as always. This time there's nothing, really nothing. Nothing can be taken from the redskins anymore, and if you come across a white, he's the one needing to get into other people's pockets. Add to that the Public Safety Committee, the devil take them! Why do those fellows have to bother about our business? What do they care where we harvest, if neither we nor they have sown there? Really, nowadays you have to be prepared to see double-barreled rifles poking from every bush you pass! But, an eye for an eye, a tooth for a tooth! We'll hang without mercy everyone we suspect is a vigilante. Have you noticed any such kind around here, Paddy?"

"Hmm!" snorted the innkeeper. "You think me to be all-knowing? Can you tell from a person's nose whether he is a spy or, like you, an honest crook?"

"But, Paddy! A pointer is easily distinguishable from a bloodhound, even if both are human. I give you my word that I can tell at a distance of over fifty feet whether a man belongs to that committee. But something else first! We're hungry. Do you have any meat?"

"Not enough even to put on the tip of your tongue."

"Eggs?"

"Not a single one. You can run about for hours without finding a beast to slaughter, nor a hen. This is thanks to your kind, who've cleaned everyone out."

"Bread?"

"Only tortillas, and those need to be cooked first."

"Go ahead. Have your Negro woman cook. We'll supply the fresh meat ourselves."

"You? I've told you already that there's nothing to be found."

"Pshaw! We've found it already."

"What?"

"An ox."

"Really! Impossible! Where?"

"Under way, back in the valley of the Santa Cruz River. These oxen belong to a wagon train we met, or, rather, rode past."

"A wagon party? Immigrants, maybe?"

"Yes! Four wagons, each hitched to four oxen."

"How many people?" asked the innkeeper.

"Don't know exactly," said Buttler. "Besides the drivers, a few horsemen were with the wagons. I couldn't see how many people sat inside."

"But surely you talked to them?"

"Yeah. They intend to cross the Colorado and will make camp here tonight."

"Here? Hmm! I hope nothing happens that may discredit us, sir!" With these words the innkeeper made an unmistakable gesture.

"Not to worry!" responded Buttler. "We know how to spare our friends. Naturally, the wagon train must become ours, but only after they've passed Tucson. But now we'll get just one ox, because we need meat."

"Do you intend to pay for it? These people won't consider selling a draft animal."

"Nonsense! What are you thinking, Paddy? We take, we never pay. You know that. It's only different when we stop by your place. You're our fence. We not only pay you, we even let you cheat us. Besides, these folks won't offer much in the way of resistance. There are the four drivers, whom we hardly count, two boys on horseback, and the scout these immigrants have hired. He's the only one we'd need to watch out for, but the twelve of us will take care of him. He'll get the first bullet. Who rides in the wagons I don't know, as I said before. But we don't expect to receive serious opposition from a tenderfoot who'd ride below the tarp. There was also someone at the rear, but I can't say whether it was a man or woman, although he or she carried a rifle and even seemed to be wearing a sword under his coat. I also addressed this ghost, but received such a curt response that I didn't understand it. If I'm not mistaken, it was in German."

"What a joke!" scorned the Irishman. "Whoever carries a sword here is crazy and surely not to be feared. Then you're going to hold up this wagon train?"

"Certainly."

"I hope you'll cut me in on this deal."

"Of course. These are the conditions."

Just then the old Negro woman stepped from the cabin to serve the guests, so the two put their heads together to continue their conversation quietly. The other eleven paid little attention to them, talking to each other in overloud voices, all the while copiously imbibing brandy, so that the emptied bottles soon needed refilling.

The village Indians, who had to keep at their tasks, made rather wide detours around the liquor shack. They were afraid of the noisy whites, with whom they probably had had bad experiences.

The Irishman had called the twelve horsemen the "Finders." This was the name of a group of freebooters feared everywhere and who had, for some time now, been notorious throughout southern Arizona. They appeared, now here, then there, often split up and at different places simultaneously. Because the group's members were very well mounted, they were so mobile that no one, not even the vigilantes, had succeeded in catching any of them. Though they were called the Finders, one might have called them the "Resourceful," because little booty escaped this gang.

Suddenly, the gabble in front of the tavern fell silent as all eyes fell on three newcomers. Indeed, the appearance of these three men justified the surprise of anyone seeing them for the first time. After dismounting, and appearing to ignore the Finders, they moved to an empty table.

Their leader was a droll little chap. From beneath the woefully drooping brim of a felt hat whose color, age, and shape would have caused even the sharpest thinker a serious headache to determine its original state, there peered from a forest of scraggly, gray-black beard a nose of almost scary dimensions, which could have served any sundial as its shadow hand. His mighty growth of beard hid all but the so lavishly equipped olfactory organ and two small, canny eyes. These appeared to be gifted with exceptional mobility as they scanned the Irishman's "poison shack" with an expression of roguish craftiness. His surreptitious glance was in truth taking in the twelve Finders, however.

The head and neck of the little man rested on a body entirely invisible down to the knees, as it was covered by an old leather hunting coat, which, evidently, had been made for a significantly taller person. It seemed to consist of patch upon patch upon patch, giving the little man the look of a small child who, just for fun, was trying on his grandfather's dressing gown. From these more-than-adequate covers peeked two thin, bowed little legs stuck in worn-out leggings.

These leggings were so aged that the little man should have thrown them out decades ago. They afforded a sweeping view of a pair of Indian boots wherein their owner, in an emergency, could have found room for his entire body. The feet were of that extraordinary size of which one colloquially says in Germany "crossing the Rhine bridge in five steps." He held a shooting iron that looked like an old stick cut in the woods. If he had weapons stuck in his belt, they were not visible, for the hunting coat concealed them.

And his horse? It wasn't a horse, but a mule—so old that its sire must have lived just after the Flood. Its long ears, rotating like windmill vanes, were bare; it long since had lost its mane; the tail consisted of a naked stub on which ten or twelve small hairs dwelled; and, in addition, the animal was frighteningly thin. But its eyes were as clear as a young filly's and of such liveliness as would command an expert's instant respect.

The second of the three men was no less strange-looking. Infinitely tall and terribly skinny, his dried-out, bony figure hunched so far over that it seemed as if his eyes always stared at his feet, which were attached to two legs of almost frightening length. Over his solid hunting boots he had buckled a pair of leather leggings, which covered a good portion of his thighs. His body was clad in a tight-fitting hunting shirt, girded by a belt, on which hung, besides a knife and revolver, various small leather bags. Over his broad, angular shoulders was draped a woolen blanket, whose threads had been given the broadest permission to spread in all directions. On the short-cropped head sat a thing not cloth, not cap, also not hat— impossible to describe. Over one shoulder was slung an old, long shooting iron that from a distance looked more like a water hose attached to a stick than a rifle.

The last member was as tall and skinny as the second. He had a large, dark piece of cloth wrapped around his head like a turban and wore a red hussar's jacket, which, for some unknown reason, had found its way to the West. Furthermore, he sported a pair of long linen pants stuck into wading boots to which two immense spurs had been attached. Stuck in his belt were two revolvers and a knife of the best Sheffield steel. His rifle was one of those double-barreled Kentucky rifles, which, in the hands of an expert, never fail and never miss their target. If one had wanted to explore the man's face for any detail, the broad mouth was most prominent. Both corners seemed to be greatly attracted to the earlobes and approached them in the friendliest fashion. His face possessed an expression of the fairest guilelessness. In any case, its owner was surely an upright man in whom no false note could be found.

The latter two rode horses that must already have had a good many experiences behind them, but that appeared capable of undertaking more.

After the three had sat down and the innkeeper had stepped toward them to ask for their orders, the little one inquired, "What do you have to drink?"

"Brandy, sir," answered the Irishman.

"Fetch us three glasses, if there's nothing else!"

"What else should there be? Or would you perhaps like to drink champagne? You don't look as if you could pay."

"Unfortunately, unfortunately, yes," the little man nodded with a modest smile. "You, on the other hand, appear to me to be someone who would have here a few hundred thousand bottles of the very finest drink, if I'm not mistaken."

The innkeeper disappeared, brought the order, and sat down again with the twelve. The little one brought the glass to his lips, tasted the brandy, spit it out, and dumped the contents of his glass on the ground. His two companions did the same. The one in the hussar's jacket stretched his mouth even wider than it was already and exclaimed, "By the devil! I think this Irish rogue intends to murder us with his brandy! Don't you think so, Sam Hawkens?"

"Yes," answered the little one. "But he'll not succeed at that. We three can take such poison, especially because we don't drink it. But why do you call him an *Irish* rascal?"

"How did I arrive at that conclusion? Anyone who doesn't recognize him on sight as being an Irishman is as big a blockhead as I ever saw."

"Quite true! But that you figured this out immediately I find truly amazing, *heeheeeheehee!*"

This "*heeheeeheehee*" was a very peculiar, one could say, inwardly directed laugh, during which the little man's eyes sparkled merrily. Obviously, it was a habitual laugh.

"Are you trying to say," asked the first, "that I am otherwise a blockhead?"

"Otherwise? Why otherwise only? No, always, always you are one, Will Parker! For fifteen long years now I've told you that you're a greenhorn, a greenhorn such as I have never seen. Do you finally believe me now?"

"No," declared the other man, without losing his composure in the least at this insult. "Anyone who's spent fifteen years in the Wild West is no longer a greenhorn."

"On average, yes! But anyone who hasn't learned anything in fifteen years is still a greenhorn and will remain one forever, if I'm not mistaken."

And the fact that you don't realize this is the best confirmation that you are still a greenhorn. What do you think of the twelve gentlemen over there, who are looking us over so inquisitively?"

"Not much good. Do you see how they laugh? That's at you, Sam, old man."

"At me? How so?"

"Because everyone who sees you has to laugh at you."

"That pleases me, Will Parker, pleases me immensely, for, you know, it is one of my many advantages over you. Whoever casts an eye on you is bound to cry, cry bitterly. You're just such a sorry chap, a very sorry one, *heeheeheehee.*"

Sam Hawkens and Will Parker seemed to enjoy an perpetual, happy feud. Neither took insult.

So far, the third man had remained silent; now he casually pulled up his sagging leggings, stretched his long legs, and said with a bluntly ironic smile spreading across his face, "Don't know what to make of us, these gentlemen. Put their heads together and still aren't any wiser. Fine company that is, isn't it, Sam Hawkens?"

"Yep," the other man nodded. "Let them rack their brains, Dick Stone! The better then we'll know what to think of them! Thieves! Right, Dick, old man?"

"Yeah. I suspect we'll have to have a word with them."

"Me, too. But not just suspect! I figure for sure we'll have to pound our fists on their noses. It's the twelve whose tracks we picked up."

"And who followed the wagon train secretly to observe it."

"Yep, and then one of them rode over to pump the folks. Looks suspicious, very suspicious! Say, Will, have you ever heard of the Finders?"

"Heard of them!" exclaimed Parker. "Have you lost your memory, you old coon? You yourself have repeatedly talked about them!"

"I know. Just asked to find out whether you've finally learned to pay attention when experienced people talk to you. You know, then, how many Finders there are?"

"Twelve."

"And how many persons do you see sitting here, my dear Will?"

"Thirteen," said Parker, laughing merrily.

"Subtract the innkeeper, blockhead!"

"How do I do that? Will he quietly accept my subtracting him?"

"You are and will remain a greenhorn through and through! Wouldn't mind if you'd subtract yourself! Haven't learned even to subtract an

Irishman. That's why I will assist your weak mind and tell you that without him twelve persons are sitting over there. Do you get this, my dear Will?"

"Yes, dear Sam. I know you well enough to know that you'd subtract him. That's why I played dumb and pretended that I was just as bad at subtracting as you are. There, twelve there are! Not badly figured, son. I hope that, just as now, you'll make similar efforts in the future. Twelve, hmm! That's sure interesting!"

"You find this interesting?" mocked Hawkens. "Then the greenhorn has finally betrayed a trace of reflectiveness! But now tell us, why interesting?"

"There are twelve of them, and there are supposed to be twelve Finders," replied Parker with stoic calm.

"And? Continue!"

"Consequently, it can be assumed that they are perhaps the Finders."

"So it can, honorable Will. I rather suspect that they are! Supposedly, their leader's name is Buttler. We'll inquire whether there's an esquire of that name among them."

"You think they'll tell you right away?"

"Don't worry! They're curious about us, these gentlemen. Can see from the tips of their noses that soon one of them will come over to pump us. I wonder how they'll go about it."

"Not courteously, that's for sure," ventured Dick Stone. "We'll snub them good."

"Why?" asked Sam Hawkens. "Do you think we should be rude?"

"Very much so!"

"I won't do it! We three together are called the Shamrock. It's an honorable name. Can't shame it. Sam, Dick, and Will are known as three gentlemen, famous for achieving more by cunning and courtesy than by crudity and violence. That's how it'll be here, too. No other way."

"Well! But then these fellows will think we're afraid of them!" protested Dick.

"Let them, let them, Dick, old man. If they do, they'll soon enough find out they were mistaken, and very much so at that, *heeheeheehee!* The Shamrock afraid! I swear, we'll have a run-in with them. They want to hold up the wagon train, which we will not tolerate."

"Do you want to render them harmless, if they truly are the Finders?"

"Yep."

"'That'll hardly come off without a fight!"

"You think so? Pshaw! This old coon"—with that, Sam pointed at himself with obvious pleasure—"sometimes has ideas that are better than knife thrusts or rifle shots. I love to joke, and if by joking I can gain an advantage over my adversary, so much the better. Don't like to spill blood. You can overcome your enemies without killing them, wiping them out."

"A ruse then?" Parker interjected.

"Yep."

"What?"

"Don't know yet! But it'll come to me at the right time. We'll have to fake it a bit at first, make ourselves a laughingstock, act inexperienced."

"Like greenhorns?"

"Yes, like greenhorns, which for you, Will Parker, will be easy, since you really are one. Look how they laugh at my Mary, my mule!"

"But she really is no beauty, Sam!"

"A beauty? Rubbish! An ugly beast she is, a magnificently ugly beast. Nevertheless, I would not trade her for a thousand thoroughbreds. She's smart, experienced, and sensible like—like—like, yeah, like Sam Hawkens himself—and has saved my life a hundred times. I've never, ever forsaken her and would give my life to get her out of danger. My Mary is simply my Mary: unique, unsurpassable, and not comparable to any other beast."

"Just like your Liddy," Dick Stone threw in.

"Yes, Liddy, too," nodded Sam Hawkens, while his small eyes sparkled and his hand tenderly stroked his old, odd rifle. "Liddy is just as precious as Mary. She's never failed me. How often freedom and life have depended on her, and she's always done her job. She sure has her notions, and someone who doesn't know her will find his pumpkin floating upstream—what us old trappers call failure. But I know her, I've studied her as the doctor has studied boils. I know her strengths and weaknesses and where I must stroke and caress her to keep her in good spirits. She'll not leave my side until I die, and once I'm dead—should you be around—do me a favor and put my Liddy with me under the sod you use to cover me up. No one who doesn't know and love her is ever to get his hands on her. Mary, Liddy, Dick Stone, and Will Parker are the four I care most about. Beyond those I don't own or desire anything else in the whole wide world."

A moist gleam displaced the bright sparkle in his eyes, but he brushed both hands quickly across them and once again in a merry voice said, "Look, one of the twelve is getting up, the one who whispered so secretly with the innkeeper. He'll most likely come over here to monkey with us. Well, the comedy begins. But don't spoil it for me by accident!"

One should not wonder, much less smile, about Sam Hawkens giving pet names to his mule and his rifle and talking about them in such endearing terms. Old-time frontiersmen—unfortunately, their kind has died out except for the few you can count on the fingers of one hand—were a very different breed from the rabble that has followed them. The term "rabble" here refers not merely to depraved people. When a millionaire, a bank director, an officer, an attorney—for all I care, even the President of the United States himself—goes West, he is equipped with today's weapons of mass destruction and anxiously watched over and protected by numerous attendants so that not even a fly may prick his corns. When, from a safe position, he kills game by the hundreds and doesn't use the meat to feed his hunger, then this high and mighty gentleman will simply be considered "rabble" by the true frontiersman. In the old days, one could find herds of mustangs five thousand head strong. Then the bison came like an ocean wave, twenty, thirty thousand, and more. Where did these immense masses go? All gone! Across the prairies not a single mustang can be seen anymore. Exterminated, destroyed! In a national park up north, some bison are being "preserved" now. Here and there, one can still see a single one in a zoo. But on the prairies, where they earlier roamed in the millions, they are extinct. The Indians starve physically and morally, and a real, true frontiersman can be seen only in picture books. This is the fault of what the trapper calls "rabble." Don't say it is caused by the advance of civilization. Civilization's task is not extermination and destruction. Once the Pacific railroad began running, how often did companies of a hundred or more "gentlemen" gather for a hunting trip? They steamed to the West, had the train stopped on the prairies, and from their safe compartments shot at the passing herds of bison. Then they moved on, left the corpses to rot, boasted of being successful prairie hunters and of having been greatly entertained. But for each animal killed in a hunt, ten or more were wounded and painfully dragged themselves on, only to perish miserably. From afar the Indian looked on in powerless rage as he was robbed of his sustenance, driven to hunger, and unable to fight it. If he complained, he was laughed at. If he fought, he was slaughtered like the bison he thought were his property and he had therefore preserved.

Totally different was the real frontiersman, the true hunter. He did not shoot more than he needed. He obtained meat at his life's peril. On his horse he rode into the midst of the bison herd. He struggled with the mustang he wanted to catch and tame. Even the grizzly he faced courageously. His life consisted of a never-ending, but chivalrous, battle against hostile conditions, hostile animals, and hostile people. All he had was his ability to rely on himself, on his horse, and on his rifle if he did not want to be wiped out. The horse was therefore his friend, as was his rifle. Many a hunter often risked his life for his horse. And with what love did he care for his rifle, this inanimate, soulless object upon which his grateful fantasy nevertheless bestowed a soul. He hungered and thirsted, only to have his horse eat and drink first, and he looked after his rifle before himself. Both objects he named as if they were human beings and talked with them when he camped alone on the grasses of the prairie or the mosses of the forest.

Sam Hawkens was this type of frontiersman. The harshness of his rough life had not corrupted his heart; he had remained a tender-hearted, though extraordinarily crafty, child.

What Sam Hawkens expected did happen: Buttler arose and came over, planted himself imperiously in front of their table, and said sneeringly, without any greeting, "How well you people look! You seem to be a most peculiar, extremely ridiculous trio!"

"Yes," confirmed Sam in a very modest and serious tone.

This confession sounded so funny that Buttler laughed aloud, and while his companions joined in the laughter, he continued, "Who are you, actually?"

"I'm the first," answered Sam.

"I'm the second," added Dick Stone.

"And I'm the third," chimed in Will Parker.

"The first, the second, the third? What else?" asked Buttler.

"Well, triplets, of course!" said Sam with a very innocent countenance.

General laughter again followed these words. Buttler had been beaten. Annoyed, he bellowed at the little one, "Quit making stupid jokes! I'm used to being talked to seriously. That you can't be triplets is obvious. I want to know your names. Out with them now!"

"I'm called Grinell," answered Sam dejectedly.

"And I'm Berry," confessed Dick timidly.

"Mine's White," Will fearfully sputtered forth.

"Grinell, Berry, and White," said Buttler. "Hmm. Now tell me what you are!"

"Trappers," explained Sam Hawkens.

"Trappers?" laughed the interrogator. "You don't look to me as if you could ever have trapped a beaver or a raccoon!"

"Which we haven't yet," little Sam modestly admitted.

"Ah, haven't yet! Still want to?"

"Yes."

"Good, very good! Where do you come from?"

"From Castroville, Texas."

"What did you do there?"

"Had a clothing store, the three of us."

"That so! Probably didn't make it?"

"No. Had a little bankruptcy. Lent too much, gave credit, but didn't get any ourselves."

"Righto! Clothing merchants, maybe even tailors. Three tailors who went broke through clumsiness and now had the smart idea to get a new start as trappers! Did you hear that?"

This question was directed at his mates, who were following the conversation with mocking pleasure. A third wave of laughter arose from them. But Sam Hawkens shouted back in feigned anger, "Clumsiness! There you're very much mistaken, sir! We knew what we were about. We had to get something out of the bankruptcy, otherwise we wouldn't have gone through with it." He opened his leather hunting coat, tapped his broad belt, which produced a metallic sound, and added proudly, "Here's the money, sir!"

Buttler's face took on the expression of a raptor searching for prey. In a most disingenuous voice he asked, "You've got money? Then you certainly have been smarter than you look. How much did the bankruptcy bring in?"

"Over two thousand dollars."

"You carry it on you?"

"Yes."

"While traveling in this unsafe territory!"

"Pshaw! We've got weapons."

"They'd be of damn little use to you if the Finders should come, for example. They'd take you three tailors before you could open your eyes. Why didn't you entrust that much money to a bank?"

"We'll do that yet. Up in Prescott."

"That's where you're going?"

"Yes."

"As trappers?"

"Yes."

"Have you got traps?"

"No."

"Where do you expect to get them?"

"Buy them in Prescott."

"By heaven! You people! What do you think to catch up there?"

"Beaver and—and—and— ." Embarrassed, Sam stopped.

"And—and—what else?" Buttler pressed the little man.

"Grizzlies."

That's when a truly Homeric laughter arose from the other tables. Buttler laughed, too, tears filling his eyes, and, once he had regained his breath somewhat, called, "You want to trap grizzly bears? Grizzly bears, which grow nine feet tall and may weigh a thousand pounds! Catch them in traps?"

"Why not?" grumbled Sam, "if the traps are big and strong enough!"

"But there are no grizzly bear traps and will not be!"

"Then we'll have some made by a blacksmith in Prescott."

"How? What design?"

"We'll tell him in good time."

"You three tailors? Stop, little one, fat one, stop, or I will choke!"

Again Buttler laughed uproariously and only after a while was able to continue, "Even if you had been joking and really had your sights set on beaver, thinking that you wanted to trap beaver up in Prescott might make a person die from laughter."

"To Prescott for that? No! We only want to buy the traps there. Then we'll ride to the headwaters of the Verde River."

"Which has almost no water. So where are the beavers to come from?"

"Leave that to us, sir! I've read a book about everything, even about beavers."

"Fine, fine, excellent! If you're so smart as to follow a book, nothing more can be said. I wish you as many beavers and bears as you want. But you will find other things."

"What?" asked Sam, asked innocently.

"Savage Indians, sneaking up on you by day and night."

"We'll defend ourselves."

"With your weapons perhaps?"

"Yes."

"For instance, with this rifle of yours?"

"Yes."

"Jeez, you are going to perform monstrously heroic deeds. Let me have a look at this musket! We positively have to see it."

He took the rifle from Sam Hawkens's hand and went over to his companions, who looked it over with the most raucous comments. Dick Stone, too, had to show his long rifle, to the same mocking approval.

Upon returning the rifles, Buttler said, "All right. I just hope for your own sake that you can handle your rifles now as well as you did your sewing needles before."

"Not to worry!" claimed Sam with assurance. "We hit what we want to hit."

"Really?"

"Really!"

"Shooting contest, shooting contest!" whispered those sitting closest to Buttler.

In the West, where just about every man is a good shot, no one misses the opportunity for a shooting contest. The shooters like to compare themselves. The victor's fame travels far, and substantial sums are often wagered. Here the opportunity offered itself not just for betting, but even for fun. The three tailors most likely had not learned how to handle rifles, and since theirs weren't worth much, there would be lots to laugh about while getting them to demonstrate their supposed skill. Therefore Buttler said in a doubtful tone to goad Sam, "Sure, even a blind man can hit the sleeve of a coat with a sewing needle. But shoot, shoot, that is something very different. Have you ever fired a shot before, Mr. Grinell?"

"Yes," answered the little man.

"At what?"

"At sparrows."

"With this rifle?"

"With a blowgun!"

"With a blowgun!" Buttler laughed out loud. "So you think you'll also be a good shot with a rifle?"

"Why not? Aiming is aiming, isn't it?"

"So, then. From how far away can you hit something?"

"From as far as a bullet will travel."

"Say, two hundred paces?"

"Well."

"That's about as far as the second shack over there. Do you believe you can hit it?"

"The shack?" Sam exclaimed indignantly. "A blind man can hit it, the same as the needle hits the coat's sleeve."

"Are you saying the target should be smaller?

"Yes."

"About how large?"

"The size of my hand."

"And you think you can hit it with your gun here?"

"Yes."

"Nonsense!" snorted Buttler. "This barrel will burst on the first shot, and if it doesn't, it's so crooked your bullets will travel around the corner of any house, but will never fly straight."

"Let's try it!"

"Shall we bet? You've got the money. How much is it to be?"

"Whatever you say."

"A dollar?"

"Agreed."

"Then the bet stands," announced Buttler. "But we won't shoot at that shack over there, since its owner may not like that, but I—"

"Shoot at mine!" interrupted the innkeeper. "I'll stick a piece of paper as large as my hand on the back. That'll be the target!"

This suggestion was accepted. Everyone went around back. The paper was put up, and Buttler counted off two hundred paces. He pulled out a dollar and Sam gave his. Then they drew lots for who was to shoot first. The lot fell to Buttler. He took his position at the measured distance, aimed only very briefly, fired, and hit the paper.

Now it was Sam's turn. He placed his crooked little legs as far apart as he could, leveled his Liddy, bent way, way forward, and aimed for a long time. In this position he looked like a photographer bending under his camera cover to adjust the focus. Everyone laughed. Finally the shot rang out and Sam fell sideways, dropping the rifle and holding his right cheek with his hand. The laughter turned to hooting.

"Did the gun butt you, even kick you?" Buttler asked sympathetically.

"Yes, it sure was a slap!" responded the little man sadly.

"Then the thing kicks. It seems to be more dangerous to you than to other people. Let's see whether you've hit the target."

Not a trace of Sam's bullet was to be seen on the paper. Finally, somebody called to the others amidst roars of laughter, "Come over here! There it is, there, in the barrel. The liquor is running out the hole!"

Standing beside the house, maybe ten paces away, was a full barrel of brandy, obviously intended for shipping. The bullet had entered this barrel, and everyone could see its contents streaming out of the bullet hole in a finger-thick jet. The laughter rose and seemed like it would never cease. But the innkeeper cursed and demanded compensation. When Sam agreed, he calmed down and pounded a wooden peg into the hole to close it.

"You didn't even hit the house!" shouted Buttler at the very nonplussed little man. "Didn't I tell you that your bullets would fly around every corner? The dollar's mine. Would you wager another one, Mr. Grinell?"

"Yes," answered Sam.

His second shot at least hit the house, but very low down at the corner, although the target was in the middle of the wall. He fired four or five more shots without getting closer to the paper and lost just as many dollars. Then he got angry and shouted, "It's only because we're betting a measly dollar. I believe I can hit closer if more is at stake."

"Suits me fine," laughed Buttler. "How much do you want to bet?"

"Whatever you say."

"Shall we say twenty?"

"Sure."

Sam also lost the twenty, because he hit exactly the same corner. Buttler raked in the money and said, "Do you want to try once more, Mr. Grinell?" At that he merrily and surreptitiously winked at his mates.

"Yes," said Sam. "It must work at least once."

"I think so, too. How much?"

"Fifty dollars."

"Okay."

"Or shall we say a hundred?"

"That's too much. I am convinced that I will finally hit the target, but I'd hate to take such a sum from you. Mr. —What's your name, sir?"

"Buttler," answered the other rather too quickly and incautiously. He would probably have used another name had he not been so taken by surprise by Sam's question.

"Fine, Mr. Buttler," Sam continued. "But not a hundred. That's too much."

"Nonsense! What I've said, I'll do. It's just a question of whether you have the guts."

"Guts? A tailor always has guts."

"A hundred then?"

"Yes."

Buttler was so sure he'd hit the target and Sam's shot would go astray that he aimed even more briefly than before. Maybe the size of the bet excited him, but for whatever reason, his bullet hit beside—close, but still beside—the target. His shot did not rob him of his good mood, however, for his adversary still would not come as close. In the worst case, they would tie, and a tie would assure his victory.

Now Sam aimed, but at what? For the wall's corner, where, except for the first shot, bullet upon bullet had hit.

"What are you thinking, Mr. Grinell?" called Buttler in surprise. "You're aiming for the corner!"

"So I am," answered the little man confidently.

"But why?"

"I have just now figured out my rifle."

"How so?"

"Seems to have its own mind, its moods. If I aim for the paper up there in the middle, the bullet goes down there into the corner. If I therefore aim for the corner, it should head up there for the paper."

"This is madness!"

"Not mine, but the gun's. Watch!"

He fired, and the bullet hit—exactly at the target's center.

"Now you see that I was right!" laughed the little one. "I've won! Shell out the hundred dollars, Mr. Buttler!"

The monies had not been placed yet. Buttler hesitated. He considered denying payment. But then a thought struck him. He pulled the gold pieces from his pocket, gave them to Sam, and said, " Shall we quit?"

"As you like."

"Or shall we bet once more?"

"Fine by me!"

"But not a hundred—two hundred!"

"Good! My buddy, Mr. Berry, can be the referee and hold the money, and let's take a new piece of paper and mark a point at its center. Whoever's bullet is closest to this point is the winner."

"Agreed," declared Buttler. "But we don't shoot from a distance of two hundred, but three hundred paces."

"I won't hit anything from there!"

"Isn't necessary. Get going, Mr. Grinell, two hundred dollars on the table!"

Sam gave the money to Dick Stone. Buttler didn't seem to have that much anymore, for he went to several of his mates for assistance. When he had the sum together, he also gave it to Dick, who knew very well why Sam had proposed him as referee. After a new piece of paper had been put up, three hundred paces were measured off, and Buttler prepared himself for his shot.

"Aim better than before!" one of his men called out.

"Be quiet!" he responded angrily. "A tailor will not beat me!"

"He did before!"

"It was a fluke, nothing else."

Nevertheless, this time he aimed more carefully and took much longer than before. His shot hit the paper, although not its center.

"Great shot, top-notch shot, fine shot!" his companions praised him. Now it was Sam's turn. He aimed and the shot rang out. Multiple shouts of shock and anger ensued. He had hit the exact center. Dick Stone hurried over to him and held out the money, murmuring, "Take it quickly, Sam, old man, or you won't get it!"

"Well, I'd have had to hand it over later, anyway." Pocketing it, he stepped toward the cabin.

"Unbelievable, damned luck!" Buttler shouted at him angrily. "I've never seen such luck!"

"Not by me, that's for sure," admitted Sam, that being the truth, for he was such an excellent shot that it did not take luck. Buttler, however, took these words in a different sense and said, "Then return the money!"

"Return it! Why?"

"Since you just admitted that the target wasn't hit by you, but by luck."

"Fine! But Lady Luck guided my hand and my rifle; she guided my hand, which did hit the target and thus won the bet. The money belongs to her, and I will turn it over to her as soon as I meet her again."

"Is that meant to be a joke, sir?" inquired Buttler threateningly, while his men formed a tight circle around him and Sam.

The little man did not show the least concern and replied calmly, "Sir, tailors are not in the habit of making jokes when money is involved. Shall we continue shooting?"

"No. I was betting against you, not against your luck. Does it always favor you?"

He winked furtively at his companions as he told them not to start anything. Sam noticed, though, and answered smilingly, "Always, when it's worthwhile. Not for a lousy dollar, though; in that case, my bullet would much rather hit the corner."

Just as they started to round the corner to return to the front of the cabin, someone approached from the opposite side. This somebody was— Sam Hawkens's mule, who was looking inquisitively for its master. Buttler, who was in the lead, almost collided with the animal.

"Ugly beast!" he shouted and hit Mary on the head with his fist. "It's a real, true tailor's steed! In his entire life it would never occur to another man to mount such a beast!"

"Absolutely true!" agreed Sam. "There's only the question, 'Why?'"

"Why? What do you mean? Are you perhaps saying your billy goat cannot be mounted?"

"No, sir. I simply meant to say that only a very good horseman can mount her."

He had voiced this statement in such a peculiar tone that Buttler inquired at once, "Are you implying that I am not a good horseman, that I could not get your beast to move?"

"Don't know, sir, although I would expect her to throw you within a minute."

"Me? The best horseman between Frisco and New Orleans? You're crazy!"

Sam gave him a curiously measured look from head to toe, then asked incredulously, "You, the best horseman? I don't believe that. You are not built for riding. Your legs are too long."

"Not built for riding!" cried Buttler, cracking up. "What does a tailor know of horsemanship! When you arrived earlier, you were perched on your beast like an ape on a camel. You want to talk about horsemanship? You are laughable! I'll take your mule between my legs, and it'll collapse within five minutes!"

"Or throw you off within one minute! Want to bet?"

"I bet ten dollars!" cried Buttler, who no longer had enough money to bet at a higher level.

"Me, too!"

"Fine, ready, out with the ten dollars!"

Sam pulled out the money, giving it again to Dick Stone.

Buttler borrowed money from his companions and also handed it to Dick. He would much rather have entrusted it to one of his people, but did not want to arouse suspicion.

"A horrible bet!" the innkeeper told him. "To mount such a monster just to make ten bucks! But this time you'll surely win."

Buttler took old Mary by the bridle and led her away from the corner and toward the open space in front of the house. "Off within the minute, then!" he called to Hawkens. "If I'm still on then, I've won."

"May I talk to the animal?" asked Sam.

"Why not? Talk to her, whistle at her, or sing with her, just as you please!"

Two groups had formed: here Sam with Dick and Will, there the innkeeper with Buttler's people. Buttler mounted. The mule let it happen,

"Throw him off, my dear bucking Mary!"

standing quietly and motionless as if carved of wood. That's when Sam spoke, "Throw him off, my dear bucking Mary!"

Immediately the mule made a round, high cat's hump, leapt into the air with all four legs, then stretched out and returned to the ground simultaneously with the rider, meaning Buttler no longer sat in the saddle, but beside Mary on the ground. His men cried out in surprise. He jumped up, shouting angrily, "This beast is the devil's!! First it stands piously like a lamb, then it suddenly rises into the air like a balloon! I'm not sure I understood right. Did you tell the animal to throw me off?"

"Yes," nodded Sam, pocketing his winnings.

"Sir, I won't allow that!"

"Pshaw! You said I could talk to her as I pleased."

"But not to my detriment!"

"It was to your advantage. You have only to listen to what I say to know what the animal is going to do and what you have to do in response, if you are as good a horseman as you claim."

"Well, then, I'll win for sure next time. I will not be thrown off again. Will you bet another ten dollars?"

"With pleasure."

Buttler once more borrowed the money, gave it to Dick, and told Sam while mounting again, "Now tell the rogue once more what to do!"

Sam briefly laughed merrily and told the mule, "Strip him off, my dear stripping Mary!"

Mary immediately fell into a gallop, against which all of Buttler's efforts were in vain, took a turn toward the cabin's lower corner, then paralleled the wall so closely that Buttler's right leg got hung up at the corner. If he did not want to have it severely scraped or even broken, he had to get out of the saddle. He was "stripped off" and once again landed sitting on the ground.

"Nine and ninety thousand devils!!" he raged while getting up and checking his knee. "This brute is truly a hellish beast. Naturally, I was prepared for being thrown off."

"And I advised Mary to strip you off this time," grinned Sam. "We agreed that I could talk, whistle, or sing with the mule, just as I pleased. I'll keep to that. The money's mine."

He took it. Buttler limped to the innkeeper and asked him in an undertone, "Give me twenty dollars! My people are broke."

"You want to bet again?" asked the Irishman.

"Naturally!"

"You'll lose again! Who'll pay me back?"

"Me, you blackguard, me!"

"But when?"

"Early tomorrow."

"Tomorrow morning? When he has taken everything from you?"

"Blockhead! It's borrowed only. Would my people look on so quietly if they didn't know that by tomorrow morning I would have my money back and plenty more besides?"

"Ah, the two thousand dollars that belongs to these tailors?"

"Yes."

"Be careful, sir! This guy isn't as stupid as we thought."

"Pshaw! All luck!"

"The shooting, yes, but probably not the thing with the mule."

"That, too! The animal is an old discharge from a circus he bought for a few dollars. It knows these two tricks; that's it. Come, give me the money! I've got to get at least the last two ten-dollar bets back."

When the innkeeper had fetched the money from the cabin, he called to Sam Hawkens, "Will you wager once more?"

"Sure, but this is the last time."

"Agreed. But for twenty dollars!"

"Okay."

"Here's the money. To that I add my most sacred assurance that your monster will not get me off this time, no matter what it tries."

He mounted, took Mary's bridle, gripped her firmly between his legs, then listened for Sam to command either throwing or stripping. The little man, though, ordered neither of the two, but called, "Roll him off, my dear rolling Mary!"

The mule immediately fell to the ground and rolled like a barrel. If Buttler did not want to have all his limbs crushed or even broken, he had to let go of the reins and take his feet out of the stirrups. Hardly had Mary felt she was rid of him than she jumped up, trotted to her master, let out a triumphant bray, and rubbed her muzzle on his shoulder.

Buttler rose slowly, felt himself from top to bottom, front to back, and produced a most indescribably silly face. Although he was furious for the multiple losses he had suffered, he did not want to let on. All his muscles and bones hurt, though, since Mary had felt like a steamroller running over him.

"Do you perhaps want to bet once more?" Sam Hawkens asked him.

"Go to the devil with your infamous beast!" growled Buttler, sitting down.

"I'll have no business with Satan, Mr. Buttler. That's why I will go where I please."

"To Prescott?"

"Yes."

"Today?"

"No. We'll stay overnight in San Xavier del Bac."

"Have you found lodging already?"

"No, it's not necessary. We'll sleep in the open."

"Have you got food?"

"Not yet. Thought we could get something here."

"Fat chance. Nothing's to be had anymore. You can fill up only if you'll be our guests. Will you accept my invitation?"

"Done, sir. When shall we eat?"

"When the meat has arrived. I'll let you know."

This ended the wagers, and the two groups once more kept to themselves.

A large, covered wagon drawn by four oxen had appeared
in the open space, followed by three others.

# 2

## THWARTED PLANS

"YOU DID A FINE JOB!" said Dick Stone to Sam. "I would have loved to help!"

"Wasn't necessary, if I'm not mistaken. They truly think we are tailors, *heeheeheehee!* And Buttler is the fellow's name!"

"That means they *are* the twelve Finders. Bad company, and that for dinner!"

"It wouldn't have been necessary to accept their invitation; we still have provisions for an entire day in our saddlebags, enough to last us until we get to Tucson. But I intend to arrest them, you know."

"Arrest them? How?"

"We'll see."

"We should have taken off. It's a very dangerous neighborhood here for us. Surely the Finders will want to relieve you of the winnings!"

"That's a given. But we'll make it hard for them. I'm not afraid of them, especially since I saw how easily they can be duped. Believing us to be tailors, us, the Shamrock!"

"You're a slyboots, Sam, old man!"

"I'm quite happy with my head, although it's a bit off-kilter already! Once I even owned my own hair together with the skin to which it was attached. I had worn it honestly and lawfully from childhood on, and no lawyer had dared contest it, until about one or two dozen Pawnee turned up around me, cutting and tearing the hide off my living head. Went to Tekama, then, and bought myself a new skin. They call it a wig, and it cost me three thick bundles of beaver skins, if I remember rightly. No harm done, though, for the new coat is at times more practical than the old one, especially in summer. I can take it off when I'm hot, can wash it and comb it, all without scratching my head. And if a redskin should demand my scalp once again, I can present it to him, eliminating any effort on his part and pain to myself, *heeheeheehee.*"

"And how silly," interjected Will Parker, "to truly believe we wanted to trap beaver, even grizzlies, up on the Verde River!"

"Wasn't as silly as you think," explained Sam. "They've clearly noticed that you're a greenhorn, and anything can be expected of a greenhorn, even that he wants to trap seals and whales in a hayloft. They spoke of expecting meat to arrive. But from where? From Tucson maybe? Can hardly believe it. They'll steal it— Look, there they come," he said suddenly, interrupting himself. "We'll get to know them now."

He pointed toward the front, where a large, covered wagon drawn by four oxen had appeared in the open space, followed by three others. A very well armed horseman rode up front, Mister Poller, the scout. Beside the wagon rode two boys, or young men, who also carried knives, revolvers, and double-barreled rifles. The drovers went on foot. Two of the wagons carried passengers. One could see them peering curiously from beneath the cover.

The scout seemed to have intended to stop here, but when he saw the lot in front of the tavern, his face darkened and he rode on. The wagons followed him.

"Damn!" said one of the Finders in a low voice to the innkeeper. "There goes our roast for the night. Who knows how far from here they'll stop now."

"They won't get far. You could see the oxen were tired. Did you watch the scout's face?"

"No."

"It changed when he saw you." The Irishman continued, "I bet he's suspicious of you because you pumped him too much. He would've made camp here, but continued because of you—probably only to the other end of the village, though, where there's grass for the oxen."

"We'll have a look."

"Don't do it. If he sees you, his suspicion will increase."

"That's true," Buttler agreed. "We'll have to wait until dark. Then I'll follow them with a few of my men. They'll let the oxen graze freely. We'll lead one away and butcher it."

"And will be caught!" the innkeeper threw in.

"What do you mean, caught? If someone comes, we'll be sitting here at your place eating roast beef. That's all. The missing ox, though, lies butchered far outside the village. Who'll be able to prove that we're the perpetrators?"

"We'll be eating the piece of meat missing from the dead ox!" pointed out the innkeeper.

"That's no proof," Buttler replied, "for we'll have just bought it from an unknown redskin. And if they bother us further, we have rifles and knives to keep them off our backs."

"The three tailors over there will eat with us?"

"Yes. You know, Paddy, I have a thought. Let's get them drunk!"

"To get them—?"

"Yeah, to get them—just what you think."

"At my house?"

"Yeah, inside the tavern. It would be impossible here in the open. There could be hidden witnesses."

"But it's really dangerous for me to have something like this take place in my house, in my tavern—"

"Be quiet! You'll get three hundred dollars from what we find on them. That's enough for the small inconvenience—agreed?"

"Yes, since there's no alternative. But I'm afraid these guys will be difficult to get drunk."

"On the contrary! Easy, very easy. Didn't you see them spill your booze?"

"Any innkeeper would notice that!"

"It follows that they are no drinkers and can't stomach anything. After a few glasses, they'll be skunked, totally drunk."

"From this I conclude that they're not drinkers and therefore will not drink anything," the Irishman noted wryly. "How do you propose to get them drunk?"

"Hmm, that's also possible. Don't you have anything but liquor?"

The innkeeper made a face he supposed to be sly and answered, "For good friends and for honest payment, somewhere in the house I have a small barrel of very powerful Caliente wine from California—"

"Caliente wine? The devil you say! Serve it, get it out for us!" Buttler exclaimed. "A single quart of it will topple those three tailors, and for us the Caliente will be a true delight. How rare to come across a fine drop like this! How much will it cost?"

"Sixty dollars for the ten gallons."

"A bit expensive, but agreed. Then you will get $360 from what the next night will net us."

"Why do you want to go out of your way with those tailors, sir? Invite them, eat with them, entertain them, get them drunk, and so on? Isn't there a shorter and better way?"

"Maybe. But, Paddy, I've got to tell you: there's something in the manners of those three men that doesn't quite convince me that they're tailors. I've thought about it. I'm starting to think that the shots the little one fired were masterly, even the first two misses. We saw him aim at the paper and yet, it's possible, with a lightning-fast movement of the rifle we didn't even notice, that he sent bullet after bullet into the corner intentionally. Look at how they sit there! Never mind that they don't look over here even once. I tell you they know everything anyway; it's like their eyes are on us all the time. I'm aware of their masked, spying glances. And their stance! As if they were ready to draw their pistols at a moment's notice. To attack them, to take them by surprise wouldn't be easy, especially if they happen to be lightning-fast with their knives and bullets."

"But twelve or even thirteen against three! That should assure the result!" reasoned the innkeeper.

"Indeed. But of the twelve of us, some will surely be wounded or even killed. Incapacitation by getting them totally drunk is the safest and least dangerous—"

Buttler stopped in midsentence, pointed to the open courtyard, and continued, "Here comes the strange figure that followed behind the wagons. It fell behind, doesn't see the wagon train any more, and is obviously at a loss as to where to go."

The description "strange figure" was definitely appropriate, saying too little rather than too much. While it slowly rode closer, the figure made regular, almost exactly timed pendulum movements on its horse: now with the legs far back, the head sunk forward, then quickly back with the head, the legs moving forward. The body was clad in a long, wide raincoat, the head covered by a large piece of cloth, the end of which fell to the back of the horse. The figure's feet were shod in riding boots. On its shoulder hung a rifle and below its gray coat seemed to hang a saber. The face, peering from the cloth, was beardless, full and red, and, by the way the figure was dressed, one really could not tell whether a man or a woman sat on the slow, scrawny mount. And the enigmatic being's age? Perhaps between thirty-five or forty years old.

The figure arrived near the tables, checked the horse, and greeted everyone in a high falsetto voice, "A good day to you, gentlemen! Have you perhaps seen four ox-drawn wagons?"

This lady-gentleman, or gentleman-lady, spoke in German, of which those questioned had no knowledge, which is why no response was given. When the question was repeated at a D-natural pitch, Sam Hawkens got up, stepped over to the horse, and responded in German, "Don't you speak English?"

"No, only German."

"May I ask who you are?"

That's when he heard at a minor third higher, that is, at an F-natural, "I am Mr. Cantor Emeritus Matthäus Aurelius Hampel from Klotzsche near Dresden."

"Klotzsche near Dresden? Then you must be from Saxony?"

"Yes, a born Saxon, but now retired."

"I am a German, too, at least, of German descent. I've been roving about America for some time. You probably belong to the four wagons, Mr. Cantor?"

"Yes. But if you please, address me by my correct title: Mr. Cantor Emeritus! Then everybody knows right away that I have retired from organ and church service to dedicate my outstanding talents exclusively to the harmonic goddess of music."

Sam's little eyes sparkled with mirth, yet he spoke seriously, "Well, Mr. Cantor Emeritus, your wagons have long passed and will, I suppose, have stopped on the other side of the village."

"How many beats will I have to ride on yet?"

"Beats?"

"Hmm—'paces' I meant to say."

"Like you, I don't know that, either, since I, too, am here for the first time. Will you permit me to guide you?"

"Very well, esteemed sir. I shall be the melody and you the accompaniment. If, on the way, we do not make any long quarter intermissions and fermata, we will presumably arrive at the wagons with the finale."

Sam shouldered his Liddy, whistled for his Mary, who followed him like a dog, took the horse of the enigmatic human being by the reins, and proceeded in the direction the wagons had taken.

He continued the conversation, "So you compose, Mr. Cantor Emeritus?"

"Yes, day and night."

"What?"

"A great theatrical opera for three evenings in twelve acts, four acts for each evening. You know, a work like *Der Ring der Nibelungen* by Richard Wagner, but this time not by him, but by me, Mr. Cantor Emeritus Mattheus Aurelius Hampel from Klotzsche near Dresden."

"Why can't you compose this at home?" asked Sam. "What is it that drives you to America, even Arizona, the most dangerous part of the Wild West?"

"What drives me? The Spirit, the Muse, who else? The gifted son of the Muse must follow the goddess's inspirations."

"I don't understand. I do not follow any goddess, only my intellect."

"Because you are not gifted. One does not compose an opera with intellect, but with general bass and counterpoint, that is, when a fitting libretto exists. And text is the spring that catapulted me to America."

"How so, Mr. Cantor?"

"Kindly repeat correctly: 'Cantor Emeritus'! Only to be accurate. One might otherwise think that I still play the organ at Klotzsche near Dresden, whereas I have had a successor for two years already. You know, in my head my opera is already finished, but I am still missing suitable text. I need a powerful, gigantic, cyclopean plot, for my opera is to be a hero's opera. That is why I have had to search out heroes on my own, but, unfortunately, I have not found any truly suitable ones, for I want new, original heroes, not yet put on the stage. Then from time to time there resides close to Dresden my friend and patron Hobble-Frank, and he—"

"Hobble-Frank lives there? You know him?" Sam quickly interjected in surprise.

"Yes. You, too?"

"Very well, very well! Go on, go on!"

"And he directed my attention to the kind of heroes I require."

"You don't say, Mr. Cantor!"

"For the third, if not the fourth, time I have asked you: Mr. Cantor Emeritus! Only to prove my integrity. One might otherwise think I pretend to a position I have not held for two years. Well, then, Hobble-Frank made me aware of heroes suited to an opera, first, naturally, in his own person and, later, through other men with whom he had earlier performed exceptional deeds here in the Wild West, and whom he has probably met up with once more."

"Who are these people?"

"An Apache chief by the name of Winnetou, two white prairie hunters named Old Shatterhand and Old Firehand, and many others. Do you also possibly know these three?"

"I think so, *heeheeheehee!* I tell you, from me you can hear so much about these men that you'll be able to compose twenty operas. To be sure, you'll have to write the music to it yourself."

"Naturally, naturally! Hobble-Frank has told me about all the adventures he has had with these gents. It would be most welcome if I could learn of other deeds from you, since it enriches my material."

"You shall learn more than you'll need. But didn't you say just now that Hobble-Frank has again met up with the others?"

"Yes. That is what I said. I suppose it to be the case, but I cannot confirm it with certainty. As it was, I had not been home for several days. When I returned, I found a note in which he invited me to join him immediately, were it still my intention to accompany him to America, to get to know the heroes for my opera personally. Naturally, I looked him up at once, but it was too late, for his villa "Bärenfett"* was closed up—locked, no one there—and from his neighbor I learned that Hobble-Frank had been traveling for some time. I took it as self-evident that he went to America, and I simply followed."

"Why, however, to this wild Arizona territory? Do you have reason to believe him to be in this area?"

"Yes, for he spoke frequently to me about Arizona and Nevada and mentioned that he would take off for there immediately, should he hear that one of his former companions was going there. He keeps in touch with them. Since he departed so suddenly without waiting for me, I presume he received such notice from one of his friends."

"And on that basis, just on that, you have embarked on this distant journey?"

"Why not? A country is a country, whether it is called Saxony or Arizona. Why would one meet greater difficulty in one versus the other?"

"What a statement! First, you have to consider that Arizona and Nevada are much larger than Saxony, and to that you have to add the conditions here. Do you have any idea how many and which Indian tribes live here?"

"They do not concern me!"

---

* "Bärenfett" means Bear Fat.

"Have you heard of the country's impassability, the wild canyons, the desolate mountains, the wretched deserts, particularly the one between California, Nevada, and Arizona?"

"Does not concern me either!"

"Do you understand the Indians' language, or the local whites'?"

"Do not need it! My language is music."

"But the Indian will absolutely not speak and deal with you musically! It appears you are totally unaware of the dangers you expose yourself to if you want to find Hobble-Frank."

"Dangers? I have told you already what I think about it. A disciple of the arts, a son of the Muses, does not have to fear dangers. He stands high above ordinary life. Just as the violin is above the double bass. He lives and breathes the ether of heavenly harmonics and does not have to deal with earthly dissonances."

"Well! Then just once have an Indian pull the scalp from your ears and tell me what heavenly harmonics you have perceived! Hereabouts there's only one music, and that's this one." Hawkens tapped his rifle and then continued, "This musical instrument plays the tunes to which one dances in Arizona and Nevada, and—"

"Dancing? Shame!" interrupted the cantor. "Who spoke of dancing? A musician, never! Dancing is a hurried and continuous variation of the fixed position in which one becomes unaesthetically sweaty."

"Then I hope you'll not get into a position here where, entirely against your artistic will, you lose this fixed position, and with it a few more things, maybe even your life. Unfortunately, I fear that very soon you will be forced to dance a few steps, which can hardly take place without your becoming sweaty."

"I? Would not think of it! Who would or could force me to?"

"The gentlemen sitting behind us there in front of the tavern. I will explain this to you later."

"Why not now?"

"Because I have to tell the others, too, and because we have now reached our destination, if I'm not mistaken."

They had left the village and were now on the road to Tucson. During their entire passage, the cantor had continued making the odd pendulum movements on his horse, with his torso now swinging forward, now backward, his legs and feet in the stirrups pointing in the opposite direction. This caused little Sam Hawkens no small amusement, as a merry sparkle in his eyes indicated. Now they noticed the four heavy immigrants' wagons in front of them.

The wagons' occupants had gotten out and unhitched the oxen, which grazed on the scraggly grass.

The wagons had been stopped closely side by side, with all the hitches pointing in one direction, a big mistake in this area where Indians and roving outlaws made it advisable to circle the wagons. The people were busily engaged with various chores. Two women were collecting thorny mesquite branches, the only wood found here to make a fire. Two others carried cooking pots. Some children were helping the women. Two men brought in buckets of water; a third was checking the wagon wheels. These three were rather young. A fourth, surely past fifty, but still in full manhood, broad and heftily built, stood amidst this bustle, watching, and from time to time calling out a short command in a clear voice. He seemed to be the leader of these immigrants. When he saw the two arrivals, he called, "Where have you gotten to again, Mr. Cantor?! We always have to worry about you and—"

"Please, please, Mr. Schmidt," interrupted the addressed, "Mr. Cantor Emeritus, as I have already said a hundred times. It is truly for completeness only and since I must not presume to a position I no longer hold."

At that he reined in his horse and dismounted—but how! He first lifted his right leg in order to dismount on the left; however, this appeared to be too dangerous to him. Hence he pulled his left foot out of the stirrup and tried to reach the ground on the right, although this must have looked just as precarious to him. Therefore, using both hands, he propped himself up on the pommel and pushed himself backward, to come to rest on the horse's hindquarters. From there he slowly pushed himself further backward, at last sliding down over the tail. The animal, as gentle as a lamb and tired, submitted to this odd and ridiculous procedure quietly. The immigrants had witnessed this descent many times, so it did not interest them. Good Sam Hawkens, though, had never seen anything like this before, and he made the most serious effort not to laugh out loud.

"Oh, so what, Emeritus!" responded Schmidt forcefully. "To us you are still Mr. Cantor. Your retirement was your own choice. But that is no reason for us to chew forever on this foreign term. Why do you always lag behind? We have to watch out for you all the time!"

"*Piano, piano*, dear Schmidt! I hear you very well, even without your shouting. I had a musical idea. You know, I believe that, for an overture, if the cello is missing in the orchestra, its part can be assigned to the third trumpet. Is that not so?"

"As far as I am concerned, you can assign it to the large kettledrum! I do know a wagon must be lubricated if it is to run well, but I do not know what needs to be trumpeted in an overture. What kind of clown have you brought along there?"

At these words, he pointed to Sam Hawkens. The cantor answered without correcting the strong and insulting word, "This gentleman is—is—his name is—hmm, I do not know myself yet. I met him in the village and asked him for your whereabouts. He was kind enough to guide me here. The main thing is, he, too, is a Saxon."

"A Saxon?" Schmidt asked in surprise while looking Sam over from head to toe. "That is not possible! If someone were to run around in Saxony in such clothes, he would be arrested immediately!"

"But, happily, we are not in Saxony now," Hawkens interjected with a courteous smile. "That's why I will probably keep my freedom, if I'm not mistaken. Here you will see very different costumes from mine. In the Wild West you will not find ten clothing shops every twenty paces. May I perhaps inquire where you all are traveling to, gentlemen?"

"You all?" voiced Schmidt dismissingly. "I am used to being addressed personally and would like to know first who you are and what you do."

"Well, I can tell you. My name is Falke, I'm of Saxon extraction, live as a frontiersman, and extend to anyone the courtesy he's due. Whether you all now want to answer my question is at your pleasure."

"You and you all? Mr. Falke, I have told you already I am accustomed to—"

"It's all right, it's all right!" interrupted the little man. "And I have said already that I extend to anyone the honor he is due. I don't consider anyone who calls me a clown fully grown."

"Damn! Does this mean me?" roared the old man, stepping threateningly closer.

"Yes," answered the little man while facing him in a friendly and fearless manner.

"Then get out of here quickly, if you wish your bones to stay together!"

"That I will do. But as your fellow countryman, I consider it my duty to warn you of the twelve horsemen who passed you today."

"Not necessary. We are smart enough to know what to make of them. Right off, we did not think much of these fellows and did not give them any information when they pumped us. You see, therefore, that your good advice is superfluous."

He turned, indicating to Sam Hawkens that he was finished with him. The latter made a move to leave, but then, driven by his good-heartedness, remained standing and said, "Mr. Schmidt, one more word!"

"What?" the old one asked gruffly.

"If you truly do not need good advice, I will happily keep it to myself. But permit me to ask you one more thing: are your wagons positioned like that only for now?"

"Why?"

"Because this is the most convenient way to be robbed or even attacked. If I had anything to say about it, all four wagons would be arranged in a square with all the people and oxen—*heeheeheehee*—people and oxen inside for the entire night. In addition, a guard would keep watch from dusk to dawn."

"Why?"

"Because you are in Arizona, not at home in Dresden or Leipzig County."

"We know exactly where we are. To learn this, we need not ask a clown. Get out now, or I will make you run!"

"Well, I will, if I'm not mistaken. Have meant well. Now the clown will quit this monkey camp!"

He turned abruptly to leave for the village. In an annoyed tone, Schmidt bellowed at the cantor, "A fine fellow you have brought us. Looked like a clown and was rude as a cuss. I do not need countrymen like that."

"But to me he was very courteous and friendly," the cantor emeritus dared to interject. "This was probably the consequence of my addressing him *dolce*, as we musical artists are used to saying, while you came at him very *sforzando*."

"Since he looked like a tramp and—"

Schmidt was interrupted by a loud exclamation. The two young men the Finders had talked about who were accompanying the wagons on horseback had been at the river to rinse out their dusty mouths. Now they came riding back. One of them had a bright face of the type and complexion of a European, although his skin had been heavily tanned by the Arizona sun. He might have been eighteen years old and was rather more broad than tall. The other's bold features were Indian, yet his cheekbones were not very prominent. Vividly in contrast to the matte bronze color of his face was the pale gray of his sharp eyes as well as the semiblond hair. Of more slender build but no less athletic than his companion, he seemed to be about the same age. Both were dressed in European fashion and, it appeared, very well armed. They also knew how to ride, particularly the gray-eyed youth, who seemed like one with his horse. He was the one who had called out, interrupting Schmidt, upon approaching the camp and seeing Sam Hawkens's quick departure.

"What's the matter? What do you want?" Schmidt asked the approaching riders.

The young man quickly urged his horse closer and, stopping in front of Schmidt, answered in German, with an accent, "Who was the little man who just left?"

"Why?"

"Because he looked familiar. I did not get a good look at him, but his gait struck me somehow. Did he have a beard?"

"Yes, thick as a jungle!"

"That matches! The eyes?"

"Very small."

"The nose?"

"Terrible."

"Fits, too! Did he give his name?"

"Yes."

"Maybe Sam Hawkens?"

"No. His name is Falke and he's German."

"Peculiar, but explainable!" the young man wondered aloud. "'Falke' in English means 'hawk.' Many Germans take English names after they arrive here. Why should a frontiersman by the name of Falke not call himself Hawkens? I did not know that Sam Hawkens was a German, though. But this figure and his peculiar sneaking gait! Every good frontiersman has learned sneaking up, but only Sam Hawkens is used to sneaking along like that. But wait, one more question: did this man laugh maybe once during the conversation?"

"Yes."

"How?"

"Very sneeringly, when he spoke of people and oxen."

"I mean with which vowel, which sound did he laugh. People laugh using an *a* or *i*, even *e* or *o*."

"He used *e*, and it was more a giggle than a laugh."

"Really, really?" asked the young man keenly. "Then it was he after all! Sam Hawkens has a very peculiar 'heeheeheehee,' not heard from anyone else. One hears it quite often from him. It sounds so sly and yet so serene. He swallows it halfway."

"True! But you are mistaken—that fellow was a tramp, not a frontiersman!"

The little man had returned to the tavern and rejoined Dick and Will at the table. In order to consume something, they each had themselves served a whiskey, which they drank diluted with water. The Finders laughed about this, but otherwise left them in peace.

When it turned dark, the Irishman lit a lantern, which, once hung, barely illuminated the space in front of the house. After a while, Buttler got up, signaled three of his companions, and they left.

"They're up to something," said Will Parker quietly.

"Where would they be going?"

"Can't you figure that out?" Sam asked him.

"No. I'm not all-knowing."

"Me, either. But someone who's not a greenhorn like Will Parker should know what they're after."

"What, you smart old coon?"

"Meat."

"From where?"

"From the immigrants. The Finders are greedy for fresh meat, and out there at the wagons are sixteen oxen. Do you get it now, my clever Will?"

"Ah, the oxen, sure, sure!" nodded the other. "These gentlemen might be expected to steal an ox, which is much easier than entering a wagon to fetch a ham. You lie down on the ground, sneak up on the animal, and slowly and carefully lead it away from the camp until you have it safe."

"That's the way! Yep, that's how it's done, *heeheeheehee!* You must've been a fine thief of oxen in earlier times, if I'm not mistaken."

"Be quiet, old man! I pity these people if they lose a draft animal. Did you figure this out only now?"

"No, as soon as Buttler talked about meat."

"And you were with the immigrants and didn't warn them?"

"Who says I didn't warn them? But I was called a clown whose good advice wasn't needed. Sam Hawkens a clown, *heeheeheehee.* That was lots of fun. Although I'm not quite dressed for a reception, this cantor emeritus looks rather more like a harlequin than I do, if I'm not mistaken."

"You laugh. Do you remember, though, that we're invited to eat with the Finders?"

"Certainly, I remember!" returned Sam. "I have an appetite like a prairie wolf who hasn't had a bite to eat for two weeks."

"So you'll accept the invitation and partake in stolen meat?"

"Yes, indeed!"

"Sam, I have difficulty believing this, since you are such an honest old soul. But do as you please. I will not take part in this. Will Parker does not consume stolen goods!"

"Sam Hawkens, either, unless he knows there will be payment afterwards."

"Oh, you mean—?"

"Yes," nodded the little one. "I've been called a clown, had my advice rejected, and will therefore not prevent anything. Punishment is necessary, particularly when it serves as education and for a change in conduct, as may be. I will eat with the greatest enjoyment, but then take care that the robbed are fully compensated."

"If that's so, I'll join in, too. But we'll have to be very careful. I'd be very surprised if the Finders were to let us get away unscathed."

"They'll lose some of their own skin. You'll see!"

Buttler and his companions were gone for about three quarters of an hour before they returned. They brought along a beef loin, which was taken into the house for roasting. Before it was done, several additional bottles of whiskey were emptied. When the Negro woman finally announced that the roast was done, Buttler came over to the Shamrock and invited them to join the others in the house.

"Can't we have the pieces you want to share out here?" asked Sam.

"No," was the answer. "Whoever wants to be our guest must sit with us. You should also know that wine tastes good only in company."

"Wine? Where's that to come from?" Sam asked, feigning surprise.

"Yes, where from?! You wonder, don't you? I tell you, you are invited by real gentlemen. We saw you didn't like whiskey, so for your pleasure and in your honor we persuaded the innkeeper to let us have the last barrel he had in the house. It's a wine like you've never tasted before. Come on, gentlemen!"

He turned for the door behind which his men had already disappeared. Sam Hawkens had the opportunity to whisper to his friends, "Want to get us drunk, then rob us. Think we can't take much, since we refused the Irishman's poison. *Heeheeheehee,* they delude themselves, if I'm not mistaken. Sam Hawkens drinks like a bottomless barrel. We'll act as if we can't drink anything, boys, but drink them under the table nevertheless."

They stepped into the house. To the right was the kitchen, with a poor-looking range. On its fire the Negro woman had roasted the meat. To the left stood two long tables consisting of unfinished posts and boards each with two benches, enough seating for all those present. The wine barrel lay on a wood block in the corner. The Irishman filled two jars from which everybody drank. There were no glasses.

The Finders intended to drink little until their three guests were good and drunk. Therefore, they passed the two jars continuously as they faked heavy drinking, while taking only small sips.

The wine, however, was truly excellent. They really enjoyed it, and so their sips became larger and larger.

The roast, too, was excellent. Everyone had dug in and it had almost disappeared when the meal was interrupted. Poller, the immigrants' scout, appeared in the doorway; behind him old Schmidt was followed by the other three men. They had their rifles with them, but the diners had put theirs aside. When they had surveyed the situation in the room, Poller stepped a few paces closer and said, "Good evening, sirs! Permit us to wish you a blessed dinner."

"Why not?" responded Buttler. "We would love to invite you, but most everything is already eaten."

"Too bad! We see there are no bones. I've the impression it's loin you were able to afford?"

"Yes, a fine buffalo loin."

"Are there still bison around here? It more likely came from tame cattle?"

"Also possible. But we bought it as buffalo loin."

"Where, if I may ask?"

"At Rhodes Rancho in the valley of the Santa Cruz River, when we passed by there."

"That should have been a hefty bundle, but we didn't notice anything on you when you passed us."

"Because each of us carried his own piece, if you don't mind, sir," Buttler said sneeringly.

"Well, mister, how is it, then, that we are missing an ox?"

"You're missing an ox? Ah, how many were you, then?"

The Finders honored this coarse joke with uproarious laughter. Poller seemed unfazed by it and continued, "Yes, we've lost a draft ox. Do you perhaps have an idea where it may be?"

"How would we know? Go look for it!"

"We already have, and we've found it."

"Then be happy, sir, and leave us in peace about your ox! We haven't got anything to do with the beast."

"Probably! The thing is, it was lured away and killed noiselessly by a workmanlike thrust between the vertebrae. This is very like the way cattle rustlers butcher their ill-gotten gains."

"Then you think the ox was stolen from you?"

"We just don't think this; we are sure of it."

"So, chase the thieves! Maybe you'll catch them. That's the single best piece of advice I can give you."

"We've done so already. Oddly enough, it's only the loin that's missing from the dead ox!"

"I don't find that odd, but rather easily explainable. The thieves must have known the loin to be the best and tastiest piece of beef."

"Well, we are of the same opinion. I cannot help but notice that your roast was the loin."

That is when Buttler rose from the bench and asked threateningly, "What is that supposed to mean, sir? Do you, by chance, associate our roast with the loin of the stolen ox?"

"Yes, I do, and I hope you don't mind."

Quickly, Buttler had his rifle in his hand. His companions, too, jumped up and went for their rifles.

"Man," he shouted at the scout, "do you know what you dare? Look at these twelve rifles trained on you and repeat your accusation!"

"Wouldn't think of it! I've done my duty and am finished now. I am the scout for these people standing behind me. They are Germans and do not speak English. What I said, I said in their name and will go now, because I am not the shepherd of their oxen. What still needs to be done here, they may take on themselves."

He turned and left. The man was entirely right from his point of view. He was a hireling and did only what he was paid for. He had actually already done too much, in that he had dared step in front of the threatening rifles of these dangerous people for a stolen head of cattle. Buttler and his Finders sat down again. The Germans had probably thought the scout would finish this matter, for they stood there helplessly until old Schmidt remembered a source of information. He turned to Sam Hawkens, who had quietly continued eating with both his friends and seemingly had paid no attention, "Mr. Falke, did you hear what our scout said?"

"Most of it," responded the little man while putting a piece of meat into his mouth.

"We did not understand it. Did he think these people to be thieves?"

"Yes."

"And what was the result?"

"The result? Hmm, the result was, he left."

"By the devil! Must I have my ox stolen, then?"

"Must have it stolen? You have already had it stolen, if I am not mistaken, *heeheeheehee*."

Having been made aware of it, Schmidt paid special attention to this merry laughter. Then he continued, "So, help me get back what is mine! You are German, a fellow countryman, and must take care of us."

"I must? What can you expect from a clown? Had you followed my advice, had you circled the wagons and guarded your cattle, the ox wouldn't have been stolen. I can't do anything for you, nothing at all."

"But sit here in cahoots with these rascals, eating the stolen roast, that you can do, can you not?"

"Yes, that I can do, since they invited me for dinner, if I'm not mistaken."

That's when the German angrily slammed his rifle butt on the floor and shouted, "Then I thank you for being a fellow countryman and will help myself!"

"How do you plan to do this?"

"I will force these bandits to pay me! We are four men and have our rifles!"

"And here you are faced by twelve bold men, whose rifles are just as good. Don't do anything foolish! The ox cannot be brought back to life by your exposing yourself to mortal danger."

"I know that, too. But where is the money it cost me?"

"These people have no money, and even if they had, you could not take it from them by force."

"Should I perhaps use a ruse?"

"You are not the man for that. A bear is no fox and a nitwit is no slyboots either, *heeheeheehee*."

Schmidt intended to respond rudely to the "nitwit," but the giggle kept him from it. He asked quickly, "Is your name truly Falke?"

"Yes, if I am not mistaken, *heeheeheehee.*"

"But you resemble another frontiersman."

"Which frontiersman?"

"Schi-So told me his name. But I have forgotten it again."

"Schi-So?" Sam asked in surprise. "Who is that?"

"A young companion of ours, the son of a Navajo chief by the name of Nitsas-Ini.

Sam gave a sign of joy and exclaimed, "Nitsas-Ini? His son is with you? He's back from Germany?"

"Yes. He has come back with us."

"Excellent, excellent! Since that is so, you have not asked for my help in vain. Return quietly to your camp now! You will get compensation for your ox."

Though he had said "you all" to Schmidt before, Hawkens now began to address him with the singular "you." The news he had just received must have changed his mind.

"Are you saying this only to get rid of me?" Schmidt asked suspiciously.

"No. I give you my word, you will be fully compensated, and maybe more than that. How much did the ox cost you?"

"$130.00."

"You will get it. Because I'm telling you this, you can believe it, *heeheeheehee.*"

"Then you are the frontiersman Schi-So mentioned?"

"I sure am, for I have seen Schi-So many times when I was a guest of his father's tribe. Tell him I will be coming to the camp in the early morning to greet him. Where was he when I came to the camp?"

"He had gone to the river."

"And I did not see your scout, either?"

"He was off hunting for wild turkey. I will lecture him for leaving us here so disgracefully."

"That'll do you no good. But leave now! If you stay here any longer these people will only get mad at you."

"Then I will go, and next time will be smarter if someone gives me good advice."

"A commendable intention!" nodded Sam Hawkens. "In the Wild West, it just isn't smart to judge a person solely by the way he is dressed!"

After Schmidt and his three men had left the house, Buttler asked the little man, "We didn't understand a word. What did the fellow say?"

"He asked for compensation."

"And what did you tell him?"

"I sent him away," Sam responded innocently.

Satisfied, the Finder opined, "His luck to have listened to you. We don't usually bother much with such characters. But now sit down again! Let's make sure these blockheads don't spoil our mood."

The feasting was renewed. Yet eating did not go on for long; instead, drinking became more ardent. When half the barrel had been emptied, Sam, with Dick and Will following his example, gave the impression that the wine had made him drunk. This pleased the Finders enormously. They felt it would take only a short time now for their victims to fall asleep and therefore passed the jars ever more eagerly. Thus passed quarter hour after quarter hour. Sam pretended he could barely keep his eyes open. The eyes of the Finders, though, began to shut because of true drunkenness. The liquor they had drunk earlier was having its effect.

The first to succomb to the alcohol was the Irishman. He sat down by the range, fell asleep, nodded lower and lower until, finally, his entire length slid to the floor without his waking up.

Sam had toasted frequently with the leader, and Buttler had become so intoxicated that he had to prop his head up on his hands and elbows on the table. He was aware of the wine putting him under, but did not want to show his vulnerability in front of his men. That's why he winked at his men surreptitiously, or thought he did. He wanted them to think his inebriation was a pretense. The obvious result was for them to believe they should follow suit. They, too, "faked" drunkenness; soon silence reigned over the formerly loud party.

At that point Sam Hawkens rose to fill the jars anew. As long as the barrel held a drop, he woke up first one, then another, to get them to drink more.

Finally, the barrel was empty and the Finders fast asleep. Sam checked by waking some of them. They stammered incomprehensible garbage without ever coming to their senses and sank down again. One of them, staring ahead with lifeless eyes, asked, "Are you finally drunk, Buttler?"

"Yes, very much so," answered Sam.

"Then outside with them and a knife between their ribs. We share the money and bury them."

When Sam did not comment, the man continued stammering, "Why don't you answer? Do you want to let them go? That cannot be! We decided to kill them. Shall I—start—with—my knife?"

"Yes," said Sam.

"Then—I take—the little—r—r —round one and—." With his hand he reached for his belt to draw his knife. At that he stood up, but being unable to steady himself, slid to the floor, where he remained unconscious.

"There, we've heard it," whispered Dick Stone. "We were to be murdered, robbed, and buried. Your guess was right, Sam, old man. What do we do now?"

"We tie them up. There should be belts and rope in the house."

There was plenty of rope, and soon the three had not only tied the Finders' hands and feet, but also those of the innkeeper and the old Negro woman, who was also quite drunk. Leaving his two friends as guards, Sam then went to the German immigrants' camp. As he approached, a young voice called out, "Who goes there? I shall shoot!"

"It's Sam Hawkens," was the response.

"Already? That's wonderful! Come in, sir. Step over these hitches!"

"I'm too small for that. I'd rather creep underneath."

Sam had noticed that the wagons had now been arranged in a square, with the animals driven inside. His advice had been followed, unfortunately, only after harm had taught them better. The guard on duty offered him his hand in greeting. It was Schi-So, the Indian chief's son. He had spoken in clear English. Now Sam asked him, "I hope you also speak German, young friend, after having been in Germany for six years?"

"Rather well."

"Then let us wake the sleeping and speak German with them! But listen! Who comes there?"

They listened into the night. They could hear a horse approaching from the village. "It's a horseman, a single one," whispered Schi-So. "Who could it be?"

"It's no horseman," answered Sam. "I know it from the hoofbeat. It's my good old Mary following me. You remember her?"

"Yes, I remember her. But, please, do not address me with the formal "Sie" when we speak German, but rather with the familiar "Du," just as in Navajo! I am Indian and want to remain one and do not want to become unfaithful to the customs of my tribe."

"Right on, my boy! Haven't become too proud over there. Old Sam loves you for it. You'll have to tell me a lot, but now is not the time; must keep it for later."

The mule came up to the wagon hitch where Sam still stood and rubbed its head on his shoulder. The loud conversation had wakened the sleepers. They came over to inquire about who had arrived, since they could not make out Sam with the fire having died. Schmidt now received him very differently from the first time and gave instructions to rebuild the fire. Once it lit up the encampment Schi-So introduced him to those present. The names of the three younger, but also married immigrants, were Strauch, Ebersbach, and Uhlmann. Schi-So's young friend's name was Adolf Wolf. More than that Sam did not want to know at this time. The women and children, none of the latter being small, approached too. Naturally, the scout could not stay away and so all were gathered when Sam Hawkens in his peculiar style began his account of today's meeting with the Finders. Except for the young Indian, none of those present had acquaintance with the cunning Sam Hawkens until now. As they presently learned how he had won the wagers and had drunk the Finders into sleep to have them secured afterwards, they recognized, despite the simplicity and modesty of his presentation, that this small, odd man was by no means an ordinary frontiersman. Old Schmidt felt so, too. When the story had come to an end he offered his hand and said apologetically, "I see now that I have to ask your forgiveness. I've misjudged you. I hope you will bear me no grudge?"

"Heavens no!" laughed the little one. "Have enough to carry of my own and will surely not tote along other people's errors. The clown is forgiven and forgotten, if I'm not mistaken, *heeheeheehee.*"

"You claim, then, that the twelve people are the Finders?"

"Yes."

"And that you were to be murdered together with Stone and Parker?"

"Yes."

"Then we have reason enough to hang them or at least put them in jail. We will guard them through the night and tomorrow turn them over to the authorities."

"No, we will not."

"What, then?"

"We let them go."

"Let them go? You barely escaped from these bandits with your skin intact! Do you have any sense?"

"Maybe there's some in there. At least it's not in my boots, Mr. Schmidt. It's very obvious you are new to this country. What authorities are you referring to? Where are they? And if we find them, do they have the required power? Can I prove my claim?"

"I rather think so!"

"No. I think those men are the Finders, because there are twelve of them and one of them is named Buttler. Is that proof before a judge? I state that they were intent on killing us, for a drunkard said so. I say that I figured you were going to be attacked. What will be the judge's opinion? And if he accepts the claims and locks up the Finders, we will have nothing but a lot of trouble and delay until we turn blue with anger."

"Well, then!" blustered Schmidt. "We ourselves will form a court of law! We'll sentence the bandits to death with a bullet for each of them."

"God forbid. I am not a murderer. Only in defense of my life and of necessity will I spill human blood.

"Then you really want to let the scoundrels go?" Schmidt asked incredulously.

"Yes."

"And they are not to receive any punishment?"

"Sure they are! It's because they are to be punished that I will let them go," said Hawkens.

"That's a contradiction!"

"Not so, Mr. Schmidt. It makes the best sense there is, if I am not mistaken. It takes just a bit of intelligence to grasp it. Have you got any, *heeheeheehee?*"

"Sir, you are insulting!" roared Schmidt, who, despite his promise, could not check himself.

"Insulting? No. I speak only as I am spoken to. Didn't you ask me earlier if I had any sense? I will explain to you why my plan is not contradictory. At present, we have only assumptions about this gang. Have to fish for proof. If we let these fellows go now, they'll hold up your wagon train and then we'll take them. Then we have the proof that will do them in, if I'm not mistaken."

"What? Let ourselves be held up? But that means the danger of our being killed!"

"I don't think so! It depends very much on how you bridle the horse, from the head or the tail. You just leave that to me! Old coon, Sam Hawkens, will come up with a trick to trap the Finders. I'll get back to that. First, I must talk it over with Dick Stone and Will Parker. The main issue now is fulfillment of my promise: compensation for the stolen and killed ox. Do you want it now?"

"If I can obtain it—at once. It is doubtful, however, that the Finders will pay the entire amount."

"Why shouldn't they?"

"Because they took only the loin, while we eat the rest."

"It's all the same. The ox is dead and must be paid for. So, come along and pick up your compensation! While there, though, be careful not to call me Sam Hawkens! I have good reasons for these people not to know my frontiersman's name yet."

"Who of us is to come to the village?"

"Only you, Mr. Schmidt. The others should stay here, start packing, and hitch the oxen to the wagons, so that your wagon train can depart for Tucson immediately upon our return."

"Right now, while it is still night? We have to rest and don't want to leave until daybreak."

"That will not be possible now. Conditions dictate that you will have to do without further rest."

That's when a deep, hearty, basso voice in true Saxon dialect sounded from the vicinity of the women, "Listen up, nothing doing! A human needs his proper rest and the beasts, too. We'll stay here!"

Sam looked at the speaker in surprise. An objection from a female, and that in a tone he had not expected! She was a heavy-boned figure of mas-culine, self-confident appearance. Had the fire burned brighter, or had it been daylight, the little man would have noticed the dark line below her sharp nose, which could not be called anything but a mustache.

"Yes, look at me!" she continued, as she noticed the surprise with which the frontiersman regarded her. "Nothing else is going to happen. Travel is by day and sleeping by night. Otherwise, anyone could come and mess up our routine!"

"But my request is only for your safety, to your advantage, my dear woman," answered Sam.

"You cannot pull that one on me!" she responded disparagingly. "A decent human being does not shuffle around in the middle of the night and in such darkness in America. Yes, if we were at home, I could see it. But in a foreign country, you wait nicely for daybreak. You understand me?"

"Sure I understand you, dear woman. But I think—"

"Dear woman?" she interrupted him. "I am not your dear woman! Do you know who I truly am and what my name is?"

"You are naturally the wife of one of these four gentlemen."

"Gentlemen! Why do you not speak German, with a German woman facing you! I am Mrs. Ebersbach, née Morgenstern and widowed Leiermüller. That one"—at that she pointed to one of the three younger immigrants—"is my present husband, Mr. Master Blacksmith Ebersbach: That is how it is spelled, spoken it is Eberschbach. And just so you know from now on, he does not dance to your fiddle, but has to listen to me, since I am eleven years older and therefore have more brains and experience. I will stay here and he, consequently, will, too. Nighttime is no time to traipse around in the world."

Since none of the immigrants offered a response, Sam Hawkens let his lively eyes wander merrily across the circle and then ventured, "If the gentlemen are used to obeying this imperious lady, I can only plead to make an exception at least this once."

He wanted to continue. She, however, quickly cut in, "Eh, you do not say! An exception! As if I would put up with that! You do not know me well yet! Why do you stare at me like that? No need to make a face like that! You know, I am the one everybody has to take his bearings from here, I, you understand? Who has paid for everything? For the ocean crossing and for the land trip, too, up to now? And who will have to chip in further? I! I am the capital! Now you know it all and now we want to go back to sleep!"

Once again none of the men said a word contrariwise, not even Schmidt, who had seemed to be the leader and in the afternoon had played himself up before Sam. That's when the little hunter stood up from the fire where he had been sitting and said in an indifferent tone:

"As you please. Then say good night, if I am not mistaken. It will be the last time you will be saying it, for I am convinced that tonight's sleep will be your last, *heeheeheehee!*"

He turned to leave. The woman quickly rose, too, reached for his arm, and asked, "Our last sleep? What do you mean by that, you little man, you?"

She was indeed taller by a head than he as she stood beside him. He replied cordially, "I mean to say that you will not wake up tomorrow morning."

"Why not?"

"Because you will be dead."

"Dead? I would not think of it! Mrs. Rosalie Ebersbach is not going to die for a long time yet!"

"You think the twelve bandits you dealt with intend to listen to Mrs. Rosalie Ebersbach?"

"They cannot do anything to us; they have been caught and tied up, as you told us."

"But they will free themselves and attack you as soon as I have left the tavern with my two companions."

"You want to leave, go away? Is it not your duty to watch those prisoners until we are safe? What am I to think of you if you forsake us and disappear from here like butter in the sun!"

"Think what you like!"

"Nice talk this, very nice talk! Have you not heard that men are supposed to be attentive to ladies and should protect them? And Mrs. Rosalie Ebersbach is a lady, understood?"

"Very true! But whoever enters into my protection has to follow my instructions. Also understood? You will be held up. If this happens here after you have gone back to sleep, you will be lost. If nothing happens, we cannot prove anything against the Finders, and they'll remain unpunished. To obtain evidence of their misdeeds, we must depart for Tucson, where I will request a small detachment of soldiers from the commander. That's why we have to be in Tucson in the morning, to get the trap ready for the Finders before they're aware of what we're doing. Can you grasp this, Mrs. Ebersbach, née Leiermüller?"

"Why did you not say so right away?" she asked in a very different tone. "By the way, I am widowed as Leiermüller, not born as such. If you talk with me as reasonably as now, I am reasonable, too. I have not been hit on the head, you know. Keep that in mind. Then we will hitch up the oxen and get ready for departure. But to take only Schmidt is not going to work. I want to look these fellows over, too. Wait for a moment. I want to get my rifle."

She went to her wagon for the rifle.

When she returned, her husband pleaded with her, "Stay here, Rosalie! This is not for women. I will go in your place."

"You?" she answered. "You are just the fellow for it! Just do not pretend to be a man and hero. You know I cannot stand this. You stay here and wait until I return!"

She turned to Schmidt and the quietly giggling Sam to walk to the village. When they arrived at the tavern, the Finders had awakened from their knock-out drunkenness because the bindings were cutting into their flesh. Buttler was speaking angrily to Stone and Parker.

"What does the man want?" Sam Hawkens asked his two friends.

"What he should want," ventured Stone. "He naturally wonders why we've got them and not they us. Asks whether this is how we show our gratitude for having eaten and drunk with them."

"Yes," Buttler shouted angrily while pulling on his bonds and trying to at least sit up, "what are you thinking, assaulting us in our sleep and now treating us like this? We received you hospitably, didn't insult you, didn't do the least thing to you, and for that—"

"Didn't do the least thing?" interrupted Sam. "I'm sure this annoys you a lot. By the way, why talk so much! We know your intentions toward us, and to thank you for it, we intend to turn you over to a judge."

That's when Buttler laughed disdainfully and sneered, "And who will believe you without any evidence?"

"You have talked in your drunkenness and confessed your wicked intentions!"

"Even if this were so, no judge would listen to the words of a drunk. Your evidence is just too weak, sir."

"Sure, I can see that turning you in is useless," nodded Sam. "We would lose too much time with you and the judge, so we'd rather forget about it."

"That's the best idea you could have. But now I hope you will untie us."

"Not so fast, sir! Still have something to say to you."

"Then hurry up! What else do you want?"

"Payment for the ox you killed."

"What do you care about the ox!"

"I care very much. We have joined up with those immigrants. They, too, are on their way to the mountains to trap bears and beaver, just like us. We have become companions and now have the duty to see that they are compensated."

"We won't give them anything!" shouted Buttler.

"No matter! What you will not give, we will take. What do you think the ox's value is, Mr. Buttler?"

"I don't care," replied Buttler. "We have no more money. You know you took it all from us through the wagers."

"You weren't very worried, though, since you intended to rob us of it again. Let's say $150. Okay?"

"Don't care if it's a hundred thousand. We can't pay."

"Certainly not with money. But that's not necessary. You ought not to have totally empty pockets."

"Damnation! Do you intend to empty our pockets? That would be robbery!"

"No matter. I'm glad to pay you once in like manner."

"We are no robbers. If you touch our property, we'll turn you in!"

"That's all right with us. Would like to hear the judge's comments when he gets to see you. Come on, Dick and Will! Let's have a look in their pockets."

With the greatest pleasure, the two friends went to work. The Finders resisted as best they could, but without success. Their pockets were emptied. A plethora of items came to light, particularly several valuable watches, which one could surely assume to have been stolen. Sam took the watches, showed them to Schmidt, and asked him, "These fellows do not have any cash. Would you take these watches in its place?"

"If they have no coin, yes," answered Schmidt. "But I do not want to lose anything! I would have to sell the watches, and no trader would pay their true value."

"Don't worry. You'll not lose a penny. These watches are worth four times the value of an ox. You can be sure of that."

"But my conscience, sir! If these items were stolen!"

"They probably are."

"Then they belong to the ones from whom they were taken, not to me."

"True. But those people will never get their watches back. They were probably murdered and, even if not, you can safely take them. Who is going to look for and establish their owners? Totally different conditions exist here from those in your home country."

"But is it not your obligation to turn stolen objects over to the authorities if you cannot find their rightful owners?"

"That is true at home! Here in the Wild West, you've got to watch out for youself if you want to assert your right against rabble. So just pocket the watches and don't worry about it. If you still feel you are committing a wrong, I will accept the responsibility on my conscience."

"If that is so, it would be stupid of me to refuse any longer."

He then put the watches in his pocket. When Buttler saw this, he exclaimed, "What does that mean? What does this guy want with our watches? That's—"

Switching into English, Sam cut him short. "Be quiet, rascal! He considers this payment for the stolen ox, and you are lucky if this is to be the entire punishment. We are, by the way, not unwilling to evade justice. We are traveling to Tucson from here, and tomorrow evening will make camp beyond town. You can follow and meet us there with the police, whose questions we'll be pleased to answer."

"Yeah, sure, we'll do that, we'll certainly do that!" Buttler's voice dripped with sarcasm. "And now untie us, since you're now surely finished with us!"

"Fools *we* would be! If we freed you, you'd still pay us a visit in camp today instead of tomorrow. You stay where you are. Come the new day, someone will come by to turn you loose."

"Then receive your reward for our treatment later in hell!"

"Thank you, sir!" Hawkens responded politely. "And so that you cannot do us any imaginable damage, we will now take your ammunition. You can pick it up tomorrow together with the watches. We will honestly safeguard everything for you until then."

Hawkens, Stone, and Parker unloaded the rifles and took all bullets and powder, to the great chagrin of the Finders.

Mrs. Ebersbach had remained a silent spectator to the entire event. Without understanding what was spoken, she nevertheless figured out everything easily. And there was another silent watcher standing by as well—Mary, Sam's mule, who once again had followed her master, standing with her head inside the house, following all his movements with the greatest attention.

When they were done with the Finders, the door was closed and a heavy rock pushed up against it. Then the five people walked back to the immigrants' camp. Mary trotted behind them good-naturedly. She was used to following her master at every turn like a faithful dog.

# 3

# DEPARTURE FOR TUCSON

URING SAM, Schmidt, and Mrs. Rosalie Ebersbach's absence, all preparations had been made in camp for immediate departure upon their return. The scout, accompanied by the two young men, rode ahead. Then followed the wagons, led by Dick Stone and Will Parker, while Sam and the cantor made up the rear guard. Sam had intentionally chosen his companions, since he thought this the best way to acquire information about the relationships of the small, curiously mixed group. Peculiar these relationships must be, he told himself after what he had seen and experienced so far. There was the musical cantor, the weighty Mrs. Rosalie Ebersbach, the Indian chief's son returning from Germany, and the young German who was seemingly a friend of the redskin and apparently did not belong with any of the others. These were truly peculiar people and circumstances. The cantor accommodated the little man's curiosity, for shortly after the wagons had started moving, he struck up a conversation with the question, "Our Mrs. Rosalie went along to see the Finders. I suppose she told them off, since she knows how to use her powerful tongue, if she wants to. She surely must have talked with them?"

"Not a word."

"I am surprised. I would have thought just the opposite, that she would have dealt with them *fortissimo.*"

"Does she speak English, then?"

"Only a few words she has picked up along the way."

"How could you think, then, that she could have talked with those people who know only English or Spanish! Ten or twelve words picked up by chance do not suffice for a long lecture. It also appeared that her courage for such a lecture dissipated once she saw those wild characters."

"Her courage? Do not believe it! Mrs. Rosalie is not afraid of anybody no matter how daredevilish he may look. She has hair on her teeth and is used to being obeyed."

"I noticed that. You all kept your mouths shut when she contradicted me."

"Yes, you must do that, if only to avoid a mighty hailstorm. For all that, she is very kindhearted. She just does not put up with any opposition."

"That's a big mistake, if I am not mistaken. If you're not competent at a subject, you must be prepared to accept advice."

"Oh," ventured the cantor, "this Mrs. Rosalie understands quite a bit of everything!"

"Nonsense!" retorted Sam. "She cannot know anything of the conditions here. And if scenes such as today's are repeated, she must expect sooner or later to get the entire group into danger, into harm's way."

"Do not believe it. Even when she does not know or understand something, she speedily will become knowledgeable and accepting of it. You saw how quickly she agreed with you."

"And you seem to have great respect for her, Mr. Cantor."

"Mr. Cantor Emeritus, if you please! Only to preserve my integrity, since I took my leave and am therefore no longer in office. Yes, I respect her and she deserves it. She is an able and musically educated woman."

"Ah, musically educated, *heeheeheehee!* Does she by any chance also compose?"

"No, but she plays the accordion."

"You don't say! The accordion! Sure, if she plays the accordion, one must respect her, *heeheeheehee!*"

"Mrs. Rosalie has earned herself many a nice piece of change with it."

"By chance with an itinerant ladies' orchestra?"

"No, she played for dances."

"For dancing? I thought you considered dancing bad form?"

"That I do. But this is different. Mrs. Rosalie was born a Morgenstern, you know—"

"That I know, since she told me."

"And married into the Leiermühle near Heimberg—"

"A widowed Leiermüllerin," nodded Sam Hawkens smilingly.

"The mill owned a liquor license together with a small dance hall. Business was bad until she started to take care of it. Mrs. Rosalie purchased an accordion, learned to play, and by this means attracted the dancing youth of the entire area. As she played for the dances, she did not need to pay a musician, and thus earned a nice bit of money, since every dance cost two pennies a person. She did not work for less, for one who has been ennobled by the Muses has the duty to maintain one's value. There was not only dancing, but also eating and drinking. The business took off, and when old Leiermüller died, he left a widow sitting on a bag full of money. Mrs. Rosalie was now the richest woman in the village. She later sold the mill at a high price and then became the wife of our master blacksmith."

"Who's just as obedient as all of you!"

"Why should he not be?"

Ignoring the question, Sam asked, "How and for what reason, though, has she come to America?"

"I gave her this excellent idea."

"You. Hmm! The woman could have stayed home. She wanted for nothing there."

"Then you think one emigrates because one is poor?"

"No. But a force, an internal or external force, that is usually the reason."

"Here, too, that was the case, namely, a pressure, a *stringendo* for the New World, where things were supposed to be better. Because the smithy was not doing well. The woman was not happy at home anymore. When she heard all Hobble-Frank had told me and that I wanted to search for my heroes here in America, she was all enthused and wanted to come along."

"How did you get to know someone who lived in Heimberg, whereas you hail from Klotzsche? Are these two places close to each other?"

"No. Heimberg is located up in the mountains, whereas Klotzsche is close to Dresden. But I was born in Heimberg, corresponded frequently with people in my hometown, and also visited often. Despite all of this, the thought of going to America would not have struck her with such force had there not be the matter of the Wolfs."

"What matter?"

"You don't know about that yet?" remarked the cantor.

"No."

"Wolf, the forester of Heimberg, has a childless brother in America who owns extensive forest tracts, large herds, and, I believe, silver mines.

This brother had asked the forester to send him his son, for he wanted to train him as his successor and to make him his sole heir, if he liked him. The forester asked his son, who was at the time attending the Tharandter Forestry Academy, and the son expressed immediate interest in following this call once he had graduated. It suited the father fine, for he had a large family, but only a small salary. That meant a tight budget, and the oldest going to the academy had amounted to a sacrifice and had weighed heavily on him. It was also impossible to have the other sons acquire a better education, although they were very gifted. Hence, although Adolf left his country and parents, he told himself that becoming the rich uncle's successor would soon put him in a better position to help his siblings."

"That is an honorable principle. And now the forester's son is among you here?"

"Yes," said the cantor, pointing. "He is riding over there."

"That's him? This young man?" asked Sam, incredulously. "It's impossible for him to have already completed the forestry academy."

"Indeed he has, and he finished with excellent grades. Since his uncle has these large forests, he will be able to apply his knowledge very well. He had another reason for deciding so quickly and willingly to go to America, however, and this reason is explained by the Indian word 'Schi-So.'"

"That is the name of the chief's son?"

"Sure. You are, as I heard, a friend of the chief. Do you know perhaps why he sent his son to Germany?"

"Yes."

"I am glad to hear it. Can you tell me," asked the cantor, "or is it a secret?"

"There's no reason to keep it a secret. It is to the chief's credit as a forward-looking and progressive individual. When he was still a young man, a hostile tribe attacked a group of immigrants. All were killed; only a girl was spared and taken prisoner, a German. The chief rescued her and brought her to his tribe. There she recovered from her bad luck and suffering, after which he wanted to escort her to the next white settlement. She was treated well. Her relatives had been murdered. She had no one who knew her. The settlement she was to be taken to was strange to her. She liked it with the Navajo, and she fell in love with Chief Nitsas-Ini (Big Thunder), who had rescued her—in short: she stayed on and became his wife."

"That is something!" the cantor cried. "A redskin with a white wife!"

"Why do I hear disapproval?" said Sam. "I tell you that God the Father is the Creator of all mankind. The color of the skin makes no difference.

Before God all men are equal; he loves each and every one, whether they are red or black, yellow or white. I have gotten to know Indians compared to whom a thousand, if not a hundred thousand, whites ought to be ashamed. Nitsas-Ini is one of those. While his white wife was a simple girl, she nevertheless was above all the tribe's women and girls. She thus became the model for all the squaws. A different style arose. Different lifestyles took shape with the Navajo. Her husband, the chief, was her first and most eager pupil and later did not object to her speaking German with their children, educating them, buying them books. That's when she became acquainted with Winnetou, the great Apache, and, through him, with Old Shatterhand, the friend and protector of all well-meaning red people. With pleasure they saw what the white squaw had accomplished, what blessings she had brought. For some time, they stayed with the tribe and later returned frequently to support and further her efforts. Never again did this tribe go on the warpath, but took up weapons only for defense. Its members became friends with the whites. Nitsas-Ini had enough insight to know that his successor would have to learn substantially more than he himself had learned. He therefore decided, influenced by his smart white wife, to send his first-born to a white school. When Old Shatterhand came to visit, he wholeheartedly agreed. He was German and the squaw a countrywoman of his; thus both convinced the chief to send his son to Germany and there to entrust him to an educational institution."

"I know, I know," the cantor injected. "I know this institution. It is the same one at which Adolf Wolf received his primary education before entering the Tharandter Academy. Why, then, did Schi-So have to study forestry?"

"Because of the large forests owned by his tribe. As the future chief, he needed the knowledge not only to maintain, but, if possible, to increase the riches of these forests. It is well known that the United States employs poor forestry techniques; from the potentially great losses that might result from this, Schi-So is to protect his tribe in the future. But let's continue! Didn't you want to tell me what influence these two young forestry scholars exerted on the former Leiermüller woman, Mr. Cantor?"

The musician contorted his face in desperation.

"Yes! But first, please, finally be so kind as to observe that I no longer hold office and that you therefore have to say 'Mr. Cantor Emeritus' to protect my integrity. I am not supposed to dress up with a title I gave up long ago, and the continued omission of this most necessary word gives me reason to suspect that you believe me to still be in office and doubt my musical talents, which alone caused me to request my retirement!

"To continue, Schi-So and Wolf often traveled from Tharandt to Heimberg and visited the Leiermühle, later also the smithy, after the miller's widow had married the blacksmith. Just when Hobble-Frank had talked me into going to America to search for his heroes, the uncle's letter arrived and also the news that Schi-So was to return to his tribe. This uncle is immensely rich and, as was soon found out, lived near the Navajo. This news traveled quickly in the village, whose inhabitants were mostly poor. That is why it was not very difficult for me to convince some of them to join me in emigrating!"

"Then, so to speak, you seduced these poor people!" Sam put forth accusingly.

"Seduced? What a word! I want to lead these people to their fortune. I am convinced that Wolf's uncle will receive them very well. And money to purchase land or to start a business is also on hand."

"I thought those three were poor," mused Sam.

"Yes, the Schmidts, the Strauchs, and the Uhlmanns are poor. But the Ebersbachs are well off, as you heard, and Mrs. Rosalie has lent them the requisite money. Thus you can see what a good woman she is. She could very well have remained in the fatherland; only because of her consideration for the three, her friendship for me, and her urge to get to a foreign country did she decide to come along. She was particularly taken by the information that in America ladies are extremely well regarded and well treated."

"So that's it," Sam smiled merrily, "and Mrs. Rosalie Ebersbach, née Morgenstern and widow of Leiermüller, is also a lady! That explains the previously inexplicable. Then you all intend to settle with Wolf's uncle?"

"The settlers want to ask him. If he refuses, they will move on."

"And you? What will you do?"

"I? I will look for Old Shatterhand, Old Firehand, and Winnetou. In the process, I will also find Hobble-Frank."

"As I said before, you seem to imagine this to be very easy, yet you could travel for years in the West without finding one of these men."

"That means I have to ask about them, inquire!"

"Do you think it's like a German village or town out here, where you simply inquire about Mr. Müller, Meier, or Schulze? The people you are looking for may easily pass near you ten times, or camp only a very short distance away without your suspecting it."

"Oh, no. I foresee success. You can rest assured. Nothing is too difficult for a musician. For him who is marked and favored by the Muses, all
notes gather into harmonics. Thus all the men I seek will assemble around
me like well-trained musicians around their conductor."

"I wish you well with that! But now you should lie down in one of the
wagons to sleep."

"To sleep? What for?"

"Because we'll probably not be able to sleep tomorrow night. We'll
have to be awake, since the Finders will try to attack us."

"Are you truly convinced of that, Mr. Hawkens?"

"Yes. Someone will come to or pass by the tavern early in the morning,
will hear their shouts, and will set them free. Then they'll mount their
horses to follow us."

"To Tucson?"

"They wouldn't think of it. They surely wouldn't let themselves be seen
in that town. Circling around Tucson, they'll follow our wagon tracks until they notice that we have made camp. Just to be safe, I have taken their
ammunition. But they are surely smart enough to pick up a new supply in
San Xavier del Bac, which, however, should not be easy, since nothing
much is to be found there. Therefore, follow my advice and get into one
of the wagons!"

"Thanks! I will not sleep," announced the cantor.

"Why not?"

"Because the most beautiful musical ideas enter my mind during a
nightly ride. That is when I do the studies for my opera. Maybe I will have
an ox-drawn wagon cross the stage right in the first act, which, by the light
of a rising moon, will make a special impression, the more so, since the
instruments must imitate the cracking of the whips, the bellowing of the
oxen, and the creaking of the wheels."

"I would love to hear it!" Sam said earnestly. "It will be an exceptional
artistic experience! Never mind, then, do your studies and stay awake. But
why do you continuously throw yourself first forward, then backward? It
must be terribly tiresome!"

"That is true. But, unfortunately, it cannot be helped."

"It cannot be helped? Inconceivable! How so? It also taxes the horse
and tires it."

"I cannot do otherwise, dear Mr. Sam. I compose all the time, even
now while I am talking with you. While the melodies sound in my mind,
I must examine them for timing. That actually requires a metronome. But

since it is impossible to carry one along through the Wild West, I have invented a much more convenient one. I simply swing back and forth in the saddle at regular intervals. Certainly, the horse at times becomes confused, thinks I want to dismount, and stops. But that does not matter! As soon as I am finished with the composition, I urge the animal on again."

"But that way you will often fall behind."

"That certainly happens."

"This can become highly dangerous to you, you careless man! When you fall behind, you can easily be held up by red or white bandits."

"I will not be held up by bandits. I am immune!"

"Nonsense!"

"Do not speak of nonsense, dear Mr. Sam," continued the musician blithely. "I know what I am talking about. As the composer of a great heroic opera and self-styled poet of the requisite text, I am under the special protection of the Muses. They will not first inspire me with great musical ideas and then not guard against having me held up and killed, thus causing those ideas to be lost to the world forever. That would be akin to having a shoemaker make a pair of new boots for me then put them in the oven to destroy them. Or do you think the Muses to be less clever than a smart shoemaker?"

"Can't tell. Haven't seen or spoken to any of these maidens," said the pragmatic Hawkens. "But I cannot remain with you for the entire night and cannot impose on someone else to watch out for you all the time. Since in no case are you to fall behind with enemies behind us, I will tie you, or, rather, your horse to the last wagon here."

"Do you think this is practical?"

"Very! The horse cannot stop then, but must continue its pace, despite your swinging. At the same time, you will be by yourself and can pursue your musical creations without being disturbed."

"True, very true! This is a great idea! I am very grateful for it and, at the premiere of my opera will be pleased to offer you a free ticket. Or would you care for two?"

"I will think about it, Mr. Cantor, should I by chance—"

"Please, please, Mr. Cantor Emeritus! I swear to you, it is only to protect my integrity."

"I know, I know! And I assure you that, on my part, it is only forgetfulness."

Sam pulled a strap from his saddlebag and tied the cantor's nag to the end of the wagon. Thus he provided for the safe, regular progress of the horse as well as the opera, and the gifted composer no longer needed to be watched over continuously.

The drive proceeded through the night at the slow pace of the oxen. Finally, the travelers saw the town ahead of them only two hours after daybreak, although the distance between San Xavier del Bac and Tucson is rather short.

The sight of this capital was not very pleasant. Although it was early in the day, the sun was already blazing on the bare mud huts and masonry ruins with an almost unbearable heat. Extremely ugly, coyotelike dogs barked and howled at the wagon train and parched human figures draped in colorful rags loitered in the doorways and on the street corners. Their sunburned faces broke into contorted grins after the last wagon had moved creakingly past them and they saw Mr. Cantor Emeritus on his tethered horse. He nodded at them in a friendly manner, without taking offense at their laughter. They might consider his situation humorous; he was happy he did not have to control his horse.

On Sam's order, they stopped in an open space, where soon a large number of yapping dogs, screaming children, and idle but nosy scoundrels gathered to loiter around the wagons and focus their attention on the Shamrock and the cantor.

Since the German immigrants had learned little English on their travels and had picked up only a few Spanish words, Sam Hawkens took it upon himself to inquire whether animal feed and water for everyone could be obtained here. Yes, hay and water were to be had, but both in poor condition and at high prices. Ten, twenty and more of the lazybones were willing to fetch it in order to make a few centavos for a task that really wasn't much work.

After this the little man went to the town's commandant to present his request. He was told that the person he sought had left for Prescott with a great deal of company and that almost the entire garrison had departed for the Guadalupe area to subdue the rebelling Mimbreno dwelling there. Hawkens was ushered in to a captain, the commandant's deputy, as he sat drinking his morning chocolate and reading an old newspaper that, here in Tucson, was considered up-to-date. At the first sight of the new arrival, his face took on an expression of surprise. Then it became more and more filled with exhilaration. Finally, he laughed out loud, rose from his chair, and said, "Man, who are you? What is it you want? I haven't seen a tomfool like you before!"

"Me, either!" responded Sam, with a gesture indicating that he meant the officer.

"What do you mean by that?" the officer bellowed at him. "Do you mean to insult me?"

"Is it an insult if I agree with you?" Sam asked quietly and earnestly.

"Oh, so that's it! Then I commend you on your noble self-knowledge. Let me repeat, that I have never come across such a yokel as you seem to be. You probably come here for permission to give an entertaining performance?"

"Yes, that's it," laughed Sam. "You guessed it, sir, and you will help me with it, if I'm not mistaken."

"Help you? I? Do you take the commandant's deputy, an officer of the United States Army, to be clown like yourself?"

Sam let go his well-known giggle, but did not respond. Even-tempered, he pulled up a chair and sat down. Irritated, the officer was going to yell at him, but Hawkens forestalled him with the friendly question, "Have you perhaps at one time or another heard about the well-known 'Shamrock,' Captain?"

"Shamrock? What Shamrock do you mean?"

"The three prairie hunters, if I'm not mistaken," replied Sam.

"Yes, I know this Shamrock. It consists of Dick Stone, Will Parker, and Sam Hawkens, of whom it is said that—"

"Well, sir, well!" interrupted the frontiersman. "Then you have heard of the three. I'm pleased, very pleased! We'll soon be done, then, with our entertaining performance and find out who takes on the role of the joker. Perhaps you also know that Sam Hawkens was a scout in the last war?"

"Yes, under General Grant. Because of his outstanding service, through his cunning and boldness, he made captain. But what has that got to do with you?"

"Much, very much, sir. In any case, more than with you, for I figure that at that time you did not even wear this uniform. Do you know that the Shamrock is in town at present."

"Here? In Tucson?"

"Yes, sir. And Sam Hawkens, the meritorious captain of the United States Army, is even closer to you. At this moment, he is sitting here in your room."

"Here? In my room?" shouted the deputy, perplexed, while his eyes widened. "Then—then—then you—you would be this Sam Hawkens?"

"Yes, the very one, if I'm not mistaken, *heeheeheehee!*"

"Hell and high water! You are really Sam Hawkens? You?"

"Think so. Why should I not be?"

"Because—because—because," stammered the captain in embarrassment, "because you do not look like it. Impossible, no officer can drape himself in such clothes!"

"Don't know why he shouldn't! It happens to be my taste, the taste of Sam Hawkens, to dress like this, and whoever considers me to be without taste may do so. I don't mind as long as he keeps silent about it. But if he dares tell me to my face, he must face me with his rifle to his cheek in order to learn whose bullet will hit the heart of the other!"

All this was spoken in a tone that, despite Sam's ludicrous figure, visibly impressed the officer.

With an dismissive gesture of his hand he answered, "It's not necessary, sir, not necessary at all! Why should gentlemen, comrades in arms, shoot each other down for no reason!"

"Hmm! Since you have realized that the apparent yokel is a gentleman and a comrade, take my hand. We'll talk in peace about the entertaining performance I wish you to participate in."

They shook hands. Then Sam told him of yesterday's meeting with the twelve horsemen he thought to be the Finders.

The captain listened attentively. His face took on an ever-increasing expression of anticipation and, when the little man had finished, he jumped up excitedly, shouting, "If only you are not mistaken, Hawkens! If they're truly the Finders! What a catch!"

Sam winked at him with his little eyes and asked, "Do you think Sam Hawkens to be so stupid as not to be sure of what he claims? It's them, I tell you, it's them!"

"But why did you leave San Xavier del Bac without taking them along? They were tied up and in your power!"

"Could I prove that they were thieves, bandits, murderers, that they were truly the Finders? This proof has yet to be established by giving them the opportunity to hold us up. If we catch them at that, it will assure their conviction."

"Catch them! You want to have yourself held up?"

"Naturally! Or do you think I'm only to dream about it?"

"Just joking. But I am serious. I could not better recommend myself to my superior than with the capture of this notorious gang. But by waiting until they attack, you expose yourself to great danger!"

"By just standing there, yes. But by then Sam Hawkens will already have disappeared with all his people."

"Then we cannot speak of a holdup!"

"Why not? The wagons will be attacked and, although we will no longer be there, the deed nevertheless remains a crime on which the death sentence is pronounced in this country."

"Well! But how do you want to catch them at it without a fight and by exposing yourself to the danger of losing your life?"

"That we shall see, we'll see for sure, sir, if you are prepared to support us in this venture. Just mount your horse and accompany us with a detachment of your soldiers!"

"I would be happy to do this. But I am not permitted to leave my post here. And since I have so few people here, I could at most spare a lieutenant with twenty men!"

"That will suffice totally, sir."

"Well, then, so be it. But beforehand I absolutely need to know how you figure to handle this. Are you really that sure the Finders will follow you?"

"They'll come, as sure as my old felt hat is here, *heeheeheehee!* Obviously, they won't dare show themselves here in Tucson, but will bypass the town. But it's possible that they'll send a single scout into town. Therefore, none other than ourselves, except maybe the lieutenant, are to know of our intentions. I expect the Finders to detour the town until they again pick up our wagon tracks and to follow them until they find out when and where we've made camp for the night. They'll naturally stay back and rest until dark. After that, the attack can and will take place, if I'm not mistaken."

"And you? You don't intend to stay with the wagons, as you indicated earlier?"

"I'll be careful not to do that, *heeheeheehee!* Do you know the place where the road from Guadalupe meets the one coming from Babasaqui? And will the lieutenant you want to dispatch also be familiar with this location?"

"We've both been there several times."

"Well, fine by me, then. That's where we'll camp. There's water, which is important for our draft animals. Send the lieutenant there ahead of us with his people. But he has to keep away from the trail so that the Finders will not discover his tracks by chance and become suspicious. We'll follow later and meet him there. When it gets dark, we'll light a large, bright fire so the Finders can find us easily. Then we'll leave the wagons and hide out in the bush. When the fellows approach, we'll grab them and take them prisoner."

For a while the captain paced the room rapidly but quietly. Then he stood before Sam and said, "As you tell it, it sounds so smooth, so easy, as if it would happen just so and no other way. But the Finders will not undertake the attack without having sent a scout to your camp."

"That they will and should."

"But then the spy will notice that no one is in camp."

"No, he won't, for we won't leave before he's been there."

"That requires that you know about his coming and going!"

"That we shall, sir. You seem to believe Sam Hawkens to be more stupid than he is, *heeheeheehee!* You credit the Finders with sending a spy first. Can't we do the same? I tell you, sir, I shall spy on these fellows much earlier than they will on us."

The officer shook his head doubtfully and replied, "That should be well nigh impossible. You would have to creep up on them in broad daylight, here, where there are no woods to take cover in. Even you may not succeed at this. You also don't know where they'll be!"

"You think so? Sam Hawkens won't know where these gentlemen are hiding, *heeheeheehee!* That's saying my head wouldn't know that it's stuck beneath my hat! Don't worry, and tell me straight out whether you want to tackle this thing or not! Even alone we'll take care of these scoundrels. Only then, we'd have to have them taste some of our lead. But since I don't wish to spill any blood, I turned to you. If you supply me with twenty men, we'll accomplish with fists what we otherwise could manage only with the help of powder and lead."

"Very well, I reckon I can go along with that," the captain responded, "but I'd first like to hear the lieutenant's opinion."

"Then call the man, sir! I don't think he'll turn this venture in a different direction."

The captain called in the lieutenant and, at the end of the conversation that followed, Sam's proposal was agreed upon. After discussing some incidental details, Sam left, satisfied with the result of the negotiations with his "comrade."

Sam finally reached the top and stopped. His sharp eyes
accommodated to the dark and saw his adversaries ahead of him.

# 4

## THE HOLDUP

WHEN SAM HAWKENS RETURNED to the wagons, the entire population of Tucson seemed to have gathered curiously around them, just as in Germany the idlers congregate around a camp of gypsies to watch their activities. The settlers sat at breakfast, paying no attention to the spectators. Sam sat down with them to partake in the simple meal and to report on the result of his discussion with the captain.

Later, some of the curious came closer to talk with the travelers. However, they were somewhat successful only with the cantor, since he had acquired a larger number of English words than the others. Among those people was a young man who finally went after the scout to engage him in a conversation between just the two of them. Sam kept a close eye on him and noticed that the stranger had a military bearing and kept looking toward Sam, Dick, and Will with particular attention during this conversation. The little man, therefore, got up and approached the two. Coming closer still, he heard clearly the scout's answer to the question directed at him, "Yes, it is the Shamrock. I can assure you, although at first I did not believe it, either."

That's when Sam took the stranger by the arm and asked him in a very firm voice, "Sir, you are a soldier, right? You belong to the local garrison?"

One could see from the man's reaction that the question embarrassed him. He stammered something incomprehensible. But Sam continued, "I know who sent you. The captain doesn't know me personally, but having given me his promise of assistance, he needs to establish whether I am truly Sam Hawkens. That's why you had to take off your uniform and come to us in these clothes for verification. Admit it!"

"Yes, sir, you are not mistaken," was the response. "Since I now know that you belong to the Shamrock, I may admit to it."

"Then report to the captain what you have learned. But do not speak about it with anyone else!"

"Not a word, sir. I know what this is about. I am a second lieutenant and am among those twenty people who are to ride with the lieutenant. We'll be leaving in half an hour."

The man courteously said his good-byes, after which Sam turned to the scout, "Tell me, Mr. Poller, what possessed you to provide information about us!"

"He asked me!" the other responded curtly.

"So! Then whenever someone asks you, you offhandedly provide information?"

"Are you by chance asking me to keep my mouth shut?"

"Yes, that is indeed what I'm asking! You are aware that no one is to find out that we are the Shamrock, but you immediately gave it away to this inquirer. You want to be a scout, a frontiersman, but do not seem to know even the first thing about caution. I would not want to entrust myself to your guidance."

"You won't have to. Before you met up with us, everything went according to my instructions and my will. But now you act as if you were our lord and master. I have been hired by these people to lead them—"

"—into disaster!" Sam interrupted. "You must protect them. Are you doing that? If we had not shown up, you would have led them into being held up tonight and murdered!"

"Pshaw! I also keep my eyes peeled. Let me tell you, Mr. Hawkens, that I am to guide these people to Phoenix on the Salt River. Until then I am master of the wagon train. If you want to come along, you'll have to submit to my orders. After that, you can command as much as you want! That's it!"

That's when Sam tapped his shoulder and, with his kindest smile, but backed up by a strong will, said, "That's not it by a long shot! I know where these people want to go. It is not necessary for them to go via Phoenix. There is a shorter way that you don't seem to know. You will stay with us until tomorrow morning, then you may go wherever you please."

"Suits me fine as long as I receive my pay up to Phoenix!"

"That you will get. Then I will lead these people without asking for payment. They'll never again be endangered by the talkativeness of their scout."

The scout sullenly sat down on one of the wagon hitches. Sam turned away toward his companions.

"You've made a mistake, old man," Will Parker ventured. "I don't understand you."

"I've made a mistake? What kind?" asked the little man.

"Why should this Poller remain with us until tomorrow? You should have sent him away at once."

"That's the mistake? Will Parker, the greenhorn, wants to give Sam Hawkens good advice. Can't you see, dear Will, that I cannot send him away today?"

"No, I don't agree with that."

"Oh, dear Will, it's so sad about you! You'll never be a frontiersman. I'm ashamed to have an apprentice who doesn't comprehend a thing! But you may consider yourself lucky that I'm your teacher, for without me and Dick Stone you would long ago have been killed. Do you know what this so-called scout would do if I chased him away today? Out of pure revenge, he would go to the Finders to tell them our intentions."

"Yes," Parker agreed openly. "When you're right, you're right, Sam, old man. It's truly my sin and shame that none of your good advice and exhortations stick to me like ink stains. I don't understand at all how you can stay around me."

"That's no wonder, since you cannot comprehend anything at all. The reason is that I feel about you like an indulgent mother who loves that child most dearly who is causing her the greatest sorrow, *heeheeheehee!*"

Later, the twenty soldiers passed by. The wagon train, however, remained a little longer in town and didn't move out until noon.

The place where they were to camp for the night was approximately nine miles away, and to arrive there by evening they had to take the slow pace of the oxen into consideration. The area traversed by the wagon train was a rocky desert with only a skinny cactus or poor mesquite bush here and there. Dry wood was taken along so that a large fire could be built in the evening. On the whole, the distance between Tucson and the Gila is rocky desert country, where water for the animals can be found only in a few pools and in two or three functioning wells dug by the now-defunct mail company. This area is known as the Ninety-mile Desert. There are other watering holes, but the hostile Indians keep these sources a secret by covering them with skins that, in turn, they cover with sand and gravel, just as the nomads of the Sahara do with their secret wells.

Sam Hawkens led the wagon train. The scout no longer rode up front, but, instead, followed it. The looks he gave the little man from time to time were hostile. He obviously was contemplating revenge.

In the afternoon, when only two miles remained to be covered, Sam began to pay more attention to the road and its surroundings—as much as one could call it a "road." It was just that everyone passing through this area, whether on horseback or by wagon, went along the same path, and thus people speak exaggeratedly of "roads" between places.

The last two miles led through a wavelike countryside appearing as if a band of giants had dumped huge baskets of sand, gravel, and rocks side by side. Thus the wagons' progress was very slow. One of those giants must surely have filled his basket with large, man-sized rocks and thrown them beside and on top of each other so that they looked like a breastwork. Anyone who hid behind it was able to see a good distance without being seen himself.

Sam pointed to these boulders and called to his two friends, "This is the place where the Finders will hide. Or do you perhaps want to bet, Will Parker, that I am wrong?"

"Wouldn't think of it, old fellow," Parker responded. "As small as my brain is supposed to be, in your opinion, it nevertheless figured these boulders to be the gang's likely hiding place. But look over there, to the left, there are more of these types of large rocks. Maybe the fellows will hide over there."

"No, because here there's enough grass for their horses. Over there someone else will be hiding. Can you think of who this will be?"

"Sure, Sam, old man! You! You will hide over there to observe their arrival and spy on them."

That's when Sam clapped his hands above his head and exclaimed in mock surprise, "Is it possible? Suddenly this greenhorn comes up with a thought, a true idea, even a correct one! Either the world is ending soon, or the knot in old Will Parker's head has finally loosened up. Yes, dear Will, I will go back over there to wait for the Finders once I've seen our campsite."

"Will you take me along?"

"I can't risk it, Will. This takes skilled and experienced people. You'll have to attend school a little while longer yet."

After the party crossed several low rises, the countryside leveled off again, and about fifteen minutes later the barren gravel turned into soil capable of supporting a group of mesquite bushes and ocotillos. There was even water, provided by a well drilled by the former mail company. The campsite had been reached and everyone stopped.

First the people refreshed themselves with the water. Then the horses and oxen were watered. They soon began to pick the few green leaves from the thorny shrubbery. The wagons were drawn up in a square, as Sam had advised the day before.

The soldiers were not to be seen. Sam nodded, satisfied, and said, "Hasn't a bad head, this lieutenant. Didn't want to get here before us. But he'll show up soon."

As if his words had been heard by the just-named, a single horseman emerged from the north and approached quickly. It was the lieutenant. Having reached the camp, he shook hands with Sam Hawkens and said, "We've been in the vicinity for several hours already, but avoided this place, for someone easily could have come for water and then might have told the Finders. But now our horses need to drink. May we come here?"

"Yes, sir," answered the little man. "But at dusk you'll need to leave again. Enemy scouts, who should not see you, will be sent out. We'll tell you in time."

"Agreed! But where will the Finders wait for the right time to attack?"

Sam pointed southeast, where one could still just barely make out the previously mentioned boulders. "Behind those rocks over there, sir! Since the Finders will probably arrive while there is still daylight, they cannot proceed any further, because we would notice them."

"But won't they see me and my men?"

"No. I sat with them yesterday and know that none of them owns a spyglass. An eye, though, even a sharp one, can make out only the wagons over this distance and later, after dark, the fire. You can confidently bring your people here."

The officer departed and soon returned with his twenty men, who had kept only far enough from the camp to not be seen from there. They determined how far the troop was to retreat at dusk. Then Sam made ready for his scouting mission. He had to walk, since being on horseback would have meant poorer concealment. Thus he walked to his mule and gave her a little pat, telling her, "Lie down, old Mary, and wait for my return!"

The animal understood him perfectly, lay down, and didn't move from the spot. Then Sam turned to Parker, "Well, dear Will, didn't you want to come along?"

"Just go by yourself," was the response. "You can't use a greenhorn like me, anyway."

"But I must take you along after all, if you are to learn anything."

"I'll come along, though not to learn, but so that you aren't without help when the Finders catch you and want to scalp you."

"They may do it! They can have my skin. I'll just buy myself a nicer one."

Hawkens and Parker left the camp. To the southeast were the boulders behind which the Finders would hide, as Sam expected. More to the south they could make out the rocks where Sam wanted to take cover. They took off in that direction, but not in a straight line; instead, they arced to the west so as not to be noticed should the Finders already have arrived. Of course, Sam had left instructions for all kinds of contingencies.

When the two reached their destination, the sun already stood close to the horizon. In half an hour dusk would fall quickly at this latitude. Over at the other boulders no one could be seen yet. The scouts, therefore, looked toward the direction from which the expected gang had to come, but nothing could be made out yet.

"I wonder if they will come at all?" ventured Parker. "We only guessed they would."

"What you call a guess is certainty to me, if I'm not mistaken," Sam told him.

"Maybe they lost their desire; we've played some dirty tricks on them."

"The greater their thirst for revenge will be. Look! Isn't something moving there between the two second-to-last rises?"

Parker focused his eyes on the place and called hastily, "Horsemen! It's them!"

"Yeah, it's them. They are coming out of the depression. It's too far to count them yet, but there are no more than twelve."

"And certainly no fewer. It's them for sure. Sam, old man, you were right again!"

"I'm always right, dear Will, always, and it's not even difficult. Do you know how to act so as not ever to be wrong?"

"How?"

"Never say anything before you are sure you're right."

"Look, Sam, the horsemen have stopped! They're talking things over. I hope they don't intend to come over here toward us!"

"They won't think of it! Now they're moving on again. They're diverging from our trail toward the right. Knowing this area, they are aware that they must be up on the boulders over there in order to see our camp."

"You think they assume that we camped by the water?"

"Naturally! No human being would camp in the desert when water is to be had. Again, what a question! Will Parker, what more will I have to put up with you! Any reasonable person will camp where there is water. Look, they're riding up there, and I was right once again. They aren't coming over here."

It was obvious that the Finders were riding toward that other rock formation. The closer they came, the more carefully they proceeded by utilizing every possible cover, so as not to be seen from the water hole.

Finally, they dismounted, leading the horses behind them, since on horseback they would have been more visible. At last they arrived at the boulders and spied from behind them. From their movements, it appeared that they had caught sight of the wagon train. They staked their horses somewhere in the back, after which the men assumed various positions from which they could comfortably observe the camp.

"It's them," nodded Sam. "Twelve! I can count them now."

"Are we going over there?" asked Will.

"Yeah, as soon as it's dark."

The two did not have to wait long. The sun touched the horizon and disappeared quickly. Deepening shadows rose from the east, and at the water a high and bright fire flared up. The Finders could no longer be made out.

"Come on," Sam said to his companion. "Let's not waste time."

They left their hiding place and approached their adversaries' camp. The closer they came, the quieter their steps became, until at last they were totally silent. How Sam Hawkens could move so noiselessly with his gigantic boots was downright incomprehensible. And Will Parker moved with a skill that proved that he was not a greenhorn, although Sam was always calling him one.

When they reached the foot of the little rise, Sam gave his rifle to his companion and whispered, "Stay back here and hold my Liddy! I want to go up there by myself."

"Okay. But if you get into trouble, I'll follow you."

"Pshaw! Don't know what trouble that could be! Keep your ears open, Will, so you won't be caught off guard!"

"By whom?"

"By the scout they'll soon send out. There is little chance he'll pass by here, but nothing is impossible."

Sam lay down on the ground and crept forward. Now was the best time for a covert approach, since right after dusk the few stars visible would provide the least light.

The large and small boulders filling the depression might have caused someone not experienced in a noiseless approach great difficulty, since some might have rolled away under his hands and feet. Sam, however, moved silently forward inch by inch without moving a pebble out of position. He finally reached the top and stopped. His sharp eyes accommodated to the dark and saw his adversaries ahead of him. He would have noticed them even without seeing them, for they were not talking very quietly with each other. He dared approach even closer and at last squatted down behind a large boulder. Two or three of the Finders leaned against some boulders and looked over them toward the distant campfire. The others had made themselves comfortable on the ground. Two of them, Buttler and someone else, talked with each other. Just when Sam had made himself comfortable behind his rock, he heard the other man say, "If only we'd been able to get more ammunition! We'll have to save our shots."

"For a while only," Buttler calmed him. "We will take back everything and much more in addition. Poston—!" he called to one of his men. "It's time, it's dark enough. Move out! But don't let yourself be caught or heard or seen, otherwise the two of us will have a serious talk!"

"I won't be seen," Poston responded. "It's not the first time I've spied."

"That's why I'm sending you instead of someone else. You don't need to get into any dangerous situation, don't need to risk anything, and don't need to approach too closely. There's no need for that."

"But I would like to learn what they're talking about!"

"That's of no use to us. I only want to know whether they're by themselves at the water, or whether anyone else has joined them."

"But if I could overhear their conversation, I could find out whether they're suspicious!"

"Suspicious? Why should they be?"

"They must be aware that we'll follow them."

"They're too stupid for that. The Germans don't count, and the scout doesn't appear to be a man who'd risk his life to protect others. So there's only the three guys who were so lucky against us yesterday, despite their stupidity. Their brains surely are not capable of suspecting that we've followed them. To catch bear and beaver in traps on the Verde River! Have you ever heard of such foolishness? Go, Poston, hurry up! You should be back in half an hour."

The scout left, and the other speaker picked up again on the conversation. "When is the attack to take place, Buttler? Still this evening, or tomorrow morning?"

"Tomorrow? I can't wait that long. I have a burning desire to pay them back, all of them, but especially the little tubby fellow. No, it'll be tonight."

"While they're asleep and the fire has burned down?"

"No. We'll mow them down with a single volley. For that we need light."

"But they have a big, bright fire lighting up everything, so they'll have to see us coming."

"Stirring up such a hellish fire proves that they aren't the least suspicious. But sure, it is troubling to have the giant flames illuminate everything for so great a distance. Therefore, we've got to wait for it to burn down. But then we'll attack immediately. But no one is to shoot the little one; he is to die by my bullet."

He indulged in additional angry words and cussing about the prior day's experience. Sam listened calmly, hoping to hear some important miscellany. After a good quarter of an hour passed without anything of importance being said, however, he disappointedly left his hiding place, as quietly and carefully as he had arrived. When he met up with Will Parker, the latter returned his rifle and said, "Here's your Liddy. Was there anything to be learned?"

"Only that the attack is to take place when our fire no longer burns as brightly as it does now. We have to be ready for it. Did you see their scout?"

"Yes. He passed pretty close to me, but didn't notice me."

"Come, then. We must get back to our people."

They took off, first very cautiously, then with less care. They did not walk directly toward the camp, but took a detour so as not to come across the returning scout. They had barely covered half the distance when they heard a loud exclamation in English, followed by a second in German.

"Hell's bells!" shouted the first voice.

"Herrjemine!" cried the second. "Who's stumbling over me?"

"That was the cantor!" Sam whispered to his comrade. "I think the man is up to something silly. Let's get closer quickly, but quietly, so they don't become aware of us prematurely!"

They hurried toward the area from which they had heard the voices. When they were close enough, they stopped and listened.

"Who are you, I asked!" said the English speaker.

"I'm suffocating," came the German response.

Yes, it was the voice of the emeritus, and it sounded as if someone was throttling him.

"I want to know your name!" came in English.

"From the camp there."

"I don't understand you. Speak English!"

"I compose!"

"Do you belong to the people sitting over there by the fire?"

"A heroic opera to fill three entire evenings!"

"Man, if you don't talk sensibly, you will not get off! Answer! Who are you?"

"Twelve parts, four for each evening."

"The name, the name!"

"I'm looking for Hobble-Frank!"

"Ah, finally! Frank's your name! What are you doing here all by yourself wandering in the night?"

"I am from Klotzsche near Dresden. Let me go—oh, oh, finally! Thank God!"

The voice sounded less encumbered. The cantor had torn himself free and run away. They could hear his steps.

"He got away after all!" the English voice exclaimed angrily. "Should I—no, I've got to get back."

He did not follow the cantor, but quickly headed back to the Finders.

"It's the scout," whispered Sam. "That's a sorry thing. It may mess everything up. I'll run over to the Finders again to listen to what the man reports. Stay here! I must get over there before he does."

He took off. Will Parker waited. Half an hour passed before Sam returned. He reported, "It turned out better than I thought. The encounter could have cost the cantor his life or, had we interceded, it would have wrecked our plan."

"I wonder who the Finders think this bad-luck emeritus to be?" Parker said.

"No one talked about him. The crafty scout never mentioned the encounter."

"Unbelievable! It is so important that he absolutely had to report it!"

"He probably kept quiet because he was afraid of being reproached. Before he left, Buttler warned him not to be seen, but he stumbled over someone. If he had admitted this, he would have been in deep trouble. That's why he preferred to keep quiet. That suits us fine. Let's go into camp!"

They went on, but after only a few paces they stopped again, for they heard a noise ahead of them. As it came closer, they recognized it as hoofbeats.

"A galloping horse, heading straight for us!" Parker said.

"Yes, that's so," Sam agreed. "What's that now? Quick, move aside!"

The horse approached rapidly. The two had stepped aside just in time. As the horse shot past them, they noticed, despite the darkness, that two shapes sat on it, one of them groaning loudly.

"Was that one of our people, Sam?" asked Parker.

"Don't know. But it was two, you old greenhorn."

"They seemed to be fighting with one another," said Parker. "One of them sat properly in the saddle, the other was kneeling behind him and had him by the throat."

"I wasn't able to see that so clearly. Could you be wrong?"

"No. I was closer than you and saw it clearly. One of them was one of ours. But who could the other one have been?"

Well, as it turned out, both of them were from the company of immigrants, for in the meantime the following had happened:

Mrs. Rosalie had quarreled with Poller, the scout, and in the course of the tiff she finally cried out angrily, "Do not think we are your subordinates and slaves! I, Mrs. Rosalie Eberschbach, née Morgenschtern and widow of Leiermüllern, am in charge here just as much as you. Do you understand! You show us the way and are paid for it. That is how it is. And tomorrow you will leave! Mr. Sam Hawkens will lead us on. He knows his job better than you and, in addition, does it for nothing."

"Better than me?" asked the scout angrily. "As a foreigner and a woman, you cannot form an opinion about that. And women should generally keep quiet!"

"Keep quiet? You do not say! We ladies are to be quiet? Listen, you, you are off your rocker. What do you think we have mouths for? You would rather keep your mouth shut, because whatever you say is wrong and crazy. And do not pride yourself too much on your barely kept function as guide and scout!"

"I can relinquish this post at once!"

"So. Fine with us. It is only right. Your resignation is accepted immediately. Step down, then! You are herewith released from your position!"

"Not before I've received what's due me!"

"That you will have, and at once. For those few pennies we will not have ourselves put before the magistrate. Julius, do you have money on you?"

Julius was the name of her husband, who was standing beside her. He answered in the affirmative.

"So pay the man. I do not want him back in camp. I shall show him whether we ladies have to be quiet or not! I came to America only because the ladies are treated properly here, and the first Yankee I come across wants to tell me to shut up! That really takes the cake! So, pay him off and then good-bye!"

The scout had his wages paid as if he had accompanied them to Phoenix, to the Salt River. With a cunning smile, he put the money in his pocket. He had obviously started the quarrel only to get his pay and to leave while Sam was still away. He saddled his horse, took his rifle, and mounted. That's when Dick Stone stepped up, took the reins of the horse, and asked, "Won't you tell me, sir, why you so suddenly want to mount up? It seems you want to leave?"

"Yes. Do you mind?" answered Poller pointedly. "What do you need to know this for?"

"Not so fast! Dick Stone is the man you answer to. We are going to be attacked. That means we are either friend or foe here. Your wanting to leave right now tells us which you are!"

"You think you know why? Really?" sneered the scout. "Would you perhaps be so kind as to tell me?"

"Yes. You intend to go to the Finders to warn them."

"I think you've gone nuts, mister! I'll tell you where I want to go. I have been dismissed by these Germans and do not care to remain with them any longer; my honor forbids this. That's why I want to ride to the soldiers to stay with them until daybreak. So, that's my intention, and now, let me leave!"

Deceived for a moment by this lie, Dick Stone allowed the reins to be torn from his grip. The scout kicked his horse and rode off in the direction the lieutenant and his twenty men had retreated. But a second later, Dick Stone realized what was happening. He jumped to where his rifle lay and shouted, "The rascal lied to me. He is betraying us after all. I'll send a bullet after him."

That's when Schi-So jumped up and said, "'Do not shoot, sir! It is dark. The bullet will miss. I will bring the man back." With these words, the young man ran off into the dark.

"Bring him back? This boy?" wondered Dick. "Should be difficult for him. I have to follow him myself."

As he went for his horse, Adolf Wolf took his arm and begged, "Stay here! He really will bring him back."

"It's impossible!"

"He will get him! Believe me. Although he is still so young, Schi-So can accomplish even more difficult tasks."

The certainty in Wolf's voice and his convincing air had its effect.

"Hmm," growled Dick, "wouldn't accomplish anything if I were to chase after him. I can't even see which way they went. If he truly intends to go to the Finders, he will probably run into Sam and Will, who won't let him pass. So, I'll stay here. But it'll be the devil to pay if he escapes. What is Sam going to say about it?"

The latter said nothing at all, but was still standing beside Parker, listening with him in the direction the horse had disappeared. They could clearly hear it snorting, yet hoofbeats were no longer audible. After a little while, however, they could be heard again. They were coming back, getting closer and closer, and much slower than before.

"Peculiar," growled Sam. "The two riders are coming back, and more slowly. Let's lie down so that we can better see who it is."

They ducked down onto the ground.

Then the horse appeared.

Only one rider sat on it. He was pulling a dark object behind him.

"Schi-So!" Sam called out. "Is that you? How did you get here?"

Schi-So stopped his horse and answered, "The scout had himself paid and then rode off against our will. He wanted to betray us to the Finders. That's when I ran after him, caught up, and jumped behind him onto the horse. After I had knocked him out with the revolver grip, I stopped the animal and threw him off. The horse is pulling him now by my lasso."

"Hell's bells!" exclaimed Sam. "Running after him, jumping on the horse, knocking him out, throwing him off! This is pure Old Shatterhand! You are a brave fellow! I will tell your father. Have you by any chance killed the traitor?"

"No, he is only unconscious."

"My goodness! And all that done so quietly, without a shot fired, or any other noise, if I'm not mistaken!"

The young man answered simply and modestly, "There could be no noise, since the enemy was close by."

"All right. You did your job so well that any praise is superfluous. Come along to the camp now! We must hurry so we can finish with the Finders!"

They approached the fire. The pain caused by the dragging brought the scout back to consciousness. He started to moan, but no one paid any attention to him until the camp was reached. There he slowly got up. His hands had been tied with the lasso, which was then slung below his arms and tied to the saddle horn. His reception is easy to understand. Gloomily staring ahead, he did not respond to a single question addressed to him. Schi-So conducted himself just as silently in response to the praise received from all sides. He quietly stepped away, but could not prevent Mrs. Rosalie from taking him by the arm and asking, "Mr. Schi-So, have you ever heard the story of the enchanted princess?"

"Which one?" was his answer. "There are many such stories."

"I mean the one about the princess who had been magically confined in the top of a church tower."

"That one I don't know."

"The church tower was 111 yards high. That is why anyone wanting to rescue the princess had to perform 111 heroic deeds, one for each yard. The poor thing was stuck in the church tower for many hundreds of years, without anyone's ever getting beyond even the third or fourth heroic deed, until finally a young knight from Schleswig-Holstein came along and, one after the other, performed those 111 heroic deeds with his sword. That is when the top of the church tower opened up, the freed princess graciously stepped forth, offered her right hand to her savior, and led him down to the vestry."

"So!" smiled Schi-So. "And what does this beautiful and touching story mean?"

"Mean?" What do you mean by that? At least do not apply the meaning to your disadvantage! I have told you of this church tower, since I saw you as a brave Schleswig-Holsteiner. Are there also enchanted princesses among the Indians?"

"No."

"Too bad! I believe you would also make it to 111. You can count on my deep respect and gratitude!"

Before she could go on, someone pushed her aside, squeezing between her and the Indian. It was the cantor, who, grasping Schi-So's hand, said, "Honored friend and young man, you know I am in the process of composing a great heroic opera?

"Sure. You have told us often enough."

"And that the opera is to have twelve parts?"

"Yes, I believe you spoke of twelve."

"Nice! In which part do you want to appear?"

"Why me?"

"Because you are a hero, as I need for my opera. You will appear dragging the traitor by the lasso across the stage. Please, then, in which part?"

The Indian's usually serious countenance brightened with a merry smile when he answered, "Let us say in the ninth."

"Good! And do you want to drag him across the stage in flats or sharps, major or minor?"

"In a minor key."

"Very well. Then I will take C-minor for it, which has the dominant sixth of G, and is in the first degree related to the glorious E-flat. And for time we will not choose 3/4 or 6/8, but, rather, the 4/4 measure, since the horse on which you appear on the stage has four legs. You see how everything will fall into place. I will write everything down right away."

He pulled his notebook from his pocket. That's when a voice behind him spoke up, "I've also something for you to write down, Mister Cantor."

Turning, he saw Sam standing in front of him. Courteously, he replied, "Please, please, Cantor Emeritus! To maintain my integrity, since I no longer hold office—"

"—you were bumbling about outside of camp!" Sam interrupted him. "Who told you to leave the camp?"

"Told me? Artistic inspiration drove me outside, first *lento*, then *vivace*, and finally *allegrissimo*. You know, when the Muse commands, her disciple must obey."

"Then I urge you to say farewell to your Muse, for she does not mean you well."

"I do not think I will, worthy sir. I need a real thriller for my opera. Since I could not find it here in camp, I left to mull it over out there in solitude."

"For that you sat on the ground?"

"Yes."

"And waited for the thriller to come? But instead a stranger came who did not see you and stumbled over you!"

"Oh, he did not just stumble, he really fell hard over me. The next moment he had me by the throat just as one holds a violin by its neck."

"Then there was a duet!"

"Not really. We spoke only a little to each other."

"You in German, he in English, without either understanding the other!"

"No wonder. He who wants to understand me should not throttle me. He should know that! At that, I used the opportunity to leave him, once he let go of me."

84 *The Oil Prince*

"Also *allegro,* or was it *allegrissimo?*"

"It was more *con fretta,* for I suspected that he wanted to get hold of me again."

"He sure intended to and more than that! Do you know who it was?"

"No. There was no opportunity in the course of our short conversation to introduce ourselves."

"That I believe. There was no opportunity whatsoever for courtesies, intent as he was on your life. The man who fell over you was one of the Finders, who are preparing to attack and murder us."

"You do not say! You must be mistaken. Have I not had the repeated pleasure of explaining to you that there is no other danger to a son of the Muses than to not have his works recognized?"

"Then, when a murderer stumbles over you and grabs you by the throat and chokes you, you are in no danger?"

"No. You have the confirmation, dear sir. He let me go, and he himself left. You see, there is a guardian angel above me, protecting me and guarding me from evil."

"If this belief makes you happy, so be it, until such time as you are shot, slain, stabbed, or scalped. But your longing for a thriller has also endangered us. In the future, we will tie up not only your horse, but also you!"

"Sir, I must object! Genius knows no fetters. Even if bound, it will break all chains. How can you suppress the sound of the trumpet once it has been put to the mouth?"

"By simply taking it away from the mouth, if I am not mistaken. For now, I demand that you stay where I put you and remain quiet. All our lives depend on no one's making a mistake."

"If this is the case, I will follow your orders, rest assured. But should it come to a fight and someone die, I will be pleased to quickly compose a Mass for the Dead to any given text. I will at once ponder a beautiful and touching melody."

Until now the fire had been kept brightly burning. Now the camp was to be abandoned. Sam determined that only he, Stone, Parker, and the soldiers were to take part in the surprise attack on the Finders; the others were not to be exposed to danger. Schmidt, Strauch, Ebersbach, and Uhlmann agreed to this. Mrs. Rosalie, however, declared courageously, "What? Am I to put my hands into my lap, when others risk their lives for me? I cannot permit this, certainly not. If no rifle is left for me, I will take a hoe or a shovel, and woe to the wretch coming too close to me! Women, too, will get to perform in Mr. Emeritus's heroic opera, and I want to be the first one on stage. Tell me, therefore, only where I should position myself! I will do my job. I certainly will not run away!"

It took some effort to convince her that her participation would likely be detrimental, and she resigned herself only reluctantly to stay away from the fight. The four German immigrants, together with their wives, children, and draft animals, moved to where the troops were waiting. Naturally, the cantor accompanied them, with Sam telling them to watch him rigorously, so that he would not again depart on his search for a thriller. The horses, together with the captured scout, were also taken there for safekeeping. Schi-So and Wolf were also to be excluded from the fight, since they were both still very young. But the Indian declared forcefully that this would be a great insult to him, so Sam acceded to his wish and, consequently, could no longer reject Adolf. The soldiers, whose horses had been taken into the care of the immigrants, approached covertly. Sam Hawkens gave them the necessary instructions and, turning to the officer, said, "I'll sneak around the camp once more to see if the coast is clear."

Just when he wanted to leave, Schi-So approached him modestly and asked for permission to accompany him. Sam squinted his cunning little eyes fleetingly, then winked at the young man kindly and affirmatively. Immediately thereafter, both scurried away in different directions. Schi-So maintained a straight line leading to the Finders' location. After approximately ten minutes, he moved off a few paces to the side. Behind him the campfire burned lower and lower, until it glowed only faintly. That was when the Finders had expected to leave their hiding place. And sure enough, soon Schi-So heard something like a faint whooshing sound from that direction. It was the barely audible sound of furtive steps. Partly raising himself, he listened even more carefully. His sharp ears told him they were approaching and would pass him at a distance of twenty to thirty paces. Therefore, he quickly scurried a bit farther away, then lay prone on the ground.

And here they came, silently and slowly, in a tight group, not one behind the other, as Indians or experienced frontiersmen would have. They hurried by, and Schi-So rose to follow closely.

Thus they proceeded, they ahead and he, like a shadow, trailing. When the Finders entered the immediate vicinity of the camp, they halted. If the chief's son wanted to hear them speak now, he had to be very daring. He therefore crouched again close to the ground and crept so close to them that he could have touched the feet of the nearest. This bold undertaking was rewarded by hearing Buttler talk, very quietly, but nevertheless loudly

enough for him to understand fairly well, "The fire's barely glowing still. I
think they are asleep. Let's wait a little while, though, before we take them.
But let's surround them right now. If we maintain thirty paces' distance
from each other, there are enough of us to form a circle around the wagons. Once this is done, wait until I give the signal."

"What signal?" someone asked.

"I'll use a blade of grass to imitate the chirping of a cricket. On this signal, all of you creep toward the wagons. As soon as I am near the wagons,
I will chirp twice, then wait a bit to give you time to get close. When I
chirp a third time, you must creep beneath the hitches and wagons and
stab the men with your knives. Let's try to avoid any shots."

"What about the women and children?"

"Wipe them out, too. No one is to survive to tell on us later. We will
share the loot; the wagons and bodies will be burned. Get moving! Half of
you go to the right, the others to the left. I will stay here. But be careful to
avoid any noise!"

One of them asked, "But if we come upon a guard? Maybe they
mounted one."

"I don't think so. If so, stab him. Place the knife thrust well to kill him
instantly. Off to work, then, and listen for my chirping!"

The Finders moved to both sides to encircle the wagons. Buttler, however, stayed put. Schi-So thought for a moment. Should he hurry away
now to report to Sam? No. He had the leader in front of him. If he rendered him harmless, the others would be so much easier to overcome.
Thus he waited a minute, then rose behind Buttler, hitting him with such
a forceful blow of his revolver that he silently collapsed. Schi-So carefully
dragged the unconscious man aside. He knew exactly the place to which
Sam Hawkens had directed the soldiers, Dick, and Will. When he got
there, Sam had already returned from his circuit. The little hunter bent
down to inspect the body dragged in by Schi-So and said, surprised, "A
man! How so? Is he dead?"

"No, he is only unconscious," responded Schi-So.

"Who is it?"

"Buttler. I have taken him by surprise!"

"Darn! You've made a big mistake and wrecked my beautiful plan! Tell
me quickly how this happened!"

Briefly Schi-So complied. When he had finished, Sam told him in a
very different tone, "Hell's bells! Well, since it happened that way, I can't
scold you; I must instead praise you. I'll chirp in Buttler's place to the

Finders and deliver them right into our hands. Tie the fellow up and gag him so he can't get noisy when he wakes up!"

The soldiers were quick to follow this order. While this was happening, the lieutenant asked, "Then you want to give the signal in Buttler's place, sir? How will you imitate the chirping?"

"Very easily, with the aid of a blade of grass. You put both hands together, forming a hollow fist, with the thumbs placed side by side. Pinching a blade between both thumbs, pulling it tight, and blowing against it produces a sound like the chirping of a cricket. And now we'll move up silently behind the Finders, two of us behind each one of them. As soon as I chirp, the men will creep forward, with you following them. When I give the third signal and they prepare to crawl below the wagons, throw yourselves on them and strike them down with your rifle butts!"

"But I think," opined the lieutenant, "that a bullet or a knife thrust would be better! The bandits have forfeited their lives many times!"

"Certainly! But I'm neither their judge nor their executioner."

"But, sir, what do you think will happen to them in Tucson?"

"They will have ropes tied around their necks and be strung up high."

"That's true. They will be hanged. There is no difference, then, if they are executed here or there!"

"That may be. But remember that the law governs there, whereas here they have not yet been judged. No, no, we capture them alive. What then happens with them at the capital is your concern."

"Hmm, then I will do it, even if I believe that these bandits don't deserve such consideration."

They went into action. Stone, Parker, and the lieutenant took the lead. The soldiers left in pairs to surround the Finders. Adolf Wolf remained with Buttler, as a guard. Schi-So took Sam Hawkens to the spot where he had captured Buttler. The two formed a link in the Finders' circle while the soldiers formed another ring encompassing the Finders.

When Sam felt the encirclement was complete, he pinched the blade of grass between his thumbs and sounded the agreed-upon signal. Then he crept forward by himself and, when close to the wagons, gave the second signal, after which he waited a while. Creeping noises could faintly be heard from all sides. Sam saw the Finders, stretched flat on the ground, approaching like snakes.

The encirclement had narrowed enough for each link to recognize the next one.

"Buttler, it's me," someone whispered from the right.

"Everything is going well," came another one from the left. "Don't waste any time! Give the signal!"

Sam looked back. His sharp eyes saw Dick Stone together with a soldier lying behind the first speaker. Behind the second, two soldiers were also waiting. That's when he chirped for the third time and then threw himself to the left onto the Finder. The chief's son jumped up to the right, but Dick Stone already had the Finder by the scruff.

They could hear the strikes of rifle butts and repressed cries. Then it was quiet all around.

"Hello," Sam called out, "did everything go well?"

"Everything," was Will Parker's response from the other side. "We've got them."

"Bring them over here, then, and stoke the fire so that we can show them our faces, as courtesy dictates!"

A few minutes later, the captured and bound Finders lay inside the wagon enclosure. Sitting around them were Sam, Dick, Will, the lieutenant, and Adolf Wolf; the soldiers had gone to fetch the immigrants and the horses. Under Schi-So's leadership, a few others had departed for the Finders' camp also to collect their horses. The fire again burned high and brightly illuminated the entire camp.

The Finders lay side by side, with their eyes open. None of them had been accidentally slain in the attack. All of them had regained consciousness. They therefore saw and heard everything happening around them. None of them seemed to be in the mood to say even a word. From their angry glances, one could easily figure out what they were feeling. So far, no one had directed any questions at them, for Sam Hawkens wanted to wait until the immigrants' arrival. Suddenly they heard from afar a female voice shouting joyfully, "We have got them, we have got them!"

The caller came closer, reached the camp, crept in below one of the hitches, and dashed toward Sam, shouting, "We have got them, we have got them! Does the English make sense in German: We have them, we have them, Mr. Hawkens?" It was dear Mrs. Rosalie Ebersbach, née Morgenstern, widow of Leiermüller. She had run ahead of everyone else.

"Yes," answered Sam. "That is the meaning of these English words translated into German."

"Then, we have got them, we have got them! Thank God! I was so afraid and concerned for you! I almost ran away to come back here to fight and help. But then the soldiers came and told us, 'We have got them!' I knew approximately what that meant in our mother tongue and took off at once to see."

Her glance fell on the captives.

"But, what is that? They are still alive! I thought I would see only their dead bodies. I do not understand. Was that perhaps done on purpose?"

"Indeed."

"Well, it is as if Easter this time fell on a Thursday instead of on Sunday, as it is supposed to! Do you not know, Mr. Hawkens, that these killers intended to take our lives?"

"I do indeed."

"And you nevertheless did not shoot them? That is noble-mindedness I cannot approve of. Those who kill must be killed in turn; an eye for an eye, a molar for a molar! That is how it is written in the Bible and all the law books!"

"Have you been murdered, Mrs. Ebersbach?"

"No. How can you ask that! Had I been killed, would I not be standing now like a ghost in front of you. I hope you do not think me to be something like that."

"Certainly not, Mrs. Ebersbach. Well, then, a molar for a molar. You have not been killed. That's why we did not kill the Finders."

"But they wanted to murder us! That is quite the same as if they truly had killed us!"

"And I should have shot them for that? Isn't that exactly the same as if you had been shot?"

She looked at him perplexedly, then patted herself on the head and acknowledged candidly, "What a stupid Rosalie I have been! Let myself be beaten by my own words! This is the first time this has happened to me in my life, because whoever wants to match me in the use of sayings and sophistry has got to get to bed late and must be awake again by half past two in the morning. But tell me at least what is to happen now with these flunkies? Since you have been so kind to the rascals, the question arises of whether you ought perhaps to be given a reward, a prize, or one of those gold medals!"

"You will soon learn what we intend to do."

"I hope so. Keep in mind that I am one of the personalities they had their eye on. Had their attack succeeded, I would now lie here on the battlefield as a murdered and departed corpse, and the morning's red glow would rise on my early death. That demands punishment. Do you understand?"

"Punishment will not be lacking, Mrs. Ebersbach. You can rest assured of that. But that isn't to say that we must kill the guilty. We are not murderers, and you are a lady. You belong to the tender sex, governing the world with love and kindness. I'm convinced that in your heart, too, dwells the charitableness without which even the most beautiful woman is an ugly being."

The funny little hunter had not miscalculated by speaking in this manner. Mrs. Rosalie straightened up and responded, "Charity in here? It surely dwells here! I still have a heart, and what a heart. It melts like butter in the sun. I, too, belong to the tender sex you are talking about and want to rule the world with kindness. It often happens that a human is misjudged, and there have been a few moments when my kindness and charitableness were not fully fathomed, but on this occasion I want to prove publicly that my tender gender is strong in forgiveness. Your judgment of me shall not be proved wrong, Mr. Hawkens. I do not want to think about punishment any longer. Let them go!"

She might have gone on talking, but the soldiers arrived with their horses to settle in outside the wagons, and with them the immigrants returned, bringing the captured scout.

That started a brisk volley of questions and answers that did not end until the Germans had learned everything that had happened in their absence. The cantor, too, listened attentively, but did not sit down by the fire. He kept himself in continuous motion. He tampered with the bound captives, whose positions did not seem to suit him. He pushed and pulled first one than another, then this one and that one. Sam finally asked him, "What are you doing there? Are the people not lying right, Mr. Cantor?"

The cantor turned and answered importantly, "Cantor Emeritus, if you please, Mr. Hawkens! Only to maintain my integrity and to avoid confusion. Yes, you have guessed: the captives must be placed quite differently."

"Why?"

"Their grouping does not provide the proper overall effect. You do not yet seem to know, or have forgotten again, what I am working on?"

Without immediately thinking of the cantor's peculiar fancy, Sam asked incautiously, "What could that be?"

"Nothing but my opera. I am at work writing a great heroic opera in twelve parts and travel in this area only to collect material for it. One sequence of this opera, an excellent one, I have found here, namely, the 'Chorus of the Murderers.' They lie on the ground singing a double sextet;

however, that requires a very different grouping from the one you arranged. I am studying it now and will sketch it as soon as I have found it. Rest assured that I will be careful not to hurt the people while I am at it!"

"When it comes to that, don't hesitate to get a good hold on them! Fellows like these need not be handled with kid gloves!"

Following this exchange, the composer of heroic deeds continued his work, and that so eagerly and enduringly that Buttler finally broke his silence and called angrily to Sam, "Sir, what is this man doing with us? Make him leave us alone! We are not dolls for him to pull and push around at his pleasure!"

Sam did not bother to respond, hence Buttler continued after a while, "I must ask by what right you attacked us and knocked us out! We arrived like peaceful travelers and saw your fire. Since it wasn't clear who was camping there, we naturally crawled closer in secrecy in order to find out. Then we were maliciously struck down. We demand our immediate release!"

"Demand what you want. I don't mind, if I'm not mistaken. Free you shall be, or instead hang tomorrow in Tucson, from a nice strong gallows, *heeheeheehee.*"

"If you want to joke, tell better ones than that! It is no joke to manhandle honest people; you will be taught this yet. It may be you yourself who will hang from the gallows in Tucson!"

At that, Sam rose from the fire, walked over to him, and said mockingly, "To bring this silly charade to an end, let's introduce ourselves appropriately! My name's Sam Hawkens. You understand? There sit Dick Stone and Will Parker. We're called the Shamrock. Understood again? You think you're men enough to fool us frontiersmen?"

Fright caused Buttler to pale, and no more words crossed his lips.

Sam Hawkens continued, "I myself listened to your conversation over there at the boulders and overheard every word. You are the Finders, which, by the way, I knew already at San Xavier."

Frightened, Buttler exclaimed, "Heavens! The Finders! What a thought to mistake us for them! Who gave you that idea, sir?"

"You yourself. I've good ears."

"Oh, even the best ears can err and misunderstand!"

"You think so? Did I also misunderstand what you said earlier about the women and children?"

"Don't know anything about it."

"That they were also to be killed so that they could not possibly give you away later?"

"Haven't got the faintest idea!"

"Also, didn't I hear that you wanted to divide the loot and then burn the wagons?"

"No."

"Then you possess an extremely poor memory, which will, however, be refreshed in Tucson."

That's when for the first time the officer spoke up and told Sam, "Don't waste your breath on that man, sir! He may deny it as long as he wishes. It'll be of no use. It is proven they are the Finders and so they will hang tomorrow."

"Won't this require our testimony?" inquired Dick Stone.

"No. You move on with the wagons. I don't wish to detain you or even take you back to Tucson. You have told me what there was to tell. That's sufficient for me to appear as a witness before the court. We have more than enough evidence and can say without doubt that our area will finally be cleansed of this gang we have vainly tried to apprehend for so long. I assure you, they will all hang."

That terminated the discussion. The necessary guards were posted and everyone went to sleep. One of the soldiers had to sit with the prisoners and keep them in his sight.

The bound scout had been placed with the Finders and by chance had ended up beside Buttler. To that point, the two had not exchanged a word, although it would not have been difficult for them to secretly talk with one another. Later, when everyone was asleep and the scout became aware that the guard cared only that the prisoners not loosen their bonds, he punched Buttler with his elbow and whispered, "Are you asleep, sir?"

"No," was the answer. "Who could sleep in these conditions?"

"Then turn toward me! I wish to talk to you."

Buttler complied and inquired, "Weren't you these scoundrels' scout? How come you're being treated like this?"

"Because they suspected me of wanting to take up with you."

"But that wasn't true?"

"Not at first. The intention came later. My name's Poller, sir, and I ask you to trust me. The bet is a hundred to one you've lost out. But I'd like to save you."

"Are you serious?"

"Yes, I swear. These people greatly insulted me, and I'm not a man to let it pass unavenged. Alone I can't do anything. But if you'll help me, they'll be sure to get what's coming to them."

"Help you? Nobody can help here—neither you, me, nor I, you."

"Don't think that! I'm convinced they'll let me go tomorrow. You'll be tied onto the horses and taken to Tucson. I'll follow you."

"I'm grateful, sir! But don't think that it'll help me. It'll be impossible for me to get away."

"Pshaw! I've got a good plan. Are you so committed to your men that you wouldn't want to be set free without them?"

"Nonsense! It's every man for himself. If I can only save myself, they can dangle!"

"Well, then, we're agreed. Tell them during the ride to pretend that the aftereffects of the blows to their heads were more serious than they really were. Reel about on the horses. Feign weakness as much as possible! I shouldn't be surprised if the lieutenant were to order a stop to allow you to recover. For that your feet must be untied. Even with your hands still tied, you can quickly grab a horse and gallop off, back to where I'll be waiting. They'll be surprised and not follow immediately. That'll give you a head start. If one of them approaches later, I have a good rifle and will shoot him off his horse."

Buttler did not answer right away. He thought about it for some time, then said, "Your suggestion is the only thing that might work; I'll go along with it. If I really get free, then three times woe to this Shamrock and all those Germans! Let's keep together, Mr. Poller."

They concluded their secret conversation without the guard's noticing anything. Buttler now felt somewhat at peace and fell asleep.

Dawn had barely broken when everybody in camp rose. First a brief breakfast was eaten from the supplies the soldiers had brought along. Then the lieutenant declared his readiness to depart with his prisoners. He had them tied to their horses, with their hands forward, so they could hold the reins. While this was being done, the scout hollered at Sam Hawkens, "And what is to happen to me? Am I to remain lying here as a prisoner?"

"No," was Sam's response. "I just wanted to keep you safe for the night. Now that it's daylight, you may ride where you please."

"Well, then, set me free!"

"Not so fast, my highly esteemed Mr. Poller! I figure you would love to take vengeance on us and follow us. I will render you harmless by keeping your weapons."

"I protest! This is theft, robbery!"

"Pshaw! Call it what you will. It will not change anything."

Poller was released from his bonds, hopped, cursing, on his horse, and rode off in a westerly direction, only to later turn unnoticed in the direction of Tucson. Then the lieutenant said his farewells and took leave with his soldiers and prisoners toward the east. Now that the multitude of people had been reduced and thoughts could focus again on a single person, Sam Hawkens found that the cantor was missing. Just as some trackers were to be sent after him, he approached slowly from the west, gesticulating oddly. As he entered the camp, Sam bellowed at him vehemently, "Where have you been again? What is it you have to do out there?"

"A triumphal march," answered the music enthusiast, looking rather flushed.

"A triumphal march? Are you crazy?"

"Crazy? Why such an insulting question, esteemed sir? We have been victorious. We captured the enemy, which is why I disengaged myself to find in solitude the motif for a victory and entry march."

"Utter stupidity! You are not to ramble about by yourself out there. This is a grave mistake I cannot tolerate!"

"Mistake? Please permit me! A disciple of the arts does not make mistakes; rather, the scout did commit one."

"The scout? How so?"

"I was in the midst of the most beautiful composition when he rode up to me and took all my weapons. He left me only the saber, which he said he had no use for."

"Hell's bells!" cursed Sam Hawkens. "I thought so! Here I send the fellow off without weapons and you run out there to let him have yours!"

"Let him have mine! I would not say that. He took them from me and gave me as payment two—two—I cannot say it!"

"Go ahead, say it! I need to know."

"I cannot say it in German. In Latin it is called '*colaphus*.'"

"*Colaphus* means 'to box one's ears.' Then he boxed your ears twice?"

"Yes, and how! *Fortissimo!*"

"That was the best thing this fellow has ever done."

"Please, please, dear Mr. Hawkens! A composer and disciple of the Muses to be given two such enormous slaps in the face, he—"

"You have squarely earned them!" Sam interrupted him. "From now on, I will keep a closer eye on you than before. Get ready to leave. We will depart now!"

An hour later, the wagon train started moving. Ahead rode Sam Hawkens, who had taken the scout's position.

Buttler had firmly decided to follow Poller's advice. He saw no other means by which he could escape.

To feign exhaustion, then! As soon as he had awakened, he had told his men, but warned them not to start too early with the deception so as not to arouse suspicion. When about half the distance to Tucson had been covered, he raised his bound hands to his head and began to moan. When the lieutenant inquired about the reason, he was told that yesterday's blows to the head must have caused a concussion. Buttler feigned increasing weakness and finally began to sway in the saddle. Two soldiers were delegated to support him on the left and the right. When similar weakness manifested itself in some of the other prisoners, the lieutenant became concerned and gave orders to stop and dismount. The soldiers dismounted first to take off the straps holding the Finders' legs below the horses' bellies. Buttler was the first to whom this was done. He was lifted off the horse and immediately collapsed to the ground. Because of his great weakness, the lieutenant didn't think they needed to pay particular attention to him but instead turned to his people. This was Buttler's intention. He had noticed that the lieutenant's horse was the best of all; it stood free, since the lieutenant had also dismounted. So, while the horse troopers were not watching, Buttler jumped up, ran for this horse, and, despite his hands being bound, launched himself into the saddle, grasped the reins, and chased off—westward, where he expected to be met by the scout.

This happened so fast, the surprise paralyzed the soldiers. The escapee thus got a substantial head start before the first angry shout finally rose behind him.

"Shoot, shoot! Shoot him out of the saddle! But don't hit the horse!" shouted the officer.

Everyone ran for the horses, on whose saddles the rifles were slung. This took a good bit of time and, since the horse was not to be hit, aiming was difficult. At last shots rang out. But they aimed too high and the bullets flew high above the escapee. Soon he was out of range.

In the meantime, some of the other prisoners had used the muddle to run away or, if they had not dismounted yet, to gallop off. All this caused furious screaming and unholy confusion. The soldiers had to split up to chase after each escapee and thus only four or five were left to go after Buttler—and this in vain. His head start was too great and his horse too fast. He was lost from sight, so they returned amid many curses. He, however, rode on, until he saw a horseman ahead of him. It was the scout, his new ally, cheerfully greeting him. First of all, they looked for a safe hiding place. The next morning, they followed the tracks of the wagon train, only a day's travel ahead of them, to get their revenge.

# 5

## FORNER'S RANCHO

T THE LITTLE SAN CARLOS RIVER, a tributary of the Gila River, stood Forner's Rancho, named after its owner. This American owned a large piece of ranch land, but only the area located near the river was suitable for farming. Although the house was not large, it was built of heavy stone, surrounded by an equally strong wall as tall as two men. The wall was equipped with regularly spaced narrow embrasures, a highly necessary provision in this remote and dangerous area. The courtyard surrounded by the wall was large enough for Forner to drive all his livestock inside should hostilities with the Indians break out.

Now was the best time of year. The country was covered by dense green grasses for the numerous cattle and sheep. Several dozen horses also grazed in the open, watched over by attendants who, because of the currently peaceful times, were playing cards. The broad gate facing the river stood wide open. The ranchero appeared, a true, sinewy, and sturdy backwoods figure. He cast a sharp eye over the grazing livestock, then shaded his eyes with his hand to better peer into the distance. His face took on an expression of close attention, after which he turned, shouting, across the yard, "Ho, boy, get the whiskey bottle ready! Someone's coming who'll drain it to the bottom."

"Who?" came the question from Forner's son at one of the house's windows.

"The Oil Prince."

"Is he alone?"

"No. He's accompanied by two other horsemen and a pack horse."

"Well, if they drink like he does, I might as well put out several bottles right away."

In front of the house lay ten or twelve stone slabs arranged in such a way that the largest of them, in the center, formed a table while the smaller ones served as benches. Forner's son soon came out and put three full bottles of liquor and several glasses on this table. Then he crossed the yard to stand at his father's side to welcome the arrivals.

The small band had reached the opposite bank of the little river and were driving their horses into the shallow waters.

"Is it possible!" exclaimed Forner in surprise. "I must be mistaken. I sure don't know what brings this man from safe Arkansas to our unsafe neighborhood!"

"Who?" asked his son.

"Mr. Duncan from Brownsville."

"Is this by chance the banker you once had some dealings with?"

"Yes. And it's really him! I'm not mistaken! I wonder what he's looking for in the wilds of Arizona?"

The horsemen had made it to the near bank of the river and began trotting toward the rancho. From afar the first rider called, "Good morning, Mr. Forner! Have you got a hefty swig on hand for three gentlemen ready to fall off their horses from thirst?"

The speaker was a tall, slim, and very well armed man, his narrow face tanned dark by the sun, wind, and weather. He wore an almost fashionable suit not befitting the surroundings or himself.

The second rider was an elderly gentleman with a portly appearance. The fast morning's ride had apparently stressed him; he was sweating. At his saddle hung a nice hunting rifle. Whether he carried any other weapons—possibly in his pockets—was not apparent, since he did not wear a belt. It was clear that the Wild West was foreign to him, or that at the very least he was not at home there. His condition could be compared to that of a landlubber on the high seas.

The third arrival was a young, blond, sturdily built man who, although obviously not an experienced frontiersman, appeared to be a good horseman. His was an open, friendly face, lightly tanned. His weaponry consisted of a rifle, a Bowie knife, and two revolvers.

"More than a swig!" responded Forner. "Welcome, sirs! Dismount and relax at my place!"

The portly gentleman halted his horse, briefly examined the ranchero, and then said, "It appears to me we have seen each other before, sir. Forner's Rancho! Then you must be Forner. Have you been at my place in

Brownsville? My name's Duncan, and the young man here at my side is Mr. Baumgarten, my bookkeeper."

Forner nodded toward both and responded, "We have certainly met before, sir. I had my savings with you and picked them up before coming to Arizona. It wasn't an amount large enough to remember me for, though. Come in! My brandy is better than most, and you are welcome to a meal if you can live with what we have. How long do you intend to stay, Mr. Grinley?"

"Until the hot noontime sun has passed," answered the one who had earlier been called the "Oil Prince."

The saddles were taken off the horses, which were then led to pasture. The horsemen took seats on the stone benches. Grinley immediately poured himself a glass of whiskey and downed it in one swallow. After only a short while, he was able to see the bottom of the bottle. The banker mixed his brandy with water, while Baumgarten drank only water. Both Forners, father and son, had retreated to the house to prepare a meal for their guests from their simple stores.

None of these people were able to see the two horsemen now crossing the river and approaching the rancho. They definitely appeared to have had a long ride behind them, as their horses were very tired. The two men were Buttler, the leader of the twelve Finders, and Poller, the fired scout of the German immigrants. As they approached the gate, Poller asked, "Are you truly convinced the ranchero does not know you? You've described him to me as an honest fellow, and I'm afraid the name Buttler may cause suspicion."

"He's never seen me," answered Buttler. "Only my brother has seen him often."

"Whose name, naturally, is also Buttler!"

"Indeed, but here he has always called himself Grinley."

"That was smart. But brothers often look alike. This is probably true of you, too?"

"No. We are half brothers with different mothers."

"Do you know where he is at present?"

"No. When we last separated, I went south to start the Finders. He, however, was undecided where to go. Who knows where we will meet again, if ever in this life—by the devil, there he sits!"

At that moment the two arrived at the gate and saw the three strangers seated in the yard. Buttler recognized the Oil Prince at once and halted his horse in surprise. Simultaneously, Grinley's glance wandered toward the gate. He, too, recognized Buttler, but, despite his surprise, had the presence of mind to put a hand over his mouth, an unmistakable request for silence.

"Yes, it's him," Buttler continued while prodding his horse on and entering the yard. "Did you see the signal he gave me? We are to pretend not to know him."

After dismounting, they let their horses run and approached the stone benches just as the two Forners came out of the house with meat and bread for their guests. Buttler and the scout offered greetings and asked whether they could join the group. They were not denied permission and partook of food and drink without being asked for their names and destination.

The two brothers, who were not supposed to know each other, nevertheless were eager to talk to one other. This, however, had to take place in secrecy. Thus Grinley got up after the meal and told the others that he was going behind the house to lie down in its shade for a little rest. Buttler followed him soon thereafter as inconspicuously and unaffectedly as possible. The others remained seated.

Meanwhile, two more riders approached—not from the other side of the river, but instead on the near bank. They were both very well mounted. From a distance one could almost have taken them to be Old Shatterhand, the famous prairie hunter, and Winnetou, the equally famous chief of the Apache. Both were too short, however; one of them stout, the other, slim.

The slim one wore worn-out leather leggings and the same type of shirt, in addition to long boots, which he had pulled up above his knees. On his head sat a broad-brimmed felt hat. In his belt, woven of individual strands, were stuck two revolvers and a Bowie knife. From his left shoulder to his right hip was slung a lasso and on a silken string suspended from his neck hung a peace pipe. Across his back he carried two rifles, a short- and a long-barreled one. This was similar to Old Shatterhand's manner of dress. He, too, carried two rifles: the feared twenty-five-shot Henry carbine and the long, heavy bear killer.

Whereas the small, slim man seemed intent on sporting a likeness of Old Shatterhand, the other had made an effort to imitate Winnetou. He wore a white-tanned hunting shirt decorated with red Indian embroidery. The legging seams were trimmed with hair; however, it was doubtful it was scalp hair. His feet were shod in pearl-embroidered moccasins decorated with porcupine quills. He, too, had a peace pipe suspended from his neck and a small leather bag supposed to represent an Indian medicine pouch. His hefty hips were surrounded by a broad belt made from a Saltillo blanket. From it protruded the handles of a knife and two revolvers. His head was not covered. He had let his hair grow long and had arranged it in a bob. Across his back was slung a two-barreled rifle whose wooden parts were studded with silver nails—an imitation of the famous silver rifle of the Apache chief Winnetou.

Anybody acquainted with Old Shatterhand and Winnetou who beheld these two little men could not have resisted a smile. The smooth-shaven, good-natured, and somewhat saucy face of the slimmer man in comparison to Old Shatterhand's manly, imperious features; the blushing red, round cheeks, the guileless eyes and friendly smiling lips of the plump one, to the likeness of the serious, bronzed face of the Apache!

Nevertheless, these were not people to be laughed at. It's true that they possessed certain striking peculiarities, but they were honorable men through and through and had boldly and fearlessly faced plenty of danger. The stout one was the frontiersman known as "Aunt Droll"; the slim man was his friend and cousin Hobble-Frank.

Their admiration for Old Shatterhand and Winnetou was so great that they imitated them in dress, which gave them a somewhat unusual appearance. Their clothing was new and must have cost some money. They also had not scrimped on their horses.

They, too, regarded the rancho as their destination and passed through its gate. They caused something of a stir as they entered the yard due to the contrast between their martial furnishings and their good-natured demeanor. Without so much as a by-your-leave, the pair dismounted, greeted everyone briefly, and sat down on two of the still-vacant stone slabs.

Forner examined the two new arrivals curiously. Despite being an experienced man, he nevertheless could not make heads or tails of them. Unable to overcome his curiosity he inquired, "Would the gentlemen also care to eat something?"

"Not now," answered Droll.

"Later then?" asked the ranchero. "How long do you intend to stay?"

"That depends on the local conditions and what they require."

"I can tell you that you are safe with me."

"Elsewhere, too!"

"You think so? Then you don't know that the Navajo are on the warpath?"

"We know."

"And that the Moqui and Nijora, too, are in full rebellion?"

"That too."

"And you feel safe nevertheless?"

"What would make us think we are not safe, if it is necessary?" asked Droll.

It is a peculiar and well-known fact that there is rarely a frontiersman who isn't in the habit of using a pet phrase. Sam Hawkens, for instance, frequently used the words "if I'm not mistaken." Droll had acquired the expression "if it is necessary." Since these phrases were applied at every opportunity, they often came across as ridiculous and frequently expressed the opposite of what was intended. Such was the case now.

Forner looked at the chubby one in surprise but continued earnestly, "Are you familiar with these people, sir?"

"A bit."

"That's not sufficient. You've got to be on friendly terms with them, but even then it is possible to lose your scalp, once they've decided to fight the whites. If by chance your travels take you north, I warn you, it is by no means safe there. Although you are well equipped, I can see from your clothing that you have come straight from the East, and your faces don't immediately call to mind the intrepid frontiersman."

"That's very candid," replied Droll. "Then you judge people by their faces, if it is necessary?"

"Yes."

"Rid yourself of this notion as soon as possible! You shoot and stab with the rifle and the knife, not with the face. You understand? Someone may have very hostile and fierce features and yet be a coward."

"I do not want to dispute that. But you—hmmm. May I perhaps inquire as to who you are, sirs?"

"Why not? We are—well, we are what is called 'retirees.'"

"Oh, boy! Then you have come to the West for some fun?"

"To our great regret, that is not so!"

"But if that's so, then turn back at once, or you will lose your life, like a candle being snuffed out. From the way you talk, I take it that you have no idea of the dangers awaiting you in this area, Mr.—Mr.—what is your name?"

Droll reached casually into his pocket, pulled out a business card, and passed it to him. The ranchero made a face as if he could hardly suppress laughter and read aloud, "Sebastian Melchior Droll."

Hobble-Frank, too, had reached into his pocket and had given him his card. Forner read, "Heliogabalus Morpheus Edeward Franke."

He halted for a moment, but then could not keep himself from laughing, "But, gents, what kind of peculiar names are these and what kind of odd people are you? By chance, do you think the rebelling Indians will run away from those names? I tell you that—"

He was interrupted by Duncan, the banker, who asked him, "Please, Mr. Forner, do not say anything that might insult these gentlemen! While I do not have the honor of knowing them personally, I know them to be respectable people." Turning to Hobble-Frank, he continued, "Sir, your name is so unusual that I remember it. I am the banker Duncan from Brownsville, Arkansas. Did you not have monies deposited with me several years ago?"

"Yes, sir, that is correct," nodded Frank. "I entrusted them to a good friend who deposited them with you, since you had been recommended to me by Old Firehand. I was later unable to withdraw the money personally, which is why I had it sent to New York."

"That's true, that's true!" interjected Duncan. "Old Firehand, yes, yes! At that time, you had found a large quantity of gold and silver up north at Silver Lake. Isn't that so, sir?"

"Yes," Frank laughed merrily. "Some thimblefuls it was."

Forner jumped up from his seat and shouted, "Is that true? Is it possible? You've been up there at Silver Lake?"

"Certainly. And my cousin here, too."

"Really, really?!" exclaimed Forner excitedly. "At the time all the newspapers were full of the adventure. Old Firehand, Old Shatterhand, and Winnetou were along, as well as Big Jemmy, Long Davy, Hobble-Frank, Aunt Droll, and many others! Then you know these people, sir?"

"Sure I know them," replied Hobble-Frank. "There, beside me, sits Aunt Droll, if you will kindly permit me."

With these words, he pointed at his companion while the latter pointed back at him and declared, "And here is our Hobble-Frank, if it is necessary. Do you still consider us to be people who are unfamiliar with the Wild West?"

"Unbelievable, utterly unbelievable! It just can't be! Aunt Droll is never seen other than in a very peculiar dress, which makes you think he's a lady. And, as is well known, Hobble-Frank wears a blue tailcoat with shiny buttons and a big feather hat on his head!"

"Must that always be the case? Cannot a person dress differently from time to time? As friends and companions of Old Shatterhand and

Winnetou, we just happen to dress at present like these two men. It is your business if you do not believe us. We do not mind."

"I believe it, sir, I believe it! I have heard that one cannot take from Aunt Droll's and Hobble-Frank's appearance what great men they are, which is being proven here. I sure am happy to meet you, sirs. You must tell your story now. I'm extremely eager to hear from the horse's mouth what all happened then and how this magnificent placer was discovered."

The banker warded off the inquiry. "Slowly, slowly, sir! You can hear this any time. First there is something more important, at least to me." This he addressed to Forner. Then he added, turning to Droll and Frank, "I am facing a similar situation. I'm on the way to make many millions."

"Do you also know of a placer, sir?" Droll inquired.

"Yes. Not gold, though, but oil is to be found there."

"Not bad either, sir. Petroleum is liquid gold. Where is this 'placer' to be found?"

"That's still a secret. Mr. Grinley has discovered it; however, he does not have the means to exploit it. It requires lots of money, which I have. He has offered me the 'placer,' and I am prepared to buy the rights from him. Such deals require one to look things over with one's own eyes. This is why I've come here with my bookkeeper, Mr. Baumgarten, to have Mr. Grinley take us to the location itself. If his description proves to be correct, I will buy the place on the spot."

"Then you do not know yet where he will take you?"

"Not exactly. It's understandable to keep the place a secret until the last moment. One cannot be careful enough when dealing with millions."

"Very true. It can only be hoped that he is not the only one acting cautiously, for you have even greater reason to be at least as careful. But you must know approximately where the oil is to be found?"

"That I do know."

"Where, then? Provided you are prepared to tell me."

"I will be happy to tell you, for I would like to hear your opinion. It is located on the Chelly arm of the San Juan River."

Droll's full red face grew long. He thoughtfully looked downward, then said, "At the Chelly arm of the San Juan River? There—petroleum—is to be—found? Never in my life!"

"What? How? Why?" shouted the banker. "You don't believe it? Do you know the area?"

"No."

"Then how can you judge so negatively."

"Why not? One need not have been there to know that there cannot be any oil."

"I must contradict this. Mr. Grinley has been there and has found oil. You, however, have not been there, sir."

"Hmm! I have not yet been in Egypt and at the north pole. But if someone told me he had seen buttermilk flowing in the Nile or palm trees growing at the north pole, I would not believe it."

"You poke fun. In order to make a quick and definitive judgment, you would need to be a geologist. Are you?"

"No. But I am possessed of common sense and have trained it."

That's when Forner interceded, explaining to Aunt Droll, "You do an injustice to Mr. Grinley, sir. Everyone here knows that he has found petroleum. Quite a few have tried to follow him to steal his secret and to discover the place, yet always in vain."

"Of course in vain, since this place does not exist!"

"It exists, I tell you! Everybody here calls Mr. Grinley the 'Oil Prince.'"

"That does not prove a thing."

"But he has shown me samples of the oil on various occasions!"

"This, too, is not proof. Anyone can show you petroleum. It is simply unbelievable that oil should be up there. Beware, Mr. Duncan! Remember that not too long ago swindlers enticed many people into so-called gold and diamond fields. Then it turned out that there were neither metals nor gems!"

"Sir, do you suspect Mr. Grinley?"

"I would not think of it," said Droll. "It is actually none of my business. But you asked for my opinion, and I have given it to you."

"Good! May I inquire what Mr. Frank thinks?"

"Quite the same as Mr. Droll," responded Hobble-Frank. "And if you do not wish to agree with us, then wait here for a few days. Two people will come by on whose judgment you can rely."

"Who will that be?"

"Old Shatterhand and Winnetou."

"What?" asked Forner, pleasantly surprised. "They will come here? How do you know?"

"From Old Shatterhand," said Frank. "He sometimes sends me a letter, and eight weeks ago wrote that he had arranged with Winnetou to meet at Forner's rancho at the San Carlos River ."

"And you believe they'll come here?"

"Certainly."

"Something could prevent it!"

"Yes, but then one will wait for the other. As soon as I read the letter, I decided to surprise them here. My cousin Droll was in agreement, and for us to have come from Saxony should convince you that we firmly believe we shall meet here with Old Shatterhand and Winnetou."

"From Germany? From Saxony?" Baumgarten, the bookkeeper, quickly interjected. "Then you must be a German, sir?"

"Yes. You did not know this?"

"No. I am very pleased to greet a fellow countryman. My hand, sir. Permit me to shake yours!"

Hobble-Frank offered his right hand and happily called out in his native Saxony dialect, "Here, take 'em with all the fingers belonging to it! You, too, are a German? If I had not seen it, I would not believe it! From which area did you come to this side of the ocean?"

"From Hamburg."

"From Hamburg? What are the chances? Only a few hours from the geographic spot where my beloved Elbe celebrates her engagement with the North Sea. Then we have both been baptized with water from the Elbe, and, once I am back at my Bärenfett, I can send you greetings via her waters without needing postage."

"Bärenfett?" Baumgarten asked, astonished.

"Jawohl, jawohl! Bärenfett's the name of the villa I've built myself in my beautiful home country. When you come to Saxony, you must visit me there, for there you will find all the mementos and remembrances of my foreign and domestic experiences."

Baumgarten remembered that Hobble-Frank had been described to him as quite a strange human being. Now he had the man life-sized in front of him and with great enjoyment engaged in the happily flowing conversation. The latter gained in liveliness as a result of Droll's participation in his Altenburger dialect.

Meanwhile, Poller, the fired scout, got up from his place, giving the impression he was going to look after his horse. For a while, he occupied himself with the animal, but then he disappeared behind the house, where the two Buttler brothers lay side by side in the grass discussing highly important subjects.

Since one of them had been introduced at the rancho by the name of Grinley, his name was to be kept as such. In former times, the brothers Buttler, together with other like-minded people, had committed a string of outrageous acts at the borders of California, Nevada, and Arizona.

Finally, due to dire necessity, a company of vigilantes had been formed to end the disorder against which the law had shown itself to be powerless. It was successful. Most members of the gang had been lynched. Only a very few had escaped, among them, however, the two worst, the Buttlers. As mentioned before, they had separated. One of them had gone south to initiate the Finders; the other, for a long time, had aimlessly tramped through Utah, Colorado, and New Mexico, until he had hit on the vile scheme whose execution he at present pursued.

When Grinley had communicated the most important details to his brother, Buttler favored him with an admiring look. "You've always had the most cunning ideas! It's an appealing plan, indeed. Do you think that this banker will really fall for it?"

"Absolutely. He's very enthusiastic about the enterprise, which, in one fell swoop, will net me at least one hundred thousand dollars."

"He's willing to commit that much!" the other exclaimed.

"Quiet! Not so loud! At times, the grass has ears. He is convinced he will make some easy millions in a very short time! What, then, is a measly hundred thousand dollars, which will pay me off once and forever!"

"But when will he pay? He's bound to discover the fraud immediately."

"He must pay up front! I know he has the draft in his pocket. It needs only to be signed, which he will do, once the oil has made him as giddy as I expect."

"But why has he not brought a real expert with him?" wondered Buttler. "The bookkeeper he's got with him must be worthless in that respect."

"Yes, I had to play this very skillfully," boasted Grinley. "The more company, the more buyers. I am to be solely dependent on him so as not to find any other opportunity for a sale. Had he brought an engineer, the same could easily have dealt with me in secret on his own account. Duncan believes he conceived of this idea himself, although I was the one who suggested it to him. He needs the bookkeeper to immediately issue his orders to all sides. I put up with him, since he is stupid and inexperienced in the Wild West. We do not need to fear him. He would be the last to arrive at the idea that the petroleum is a fraud."

"Are you convinced your oil stores are sufficient?" Buttler pressed his brother further.

"They're enough. But you can imagine what effort it cost me to move the barrels one by one over this distance! No one could suspect anything, and I had to avoid any encounters on the way. I've slaved over it for half a year and had to do everything myself, since, except for you, I couldn't have any confidant. And you were not around."

"Would you have been able to accomplish what's left to do without help?"

"It would have been difficult. Think about it: with me being the banker's scout, I cannot separate myself from him, or he may become suspicious. And yet I'd have had to in order to dump the oil into the water. There are thirty barrels—a veritable bugger of a job for a single person, who most likely would not even have the time to do it! So I am all the happier to have met up with you, for you'll help me, right?"

"With the greatest pleasure," replied his brother. "I assume, naturally, that it will not be for nothing."

"Of course! But I don't want to give away the hundred thousand dollars, since I have honestly earned them, and you'll not have to do more than open the barrels. I'll simply ask Duncan for more and the extra will be yours. You understand?"

"And if he doesn't give more?"

"He will, I assure you. And if I am mistaken, you know me and know I'll settle with you. But you have to leave today, because if you stay any longer, something may happen to arouse suspicion should they find out that we know each other."

"I have to leave anyway, since those immigrants with their 'Shamrock' will arrive by afternoon, and they must not see me."

"Do they suspect that you're pursuing them?"

"No, at least, I don't think so, since they can't have heard of my escape. It was quite an effort today to pass them. That smart Sam Hawkens has shown them a shortcut and, in order to travel faster, has traded the slow oxen for faster mules at Bell's farm and sold the wagons and all unnecessary equipment. Now they're all riding."

"You're sure they'll arrive here today?"

"Yes. Last night I spied on them at their camp. Poller heard it, too."

"Ah, this Poller! Isn't he in your way?"

"Not yet."

"In mine, though. Can you get rid of him?"

"Hardly. For revenge, he'd give me away to the Shamrock and would surely tell them about you."

"But he doesn't know me!"

"Yes, he does. When I saw you sitting there, I told him you were my brother. While we're here, talk will surely move to your oil well. He'll for sure figure out what's going on and would betray you if I dumped him."

"That's bad. You shouldn't have told him anything!"

"It's done and can't be changed now. Besides, he can be of help; he can make my work up at Gloomy Water a lot easier."

"You want to let him in on our scheme?"

"Only partly."

"He'll still want a share!"

"Maybe. But he won't get anything. Once I don't need him anymore, I'll do away with him."

"Well, I'll go along with that. He can help us now; later, he'll get a bullet or will drown in the oil," Grinley said callously. "When are you leaving?"

"Now."

"Good! Then you can be far from here by tonight."

"You're wrong there. I wouldn't think of letting those German immigrants out of my sight."

"If you want to help me, you'll have to let them go."

"No way," argued Buttler. "One of them by the name of Ebersbach carries a lot of cash on him, and they have a lot of things that would be useful to us. On top of that, I want revenge. I can't get it out of my mind."

"I don't like it at all. It doesn't fit into my plan!"

"Why not? Their way takes them past Gloomy Water. Just join them. The rest is my business."

At this point, they saw Poller approaching. Stepping closer, he said importantly, "I must disturb you, for significant things are happening up front."

"Are they so important that you have to interrupt us?" Buttler asked, annoyed.

"Yes, because Old Shatterhand and Winnetou are expected here."

"Hell's bells!" Grinley exclaimed. "What do they want here?"

"Why do you care if they come?" Buttler asked, in a calmer tone. "It's of no consequence to you where they are. How do you know, Poller, that they're coming?"

"Right after you left, two strangers arrived who intend to wait here for Winnetou and Old Shatterhand. They're sitting there and talking with the banker's bookkeeper in German."

"How did you know it's a bookkeeper with this banker?" Grinley asked.

"Duncan himself said so."

"The devil—! Has he told them even more about us?"

"You mean about the oil? Yes, he told them about it, too."

"That's bad, really bad!" Grinley exclaimed, jumping up. "I must get back to prevent further disclosures. You said they speak German. Are the strangers Germans, then?"

"Yes. One of them is called Aunt Droll, the other, Hobble-Frank."

"You don't say! Then they're part of the group that became rich so quickly up at Silver Lake!"

"Yes, they talked about it. These two fellows seem to have a lot of money on them."

"And what did they say about my oil well?"

"They don't believe it and have warned the banker. They think it's a fraud."

"Damn! Didn't I smell trouble right away when I heard Old Shatterhand and Winnetou were coming! They haven't arrived yet and already the devil starts spinning his yarn! That just means that we must take the saddle more tightly between our legs. How did the banker respond to the warning?"

"He didn't seem to lose his confidence," replied Poller. "But they advised him to wait here for Winnetou and Old Shatterhand and get their advice, too."

"That's just what we need! Did he go along with it?"

"No, but he appeared very reflective."

"Then I must get to him to talk him out of his whims," said Grinley. "But first I have to get things cleared up with you, for you must leave. Listen to what I have to tell you!"

For a short while they spoke hastily and quietly. Promises and assurances appeared to be exchanged, for they shook hands repeatedly. Then Buttler and Poller walked to the front of the house and told the ranchero that they had to depart. They wanted to pay for what they had consumed, but he refused, stating that his rancho was not an inn. They rode off before anyone had learned their names or intentions or had even asked about them.

Shortly thereafter, Grinley came strolling around the house. He acted as if he were rested and sat down again at his place while courteously greeting Frank and Droll and trying to put on an open, honest face to gain their confidence. The banker, however, could not restrain himself. He had to air his concerns: "Mr. Grinley, here sit two good acquaintances of Winnetou and Old Shatterhand, namely, Mr. Droll and Mr. Hobble-Frank, who do not believe in your oil well. What do you say to that?"

"What do I say to that?" the other responded in an even-tempered way. "I say that I don't hold that against them. Where one deals with large sums, one must be cautious. I myself did not believe it until my oil samples had been tested by several experts. If it pleases the gentlemen, they may accompany us to convince themselves of the quantities of oil the place holds."

"They intend to wait here for Winnetou and Old Shatterhand," said Duncan.

"I don't mind that. But since I don't want to sell my placer to either Winnetou or Old Shatterhand, it is not I who have to wait for them."

"But if I should want to wait?"

"Then I wouldn't think of preventing you. I'll not force anyone to come with me. If I ride over to Frisco, I can find enough investors to jump in who will not desert me on the way. Whoever doesn't believe me can stay away!"

He downed a full glass of brandy and then walked to his horse.

"There you go," the banker said. "Doesn't his behavior convince you completely that he's sure about his find?"

"That he is," voiced Aunt Droll. "But whether this thing is true or not will show up only later."

"I've insulted him and he'll not wait here," worried the banker aloud. "I can't let him leave by himself. I have to go along, since I don't want to miss out on this big deal. You must admit that your mistrust doesn't prove anything," he said to Droll and Frank.

"Not to you, probably," replied Droll. "We thought it our duty to caution you. We have said that up there, where you intend to go, no oil is to be found. By that we do not claim that your Grinley is necessarily a cheat, since he may himself be mistaken. But let me openly tell you that I do not like his face. Me, I would think ten times before I would trust him."

"I thank you for your candidness, but it is my opinion that one cannot hold a man responsible for his face, for he has not given it to himself."

"You are mistaken there, sir," disagreed Droll. "Indeed, the face is given the child by nature, but then is modified by education and other impressions in which the soul partakes from inside. I will not trust a man who cannot straightforwardly and sincerely look me in the eye, and that is not the case with this Mr. Grinley."

"With that in mind, sir, I would not act carelessly, even without your warning. I am a businessman and used to thinking clearly. Here, in a situation dealing with a great sum, I will reflect a hundred times before I say ten words. And, besides, we are two against one, for Mr. Baumgarten is loyal and experienced."

"Hmm, Grinley may have accomplices up there waiting for you. Consider, too, that the redskins whose territory you will be crossing appear to be on the warpath just now. And even if this were not so, the fact that you are two against one does not provide the least security. He could shoot you, or take you in your sleep to force money from you or other things. That is why I suggested that you wait here for Old Shatterhand and Winnetou, on whose judgment you can rely."

For a while Duncan sat in quiet contemplation, but then spoke, "Unfortunately, I'm not able to wait for them. If I insist on staying here, the Oil Prince will surely ride off without me."

"I, too, am convinced of that," said Droll, "and I also know the reason: He is afraid of meeting Winnetou and Old Shatterhand. In any case, I have done my duty and you must decide for yourself now what to do."

"This is difficult, very difficult," worried the banker, "the more so since the decision must be made so quickly. Up to now, I've had the fullest confidence in Grinley. Now it's nearly gone. What am I to do? Give up on it? It would be the greatest stupidity were it all true! Mr. Baumgarten, you are closest to me. What's your advice?"

The young German had followed the conversation attentively without taking part in it. Now that he was asked to speak, he responded, "The issue is so important that I can take no responsibility for it. But what I would do in your place, sir, I can tell you. I would ask these two gentlemen here, Mr. Droll and Mr. Frank, to accompany us. They are two men with hair on their chests and with them on our side we can cope with any danger."

"That actually would be a good solution!" exclaimed Duncan. "But would you really ride with us, gentlemen?"

"Hmm," ventured Hobble-Frank, "actually, we would be pleased. Primarily, because Mr. Baumgarten is German, and we Germans stick together around the world. But you know why we have to stay here."

"Have to?" Baumgarten interjected. "Not really. Winnetou and Old Shatterhand can follow us, or, if they do not want to, may wait here for your return. Keep in mind that Old Shatterhand and Winnetou are masters of their own time."

"We admit that. In this respect, we frontiersmen are not just barons, but even counts and princes. Besides, we are convinced that our famous friends will gladly wait for us. What do you think of that, Cousin Droll?"

"We shall ride along," answered Droll, decisively.

"Old Shatterhand will surely follow and the Apache, too. I am eager to keep a few tabs on this Oil Prince and, since he does not want to wait, there is no alternative but to come along. There are two reasons important enough to make us come along: we are dealing with a million-dollar deal, and Mr. Baumgarten is a German with a right to our help."

"I thank you," said Baumgarten while pressing Frank's and Droll's hands. "I want to be honest now and admit that I have not had full confidence in the Oil Prince. Because of that, I asked Mr. Duncan to take me along. On the way, I watched Grinley closely, but never discovered anything that increased my mistrust. Now, however, with people like you at our side, I am no longer afraid of what may happen. Shake hands! Let us be good comrades!"

He again shook hands with both of them, with the banker happily following his example. The ranchero, having approached and having overheard the final part of the conversation, now said, "That's the way, sirs! Stick together! I don't think you will be wanting with regard to the Oil Prince, for I cannot say anything bad about him. But let me give you this advice about the Indians: the Nijora and the Navajo are on the warpath and even the Moqui, usually very peaceful, cannot be trusted anymore.

"So you won't stay here," Forner continued. "What am I to tell Winnetou and Old Shatterhand when they arrive?"

"That they are to wait here for us or, much better, follow us immediately to the Chelly River," answered Droll. "But I suggest strongly not telling the Oil Prince anything about that!"

"I gladly promise you that. He'll not hear a word. Where might he be? Let me have a look."

Forner stepped through the gate through which Grinley had gone, looking for him. That's when he spotted a group of riders advancing on the ranch from the south.

A few minutes later, they returned in extreme excitement and
without the kettle, their faces full of terror.

# 6

## A PUZZLING MONSTER

THE RIDERS WERE STILL some distance away. It was apparent, though, that they also had pack animals with them. Soon, however, Forner noticed that the group consisted not only of men, but also included women and children. Some of the riders rode horses; the others, mules.

Ahead rode a small fellow clad in a large and much too big deerskin hunting coat. Because of an extraordinarily bushy beard, only two small, crafty-looking eyes and a nose of almost scary dimensions could be seen of the face. This little man was Sam Hawkens, who, together with his two companions, Dick Stone and Will Parker, had taken over as the immigrants' guides. Putting his old mule Mary into a gallop, he stopped in front of Forner with the greeting, "Good day, sir! This is the settlement called Forner's rancho, isn't it?"

"Aye, mister, this is it," answered Forner, first eying the little man, then the rest of the riders following him. "You seem to be immigrants, mister?"

"Yes, if you don't mind."

"Fine with me, as long as you're honest. Where do you come from?"

"From around Tucson, if I'm not mistaken."

"Then you've had a difficult trip, particularly with children along. And what's your destination?"

"Toward the upper Colorado. Is the ranchero at home?"

"Yes. He's standing right in front of you. It's me."

"Then tell me if we may stay at your place until tomorrow morning."

"That's all right by me. But I hope that I won't regret having given you permission."

"We'll not swallow you whole, rest assured. And what we take from you, we'll gladly pay for, if I'm not mistaken."

He dismounted. At first the Oil Prince stood at a distance, but then he came closer and overheard everything. He now knew that these were the immigrants his brother and the treacherous scout had told him about. All the other people present in the courtyard also came to the gate just as the immigrant group arrived and began to dismount. This did not proceed as smoothly as one might have expected, however. The mule upon which Mrs. Rosalie sat seemed to have a mind of his own. It did not want her to dismount, but wanted to go on. Always the courteous little gentleman, Hobble-Frank stepped up to assist her, which greatly infuriated the mule, so that it jumped into the air with all four legs and tossed its rider to the ground. The woman would surely have had a bad fall if Frank had not been agile enough to catch her.

Instead of being grateful for his help, she jerked away from him, gave him a strong punch in the ribs, and angrily bellowed at him, "You sheep's head!"

"Sheep's nose!" he responded in his well-known, quick-witted way.

"Clown, boor!" she retorted furiously, threatening him with her doubled right fist.

"Stupid girl," he laughed and turned away from her.

She had thought him to be an American and thus had brought forth the English fighting terms known to her. The "stupid girl," however, got her so excited that she grabbed his arm and thundered at him in German, since her English vocabulary was insufficient to the task, "You ass, you magnificent one! You dare insult a lady! Do you know who I am? I am Mrs. Rosalie Ebersbach, née Morgenstern and widowed Leiermüllerin. I'll serve notice on you in a court of law! First you upset my mule, then you squeeze my hips something awful, and finally you throw in my face abuse a decent person ought not to know! Understand?"

She looked at him in a most challenging way, pugnaciously, her hands on her hips. In surprise, Hobble-Frank stepped back a pace, asking in German, "What was that? Your name is Rosalie Ebersbach?"

"Yes," she answered, following his step backwards.

"Née Morgenstern?" he continued, stepping back two more paces.

"Naturally! Or do you mind?" she responded, again following him two paces.

"Widowed Leiermüllerin?"

"Well, sure!" she nodded.

"But then you are German?"

"And how! Say another wrong word and you will get to know me! I'm used to being treated civilly. Do you understand?"

"But I have been very obliging to you!"

"Obliging? You do not say! Can it be considered obliging to lay hands on my mule?"

"I only wanted to steady it, since it did not obey you."

"Did not obey me? That is just about enough now! Every ass obeys me; take notice of that! And after that you nearly crushed me in your arms. I lost my breath and I saw stars in my eyes. I will suffer that. A lady is to be treated nice and gently. We are the more beautiful and gentler sex and ask to be treated as such. Whoever grabs like a stevedore—"

She stopped, for she was interrupted. Behind her a shout arose, a shout of astonishment and delight, causing her to fall silent. "*Herrjemine!* Is that not the famous Hobble-Frank?"

Frank quickly turned and cried out in the same amazement when he recognized the speaker, "Our Cantor Hampel! Is it possible! Dismount and come let me hug you!"

The honorable creator of operas had fallen back as usual and had only now arrived at the gate. He admonishingly raised his finger, answering, "Cantor emeritus, if you please, Mr. Frank! As you know, it is only to protect my integrity and to avoid confusion. There could easily be another Cantor Matthäus Aurelius Hampel who is not yet retired. And, before I dismount, I would like to draw your attention to another item."

"And what might that be? I am very anxious to hear it, my very dear and most honorable cantor."

"See, there you go again! You say only 'cantor' while I address you courteously with 'Mr. Frank.' A disciple of the arts may not compromise his dignity, hence I must ask you not to omit the 'mister' in future. This is not due to pride in myself, as you surely know, but only for completeness."

The cantor very carefully dismounted and hugged Frank majestically. The latter ventured laughingly, "We are here in the Wild West, where such completeness is not called for. But if it pleases you, I will henceforth address you as 'Mr. Cantor.'"

"Mr. Cantor Emeritus, please!"

"All right, fine! But now tell me how and from whence you have appeared here. You can rest assured that I would not have thought a *reservoir* with you possible here."

"*Revoir*! In German '*Wiedersehen*' you probably mean! You must have been prepared for such a meeting with me. You know my intent to compose an opera?"

"Yes, you have talked about it, an opera of three or four *actricen*!"

"Twelve! And not *actricen*, but acts! It is to be a heroic opera, and since you told me about the heroes of the West, I thought of traveling with you through the West to collect material for this opera. But, unfortunately, you left without letting me know, and, since I knew approximately where you would go, I followed you."

"What imprudence! Do you think one can meet here as quickly and easily as at home on the main floor or in the attic, you speeding Uhland?"

"You probably wanted to say Roland," the cantor corrected him.

That's when Frank finally frowned, saying in reproof, "Listen, Mr. Cantor, you have contradicted me for the third time. This I cannot and must not tolerate. The first two times I let it pass unpunished. But now it is over! Your contradictions are insults to me for which I actually would have to duel with you if I were not such a good friend of yours. Therefore, no longer correct me when I say something in the future. It could jeopardize our mutual symphony, which I would regret on your part. But now permit me to introduce to you my friend and cousin, after which I hope you will respectfully acquaint me with your companions."

The good-natured cantor complied with the request of his learned friend without any hurt feelings, giving him the names of all those who had arrived with him. Much was to be told and a thousand questions to be answered, but first it was necessary to set up camp and to take care of the animals. Everything else must be postponed.

The Oil Prince looked on for some time while everyone was occupied. He had promised to influence the immigrants and to lead them after his brother and Poller. He seized a moment when Sam Hawkens stood aside from the others, greeted him courteously, and said, "I have heard, sir, that you are Sam Hawkens, the famous frontiersman. Has anyone told you my name?"

"No," answered the little man, also courteously. The Oil Prince, being Buttler's half brother, did not look at all like the latter; therefore, Sam could have no idea that such a close relative of the brigand stood before him.

"My name's Grinley," the other continued. "Around here I'm called the Oil Prince, since I know a spot where an extremely productive oil well seeps out of the ground."

"An oil well?" Sam inquired keenly. "Then you have been very fortunate and may become immensely rich. Do you intend to exploit the well on your own?"

"No, I am too poor. I have found a buyer, Mr. Duncan, a banker from Brownsville, Arkansas."

"Then, don't let yourself be taken. Ask as much as possible! Are you traveling with him to the well?"

"Yes!"

"Is it far from here?"

"Not very."

"Well, the place is certainly your secret and I don't want to inquire any further. But you did address me, from which I conclude you to have a reason for approaching me?"

"That's correct, sir. Someone earlier said you are traveling to Colorado?"

"Indeed."

"My oil well is located at the Chelly River, and from here my route is the same as yours."

"That's so. But why tell me?"

"Because I wanted to ask permission to join you."

"Together with your banker?"

"Yes, and his bookkeeper."

Sam looked the Oil Prince over from head to foot, then answered, "Hmm, you cannot be too careful here in the choice of company, as you may very well know."

"I know. But tell me, sir, do I look like a person you cannot trust?"

"I wouldn't want to say, if I'm not mistaken. But why do you want to ride with us? If you want to keep the location of your petroleum find secret, your desire to join us strikes me as peculiar, if I'm not mistaken."

"I'm convinced that Sam Hawkens would not cheat me."

"Well, you hit the nail on the head about that. You would certainly not lose of drop of oil through me and my comrades."

"I have another reason, even two," continued Grinley. "The redskins have become restless, which is why I'd feel safer with you than if I were to travel alone with my two inexperienced companions. Surely you understand this?"

"Very well, if I'm not mistaken."

"Furthermore, Mr. Droll has put me into quite a quandary. We told him openly of our objective up at the Chelly and he returned this candidness by making the banker distrustful. He doesn't believe there's oil to be found at the Chelly."

"Hmm, I can't blame him for that. I must tell you that I don't believe it, either."

"Then you also think me a fraud?"

"No. I simply assume that you were deceived."

"No one could deceive me, since I discovered the find myself."

"Then you simply deceived yourself by believing some kind of liquid to be petroleum."

"But I've had the petroleum I discovered tested!"

"And how did the test results turn out?"

"To my fullest satisfaction."

"I don't understand that," said Hawkens. "A miracle happened, and I admit to wanting to look at this peculiar petroleum myself."

"That you can, sir. If I have your permission to join you, you'll get to see it."

"You would take me to the find?"

"Yes."

"Well, I'd be delighted. Mr. Droll didn't believe in the oil, and neither did Mr. Frank?"

"Nope."

"And you're angry about it?"

"Not about that, actually, but about their raising doubt in the banker. For my part, they could doubt ten or a hundred times, but they should not have talked him into their own disbelief. They could easily have soured my deal."

"Has Mr. Duncan truly become distrustful all of a sudden?"

"Yes. It's for just this reason that I ask you to let us join you. They'll know that they're under your protection and will no longer suspect me of scheming against them. Will you do me the honor, sir?"

"Gladly, but I must check with my companions first."

"Is that necessary, sir? Do I look so untrustworthy?"

"It's not that. I think you're a person one has to get to know and examine in order to judge properly. That's why I wanted to confer first with Dick Stone and Will Parker."

"By the devil, sir! Your candidness is hardly courteous!"

"But isn't it better than if I were friendly to your face but distrusting behind your back? And for you to see that it isn't meant quite so badly, I will not first ask my companions whether they agree to take you along, but will give you my consent right now."

"Thank you, sir. And when will we leave?"

"Tomorrow morning, if I'm not mistaken. When were you planning to ride on?"

"Today. But I will try to convince Mr. Duncan and Mr. Baumgarten to wait until tomorrow."

"Do that, sir. Our animals are tired, also the women and children, since they are not used to riding. I hope I do not regret my consent."

"Don't worry, sir. I'm an honest chap and think I have proven it by being prepared to show you the find, despite the danger I expose myself to. It is unlikely anyone else would do this."

"Yes. I at least would be very careful about revealing my secret to anyone but the buyer. Then we are agreed, sir. Tomorrow morning we will depart."

Sam turned away from him. The Oil Prince went to the yard, uttering a curse and angrily muttering to himself, "Damned fellow! You'll pay for this! Telling me this to my face! I am to be observed and tested before being accepted as an honest human being! May lightning strike you dead! I'm happy my brother wants these jackals. Wasn't much interested at first in dealing with them. After this insult, however, it will be a pleasure to take them to him."

The horses, mules, and hinnies by now had been unsaddled and were grazing on the fresh grasses or refreshing themselves at the river. Tents were set up in the yard using poles and blankets, since so many people could not be accommodated within the rancho proper. The women then became busy and soon the yard smelled of roasted meat and freshly baked corn tortillas. Hobble-Frank and Aunt Droll were invited to the feast; the others had to fend for themselves.

Frank had to smile to himself when he noticed how concerned Mrs. Rosalie Ebersbach, née Morgenstern and widowed Leiermüller, was about him. She served him the best pieces. He almost had to eat more than he was able to, and, when he was finally satiated, he thanked her emphatically when she wanted to press on him another corn tortilla. But she urged him, "Take just one more, Mister Hobble-Frank! I gladly give it to you. You understand me?"

"Oh, yes," he laughed. "I have already seen earlier how gladly you'd give me something. I almost had my ears boxed."

"Since I did not know who you really were. Had I known you were the famous Hobble-Frank, the misunderstanding would not have occurred."

"But, then, to someone else you would have been rude?"

"Clearly. Such behavior is an insult, and I just will not let myself be insulted, since I am not only an educated, but also a brave woman and know exactly how to respond if, as a lady, I am not treated with the proper respect."

"But let me repeat that you cannot speak of any lack of respect or insult. I just wanted to express my gentlemanly attention when your mule was so obstinate. You falsely directed your accusations at me, whereas it was your mule that did not act the gentleman toward you."

"But why did you have to handle him? You did not have the least reason for it. I would have controlled him myself. I know how to deal with asses of whichever sort. You will get to know me yet. I am not afraid of any ass or any mule, neither of a red Indian nor of any paleface. Mister Cantor Emeritus has told us so many kind and nice things about you that I have become fond of you and in case of need and danger am prepared to come to your aid. You may rest assured: if necessary I will go through fire for you. Here, have this little bit of beef. It is the best I can offer you."

With a "Thank you, thank you!" he declined. "I cannot eat any more, I truly cannot. I am completely stuffed and could easily get indigesticulation if I ate more."

"'Indigestion' you supposedly meant to say, Mr. Frank," the cantor interrupted. That's when the little man angrily bellowed at him, "Keep quiet, you confused emeritechnicus! What do you know of Greek and Arabic dictionaries! You may be able to play the organ and possibly compress operas. Beyond that, though, you need to be quiet—the more so to a prairie hunter and savant like myself. If I were to enter into a learned discourse with you, you would have to admit defeat any old time!"

"That I doubt very much," the cantor objected.

"How? What? You will admit that? Must I prove it to you? Now then, to what do you object about my *indigesticulation*, my dear, sweet, learned Mr. Cantor Emeritus Matthäus Aurelius Hampel from Klotzsche near Dresden?"

"It is called 'indigestion.'"

"So, so! And what is the meaning of this pretty word?"

"That the stomach cannot digest something."

"That I readily believe and with all my heart, for you yourself are highly indigestible. I, at least, cannot stomach your continued know-it-allness. But what have you got against the word I used, *indigesticulation*?"

"That it is not a true word, but plain nonsense."

"Ah, so, hmm, hmm! And what then is the meaning of 'gesticulation'?"

"It is the language of gestures, the language expressed by the movement of a hand or other body parts."

"Nice, very nice! Now I have you where I wanted you. Now you are trapped like Cleopatra by Carl Martell in the battle at the Beresina! Gesticulation, then, is a language of bodily movements, with 'indi' meaning inside, relating to the stomach, for you yourself said that 'indigestible' means what the stomach cannot digest. So, then, when I employ the ingenious term 'indigesticulation,' I am saying that I have eaten too much and indicate metaphorically that my stomach is engaged in stormy contortions telling me through the language of movement to put knife, fork, and spoon aside now. You, however, do not seem to appreciate your stomach's delicate intimations; otherwise, you would not have questioned my 'indigesticulation.' Do you know perhaps the fable of the frog and the ox?"

"Yes."

"Then, how did it go?"

"The frog saw an ox, wanted to become as big as him, inflated himself and—burst on doing it."

"And what is the lesson to be drawn from this fable?"

"The small one should not fancy himself to be big, or else he may come to harm."

"Nice, very nice! Excellent, even!" Frank agreed enthusiastically. "Take this lesson to heart, Mr. Cantor Emeritus! This fable fits both of us, you and me, exceptionally well."

"How so?"

The wily smile with which the cantor voiced this question indicated his intention to lure Hobble-Frank into a trap. The others around him looked at the excited little man with great anticipation. Frank was too enthusiastic to notice anything. He responded to the emeritus's "How so?" without considering what he said, "Because you are intellectually insignificant, whereas I am a celebrity. If you want to compare yourself with me, you must by necessity burst, for you are with respect to knowledge, skills, and the sciences the little frog, whereas I am in all these things the big o—" Frank stopped in the middle of the word. Frank's jaw dropped as he suddenly realized the predicament he was in.

" …You are the big ox," the cantor emphasized the interrupted statement. "I do not want to argue that."

Seemingly endless general laughter erupted. Frank's angry shouts only caused the merriment to increase or to break out anew. That's when he jumped up in rage, shouting as loudly as he could, "Shut up, you loudmouths, you! If you are not quiet immediately, I shall ride off and leave you sitting here!"

But no one took notice of his threat. The laughter resumed once more; even his friend and cousin Droll laughed until his belly wobbled. For his part, the little man was beside himself with fury. Shaking his fists angrily at the laughers, he shouted in a cracking voice, "Well, then! If you do not want to listen, you will have to feel! I shall shake the dust off my boots and will go my own way. I shall wash my hands in childlike innocence and leave the soap with you!"

He ran off, followed by Homeric laughter from the others.

Only one person had not taken part in the laughter, namely, Schi-So, the chief's son. His inborn Indian seriousness held him back. He, too, understood German and had heard the funny way in which Frank had caught himself in his own netting. He, too, felt amused, yet his amusement found expression only in a smile playing about his lips.

In a short while, he rose and went to the gate to look for the angry little man. In a moment he returned reporting, "He is truly serious and is saddling up his horse out there. Should I ask him to come back?"

"Nah," answered Droll in his Altenburger dialect. "He only wants to embarrass us. I know my associate. He would not think of riding off and leaving me sit here."

Nevertheless, Schi-So returned to the gate. Just as he got there, he whistled, calling out as everyone looked at him, "He's mounted. He seems to be serious."

Now everyone came running over. They arrived just in time to see the furious Hobble sitting in the saddle, guiding his horse toward the river.

Droll called after him, "Frank, cousin, where are you going? We did not mean to be so hard on you!"

Hobble, turning his horse around, answered, "Mean what you want. The prairie hunter and private savant Heliogabalus Morpheus Edeward Franke will not be laughed at."

"But we did not laugh at you, but at the cantor," lied Droll.

"You cannot tell me that. You laughed about the ox. I did not even fully pronounce the word. It came out only halfway. The other half became stuck in my mouth. Is that so ridiculous?"

"Not ridiculous, but highly dangerous to have half an ox in your mouth. None of us will be able to equal that. You have our respect. Come back, old chap!"

"Would not dream of it, especially since you yourself are laughing again about the ox. Oh, Cousin Droll, what do I have to experience and suffer from you? I would not have thought it of you! But punishment there must be. Hobble-Frank will disappear!"

"Nonsense! Come here now and do not be silly!"

"Silly? That word really breaks the camel's back! Hobble-Frank being silly!"

He once more turned, put the spurs to his horse, headed for the river, and entered it.

"Frank, Frank, turn back, do turn back!" Droll shouted after him, laughing. "You cannot leave your Aunt like that!"

But the angry Achilles rode on, crossed the river, and disappeared into the area beyond.

"I very much regret this," the saddened cantor admitted. "He is somewhat quarrelsome, particularly when it comes to the sciences, but otherwise a soul of a man. I had looked forward so very much to meeting him, and now we have lost him!"

"At most for a few hours only," answered Aunt Droll.

"You really think so?"

"Yes! I know him. If you do not agree with him, he likes to pout, but he'll soon turn around. I know that he can't live without me, and he surely will not leave me. He'll ride his anger out into the field, leave it there, and return to us later. You can rest assured of that. Just do not talk about it then. Act as if nothing happened and as if you do not even notice him. In general, you should not make him angrier by contradicting him once he starts to quarrel. He just imagines to possess all kinds of learning. That does not do any harm. Let him, therefore, keep this notion if he wants to dwell on it!"

The banker and his bookkeeper had also observed the event. Since the banker did not know any German, Baumgarten had to explain the issue to him. In retrospect, he laughed merrily and was intrigued about whether Droll's prediction would come true and Frank would return. While the two were still talking with each other, Sam Hawkens stepped up and asked, "You intend to go to the Chelly River, Mr. Duncan?" Our route will lead us past there and we will leave here tomorrow morning. Your Oil Prince intends to join us, and I have agreed to it. Do you know about it already?"

"No. He hasn't told me anything yet. What do you think of the oil find?"

"That the Oil Prince was fooled by the liquid, at the very least. I can only advise caution."

"That is what Mr. Droll told me. In any case, your offer affords me protection I may very well need. Therefore I will join you, sir, and, for the time being, please accept my thanks for the permission!"

Thus the matter was arranged to everyone's satisfaction, and Duncan, Baumgarten, and the Oil Prince, who had kept to themselves, joined the immigrants and frontiersmen. As they sat together, stories were swapped, and soon everyone was getting to know each other better. Thus passed the afternoon. Dusk fell and a fire was started in the yard to roast the meat the ranchero had supplied. After dinner coffee would be brewed. The requisite vessels were on hand, so there was no need to borrow them from Forner. Mrs. Rosalie and one of the other women took a kettle and went to the river to fetch water. A few minutes later, they returned in extreme excitement and without the kettle, their faces full of terror.

"What is the matter with you?" asked the cantor. "Where is the kettle? Why are you looking like that?"

The other woman could not speak from fright; Mrs. Rosalie answered, but only with all the signs of terror, "How do I look? Bad, do I not?"

"Pale as a corpse. Have you perhaps met up with something unpleasant?"

"Met? Really! Sweet Jesus, what we have seen!"

"What, then?"

"What? That I do not know, you are asking too much there."

Her husband ventured, "Do not be so stupid! You must know what you have seen!"

She put her hands on her hips and bellowed at him angrily, "Perhaps you know?"

"Me? No," he answered perplexed.

"Well, then! Be quiet, you understand! I know where my eyes are. But a horrible being such as we have seen I have never come across in my life."

"It was a ghost, a river spirit," explained the other woman, trembling.

"Nonsense!" answered Mrs. Rosalie. "There are no spirits, and in ghosts I believe even less."

"Was it a water nymph?"

"Not that, either. Do not be so superstitious! Mermaids exist only in fairy tales."

"What do you think it was, then?"

"That is where you ask me too much. It was not a ghost, for there are none. It was not human, either, so it must have been an animal, but what kind!"

Here the cantor took over: "If it was an animal, we will soon discover the genus, the species, and the name. I am a zoologist from my studies at school. Answer my questions, please! Was it a vertebrate animal?"

"I did not see any vertebra. It was too dark to see."

"What size was it, then?"

"When it sat in the water, I could not make this out very well. But when it jumped up, by my soul, it was as big as a man."

"Then it was positively a vertebrate, probably a mammal?"

"I cannot say."

"Let us go through the individual classes. Was it an ape?"

"Nope, because it had no hair."

"So, so, hmm, hmm! Maybe a fish?"

"No, not at all, since a fish has no arms and legs."

"But it had those?"

"Yes."

"Peculiar, very peculiar! Only humans and apes have arms and legs; but an ape you insist it was not. Then it appears to have been a human."

"God forbid, it was not human. A human has a very different voice."

"Did it have one, then?"

"Yes, and what a voice!"

"Could you perhaps imitate this inhuman voice for me?"

"I shall try," she ventured, took a deep breath and then roared, 'Uhuahuahuahuaauauauauahh!'"

At this terrible roar, all those present jumped up.

"Good God, what a monster this must be—a lion—tiger—panther!" the confused cries rang out.

"Quiet, people!" demanded the cantor. "Do not get exited! Using science I will soon explain the event. The animal had no fur and was therefore not a mammal. A fish it cannot have been either, since it had a voice. Since we have to forget about the invertebrates, only the frogs and toads remain."

That's when the other woman shouted quickly, "Yes, yes, that is it. It was a toad!"

"No, it was a frog!" insisted Mrs. Rosalie just as quickly.

"No, a toad! Like this creature, only a toad can sit in the water."

"But it jumped up!"

"Toads do, too!"

"But not like frogs, and toads keep mostly to the ground, not in the water. You know that! It was a frog!"

"But such a large frog!" the cantor doubted, all the while shaking his head critically. "You just said it appeared to be as big as a man?"

"Yes, that is how large it was, honest!"

"Hmm, hmm! The biggest frog here in America is the bullfrog. But it is not as large as a man!"

"Bullfrogs? Is there such a thing? Then it was one for sure."

"Impossible. These frogs never get to be as big as that."

"Why not? There are giants and dwarfs everywhere. Why not also among the frogs? Then it is a bullfrog giant, or a giant bullfrog, or a bull giant frog, or a frog bull giant, or a giant frog bull, or a frog giant bull—"

"Stop, stop, stop!" the cantor warded the thought off with a shudder. "What else will you make of this frog! My textbook on natural history did not include such a bullfrog giant. But I do not want to dispute this. I live more for the arts than for zoology and do not want to assert that such a monster cannot exist. You truly think that it was a giant bullfrog, Mrs. Rosalie?'

"Yes, truth and honor! I shall swear to it, for in the manner the animal jumped up on all its four legs, it cannot have been anything but a frog."

"What did the animal do before it jumped? Did it sit or swim?"

"It sat, like a frog sits! The hind part could not be seen and only the forelegs, a bit of the body, and head showed above the water. And now I recall also exactly the broad gape of its frog mouth and the saucerlike eyes with which it stared at us, Mr. Cantor."

"Please, Cantor Emeritus, for my integrity's sake! Despite the description you have supplied us, we are faced with a puzzle, and I suggest we go to the river to convince ourselves."

"You think it will still be sitting there?"

"Yes. Frogs are not migrants but stay put. This frog was born here, or has been spawned, and will, therefore, never leave the area. But since it is such a large beast, we should take our rifles. The animal could bite."

The host had to fetch some lanterns, and everyone without exception left the yard to go to the river.

When the group of the curious approached the river, there sat Hobble-Frank in the grass beside his grazing horse. He rose in surprise at seeing the many people and asked in German, "What do you people want? This looks like a real pilgrimage moseying about here!"

"Ah, you are back again, Mr. Frank!" the emeritus cried. "I am very happy for that. Perhaps you can give us some information. How long have you been back here?"

"For an hour perhaps."

"Have you observed what happened at this place?"

"Naturally! I do have eyes and ears, and nothing escapes a prairie hunter like me."

"Did you see the two women wanting to fetch water here?"

"Yes."

"And also the animal?"

"What animal?"

"The one sitting in the water!"

"Sitting in the water? I did not notice anything. What kind of animal was it supposed to be?"

"A bullfrog!"

"No, truly, nothing like a bullfrog has come into view."

"Were you really close when the ladies were here?"

"I was very close to them."

At that point, Mrs. Rosalie, stepping over to him, said, "I did not see you, Mr. Hobble-Frank, but most clearly saw the bullfrog. If you claim to have been that close to us, you must have positively seen it! It was sure big enough!"

"How big approximately?"

"Just like a full-grown man."

"Oho! Never in my life will a frog be that big, Mrs. Ebersbach, even if it is a bullfrog. I have seen enough of such critters; they get to be a bit bigger than a man's hand, no more. They do not get their name from being the size of a bull, but from their lovely voices. Their bellow is actually quite similar to that of an ox."

"That is true, that is true. We have heard the beast scream."

"That I would also have to have heard!"

"I think so, too. Where were your ears and eyes that you did not hear the beast or see it?"

"I truly do not know. Most humbly, I ask you to show me the place where the frog bellowed!"

"He bellowed only when he jumped up."

"Listen, Mrs. Ebersbach, that sounds unlikely to me. A frog does not bellow while jumping; he croaks only while sitting."

"No, that one screamed the moment he jumped up from the water. Come! I will show you the spot."

Mrs. Ebersbach led the doubting Frank down the bank and indicated a point close to which lay the empty kettle, then the water, declaring, "Here we stood to draw water for the coffee. As proof you can see the kettle lying there, where we dropped it from fear. And there in the water sat the bullfrog."

At that point Hobble-Frank's face became longer and longer, finally assuming an expression of great amusement, after which he asked, "Then you clearly saw that it was a bullfrog?"

"Well, honestly, at first we were not quite sure to which class of insects the beast belonged. But our Mr. Cantor has studied zoologistics and, with his help, we solved the puzzle in that it must have been a bullfrog."

"Excellent, excellent! This is a mighty pleasure for me, ladies and gentlemen! And why have you come to the river with lanterns and torches?"

"To look for the bullfrog and to catch him," responded Mrs. Rosalie. "If it were to bite, it would be shot. We have the rifles along, as you can see."

Here Frank erupted into merry laughter, by which Mrs. Rosalie felt insulted enough to tell him, "Do not laugh that way! It is not funny, when it is dark, at night—"

"—to take the famous and learned Hobble-Frank for a bullfrog!" the little man completed the sentence.

Stepping back a pace, she squinted at him and asked, "You, you were the bullfrog?"

"Yes, I!" he laughed. "I had ridden off into the countryside and had turned back as dusk fell. All day it had been so hot, and the ride made me hotter yet. When I crossed the river, the water cooled me off so nicely that I thought I would take a bath. I, therefore, dismounted, undressed, and entered the water."

When Frank paused, Mrs. Rosalie clapped her hands together and called out in a voice filled with premonition, "Ohlordielordie, what am I going to hear now! You stepped into the water?"

"Yes. I swam back and forth, splashed about thoroughly, and was just ready to step ashore when I saw two women coming to the river without my having noticed them because of the darkness, and now they were already very close. I quickly squatted down again, hoping they would pass me by. But they came right to the spot where the rabbit sat in the trap and Frank in the water. That is when they stopped and looked at me."

"That is actually true," Mrs. Rosalie admitted. "We saw something white in the dark water and at first did not know what to make of it. But in any case, it was a living being staring at us terribly."

"Please, Mrs. Ebersbach! I did not stare at you! I looked at you fearfully, hoping that you would remove yourself with modesty and in consideration. But this was not to be the case. That is when I decided on a strategic approach: I jumped up, clapped my hands, and roared as loudly as I could."

Mrs. Ebersbach seemed to be deeply offended by this revelation and was about to answer him in an even sharper voice when Droll interceded, "It was an error, honorable folks, an error that did not hurt anyone. Therefore, let us not quarrel any further, but honor him who is due it, namely, our Hobble-Frank, the giant bullfrog, hip, hip, hurrah, hip, hip, hurrah!"

After everyone had chimed in to the hurrah and all had finished, he continued, "There lies the kettle. Fill it full so that we may finally get some coffee. Then we shall line up to take our bullfrog home in triumph!"

That's how it was done. Hobble-Frank resisted in vain. Like a child he was lifted onto the shoulders of the blacksmith Ebersbach, the tallest of the immigrants, after whom the group marched in cadence to the yard. Once again everyone gathered around the fire to resume the interrupted preparation of the coffee.

Tomorrow's destination was a lone pueblo located at the southern slope of the Mogollon Mountains. To reach it before evening, a timely departure was required and frequent or longish breaks would not be allowed. Nevertheless, no one went to bed early. There was too much to talk about.

The Oil Prince, too, engaged in lively conversation. This was made possible by the use of English for the banker's benefit. Thus Grinley could also partake. He made a visible effort to gain everyone's goodwill, which he seemed to accomplish fairly well with the German immigrants, although they did not understand too much of the English conversation. The banker, too, appeared to waver again in his mistrust.

Time passed quickly, and everyone was surprised when Will Parker told them it was past midnight.

They would get only four to five hours of rest now, so everyone lay down. In a few minutes, all were asleep. No guards had to be posted, since the rancher's farmhands were on guard outside.

# 7

## AT THE PUEBLO

A S THE GRAY DAWN of the next day opened, Forner had already prepared a supply of fresh-baked corn tortillas and coffee, so the group would not have to lose time making breakfast. The animals were well watered, since they expected to find no water until evening. The ranchero was paid for what he had supplied and his farmhands received a tip. Then they were ready to leave.

Sam Hawkens had taken care that the women had good saddles on their animals, so the ride would not strain them any more than it did the men. The children were placed in straw-padded baskets, two each carried by a mule, hanging to the left and right of the packsaddle. Thus the riders could let their animals go at full stride in order to proceed at a fast pace.

The farther they got from the river, the more barren the land became. Where there is running water, or even moisture, the land produces luxurious vegetation, but where enlivening moisture is lacking, there is nothing but desolate desert.

During the morning the heat was not unbearable. The higher the sun rose, however, the greater became the heat, much of it reflected by the dry, rocky ground and the barren cliffs. It was barely tolerable to the German immigrants, who were not used to such fiery heat.

In the early afternoon, their route led them through shallow depressions or across vast plains with no sign of a blade of grass. The rises they traversed didn't offer visual relief, either, for nature was so stingy here that she did not grant a single tree, not even a bush. Only in hidden spots, where the sun could not reach from early to late, where there was shade for at least a few hours, a lone, fantastically formed cactus could be seen, whose pale gray didn't afford the visitor a pleasant sight, either.

During the hottest part of the day, they rested below a steep cliff, where they found some shade. Yet the opposite wall reflected the heat so agonizingly as they rested that they chose to remount and move on, since the fast-paced ride created a slight cooling breeze.

Finally—as the sun was descending in the west—the heat seemed to abate, and surprisingly quickly. Sam Hawkens checked the sky with a little frown.

"Why do you look up that way?" Hobble-Frank asked him. "It looks to me like you do not like the sky?"

"Could be right," the other answered. "The air cooled off too suddenly."

"A thunderstorm perhaps?"

"Almost afraid of it. And you probably know how thunderstorms occur in this area. There are years when not a drop of rain falls here. There have even been periods when it hasn't rained for two, even three years. But when there finally is a storm, it is usually terrible. Let's hurry and get to the pueblo."

"How far is it?"

"We'll arrive in about half an hour."

"There is no danger then. There is not even a small cloud in the sky. Hours may pass before it gets too dark and gloomy up there."

"Don't make that mistake, Mr. Frank. Look at the eagerness of my Mary, how her nostrils move, how she wags her ears and her tail."

That was true. The old mule literally hastened forward, displaying a remarkable anxiety. And yet nothing threatening was noticeable. When Frank reported Sam's concern to his cousin Droll, the latter answered, "I was thinking the same thing. Look at the yellow color along the horizon! It will rise higher and higher, and when it reaches the zenith, the storm will start. It will be good to be under a roof soon!"

"Sam Hawkens spoke of a pueblo. Our accommodation should be better there than in a tent."

Hobble-Frank was right about that. A pueblo is a peculiar stone construction. *Pueblo* is a Spanish word meaning "inhabited place," designating a single homestead, a hamlet, or a village. Those Indians living in pueblos are called Pueblo Indians, or simply Pueblo. To them belong the Tano, Tao, Tehua, Jeme, Quere, Acoma, Hopi, Zuni, and Moqui, as well as the Pima, Maricopa, and Papago on the Gila River and south of there.

A pueblo is built of rocks or adobe bricks. The building usually extends from a rock face, which serves as its rear wall, with outcroppings incorporated into the structure. The building always rises in tiers, so that each previous, lower level extends in front of the next higher one, with all covered by a flat roof. The ground floor supports the next higher floor on its flat roof, set back by several feet. By this means, an open space remains in front of the second floor and is furnished with an opening in the roof that leads down to the ground floor. The third floor is on top of the second, but again set back, so the second floor's flat roof is at its front. There is no floor-level entry at the ground floor; no level actually has a real door, but only the hole in the roof through which one enters. There are no stairs, but only ladders resting outside from level to level, which can be removed. Therefore, anyone who wants to enter the ground floor must climb to the second floor and then descend through the hole in the flat roof. The higher set-back levels thus form a series of giant tiers. You can get an approximate idea by visualizing a German vineyard rising tier by tier up the hillside.

The settled, industrious aboriginal residents were forced into this type of design by roving, rapacious hordes. As simple as its design is, though, a pueblo like this forms a fortress not easily taken with the weapons available at that time. Simply removing the ladders kept an enemy from ascending. And if an enemy brought ladders, he would have to occupy each level before moving to the next higher one.

These Pueblo Indians are usually very peaceful and are under government control. Yet there are also solitary pueblo buildings in remote areas. Their inhabitants consider themselves independent and are just as dangerous as the roving, unrestrained tribes. The pueblo our riders had chosen as the day's destination belonged to the latter kind. Its residents were wild Nijora Indians, whose chief was called Ka Maku. "Ka" means "three" and "Maku" is the plural of "finger," which meant Ka Maku was called "Three Fingers." He carried this warrior's name of honor because he had lost two fingers on his left hand in battle. He was known as a brave but covetous warrior on whose word and friendship one could probably rely in normal times. Now, however, when various tribes had gone on the warpath, it was hazardous to extend him unreserved trust.

The solitary pueblo lay in the glow of the setting sun. It had five levels in addition to the ground floor, all resting with their back against a cliff. The lower levels were constructed of mighty rocks interspersed with adobe bricks; the upper levels were built exclusively in adobe style. The building was certainly more than half a thousand years old, yet not the smallest crack could be seen.

Women and children sat on the rooftops, all busy and serious-faced, as is the Pueblo custom. An attentive observer, though, would have noticed the women, even the children, looking often and deliberately to the south, as if expecting something important from that direction.

No man, or even a warrior, could be seen.

Then three people rose from the hole on the fourth level, a redskin and two whites, who remained poised there as they directed their attention toward the south. The redskin was the chief Ka Maku, a tall, sinewy figure with an eagle feather in his hair. His face was unpainted, a sign that his pueblo was at peace. For this reason, he carried just a scalp knife in his belt. The two whites next to him were Buttler, the leader of the twelve Finders, and Poller, his companion, the German immigrants' unfaithful scout. When nothing could be made out in the direction they were looking, Buttler said, "Not yet! But in any case they will arrive before dusk."

"Yes, they will hurry," the chief agreed. "They have shrewd men among them who will not miss that a storm is brewing. They will hasten their pace to arrive here before it starts."

"You will keep your word, then? I can trust you?" Buttler continued.

"You have been my brother for a long time, and I will be true to you. Yet I hope I can trust you, too, and will receive the reward you promised me."

"I shook hands with you on it; that's as good as an oath. Just take care that I can soon talk with the Oil Prince!"

"I shall lead him to you. The weather will be very helpful. The pale-faces will not want to remain in the open, but will want to come into the pueblo so as not to get wet. There I can take them prisoner without a fight."

"As I indicated to you, however, you must keep them separate so that later they believe they were saved by the Oil Prince."

"It will be done as you said. Uff! Here come riders. That will be they. Quick, hide!"

The two quickly climbed to the next higher floor and disappeared into it. The chief, though, remained standing where he was and, with a sharp eye, observed the approaching group.

The troop consisted of riders and pack animals. At its head rode three men side by side, namely, Sam Hawkens, Aunt Droll, and Hobble-Frank. They stopped at the foot of the pueblo. The ladder used for access to the ground floor had been pulled up. In addition to the women and children, only a few men could be seen on the various levels. This gave the impression that the warriors were absent. The chief, in a proud, unmoving stance, waited for the strangers to address him. Sam Hawkens called up to him in the customary mix of English, Spanish, and Indian, "Are you Ka Maku, the chief of this pueblo?"

"Yes," he responded curtly.

"We would like to camp here. Will you let us have water for ourselves and the animals?"

"No."

This rejection was calculated. It was the chief's plan to keep the whites here. He, therefore, had to allow them water. Yet they were not to suspect that he wanted very much to hold them.

"Why not?" asked Sam.

"The little water we have is barely enough for us and our animals."

"But I see neither your warriors nor your horses. Where are they?"

"Hunting; they will return soon."

"Then you must have water to spare. Why deny it to us?"

"I do not know you."

"Don't you see the women and children among us? We are peaceable people. We need to drink. If you don't give us water, we must search for it."

"You will not find it."

The chief turned away, feigning no further interest in them. That was enough for the good Hobble-Frank to angrily address his cousin Droll, "Who does the fellow think we are? Come to think of it, I just might put a bullet through his head. That should make him more courteous. We are a select people here with hair on our chests and will not be turned away like vagrants from his high portal. I suggest we talk seriously with this man. Agreed?"

"Yes," the Aunt answered in his home dialect, "it is not very pleasant to be thirsty and not be given any water. But find it we will. We have only to look for it."

The riders dismounted to search for the spring. There was moisture enough, since grass grew next to the pueblo and not far way were several small gardens with corn, squashes, and other plants whose condition implied the diligent application of water. But they did not discover the spring, so Frank finally cried out in annoyance, "Blockheads we are, nothing but! If Old Shatterhand and Winnetou were present, they would long since have found water. I think they could even smell it."

"It does not take these famous warriors," Schi-So, son of a chief, declared. He had followed their efforts with a quiet smile. "One has to think before searching."

"Then start thinking!"

"I have done that already," he replied.

"Really? Then, please, kindly tell us the result of your mental efforts!"

"This pueblo is a fortress, which cannot exist without water. It is especially necessary in case of a siege, when the defenders cannot leave the building. Taking this into account, you can easily figure where the well is to be found."

"Ah, you think it is inside the pueblo? But where?"

"Certainly not in one of the upper levels," the young Indian smiled.

"Nah," responded Frank, "I have not seen a waterworks on top of a church tower yet, either. The well must be on the ground level."

"Where it was set up centuries ago, when the pueblo was built."

"True! That is as clear as boot polish. Listen, my dear young friend, you do not seem to be as stupid as you look. If you continue to develop like that, it is quite probable something will yet become of you. Then it is on the ground level we have to look. But how do we get in there? There is no doorway, just as there are neither straight nor corkscrew stairs. And they have kindly pulled up the ladders. But if we form an Egyptian pyramid by climbing on one another's shoulders, then several of us can get up on the roof and from there down onto the ground floor, where the *aqua destillaterium* is to be found."

That's when Sam Hawkens remarked, "This would mean forcing entry, which we should avoid, if possible, if I'm not mistaken. It appears we can forget about that. The chief's coming down. I think he wants to talk with us."

Ka Maku descended to the first level. He stepped to its edge and asked, "Did the palefaces find the water?"

"Permit us to come up to you, then we will find it," the little man responded. "It's flowing inside the pueblo."

"You have guessed right. I would give you some, but its flow is so puny that—"

"We will pay you for it," interrupted Sam.

"That is good! But does my brother perhaps know that several tribes are on the warpath against the whites! Can we trust the palefaces?"

"You don't have to fear anything from us. Maybe you have even heard of us before. These two warriors standing here beside me and I are called the 'Shamrock'; there behind me stands—"

"The Shamrock?" the chief interrupted hastily. "Then I know your names. You are Hawkens, Stone, and Parker?"

"Yes."

"Why did you not tell me this right away? The Shamrock has always been friendly to us red men. You are our brothers and we welcome you. You will have water, for nothing, and as much as you need. Our women will pass it out to you."

At his shout, a number of squaws climbed to the lowest platform and in large earthen jugs fetched water from the well on the ground floor. The travelers could easily bring it down after ladders were put out. All this made such a peaceful impression that it did not occur to Sam Hawkens, usually so wily, or to any of his companions that the chief's friendliness was only a ruse.

While the people refreshed themselves, after which the horses were watered, the sky changed in a threatening manner. First it was bright red, then dark red, and finally violet, and this violet was now turning into a cloudless, gloomy black.

"That looks bad," Dick Stone said to Hawkens. "What do you say, Sam? Looks like it might become a hurricane or a tornado."

"Don't think so," Sam responded, all the while checking the sky with a long look. "Yep, there'll be a storm, a severe storm, but with a great deal of water. It would be best if we could get under a solid roof and our horses, too, or they may bolt."

Turning again to the chief, who was still standing on the platform, he asked, "What does my red brother think of this ominous weather? What will come of it?"

"A big storm with lots of rain, so that everything here will be flooded quickly."

"I think so, too, but I don't care to swim or to have our equipment spoiled by the rain. Will you allow us into the pueblo?"

"My white brothers together with their women and children may climb up to us. Not a drop of rain shall hit them."

"And our animals? Is there a place for them where they can't get away?"

"There, around the left corner of the pueblo, is a corral where you may keep them."

"Good, we'll do that. In the meantime, may the women come up now?"

Several more ladders were lowered, by means of which the women and children made it to the fourth level, and from there down through the previously mentioned hole into the enclosure of the third one. Simultaneously, several Indian squaws and half-grown children came down to carry the baggage taken off the horses and mules up to the second level and from there through the opening in the roof onto the ground floor.

On the side of the pueblo, an open, squarish space had been enclosed by a rather tall wall, which Ka Maku had called the corral. That's where the horses and mules were taken. When they were safe, the opening was closed off with poles. Just as they finished, a lightning bolt flashed, giving the impression that the entire sky was set aflame, with a thunderclap that seemed to shake the earth. It started to rain so hard that one could hardly

see even a few paces. The mighty storm broke out so suddenly that one had
to hold onto the wall in order not to be toppled.

The men hurried to the ladders.

The banker and his German bookkeeper were not as experienced, agile, and quick as the others, and therefore arrived last. Everyone hurriedly
pushed up toward the platform and the hole through which they descended by means of a ladder into the third level. Since only one person
could descend at a time, things did not work as quickly as the pound-
ing rain made them wish it would. Everyone thought only of himself
and pushed forward. That's how it happened that no one noticed the
five or six Indians suddenly standing by the chief, who was directing
the descent.

The cover closing off the entry hole lay beside it. Close by, a few large
rocks, weighing more than a hundred pounds, were deposited. No one
noticed them, either. As mentioned before, the banker and Baumgarten
were the last. Just as the banker was about to put his foot onto the uppermost rung of the ladder, the chief called out to him, "Stop, get back! You
are not to go in there!"

"Why not?" asked Duncan.

"You will find out right away."

Together with the other Indians, he threw himself onto the two, who,
before they could think of resistance, were wrestled down and tied up.
Their calls for help were swallowed by the raging storm and the claps of
thunder. At almost the same time, the chief pulled the ladder from the hole
and put the cover on it, after which his people rolled the heavy rocks on
top. The travelers, taken by surprise, were trapped below.

Most of the whites—men, women, and children—had been caught.

Now the banker and Baumgarten were moved from the forth to the
third and then to the second level, from which they were lowered with
ropes to the ground level. Here, too, the entry was closed off by the
trapdoorlike lid. Then the chief sent one of his men away. Using the lowest ladder, the man left the pueblo and, despite lightning and thunder,
storm and rain, ran off along the cliff that supported the building, turned
a corner, and, after maybe ten minutes, arrived at a place where the rubble
of a collapsed rock face had formed a maze well suited as a hiding place. It
was here the pueblo's warriors had withdrawn with their horses to make
the whites believe they were on a hunt. The messenger reported that the
ruse had succeeded and that they could now return to the pueblo.

Yes, they had succeeded, and much more easily and faster than the chief had thought. Certainly, the sudden onset of the storm had largely contributed to this unexpected success, although not much more than the incaution of the whites.

As previously related, first the women and children had climbed from the fourth level down to the third. There they found themselves in a windowless room with an approximately ten-foot ceiling. Except for the hole in the ceiling through which they had come in, there was not even the smallest opening in the walls. Four cross walls split this level into five rooms, with the one at the center being the largest. There they were. In a niche burned a small oil lamp whose poor light penetrated only a few paces.

Shaking her head, Mrs. Rosalie looked around. When she did not find anything in the entire room except for the ladder and the lamp, she said indignantly, "Well, I have never seen and experienced anything like this! To stuff one's guests into such a hole where there is not even a couch or a single chair! This is just like a cellar! Where do you sit? Where do you hang your clothes? Where do you make a fire? Where do you brew coffee? There is no window nor an oven! I surely will not put up with that! We are ladies and you do not stuff ladies in—holy Saxony!" she interrupted herself, frightened when she heard the first thunderclap penetrating even down into this room. "I think this one struck, did it not?"

"Yes, that must have been a strike, and what a strike!" answered Mrs. Strauch. "I had just looked up at the hole and clearly saw the flash."

"Now then, all of you stand right there in the farthest corner! On the way, the men talked about thunderstorms here being quite different from those at home. If an insane American lightning bolt comes down through the hole, we are all dead on the spot. It is well that no hay, straw, or any other combustible materials are down here. You understand? Listen how the rain is hitting up there! Oh my goodness, our good men will be soaked to the skin! After that there will be colds, fever, belly and stomach aches. And who has to worry? We females, we women, we ladies, of course, that is evident! If they would only come soon!"

Her wish was fulfilled immediately, for just then the first, Hobble-Frank, came climbing down, with the others following one by one. Arriving at the bottom, he tried to shake off as much of the water as he could, looked around, and remarked in disappointment, "What kind of a mean hole is this down here? Is this perhaps supposed to be a living space? If these red gentlemen do not have a better abode for us, I will, at the next opportunity, send them a royal Saxon architect. He can show them the difference between my villa Bärenfett on the Elbe and this rotten dwelling below the ground. Really, where do you sit here, if you are tired, to take a little afternoon nap?"

"Anywhere, Mr. Franke," said Mrs. Rosalie. "There is room enough."

"Really? What did you say?" asked Hobble-Frank, irritated. "Anywhere? Why do you not sit down, then? Is it that you do not like it, either? And although it does not please you, it is supposed to be good enough for me?"

"Be quiet, Mr. Frank!" demanded Sam. "It's not the time and place for such quarrels. We have better things to do."

"What?"

"First, we must smoke the peace pipe, if I'm not mistaken."

"With these Indians?"

"Yes. At least with the chief. You know that you can trust a redskin only once you have smoked the calumet with him."

"I do know that. But should we not have smoked that outside?"

"There was no time."

"We should have taken the time, despite the bad weather. Now we are stuck in this cellar, and if the redskins are not sincere, it is just as well if— hell's bells! Look, it is beginning already! They are pulling the ladder up. Hold it, hold it down!"

He rushed over and with arms stretched out jumped up to grab the ladder, but was too late. It disappeared through the opening.

"What a mess!" he shouted angrily. "Now we are in a pickle like Pythagoras in the barrel!"

"That was Diogenes," the cantor corrected.

"Be quiet!" Frank hissed at him. "What do you understand of these men? Diogenes was the dwarf at one side of the big Heidelberg barrel. Must you always argue with me?"

"Stop!" ordered Sam. "This matter of the ladder looks rather serious to me. Why was it pulled up? Was it perhaps needed quickly for another level? That's easy to believe with this weather. Let's see whether we're all here!"

It turned out that the banker and his bookkeeper were missing. Satisfied, Sam Hawkens ventured, "That relieves me. They belong to us and need to get down here yet. The ladder must indeed have been required elsewhere, if I'm not mistaken."

"But why have they closed us off up there, put the cover on the hole?" Droll inquired.

"You have to ask that?" answered Frank. "I am really ashamed of you, being as how you are my cousin and relative! Any reasonable person will close the door when it rains. Here, it does not just rain, it pours buckets. That is why the lid was put on, to protect our valuable heads. Can you grasp that?"

"Yes, my dear friend and cousin Heliogabalus Morpheus Edeward Franke, since you so capably made it clear, I comprehend."

"Yes, this could be the reason," Sam agreed. "Until the chief comes down here, let's reconnoiter our abode with the aid of this lamp."

They were less than enthusiastic about their "abode." The rooms were totally empty. There was nothing to sit on, no blanket, not a speck of straw, hay, or leaves of which one could have fashioned a resting place for even a single person. This caused the mood of the sopping-wet people to droop profoundly. Sam still did not lose his equanimity, but said, returning to the central room, "This will change soon. Let the chief come first! Then we will get everything we need."

Schi-So, the young Indian, had not joined in the inspection of the rooms. He sat on the floor with his back to the wall and a grave expression on his face. When he heard Sam's comforting words, he broke his silence and said, "Sam Hawkens is mistaken. Nothing will change soon. We have been trapped."

"Trapped? Heavens! Why do you think that?"

"I know where we are. When we entered, I saw two ladders leaning against the next level. If you needed one quickly, why not take one of them; why not take one of those that were easier to get than ours?"

"I also saw these two ladders."

"And another thing," the youngster continued. "Where is Grinley, the one who calls himself the 'Oil Prince'?"

"Hell's bells, yes, that's true!" Sam cried, perplexed.

"Why are only the two whom he probably wants to cheat missing? He knows that we will not let this fraud come to pass. That is why he wants to separate them from us and, for this purpose, turned to the chief."

"How and when?"

"Remember the two whites who arrived ahead of us at Forner's rancho! He talked with them. I found out that he hung around with one of them behind the house for some time."

"If that's so, it establishes a connection, which worries me. But how can they dare take as many as we are prisoner? We are also armed and can break out."

"Where?"

"By opening the cover," said Sam.

"Try it! It surely will not open," responded Schi-So.

"Then through an outside wall."

"That consists of rocks and a mortar even harder than rock."

"Through the roof."

"Try to get through it with your knives!"

"But except for the chief, I've seen only women and children!"

"The warriors were hiding," explained Schi-So. "They were supposed to be on a hunt. What kind of game is there at this season and in this desolate area? You know that several Indian tribes are on the warpath. Being on the warpath, they could appear at any place at any time. Would anyone be so incautious as to leave a sturdy camp to go hunting? And since when do Pueblo Indians go hunting in a group? Do they not live on what they produce in their gardens? Sam Hawkens can believe me, we have been taken prisoner."

"Then let's prove it by trying to open that cover up there."

Having Dick Stone and Will Parker stand side-by-side, Sam climbed onto their shoulders so that he could reach the cover, then pushed against it with all his might, for naught. It would not budge.

"It's true; we are locked in," he angrily exclaimed when he climbed down. "But we will show these rascals that they miscalculated."

"How so?" asked Stone.

"We dig through, either the wall or the ceiling. Let's check the wall first."

By the light of the little lamp, they first inspected various places of the wall. It turned out that the entire length of the outer wall, as Schi-So had said, consisted of heavy rocks connected by a mortar no knife could touch. And other, stronger tools were not at hand.

That left only the ceiling through which an exit could perhaps be forced. All of the men took part in this examination by having one man step onto the shoulders of two others, then try to peck a hole with a knife. They found out that the ceiling supports consisted of iron-hard wood poles placed tightly side by side. For centuries the wood had not been exposed to moisture and offered indefatigable resistance to the knives, so they could not determine even the consistency of the layers above it.

The women had followed these efforts anxiously. When they turned out to be useless and the attempts were stopped, Mrs. Rosalie cried out angrily, "Would you believe that there could be such bad people as these

Indian rascals! If I only had these rogues here now, Lord of my life, how I would tell them what is what! Here you see again what happens when you rely upon men! They are supposed to be our natural protectors, but instead of watching out and protecting us, they lead us right down into darkest misfortune!"

"Oh, be quiet!" demanded her husband. "You are insulting the gentlemen with your perpetual complaining."

"What? How? Perpetual?" she asked angrily. "Since when have I been talking? At most, three or four seconds ago. And that you call perpetual! She who is right does not need to keep her tongue still. We have been stupid enough to let ourselves be taken prisoner. It is not my fault. But I will ask what we can expect now and what will happen to us."

"You have to ask that?" Hobble-Frank cut in, with the corners of his mouth twitching cunningly. "It is evident that we will be tied up first."

"We ladies, too?"

"Naturally! Then they will tie us to the stake—"

"The ladies, too?"

"Of course! And thereafter we will be killed nice and slow—"

"We ladies, too?"

"All of you! And once we are dead, we will be scalped."

"Holy Saxony! Not we ladies, too?"

"Certainly! The redskins commonly scalp the women even while alive. They do not wait for them to die, you know, since the ladies have nicer and longer hair, making the scalp much more valuable—"

"Thank you most humbly for this flattery!" Mrs. Rosalie interrupted Hobble-Frank.

"My pleasure!" he responded. "And also because the scalp is not so easily pulled off of a dead body as from a living."

"Is that true, or do you only want to scare me, Mr. Frank?"

"It is the truth, and nothing but the truth, you can rest assured."

"Then these redskins are true and veritable barbaric murderers! But I shall not have myself scalped, dead or alive. My skin they will not get, at any price. I shall defend my hair until the end. I am Mrs. Rosalie Ebersbach, née Morgenstern, and widowed Leiermüllerin. They are going to know who I am!"

With the other group of prisoners, that is, the banker and his bookkeeper, things were not as lively. Together they lay on the ground floor. No lamp was burning, so it was dark. The humidity and an occasional burble made them think they were close to the spring. Down here the walls were so thick that the storm's rage could barely be heard. After they had been lowered by the ropes and the lid had closed above them, the two at first listened. Everything remained silent around them; nothing hinted of the presence of another human being. Then the banker spoke up, "Have you fainted, Mr. Baumgarten, or can you hear me?"

"I hear you, sir. But I could faint. What have we done to the Indians that they treat us in this manner?"

"Hmm, I wondered about that, too. Why have they taken just us two prisoner and not the others?"

"I guess that they'll not be any better off than we."

"You think they've also been imprisoned?"

"Yes."

"You have a reason to think so?"

"Several. Foremost, the redskins cannot take us prisoner without doing the same to our companions, since they would otherwise free us."

"That's true, but at the same time sad for us, since we must abandon all hope of being liberated by them."

"Would not think so! I shall hope until the last moment. I would not exclude the possibility that, despite everything, we can count on our companions. They are probably locked up like us, but not tied. They have their weapons. Add to that the kind of fellows they are! Although this Hobble-Frank is quite a funny little fellow, he is certainly a brave, intrepid person and an able frontiersman. One can say the same of Hawkens, Parker, Stone, and Droll, and as for the others, except for the unreliable cantor, surely none of them would sit with their hands fearfully folded in their lap."

"Well, I think you are right. But why did they take us? Perhaps for ransom?"

"Hardly. That would be typical of white bandits, but not of Indians. I assume the redskins' behavior is the result of squabbles between them and the whites."

"The devil you say! Then we have no hope, for we are prisoners of war, and it will likely cost us our lives! That's a nice prospect! To be burned at the stake and to be scalped!"

"We aren't that far yet! Let's first try to get free of our bonds."

They made every effort, used their strength to the utmost, but in vain; the straps were too tight. They did not think of untying each other, but they could, even with their hands bound, at least have made the attempt.

They now lay quietly beside each other and waited—a long, long time, it seemed. Then the cover was lifted. They saw dark, starry sky. The thunderstorm had moved off and evening had come. They saw the ladder being lowered and the chief coming down. He bent down to check their bindings. When he had convinced himself that they were still bound, he said, "The white dogs are more stupid than the howling coyotes. They come to the dwellings of the red warriors without taking into account that the tomahawk is now between us and them. They have taken our land, our holy places, and driven us off; they pursue and cheat us again and again. First they came singly, then swelling to millions. Although we were millions, we are disappearing like the mustang and the bison of the prairies. But we shall not die without taking revenge. We are on the warpath and all palefaces falling into our hands are lost. Tomorrow morning at daybreak, we will erect the stakes and your howls of pain shall be carried aloft to the sky! That is how it shall be, for Ka Maku, the chief, has spoken!"

After these words he climbed again, pulled the ladder up, and once again put the cover on the hole.

His threats had shaken the two to their bones. They were unaware that this was all make-believe, that he painted their fate in such gloomy colors only for them to later be the more grateful to their alleged rescuer. The chief's visit totally depressed the banker, and Baumgarten, too, was no longer as confident as before. Tomorrow morning at the stake!

They confided their fears in one another. They racked their brains to find an escape. They began once more to pull on their bindings, only to have them cut their flesh. All without the least success.

Again—several hours might have passed—they heard a noise. They looked up. The cover was moved aside and a head peered through the opening.

"Pssst, pssst, Mr. Duncan, are you down there?" they heard a whisper.

"Yes, yes!" they answered aloud, joyful in newfound hope.

"Quiet, quiet! If we are heard, I am lost. Is Mr. Baumgarten with you, too?"

"Yes, I'm here, too," answered the German.

"At last I've found you! Under a thousand threats to my life I've looked for you to save you. Did you fight back? Are you hurt?" The words carried an almost affectionate worry.

"No, we are healthy and unhurt," declared Duncan.

"Wait a little, then. I'll see whether I can get a ladder."

The head in the opening disappeared.

"Thank God! We will escape!" the banker let go with a sigh of relief. "That was Grinley, our Oil Prince, right?"

"Yes," answered the bookkeeper. "I recognized him by his voice, although he could only whisper."

"He will get us out. He is risking his life to free us. Is that not brave of him?"

"Very brave!"

"There, you can see how even sharp-minded people can be mistaken about a person! He was cast as a cheat. This should prove that we can extend him our full confidence. I will no longer doubt him."

Once again the Oil Prince appeared in the hatch. He lowered a ladder and in a low voice told the two, "I was in luck; come on up!"

"We cannot because we have been tied up," answered Duncan.

"That's bad. Then I must come down to you and we'll lose valuable time."

He climbed down to them, felt for their bindings, and cut them. Both stood up and stretched their limbs to get the blood flowing again. Duncan offered the alleged rescuer his hand and whispered, "I will not forget this, sir! But tell me how you succeeded—"

"Psst, quiet!" the Oil Prince interrupted. "Later. Now we need to get away quickly, since someone may be looking for you at any moment, and we'll be out of luck. Come up quickly! But do not stand upright up there. Otherwise, you'll be noticed immediately. We need to get away on our bellies."

He climbed up, the two following him. They lay flat on the roof.

"Look up! Do you see the guards?"

Under the bright, starry sky, they saw Indians on the uppermost platform. In their inexperience, it did not occur to them that down here, where a guard would have been most necessary, none was present. It was even less obvious to them that this was precisely the spot from which they could be seen best. The Oil Prince left the hole open with the ladder inside. He whispered, "Follow me silently to the edge, where I have put a second ladder. Once we're down, we have nothing to worry about anymore."

They crept to the edge of the first platform and found the ladder. In their relief, they didn't find this remarkable, either. They descended one after the other and were soon outside the pueblo.

"Finally!" the Oil Prince said. "It worked. Let's get away from here quickly!"

"Not yet, Mr. Grinley," said the conscientious bookkeeper. "Our companions must also be prisoners? Are we going to leave them? It is our duty to—"

"Nonsense!" Grinley interrupted. "What are you thinking! The chief lied. His warriors are not out hunting, but are here. What can the three of us hope to achieve against sixty to seventy well-armed Indians? It would lead only to our ruin. Be happy that I was able to get you out!"

"That may be true, but I am still sorry for my comrades."

"They'll take care of themselves. They are knowledgeable fellows who will surely find a way out."

"That's small consolation. But how do we get away from here? They will surely pursue us. If we only had our horses and weapons. We'll also miss our baggage."

"Everything is here. I've retrieved everything!"

"What? How? That's not possible!"

"Oh, for the sake of his friends a brave man makes the impossible possible. Alone, however, I would probably not have made it. I found help and support."

"From whom?"

"From two gallant gentlemen I'll take you to. Come quickly now. We should not remain here a moment longer."

Grinley led the two along the outside wall of the pueblo and out to the rock fall where the Indian warriors had hidden. There they were met by Buttler and Poller, who had with them not only their horses and weapons, but also all their other property. This quite surprised them. The Oil Prince evaded their questions by demanding, "We must leave now, at once, since, as you suspected, we will be pursued, which necessitates that we get the best possible head start. We'll tell you on the trail how everything happened."

He had fabricated a believable tale and was convinced that it would be accepted. They mounted and rode away in a gallop. The banker, grateful to his rescuer, worried little for those left behind. Baumgarten, however, could not help thinking that it was their duty at least to have attempted their companions' liberation.

The latter found themselves in an unpleasant situation. At first, they were convinced that the trapdoor cover would open again for the banker and the bookkeeper to follow them in. After they had waited for a long time, even hours, without the cover's opening, it became obvious to everyone that they had become prisoners of the Indians. The experienced frontiersmen took this with their customary restraint, but the German immigrants were more excited. Only one of them kept his wits about him, the cantor, who wouldn't believe that his artistry, composing, and striving would find a violent end here.

As one might guess, Mrs. Rosalie got in the first word. She first railed mightily against the Indians, then against Sam Hawkens and his companions, whom she blamed for their having been duped.

"Who would have thought this of the old redskin lord mayor!" Mrs. Rosalie railed. "The man was so friendly, like good yellow margarine. He acted so nice that I thought he would ask me to dance a waltz with him. And then it turns out that it was all falsehood, deception, and cunning. What does he really want? Our possessions or our money? Tell me, Mr. Hawkens! Talk to me! Say something! Do not stand around like a Chinese statue, which cannot speak a word!"

"Of course, they are out for our property," responded Sam.

"Of course? I just do not find that as 'of course' as you do. My property is my property, and no one else may tamper with it. Whoever puts his hand on my legitimate and legal belongings is a thief, do you understand me! And there are certain legal clauses in Saxony the police strictly enforce. Whoever steals is incarcerated!"

"That is very true. But, unfortunately, we are not in Saxony."

"Not in Saxony! What are you saying! I am not an American yet, not by a long shot. Despite currently being an immigrant, I have not yet relinquished my Saxon citizenship. I am still a daughter and citizen of the beautiful Saxon lands on the Elbe. The Saxons have been victorious in more than twenty battles, and I, too, will fight my way out of here. I will not let myself be robbed and then chased off without a penny in my pocket."

Sam gave her one of his oddly sparkling looks and told the excited woman, "You are mistaken, Mrs. Ebersbach. They will not rob you and then chase you off."

"No? What, then?"

"When the Indian commits a robbery, he also kills. If they take our belongings, they will also take our lives, so that we cannot take revenge later."

"Lord, my soul! Really, that is the end of everything! And you knew this and brought us here anyway? Mr. Hawkens, do not take this wrong, but you are a monster, a weasel, a serpent unlike any other!"

"Excuse me! How was I to know what the Indians planned! These Pueblo are known to be friendly and reliable. It was almost impossible to think they would set such a trap for us."

"Did you have to jump into it? We could have stayed outside."

"During this weather?!"

"Nonsense, weather! I would rather have ten buckets of water dumped on me than have myself robbed and killed. Can you not figure that out yourself? Heavens! To be murdered! Who would have thought that! I have immigrated to live the American way for a few years more and barely have I set foot in this country and begun to live than death is staring me in the face. I would like to see the person who could tolerate this!"

That's when the cantor stepped up to her, put his hand on her arm, and told her in a calm voice, "Do not get excited for nothing, my dear Mrs. Ebersbach. As long as I am with you, you are safe from any danger. I shall protect you!"

"You?—Me—?" she asked, her eye wandering doubtfully up and down his figure.

"Yes, me, you! You are under my protection. On behalf of my great opera, the Muses will make certain that I return home happy and healthy, since the world would otherwise lose an irreplaceable work of art. On my travels in America not a hair on my head will be hurt. Consequently, everyone with me is safe from any accident."

"Wonderful! If you are so sure that nothing can happen to us, why do you not do us the favor of getting us out of the predicament we are in!"

The cantor scratched behind an ear and answered in a grumble, "You seem to have misunderstood me, my dearest. One cannot play a composition '*allegro vivace*' when it is designated '*lento*.' If I said that no misfortune would befall you in my presence, I by no means meant that I was the one to open the gates to freedom from our present imprisonment. For this there are other people. I need mention to you only Mr. Frank, who has already performed many great deeds and will by no means let us down. Am I not right about that?"

He amicably directed this last question to Hobble-Frank.

The latter felt flattered and responded as was his wont, "Yes, you speak correctly, very correctly, Mr. Cantor Emeritus, and the trust you honor me with shall not be in vain. Even if everything else fails, I shall set you free!"

"How?"

"You do not believe me? While you have been wasting time quarreling, I deliberated quietly and have found the way to get us out."

"I'm curious to hear it," voiced Sam.

"You have pecked on the wall and poked at the ceiling, but your knives could not penetrate the rocks. But I will bet there are holes here to which we can set the levers to freedom!"

"Holes? Where?"

"Where?" said Frank. " Yes, that we have to establish first."

"Then we are just as well off as before."

"Be quiet! Your eyes are struck by blindness and all your noses not worth three pennies. The cover up there is shut and, except for it, there seems to be no other opening. If that were true, we would suffocate here, since the air would become depleted of oxygen. Now look at the lamp, how nicely it burns, and strain your olfactory tools for even a bit of bad air! I am convinced the air is being renewed. Therefore, there must be holes down here or up there, as in my villa Bear Fat on the Elbe. There is a continuous draft here, which we must find. And do you know how one best finds this out?"

"With the lamp, you think?" asked Sam.

"Yes, with the flame. This shows there are times that you all have not banged your heads too hard! Take the lamp and move with it along the wall down at the floor and up at the ceiling! You will find the openings where the good air comes in from outside and the bad goes out."

"Mr. Frank, this idea is truly not bad!" cried Sam Hawkens. "Your observation is correct. We have here completely fresh air; therefore, there must be a draft. We shall search for it."

"See, you old rascal, this fellow knows a thing or two! If it were not for me then—listen!"

He stopped in the middle of his sentence and the others also listened to a noise coming from above. The storm had passed. There was no more thunder and thus they could hear quite clearly what was taking place on the flat roof. Heavy rocks were being rolled about and the cover was opened, but only a small crack. Then the chief's voice could be heard, "Listen, white men, what I tell you! You are aware now that you are my prisoners. There is war between us and the palefaces and I should kill you. But I will be merciful and let you keep your lives if you surrender all you have of your own free will. Your leader shall answer me!"

The designation "leader" referred to Sam Hawkens, who responded, "You shall have everything you desire. Let us come up and we will give it to you!"

"My brother is cunning like a snake. If I let you come up, you will not give anything to me, but will fight."

"Then come down and take what you demand!"

"Then you would keep me down there. The palefaces shall first bundle up their weapons with the straps I am going to throw down. We will then let down our ropes and pull the bundles up. Sam Hawkens, tell us if you agree!"

"Will Ka Maku, the chief, keep his word and release us once we have given him everything?"

"Yes."

"Yes? *Heeheeheehee!* Don't think us to be as stupid as you are, and move away quickly up there or I will put a bullet through your head! We know exactly where we stand with you liars and traitors. You will not get as much as a fingernail clipping from us."

"Then you must die!"

"You just wait! Death threatens us even if we give you everything. You miscalculated. We have rifles and will force you to let us go without paying ransom."

"Sam Hawkens is wrong. Your weapons will be of no use to you, since there will be no fight. You are locked up and cannot get out. We will not attack you and you will not have to defend yourselves. But there is no water and nothing to eat. We shall wait until you have expired and then get what we want without having to fight. Howgh!"

The cover was replaced and they could hear the big rocks being rolled on once more.

"Stupidity!" Dick Stone rumbled. "You could have done better! Not even answered, but put a bullet through the treacherous bandit."

"Do you believe, Dick, old man, that this would have helped us any? On the contrary, our situation would only have worsened. No, if it's not necessary, I will not spill blood. Let's try instead to free ourselves by cunning!"

"Then let's follow Frank's advice. But we must hurry, since the lamp will not burn much longer. Then we will be sitting in the dark."

It turned out that Hobble-Frank was right. Holes were found in the outside wall permitting the entry of fresh air, and soon they also discovered small openings in the ceiling for the escape of exhaled air.

These openings led diagonally through the masonry so that daylight would not give them away. Their diameter was barely more than an inch.

"This will probably be of help to us," ventured Will Parker. "The holes offer us points where our knife blades can start biting. There remains only the question of where we want to get out. Through the wall?"

"That's too thick," said Sam. "That takes too much work."

"Then through the ceiling?"

"Yes, although this will be difficult, since the one working will have to stand or sit on the shoulders of two others. But once we have removed some of the wood, it will go that much faster. It's too bad we will have light for at most half an hour; then we will be in the dark. Let's find the best place, then!"

They found it quickly. Sam and Droll asked to work first. Sam stood on Stone and Parker, Droll on the shoulders of the two Germans, Ebersbach and Strauch. When they tired, they would be spelled. Shortly after starting their work, Schi-So suggested, "The light will not last. Later it may be of greater need. Why let it burn down now?"

He was right, and it was extinguished. Now it was totally dark in the room. They could hear the quiet pecking and grinding of the knives and the breathing of the two men at work. They labored so hard that they had to be relieved after only a quarter of an hour. There was no talk of sleep. They drilled, cut, and pecked throughout the night. By then, enough wood had been cut from the ceiling that a man could snake his way through. Now there was still the task of continuing the hole through the ceiling's upper layer. This layer consisted of pounded clay hardened almost to stone. It was slow going, but by noon, the noise of the knives told them that the upper layer would soon be penetrated.

"Work quietly now, as quietly as possible," demanded Sam Hawkens, "or else they will hear you up there."

He had barely spoken when a shot rang out from above the laborers and little later Dick Stone, working beside Schi-So, called, "Darn it! I've been hit."

"Where?" asked Sam.

"In the upper arm. The rascals are shooting at us."

"Through the roof? Then they have heard the noise of our knives. Is it bad?"

"Don't think so. Just a glancing shot. The bone's not hurt, but I feel blood running."

"Come down quickly, then! They may shoot again and hit you in the head. Let's look at your arm."

It turned out to have been wise not to have let the lamp burn out. The space below the hole had barely been vacated when two or three more bullets penetrated the ceiling. They heard them hitting the floor. Sam Hawkens let out an overloud howl.

"Why are you screaming?" Parker asked concerned. "Have you been hit?"

"No. Just want to know where the rascals are."

A joyous howl rang out above them. The Indians had heard Sam's voice and thought they had hit him.

"Very good!" Sam laughed. "They are lying or are squatting right above our hole to listen. Let's give 'em some bullets, too! Frank and Will, come here! There are six bullets in our double-barreled rifles. Each of us, two shots, quickly, one after the other! One—two—three!"

The shots rang out and howls of dismay and hurt immediately sounded above the prisoners.

"Well! Excellent! *Heeheeheehee!*" laughed Sam. "We seem to have hit a few. I don't think they'll sit down again to listen."

"But neither will I stand in the hole to have them shoot at me!" Stone grumbled.

"No one has asked you to," Sam responded. "Show me your arm."

The lamp had been relighted. By its flame they found Dick's arm had suffered only a small, glancing wound, easy to dress. When this had been done, Hobble-Frank spoke up, "We should not have dug through the ceiling but down here through the wall. The Indians on the roof can hear us. But if we break through the wall, no one can hear us."

"But the work is much harder," Sam objected.

"Rather harder work than easier, by which one risks one's life being shot!"

Everyone agreed. The air holes in the outside wall were large enough to put two rifle barrels into side by side and use as levers. By this means, but only after hours of effort, they succeeded in loosening the masonry structure sufficiently to then continue with the knives.

It was evening when the first rock finally tumbled from the wall. The first! And how many more were still to be removed! And what was the prisoners' condition! They had intended to rest at the pueblo and to recover. But upon their arrival there had been time only to quench their thirst, but not to eat. They had now been imprisoned for over a day without any sustenance. Hunger and thirst made themselves felt. It did not matter that much to the adults; however, the children asked for food and drink and could not easily be calmed.

Spelling each other, they labored in pairs on the hole through the night. Progress was very slow because the wall was so strong and the mortar almost harder than the rocks. At last another rock broke away—to the outside. The morning's early light shone through. Now things went faster. Another half hour and the hole was large enough for a person to crawl through.

"We have won!" Mrs. Rosalie rejoiced. "This hole is not a comfortable passage for a decent lady, but if it leads to freedom, I will even crawl through a chimney, especially since I can wash later. Go ahead, now, gentlemen! Who is first? Of course, courtesy demands that the ladies to be rescued first. I suggest, therefore, that I be the first."

She had already bent down to put her head through the hole, but Hobble-Frank pulled her back, saying, "Are you out of your mind, Madame Ebersbach? What has come into your head? This is not something for women. Here the lords of creation must take the lead."

"Who?" she asked. "The lords of creation? You surely do not count yourself among them?"

"But of course!"

"Well, then, I feel sorry for all creation. And have you not heard that one should be courteous to ladies?"

"I do not understand you, my most dear, honorable Mrs. Ebersbach! If I crawl out ahead of you, then this is obliging you!"

"Yes, but if you use the word that way, you employ it entirely incorrectly. You are to be obliging by letting me go ahead of you. Can you not grasp that?"

"Very well, then. But considering that the Indians heard the rocks we freed tumble out, they have surely posted a guard. They will surely greet the first one to come out with a bullet, whether he sees the morning's light first with his head or with his feet. If you now want to be first, I do not mind."

"I gladly pass that up, then! I gladly do! I am a lady and as such not obligated to act as target for the lords of creation."

She stepped back quickly. But neither did Frank gain permission to be first; Sam Hawkens claimed this dangerous right. He first hung his hat onto his rifle barrel and carefully stuck it out a bit from the hole. Everything remained quiet. Then Sam Hawkens himself slowly crawled forward, head first. When his eyes reached the opening's mouth, he quickly pulled back and reported, "It's true, several guards are sitting on the platform below. Our hole must have been detected."

"Did they see you?" Dick Stone asked.

"No."

"How are they armed?"

"With rifles."

"Then they can shoot us. They are standing on the platform onto which we must jump, and only one of us at a time can come out. The hole is probably being watched not only from below but also from above. Let's find out."

Dick took his long rifle, cocked his impossible hat onto the muzzle, and slowly pushed the barrel through the hole so that it looked from outside as if a man's head was appearing. A shout rang out, immediately followed by several more. He pulled the rifle back, carefully investigated his headgear, and said, "Two bullets went through, one from below and one from above. What do you say about that, Sam, old fellow?"

It took a while for the latter to respond. In great suspense, everyone waited for him to speak. When he finally did, he sounded rather dejected, "There are also guards above us peering over the platform's edge observing the hole. Guards above us and below. That's bad, very bad!"

"We shoot them off!" Hobble-Frank ventured cheerfully.

"Try it! Can you shoot at those sitting on the roof?"

"No. Did not think of that; but so much easier at the ones standing below us."

"How do you intend to do this?"

"Well. I only need to aim the rifle at them and pull the trigger!"

"Easier said than done. The opening is so narrow that you can aim only with the entire rifle, with both hands and your head outside. But before you can get into this exposed position, you will have several bullets in your head."

"Shucks! That is true! Now we have this nice hole and still cannot get out!"

"Alas, we have toiled for nothing. We cannot get through the ceiling or through the wall."

"Hell's bells! Is that true?" Mrs. Rosalie asked. "Is there no other way out? Possibly through the floor?"

"No, because they will also watch from below."

"Well, that means the oxen still stand in front of the mountain, just as before! And they call themselves lords of creation! If I were a man, I would know what to do!"

"What?"

"Shucks, that is just what I do not know, since I am not a man, but a lady. It is the gentlemen's task to protect us. You understand? Do your duty, then! I do not need to rack my brains about how you are to free me from this imprisonment. But I must positively get out, which is why I challenge you to strain your poor minds to find out by what means you can save me and also yourselves!"

A long pause ensued. Each and every one contemplated means of escape. But no voice announced anything. Finally, Schi-So spoke up, "There is no use mulling this over. We cannot get out, for we would have to crawl out singly and would be killed off. Nevertheless, I do think that we will be rescued."

"How? Whereby? By what means?" everyone chimed in.

"Old Shatterhand and Winnetou are to meet at Forner's rancho. Forner will tell them about us, and it is likely the two men will follow our tracks. They will, therefore, come to the pueblo."

"Yes," declared Sam with a deep sigh, "that's our only hope. They will come, I would swear to it. And if we can endure until then, we will be freed."

"But they are only two people. What can they achieve against so many Indians?" Mrs. Rosalie objected.

"Please, be quiet!" she was ordered by Hobble-Frank. "What do you know of these two heroes, who are my friends and patrons! Once they are on our track, we need not worry anymore. They will get us out, and not just us."

"Who else?"

"Also the banker, if he's still alive."

"He is probably no longer alive," Droll put forth, "not he nor his bookkeeper. This was probably primarily aimed at them; otherwise, they would not have been separated from us."

He was right, but for the wrong reason. They were the primary targets, but it was not the perpetrators' intent that it would so soon cost them their own lives.

Old Shatterhand and Winnetou met in a small clearing.

# 8

---

# THE LIBERATION

HE RESCUED BANKER AND HIS BOOKKEEPER, together with the Oil Prince, Buttler, and Poller, traveled north without stopping. By noon they reached the forest of the Mogollon Mountains, which offered them shade, coolness, and water. They dismounted to rest at the side of a brook and to let their horses recover. Here the Oil Prince explained to the banker the events of the previous evening. His tale was entirely successful. Once again Duncan was convinced that Grinley was an honorable gentleman. The banker was also delighted to have found such brave and respectable companions as Buttler and Poller.

After resting sufficiently, they remounted and rode on until, that evening, they came across a place well suited for the night's camp. There was water and enough dry wood to maintain a fire for the entire night. Neither Duncan nor Baumgarten noticed the ample provisions that the Oil Prince, Buttler, and Poller could have acquired only at the pueblo. When Poller started the fire, Buttler voiced quiet concern, "We're close to the Nijora's territory. Wouldn't it be better to do without a fire? It'll give us away."

"There's no danger," the Oil Prince declared. "I'm in good standing with the Nijora."

"But they're on the warpath, Grinley!"

"No matter. Even on the warpath they are no danger to me."

"Maybe, but they live north of here," Buttler warned. "And various Apache tribes who are enemies of the Nijora are just to the south. We're right in between the two adversaries, and it's always dangerous being in such borderlands, because this is where hostilities often occur! War parties will spare neither friend nor foe as long as they make good for themselves!"

Still unconcerned, the Oil Prince replied, "Rest assured! Except for us, there isn't a single soul in this whole area! And this place is especially well hidden. I've never met anyone here, nor have I seen any tracks. I'm sure that within a large radius we are by ourselves and can safely light our fire."

As certain as Grinley thought himself correct, he was wrong, for to the north two solitary horsemen, unbeknownst to each other, had the same destination in mind—that is, the spot where the Oil Prince and his companions were camped.

The two riders were perhaps three English miles from this camp and only one from each other, both traveling south.

One was white. He rode a magnificent black stallion with red nostrils and that particular crown in its long mane considered by the Indians to be a sure sign of excellence in a horse. Saddle and leatherwork were of the finest Indian craftsmanship. The man himself was not particularly tall or very broad in stature, but his sinews were like steel and his muscles of iron. A dark-blond, full beard framed his suntanned, serious face. He wore frayed leggings and a hunting shirt frayed at its seams, long boots pulled up over his knees, and a broad-brimmed felt hat, its string entirely decorated with the ear tips of the grizzly. In his broad, braided leather belt, he kept a good supply of cartridges, two revolvers, and a Bowie knife. Slung from his left shoulder down to his right hip he carried a lasso braided of several leather strands, and around his neck, suspended from a strong silken cord, a peace pipe decorated with hummingbird skins. Its head was engraved with Indian symbols. In his right hand he held a short-barreled rifle, its bolt of very peculiar design—it was a twenty-five-shot Henry carbine—and over his back was slung a double-barreled bear killer of the heaviest caliber, like none found today.

True prairie hunters do not think much of shine and neatness. The more worn his appearance, the greater the honor, for the more he has been through. He looks down, with the disdain of a superior, on anyone who keeps up appearances. The greatest abomination is a brightly polished rifle. It is his conviction that no frontiersman has the time to spend on rifle cleaning. But everything on this man looked as neat as if he had set out from St. Louis for the West only yesterday. His rifles appeared to have left the gun maker's hand only hours ago. His boots were immaculately polished and his spurs without a trace of rust. His suit was spotless, without a mend, and, truly, not only his face, but also his hands, were washed clean! It was not difficult to think him a Sunday hunter.

And no wonder, for this frontiersman's clean appearance had fooled many who were not acquainted with him. Yet once they heard his name, they realized their error, for he was none other than Old Shatterhand, the famous, courageous hunter, the unshakeable friend of the red man, and the inexorable foe of all villains, of which there were many beyond the Mississippi, and still are today.

Old Shatterhand was his warrior's name, referring to his shattering hand, for he spilled the blood of an enemy only when absolutely necessary, and even then he would not kill his adversary, but only wound him. In a close fight, he could down his enemy with a single blow to the temple, a feat of strength quite unexpected from a man of his stature. This is how he received the name given to him by white and red hunters alike.

His magnificent stallion, named Hatatitla, "Lightning" in Apache, had been a gift from his blood brother Winnetou.

The other horseman, a mile to the west of the white man, was Indian. The horse he rode was a look-alike of Old Shatterhand's.

There are people who, on first sight, before they have even spoken, leave a deep, unforgettable impression. Such a man was this Indian.

He wore a white-tanned hunting shirt decorated with red Indian embroidery. The leggings were made of the same material. No spot, not the least smudge, could be found on either shirt or pants. His small feet were shod in pearl-embroidered moccasins decorated with porcupine quills. Around his neck he wore a precious medicine bag, an artfully carved peace pipe, and a threefold string of the claws of the grizzly, the feared carnivore of the Rocky Mountains. Around his hips was tied a broad belt made from a valuable Saltillo blanket. From it showed, as was the case with Old Shatterhand, the handles of two revolvers and a scalping knife. His head was not covered. His long, thick, blue-black hair was arranged in a helmet-like bob and braided with the skin of a rattlesnake. Though no eagle feather adorned the hair, it was obvious at first sight that this red warrior was an outstanding chief. The features of his beautiful, manly, serious face could have been called Roman. The cheekbones barely stood out, the lips in the beardless face were finely curved, and his skin color was a matte light brown with a tint of bronze. In front of him, across his saddle, he had placed a rifle whose wooden parts were heavily studded with silver nails.

Had he met a frontiersman who had never laid eyes on him, the man would at once have been recognized by this rifle, the subject of thousands of campfire conversations. There were three rifles in the West whose fame could not be approached by a fourth: Old Shatterhand's Henry carbine, his Bear Killer, and Winnetou's silver rifle. This horseman, then, was indeed the Apache chief Winnetou, a most faithful and self-sacrificing friend, and a most feared opponent of any of their enemies.

He did not ride in the European manner, but instead leaned forward, as if he did not know how to ride, on his Iltschi, meaning "Wind" in the Apache language, the brother of Hatatitla. His look seemed tired and continually directed, dreamlike, to the ground. But those who knew him realized that his senses were of incomparable acuity and that nothing escaped his eyes.

Suddenly he straightened up. Just as quickly he leveled his rifle. A shot rang out, a short, sharp report. Winnetou directed his horse to a tree, rode close to the trunk, stood up on the saddle, reached into a cavity in the vicinity of the lowest branch, and pulled out the creature he had shot. It was an animal about the size of a mid-sized dog, with a yellowish-gray pelt with black hair tips. The tail was half as long as its body. It was a raccoon, a welcome roast for a hunter.

Winnetou barely had his quarry in hand when another shot rang out to the east of him, one with a peculiarly deep and heavy sound.

"Uff!" the Indian mumbled in surprise. "Akaya Selkhi-Lata!" meaning, in Apache, "There's Old Shatterhand!"

Oddly enough, Old Shatterhand, seemingly unconcerned and deep in thought, had been following the trail south when the Apache's shot rang out. Surprised, he had checked his horse and said, in his native German, "That was the sound of the silver rifle!" Then, quickly raising his Bear Killer, he had fired the shot by which Winnetou immediately recognized his friend.

(To the European, or anyone else, for that matter, who has never been to the Wild West, this would seem to be an impossibility. But the experienced, practiced frontiersman knows the voice of each rifle he is acquainted with. His senses are sharpened, for his life depends on their discernment. Whoever cannot develop this acuity will go under here. How particular is the human voice! The voice of a familiar person can be distinguished from among thousands. As another example: How is it with a dog's bark? Do you not recognize your Phylax, Caesar, or Nero at once by his voice? So it is with rifles. Each has its own voice, yet its particularities are known and heard only by those of a discerning ear.)

After the two shots had rung out by which the friends recognized each other, they rode toward each other, Old Shatterhand to the west and Winnetou to the east. In order to find each other, they shot once more. Then they met in a small clearing, jumped off their horses, and embraced.

"My spirit is happy to meet my good, white brother Scharlih so soon today!" Winnetou said. "We had wanted to meet only two days from now at Forner's rancho. For a long time my heart has longed for you and my thoughts rushed ahead to you during many days' travel."

"I, too, am very happy to have with me once more the best and most noble of my friends," responded Old Shatterhand. "I have longed for you. I have missed you since I last said farewell to you. Now my spirit is content seeing you before me. How did my brother fare during our long separation?"

"The sun rises and sets. The days come and go. The grass grows and withers; Winnetou, though, stays the same. Has my white brother experienced much since I saw him last?"

"Much! Not every day is beautiful, and among the prairie flowers are many that are poisonous. So it was also with my experiences at home. I had to fight envy and malice, poison, scorn, and malicious joy. My trust in God and love for humanity have not been shattered. I am still the man I always was. When we sit at the campfire, we can talk about our experiences. Does my brother know a place nearby where we may rest well?"

"Yes. If we ride for another hour, we will come to a brook flowing from a small spring. At the spring is a place surrounded on all sides by bushes no eye can penetrate. There we can light a fire to roast the raccoon I just shot. Will my brother join me?"

They continued their ride under the forest's canopy of tall trees. It was already rather dark, since the sun had traveled close to the horizon.

About an hour later, they arrived at the small, narrow brook Winnetou had talked about. Riding across they immediately checked their horses, for in the grass they saw a streak, a track, coming from the left and leading to the right along the brook. Both dismounted to investigate, to read the track, and both straightened up at the same time.

"Five horsemen," said Old Shatterhand, "on rather tired horses."

"They came by here only minutes ago," Winnetou added. "They will set up camp not far from here."

"We need to find out who they are," said Old Shatterhand. "My brother knows of the tomahawks being on the warpath. We need to be cautious."

They proceeded to some thick brush nearby, led their horses in to hide them for the time being, tied them up, and put their hands on their muzzles. This was the sign to the Indian-raised animals to remain quiet and not to give their masters away by loud snorting. The two men then returned to the brook and followed the tracks with slow, inaudible steps. They were both masters in making an approach, and for cover utilized every tree and bush, every bend of the brook.

They had advanced for only five minutes when Winnetou stopped and smelled the air. Old Shatterhand did the same and smelled smoke.

"They are close by and keep a fire," he whispered to Winnetou. "They must be whites, for a red man would not choose a place to camp that was open toward the wind."

The Apache nodded and moved on. The brook now made its way between trees, below which stood rather tall bushes. The bushes afforded excellent cover to the two hunters. Soon they saw the fire. It was set close to the water with the flames rising up several feet, betraying a lack of caution a real frontiersman would never be guilty of.

Here the forest floor was covered by soft moss, so that the steps of even those less experienced than Winnetou and Old Shatterhand would not have been heard. Four trees, below which the fire burned, stood close together, and between their trunks grew bushes that made a blind that hid the two eavesdroppers very well. Cautiously, they crept close, face down on the ground, their heads hard by the bushes through whose leafless lower stalks they could peer. That's when they saw the five men close in front of them. The fire burned approximately four paces from the trees. Close to them sat the Oil Prince and Buttler, his brother, resting with their backs against tree trunks; opposite sat the banker and Baumgarten, his bookkeeper, and to their right Poller was occupied in breaking up dry wood and throwing it into the fire. They must have felt very safe, since they did not think it necessary to talk quietly. They spoke in such loud voices that anyone would have understood every word from at least twenty paces, a circumstance very accommodating to the two listeners.

"Yes, Mr. Duncan," said the Oil Prince, "I assure you, the deal you are going to make will be splendid, even magnificent. The oil floats at least a finger thick on the water there; below ground it must therefore exist in great quantity. If that had not been the case, I would not have discovered it at all, since the place lies so hidden and forlorn that I would bet no man's foot has yet trod there and none would come across it for decades yet, although the Chelly River has often been visited by hunters and probably more so by Indians. As I said, I, too, would have passed by the place had my attention not been drawn by the smell of the oil."

"Was the odor truly that strong?" the banker asked.

"It sure was! I must have been half a mile from the spot, and yet my nose smelled the petroleum. You can imagine what quantities must be there! I'm convinced the drill will not have to penetrate the ground very deeply to hit the underground oil reservoir. Jeez, what a spout that will be when it rises! Want to bet that it will rise at least a hundred feet?"

"I never bet," declared Duncan with forced quiet, yet the sparkle in his eyes gave away his strongly aroused desire. "I just hope everything will be as you say."

"Can it be otherwise, sir? Can I lie to you if, when you get to the place, you would instantly recognize any deception? I haven't asked for a single dollar from you yet. You pay me only when you have convinced yourself that I am not cheating you and the deal is on the up-and-up."

"Yes, you are so involved in this matter that I must believe you to be an honest man. I admit that."

"Added to this is the fact that you will not pay me cash, but by draft payable in San Francisco."

An attentive observer would have noticed an expression of expectation he could not quite suppress on the Oil Prince's face. His gaze showed badly concealed avarice.

Duncan caught neither the evil look nor the emotional expression of the other and answered carelessly, "Certainly! I have some quills with me and also a small bottle of ink. I'm surprised, though, that this chief Ka Maku did not think of emptying our pockets. I truly do not understand that."

"Oh, the explanation is as simple as can be. The redskins were so busy taking you prisoner that at first they did not have any time for looting. That was to have been later."

"Do you think they also had intentions on our lives?"

"Certainly! At daybreak you would, of course, have been tied to the stake."

"Then we two should be very grateful to the three of you. I'm just sorry for our poor companions. By now none of them are probably alive."

"Yes," Baumgarten added, "I am really sorry we rode away and thought only about ourselves. It was definitely our duty to try everything to save them."

"You can say this now only because you are safe," the Oil Prince said. "I assure you, though, that the others' rescue was simply impossible. I have experience of the Wild West, and you can believe every word I tell you. We need not be sorry in the least. On the contrary, I think our escape will prove more useful to our companions than if we had attempted their rescue at the risk of our lives."

"How so?"

"Because they gained time by it. In the morning, as soon as they discovered our escape, the redskins surely set out in pursuit. They would have had no time to torture and kill their captives. I figure they'll follow us for a day and will need another one to return. That gives them a delay of two days, and you know a lot can happen in two days, especially when dealing with such clever, experienced, and brave people as those in the pueblo!"

"Hmm," the banker murmured, "what you say seems to make sense. Although this Hobble-Frank and Aunt Droll are odd fellows, they are certainly not men who let themselves be butchered and, when it comes to these three hunters calling themselves the Shamrock, they seemed even less likely to be hoodwinked."

"You mean Sam Hawkens?" Buttler asked.

"Yes. Him, Dick Stone, and Will Parker. They are frontiersmen out of a book. You did not meet them, Mr. Buttler and Mr. Poller, and I haven't told you yet how they met up with the German immigrants. You need to hear this to understand what clever men they are."

"Were you present, sir?" Poller queried.

"No, but I was told on the ride from Forner's rancho to the pueblo. That's where I heard about it."

Yeah," responded Buttler, with a forced smile. "This Hawkens especially seems to have a wily reputation. But didn't you say earlier, sir," he addressed his brother, "that we are being pursued by the redskins?"

"Indeed," the Oil Prince confirmed.

"But if the redskins find us now? If they see our fire burning so nice and bright?"

"They won't. They won't catch up with us."

"Aren't you mistaken there, sir?" Duncan asked. "I am not familiar with the Wild West, but have heard much and read even more about it. These Indians are terrible people who for months keep on a man's heels until they catch him."

"That will not happen in this case. Consider the time we left the pueblo and that they could have taken up pursuit only at daybreak! We have a head start they cannot overcome."

"Why not? They only need to continue riding while we sit here to arrive at this place even before midnight."

That's when the Oil Prince broke into a peal of laughter and shouted, "You earlier claimed not to know anything of the Wild West and were quite right there, sir. You do not know anything at all. You claim the redskins can follow us through the night?"

"Yes. At least if they are smart, they will, to quickly compensate for the head start we have on them."

"How are they to do this? Do they know where we are?"

"No, but they need only to follow our tracks to find us."

"Can one smell tracks, sir, or see them at night?"

"Well, not really."

"Can the redskins, now, when it is dark, follow our tracks?"

"No."

"Then they must stop and wait for daylight. How, then, are they to make up for our head start, particularly when tomorrow morning our tracks will no longer be recognizable? No, sir, we need not fear anything, nothing at all, and we will happily make it to Gloomy Water to bring our business to a conclusion."

"Gloomy Water? That's the place where you discovered the petroleum? Where does it get its name? Didn't you say that no one had been there yet?"

"I did, with deepest conviction."

"But you said the place had no name. If, however, its name is Gloomy Water, then someone who was there must have named it."

This put the Oil Prince in a quandary. Despite his cunning, no quick subterfuge came to his mind. He covered the brief silence with a half-loud laugh meant to sound superior. Fortunately for him, Buttler came to his aid. "Mr. Duncan, you seem to think you've made a very astute observation. Isn't that so?"

"Astute?" the other repeated. "No, I don't, but in any case, it was relevant. The place has a name; therefore, someone else must have been there prior to Mr. Grinley. Why has that person not also spoken about the petroleum he must have seen, too? You see, there are certain inconsistencies I must address."

"Eh, these inconsistencies are really easily resolved! The person you are talking about is our Mr. Grinley, the Oil Prince."

"Ah!" the banker now exclaimed in surprise.

"Yes, he was the one, and he gave the place its name, Gloomy Water, since—"

"—since," the Oil Prince quickly interjected, "the place is so gloomy that the water is almost black."

The grateful look he gave Buttler was answered with a quiet, disapproving headshake. Neither was noticed by Duncan or Baumgarten. The Oil Prince, though, seemed to have lost any desire to continue the conversation. He got up and walked away, saying he wanted to collect more firewood.

It was time for Old Shatterhand and Winnetou to withdraw, since they might be detected by Grinley. Fortunately for them, he went upstream without looking in the direction the listeners were hidden.

He had been sitting with his back toward them; thus the tree trunks and bushes had been between him and them. For this reason, they had been unable to see his face. But when he got up, he had to turn, which allowed them to see his features clearly. They crept back into the woods until the firelight no longer reached them. Then they stood up and returned to the spot where they had hidden their horses. Without speaking a word about what they had just learned, Winnetou pulled his horse from the bushes and stepped into the forest with his horse behind him. Old Shatterhand followed with his own.

The horses' hiding place had grass and water, so the two men could readily have camped there for the night without danger of discovery. But there was a possibility that the Oil Prince or one of his companions might come to this place the next morning and see them or notice the traces of their camp. Therefore they left. Their tracks would not be visible in the morning, once the grass straightened up again.

They did, however, require water and pasture for their animals, so they returned to the brook to a spot farther along. They traveled in a wide arc through the forest, since here the soft moss would by morning have recovered from the hoof- and footprints.

It took the eyes of Winnetou and Old Shatterhand, used to the darkness, to make it through the woods without bumping into trees or falling down. For about a quarter of an hour they moved among the trees as if it were broad daylight. They then turned to the right to make it back to the brook. At the spot where they emerged, a small stream entered the larger body of water. They crossed the brook and followed it upstream until they reached the spring Winnetou had spoken of and where he had wanted to camp. How acute the chief's sense of place—to be able to find this spring in the midst of this great forest, despite the darkness!

They unsaddled their horses and let them graze freely. They could do this only because both stallions were as faithful as dogs that obeyed the softest call and never moved far from their masters. Only then did Winnetou speak. "Does my brother have some food on him?"

"A piece of dried meat," Old Shatterhand answered. "I did not look for more, since I intended to stop at Ka Maku's pueblo tomorrow."

"My brother may keep his meat! We shall roast the raccoon I have shot."

With these words, the Apache left. Old Shatterhand did not ask where he was going. He knew that Winnetou was now reconnoitering the spring to assure himself of the security of the place. About ten minutes later, he returned with an armload of dry wood, which confirmed the absence of hostile beings close by. Even Old Shatterhand's sensitive ears had not heard the breaking of this wood, another sign of the Apache's incomparable skill.

Soon a fire was burning, but it was small, in the Indian way. The two men settled down to skin the raccoon. A little later, the delightful smell of roasting meat suffused the camp, an odor that cannot issue from any kitchen, but only from a campfire. They ate, slowly and with enjoyment, without speaking a word. When both were full, they roasted the remaining meat for the next day. Only then did Winnetou think the time right to speak. "How many bindings does my brother carry?"

"Maybe twenty," answered Old Shatterhand, knowing why the Apache asked for them. Every frontiersman generally carries a good supply of bindings.

"I have about the same number," the chief said. "I will, nevertheless, cut the raccoon's hide into strips in case we need more tomorrow."

"For Ka Maku's warriors," nodded Old Shatterhand. "Although this chief has never been hostile toward us, we may have to force from him what we require."

"My brother is right. Does he know the men we have overheard?"

"I have seen only one of them before, the one called Grinley and Oil Prince. I recall having seen him with a gang of no-goods."

"Even though I have not seen him before, I told myself that he must be a dangerous man. They spoke of the Chelly River. My brother and I have been there. Tell me if there can be petroleum!"

"Not a drop!"

"And did this Grinley discover Gloomy Water and give it its name?"

"No. Years ago the two of us were at this small lake and it already carried this name. The Oil Prince is planning to defraud these two men and even worse."

"A double murder!"

"Yes. Two of the five men we saw are to be cheated and then murdered. They are to find an oil well, pay for this discovery and then—disappear."

"We must save them!"

"Certainly. But it is less urgent than the liberation of Ka Maku's captives. Let the Oil Prince's two victims first become aware that they have been deceived."

"My brother Scharlih has decided to abandon our original plan?"

"Yes. We had intended to meet at Forner's rancho, but have already met here. From there it was our intention to go to Sonora to visit with some Apache tribes. This we can do later. Now we need to effect the release of the prisoners at the pueblo and then save the lives of these two palefaces. But what does my brother say about friends being among those captives?"

"Uff! What is Hobble-Frank doing here?"

"I wrote to him twice mentioning when and where I intended to meet you. The little fellow must have contracted 'Wild West fever,' which drove him here. Of course, Droll was happy to accompany him."

"And Hawkens, Stone, and Parker are in there, too! Uff!"

This was an exclamation of amazement and disapproval wrapped all in one. The reason for the disapproval was immediately clarified by Old Shatterhand, "To have themselves caught, being as experienced as they are. Hard to believe! They must surely have heard of the hostile movement among several Indian tribes, which would call for twice the caution. They should not have entered the pueblo prior to having smoked the peace pipe with the chief. Yesterday's thunderstorm may have been the culprit."

"Right!" agreed Winnetou. "The weather probably drove them into the pueblo without giving them time to assure themselves of the chief's friendship. Ka Maku is usually friendly toward the whites."

"Tomorrow we shall find out the reason for his current enmity. Think about this, my brother Winnetou: Our Hobble-Frank and his friend Droll came to Forner's rancho to meet us. He knows us well and, therefore, knew we would arrive on time. Why did he not wait for us? Why did he join these immigrants?"

"The Oil Prince!" The words spoken by Winnetou demonstrated how clearly he understood the state of affairs.

"Quite right. At the rancho, Hobble-Frank and Aunt Droll must have heard of the supposed oil find, did not believe it, and became suspicious. Of course, they would have told Sam Hawkens and his two friends, who quickly allied with them. The Oil Prince found out and got rid of them by inducing Ka Maku to capture the entire party, but then to let the two people in question escape."

"My brother Old Shatterhand speaks my thoughts. When will we leave here to free the captives?"

"Tomorrow morning. If we were to leave now, we would arrive in daylight at the pueblo and would easily be seen. What we need to do can be accomplished only by night. Setting out tomorrow morning will get us there in plenty of time."

Winnetou agreed. "By dusk we will be close to the pueblo. Let us quench the fire now!"

While Old Shatterhand extinguished the flames with water from the spring, Winnetou once more made his rounds to assure himself that they could sleep without concern. Then they stretched out side by side on the soft grass. They did not find it necessary to alternate watch, but relied on their sharp ears and on their horses, who would give away the approach of any person or animal by snorting.

The next morning, the two men awoke early and watered their horses very well, since the animals probably would not be getting water for more than a day. They could not be watered at the pueblo, which now had to be considered as hostile. The two friends then consumed part of last night's leftover meat, saddled the horses, and rode off into a day whose evening promised to be eventful.

It was a good day's ride from their resting place to the pueblo. They had no need to push their excellent horses to arrive there long before evening. For the entire morning, they followed the tracks of the Oil Prince and his companions and stopped around noon to let their horses rest a bit. They talked only about their experiences since they had last parted. Now, however, while they rested, Winnetou said, "Does my brother see that we were not mistaken: Ka Maku has been in league with the Oil Prince."

"Yes," nodded Old Shatterhand. "If not, the chief would have pursued the escapees and we would either have met him, or at least have come across his tracks."

They continued to ride until they were an hour from the pueblo. Now caution was called for, since they could be seen from this point on. They once more dismounted to let some time pass, since they wanted to approach the pueblo at dusk.

The area was flat and sandy. In a narrowing tongue the barren plain extended into the Mogollon Mountains. Here and there was scattered a solitary big rock. Behind one of those they settled down. To the south lay the pueblo. Anyone coming from there would observe neither them nor their horses.

Shortly after sitting down, Winnetou pointed to the right, calling in surprise, "Teshi, tlao tchate!" These three words in the Apache language mean, "Look, many deer," or "See, a herd of deer!" These were not deer, however, but a kind of American antelope quite rare in Arizona, thus accounting for the Apache chief's surprise. He and Old Shatterhand would have dearly loved to take off to hunt these fleet-footed animals, which make for a very tender roast; however, the task they had to complete today did not permit it.

The beautiful game moved south against the wind so as to lose neither sight nor scent of any potential pursuers.

"Wonderful game!" Old Shatterhand said, "but a bad time for us."

He checked the wind from the south.

"It can easily bring the enemy," nodded Winnetou. "The herd is moving straight for the pueblo. If they see it, we may soon see red hunters, since the wind is coming from there."

They focused now on the south. More than a half hour passed and nothing happened. It appeared that the antelope had not been noticed. Then, however, several small dots appeared, rapidly growing larger from the direction the two friends were looking.

"Uff! They are coming!" said Winnetou. "Now we will be discovered!"

"Maybe not," ventured Old Shatterhand. "If the red hunters do not split up, but stay in a group, they will pass by on one side and we can move around the rock. Let's see!"

They stood up and took their horses by the reins.

The antelope were returning, and behind them appeared four horsemen, pushing their horses to the utmost.

"Only four!" said Winnetou. "If only the chief were with them!"

Quickly, Old Shatterhand pulled his telescope from its pocket and pointed it at the riders. "He's with them," he reported. "He's riding the fastest horse and is in the front."

"That is good!" cried the Apache, his eyes lighting up. "Shall we catch him?"

"Yes, and the other three, too."

"Uff!" With this exclamation, Winnetou jumped in the saddle, taking his silver rifle into his hand. Just as quickly, Old Shatterhand was on his horse, with his Henry carbine at the ready. The fleeing game came racing by, passing them at a distance of perhaps a thousand feet. The four Indians were still somewhat behind. They could hear the sharp cries with which they drove their horses.

"Now!" Winnetou shouted.

He catapulted from behind the rock, Old Shatterhand right behind, diagonally toward the Indians. The redskins were startled when they suddenly saw two riders cutting them off.

"Stop!" Old Shatterhand shouted while, like the Apache, he reined in his stallion. "Where is Ka Maku going with his warriors?"

It was difficult for the Indians to bring their horses to a halt. The chief screamed angrily, "Why do you delay us! Now there will be no meat for us!"

"You would not have gotten it anyway. Since when do you hunt the fleeing antelope like a slow prairie wolf? Do you not know that they must be encircled so that, despite their speed, they cannot escape?"

The four Indians had finally succeeded in calming their horses and could more closely look over the two intruders.

"Uff!" exclaimed the chief. "Old Shatterhand, the great white hunter, and Winnetou, the famed Apache chief!"

"Yes, it is us!" responded Old Shatterhand. "Dismount with your people and follow us over there into the shade of the rock, behind which we rested until we saw you coming."

"Why should we go there?" asked Ka Maku.

"We must talk with you."

"Can we not talk here?"

"The sun is still quite warm. Over there is shade."

"Will my two famous brothers not follow me to the pueblo, where they can tell me everything just as well as they can here?"

"Yes, we will ride with you to the pueblo. But first you should smoke the peace pipe with us."

"Is that necessary? I did so with both of you long ago."

"Then there was peace in this area. Now people are on the warpath. Therefore we trust only those who are willing to share the calumet with us. Whoever refuses we consider our enemy. Decide, but quickly!"

At the same time, he played with the Henry carbine in a way that caused the chief some anxiety. He knew this rifle the redskins thought to be magic, and knew also what it meant when Old Shatterhand held it so suggestively in his hands. He therefore acceded, but not happily, "Since my famous brothers wish it so, we will comply."

Ka Maku would rather have ridden off, but knew he could not risk this. His horse was not as fast as Old Shatterhand's or as fast as Winnetou's bullets. Although he and his three companions also had rifles, theirs were no match for the rifles of the two hunters. He therefore dismounted, and his three companions followed his example. Leading their horses, they walked over to the rock and sat down.

There Ka Maku worked his peace pipe from its string and said, "My tobacco pouch is empty. Perhaps my great brothers have some *kinnikinnik*\* on them to fill the calumet?"

"We have tobacco enough," answered Old Shatterhand. "But before we smoke the peace pipe with you and follow you to the pueblo to be your guests, I would like to know what warriors we will find there."

"Mine."

"No others?"

"No."

"I have been told you are sheltering foreign warriors. There's discord between several tribes and between the red man and the palefaces. Ka Maku will understand that this calls for caution."

"My brothers will not find foreign warriors at our place."

"And yet a wide track leads from Forner's rancho to your pueblo, where it ends. Leading away from you, it shrank to a small track of only five men."

Ka Maku became alarmed, but did not let on. He assured them eagerly, "My brothers must be mistaken. I do not know of any such tracks."

"The Apache chief and Old Shatterhand are never mistaken when dealing with a track. We not only counted the animals' hoofprints, but even know the names of the people whose animals made them."

"Then my famous brothers know more than I do."

"Have you never heard of Grinley, the Oil Prince?"

"Never."

"That's a lie!"

---

\* *Kinnikinnik* means "mixture." This Indian mixture was made of maple and willow bark, sumac leaves, and other leaves and bark.

At that point, the chief reached for the knife in his belt and shouted angrily, "Does Old Shatterhand mean to insult a brave chief? My knife will give him the answer!"

The white hunter barely shrugged his shoulders and answered, "Why does Ka Maku commit the huge error of threatening me? He knows me and, therefore, knows very well that my bullet would be in his head before the point of his knife could reach me."

With these words and a quick draw, Old Shatterhand pulled both his revolvers and pointed them at Ka Maku. Just as fast, Winnetou had his two revolvers in his hands, keeping the other three Indians in check while Old Shatterhand continued with a quiet mien, "You know these little guns in my hands hold two times six shots. My brother Winnetou will now take your knives and guns. Whoever resists, or makes even the slightest move to resist, will receive a bullet immediately. You have been warned. This is it! Howgh!"

Commandingly, his eyes held those of the chief, who did not dare move when the Apache collected his and his companions' knives and guns. When this was done, Old Shatterhand continued, "The red men see that they are in our power. Only the admission of the truth will save them. Ka Maku may answer my questions now: why did he intentionally let several captives escape with the Oil Prince?"

"There were no captives at our place," the chief hissed angrily.

"And even now there are none at the pueblo?"

"No."

"Ka Maku seems to think Winnetou and Old Shatterhand are young, inexperienced pups who can be deceived. We know that Sam Hawkens, Dick Stone, and Will Parker are at your place."

The chief's eye twitched and betrayed his fright. Yet he did not answer.

"Also two other white warriors, called Frank and Droll, remain there together with other white men and their women and children. Will Ka Maku admit that?"

"No one is there, not a single person," was his answer. "Am I a miserable, mangy dog to have myself addressed like this?"

"Pshaw! I will say even worse to you! Will the other three red warriors perhaps admit that which their chief unwisely denies?" The question was directed at Ka Maku's companions.

"He is telling the truth," one of them answered. "There are no captives with us."

"As you will, then. We will ride to the pueblo to find out. To keep you from causing any trouble, we will tie you up. Winnetou will start with Ka Maku."

When the Apache pulled the thongs from his pocket, Ka Maku jumped up in a fit of rage and screamed, "Tie me up? That will—"

He did not get any further, for Old Shatterhand jumped up just as quickly and gave him such a blow to the temple that he instantly collapsed into unconsciousness. This was the blow that had given the famous frontiersman his name. Threateningly, he turned to the other three, "You see how much good it does to resist us! Must I hit you, too?"

The threat so impressed the three Indians that they offered no resistance as they were tied up. Ka Maku was also bound hand and foot. The ease of the victory was partly due to the fact that these were Pueblo Indians, who had settled down and lost some of their original fighting spirit. Had they belonged to a roving, wild tribe, their reaction would most likely have been different.

To prevent the captives' horses from escaping, Old Shatterhand and Winnetou staked them to the ground with long reins. Then they had to make certain that their prisoners could not move about or help each other, despite their tied hands. Therefore, the rifles of the four Indians were buried far apart, deep in the ground, and then each Indian was tied to one of them so that they could not possibly free themselves.

While this was taking place, the chief regained consciousness. Seeing the helpless position he was in, he gnashed his teeth. Old Shatterhand, hearing this, told him, "It is Ka Maku's own fault he is treated like this. I ask him once more to tell the truth. If he promises to release the captives and everything belonging to them, he shall be untied."

Ka Maku spat on the ground and did not respond. His gesture, meant to insult Old Shatterhand, produced only a pitying smile. Having once more carefully checked that it was impossible for the prisoners to free themselves without aid, the two friends mounted their horses and rode off toward the pueblo.

Ka Maku sent hateful looks after them. He hoped soon to be free again, for if he and his three companions did not soon return to the pueblo, scouts would be sent out to search for them.

However, Ka Maku was mistaken. His people did not think to look for him and his three companions. Their failing to return did not alarm anyone, because pursuit of the fast antelope can take the hunter far away and, should night fall, there may be simple reasons to delay return until the next morning.

Since the pueblo was situated on the rock cliff's south side, it could be spied on only from that direction. Because Winnetou and Old Shatterhand were coming from the north, they had to ride in an arc to see anything. Even so, they had to maintain the utmost caution, since a hostile Indian could show up at any moment.

Just as the sun disappeared below the horizon, they saw the mountain with the pueblo atop its steep rock face. They approached almost as close as the eyes could reach. There they halted their horses and Old Shatterhand pulled out his telescope. After peering through it for some time, he handed it to Winnetou. A short while later, Winnetou lowered it and said, "The prisoners have been active. Has my brother seen the hole in the wall of the third level?"

"Yes," answered Old Shatterhand. "They broke through the outer wall, but cannot get out, since the hole is being watched. They may also have tried to get through the roof."

"They will not succeed at that, either, for there are guards there, too."

"In any case, when it gets dark, fires will be lighted. That will be very troublesome for us. But let's be content that we have seen the hole, for now we know the level the prisoners are in. There's a ladder at the bottom, most likely for the chief's return. It would be wonderful if it were not pulled up!"

They dismounted and settled down to wait for darkness. When it came, they saw several fires up on the pueblo. They staked their horses and walked slowly toward the place where a truly masterly deed had to be performed.

The two men were ready to take on the entire population of the pueblo, whether by cunning or by force.

It was still too early for the daring maneuver. In a few hours, the majority of the Indians would be asleep, then only a few guards would have to be overpowered. But there were, nevertheless, sound reasons not to delay the execution of the operation. First they had to consider that the captured chief and his companions could be freed through some unexpected circumstance. One of his people out hunting might find them. If Ka Maku were to get free and make it to the pueblo, it would be nearly impossible to liberate the captives. Second, they were unaware of the condition of the prisoners and to what threats they were exposed. Any delay could very well be disastrous. And, third, the Indians would probably be waiting for their chief's return and would notice his long absence. In that case, scouts would be sent out to look for him. All this would produce general excitement and watchfulness, which would likely thwart Old Shatterhand and Winnetou's plans. Thus, it was preferable to begin their task at once.

When the two had come close enough to the pueblo, Winnetou said, "My brother may keep to the right, I will stay on the left. In the middle, where the ladder is, we will meet."

Old Shatterhand understood. First they wanted to check the area in front of the pueblo to see whether it was guarded, or whether any of the Indians were outside the dwelling. Old Shatterhand followed his friend's instructions and found nothing of concern. When they met again, they saw that the ladder they had seen lying on the ground had been pulled up.

"Uff!" the Apache said quietly. "It is gone."

"Yes," nodded Old Shatterhand. "But it won't prevent us from reaching the lowest platform. Most of all, we need to know how the enemy is distributed and where they are placed."

"Two guard fires are burning."

"Right. One is on the platform above the captives' confinement area, and one is on the level below to illuminate the hole through which they wanted to escape. At each fire I have counted three guards. But where are the other Indians?"

"Inside the dwelling," replied Winnetou. "Did my brother not see the light there?"

"Yes. The entry holes are being kept open and the lights show through to the outside. Judging by that, the redskins with their squaws and children occupy the upper levels while the two lowermost ones are unoccupied and serve as storage places."

"What my brother has said is correct. Several years ago I visited here and looked over the inside of the pueblo," said Winnetou.

"Hmm! The arrangement may have been changed. We need to be cautious. It's a beautiful evening, and we must assume that not all the Indians will be inside. Some may very well be lying outside on the flat roofs where we can't see them."

"Is this going to stop us?" asked the red man.

"No."

"Then step close to the wall so that I may climb onto your shoulders."

Old Shatterhand complied, and the Apache swung himself up onto his shoulders. He could not reach the edge of the lowest platform with his hands, so he whispered to his companion, "Stretch both arms up. I need to step onto your hands!"

Old Shatterhand lifted the chief up as easily as if Winnetou were a child.

"It is still not enough," the Apache said.

"How much is missing?" asked Old Shatterhand.

"Three hands' width."

"Never mind. Your fingers are like iron. Once you have hold of the edge, you will be able to hold on. Then I will help with my bear killer. I will count to three and will then heave you upward. Watch out and quickly grab hold! One—two—three—!"

On three, he delivered a forceful upward push. Winnetou reached the edge with his hands and latched onto it like an iron clamp. Old Shatterhand quickly took his bear killer and used it to support one of Winnetou's feet. Then the Apache swung himself onto the platform, with Old Shatterhand assisting him with a hearty push of his rifle. At first, Winnetou remained very still to listen. For a while he crouched, although he was ready to leap like a panther at any adversary and, with a grip to the throat, disable him to prevent him from shouting a warning. His sharp eyes surveyed the entire platform, but, except for him, no one else was about. Not far away, he saw the open rectangular entry hole leading into the ground floor and close beside him lay the ladder that had been pulled up.

With a silent, snakelike movement, Winnetou crept toward the hole and listened. It was dark inside. Nothing moved. No one appeared to be down there. He crept back to the ladder and lowered it to Old Shatterhand so that his friend could come up. When Old Shatterhand reached Winnetou, he lay down beside him and whispered, "Is anyone below us?"

"I have not heard anything," Winnetou responded.

"Shall we pull the ladder up again?"

"No."

"Right! We might have to get away quickly and would need it then. Now, up to the next platform."

A ladder led up to it; only the ladder from the ground to the lowest level had been removed by the natives. But the two men could not use this ladder, since it rested against the middle of the platform where the lower of the two fires was burning with three guards sitting by it, keeping watch over the hole made by the captives. The guards would have noticed them immediately had they climbed that ladder.

The platform above them was perhaps four paces wide and eighty long. The fire in its middle was a small one, in the Indian way, and its glow did not reach either end of the platform. Hence it was dark there, and that's where the two liberators had to climb up, either on the right or the left side of the flat roof. They decided on the left side, because of a reason that offered a great advantage.

The three Indian guards were seated at the fire in such a way that two of them faced the hole they were to watch. The third squatted on the left, blocking the fire's glow, and thus threw a long shadow to that side of the platform. His shadow made it possible to approach them without being noticed immediately.

The two friends pulled up the ladder leading from the first platform and very cautiously carried it to the left side of the platform. They placed the ladder against the wall of the next floor and climbed up. Once up, they again remained prone for some time to look over the platform.

"The guards are alone," whispered the Apache.

"Yes, and that is good," ventured his white friend.

"Nevertheless, this task is extremely difficult. There is no cover."

"Only shadows!"

"Well! That is not sufficient. The closest we can approach them is about twenty paces. And if the fellow throwing the shadow moves, the light will fall on us and they will notice us even sooner."

"We shall draw their attention to the opposite side," whispered Winnetou.

"With what? Small pebbles?" asked Old Shatterhand.

"Yes!"

"Well! If they are stupid enough, we can fool them that way. But we will have to cover the twenty paces in the blink of an eye. I will take care of the one with his back toward us first. You take the next one, and I will take the third."

"But without any noise!" warned Winnetou.

"If even one of the three guards on the next platform looks down and sees us, we will be given away. If that happens, we must knock out the three down here and quickly get up to the other three. Once they have been rendered harmless, we are in possession of the entry leading to the captives."

"But if things get noisy, the entire pueblo will be in an uproar," cautioned the Apache.

"Nevertheless, Winnetou and Old Shatterhand will not be afraid. We will extinguish the fires and thus cannot be seen. Then they cannot shoot at us."

"All right! Let's get some pebbles!"

It was to their advantage to consider all possibilities, for, if they were seen, they could act in unison without losing precious time with questions. On the platform they felt for pebbles and soon found some. Then they lay flat on the floor and crept toward the three guards. Old Shatterhand had guessed very well; when they were still approximately twenty paces from the guards, they had to stop. Winnetou raised himself up a bit and threw a pebble over the guards' heads. As slight as the noise was, it was noticed, and they turned to the right to listen.

Winnetou threw several more pebbles, which made them think someone was to their right, perhaps even someone hostile, which caused them to listen even more attentively in that direction.

"Now!" Old Shatterhand said quietly.

They rose. Five, six long, almost inaudible, leaps and they were at the guards' side. The fist of the strong white hunter hit the first one so that he went down noiselessly. The very next moment Winnetou and Old Shatterhand had the second and third by the throat. Firm pressure, blows against the temples, and these enemies, too, were unconscious. The unconscious Indians were quickly tied up and gagged.

"That worked!" whispered Old Shatterhand. "Let's put the ladder up to the hole. I want to talk to the captives. In the meantime, my brother Winnetou should keep the next floor in sight. One of the guards could appear at the edge of the roof."

He cautiously pulled the ladder up from the lower level, leaned it beside the hole onto the wall, and climbed up. Sticking his head into the hole, he called in a subdued voice only the captives could hear:

"Sam Hawkens, Dick Stone, and Will Parker! Is one of you there?"

He heard a voice from inside: "Listen! Someone spoke out there! There's someone at the hole!"

"Probably one of the red rascals!" opined another. "Give him a bullet!"

"Nonsense!" a third one quickly interrupted. "An Indian would not dare stick out his head so nicely that we could blow out his candle, if I'm not mistaken. It must be someone else, someone to rescue us, perhaps even Old Shatterhand or Winnetou. Make room for me!"

When he heard the phrase "if I'm not mistaken," Old Shatterhand recognized the speaker. He asked, "Sam Hawkens, is it you?"

"Think so," sounded from inside. "Who are you?"

"Old Shatterhand."

"That'll be the day! Is it true?"

"Yes. We want to get you out."

"We! You are not alone, then?"

"No. Winnetou is here, too."

"Thanks a lot! I've been expecting you. But, sir, are you truly Old Shatterhand? Or is your name by chance Mr. Grinley, the Oil Prince?"

"You should recognize me by my voice, Sam, old man!"

"Voice this and voice that! Down here in his hole one voice sounds like another, particularly since you speak softly. Show me proof!"

"What?"

"Do you have your Henry carbine with you?"

"Yes."

"Then lower it down so I can touch it."

"Here it is. But return it quickly, since I may need it at a moment's notice."

He lowered the rifle down the hole. In a few seconds, it was returned to him, and Sam said, "It's true. It's you, sir. The Lord be thanked that you have come. We cannot get out. How are you planning to accomplish that?" asked Hawkens.

"Don't you have a ladder?"

"The rascals have pulled it up. Also, the hole in the ceiling is shut."

"And weapons?"

"Those we have!"

"Who all is with you?"

"Good friends of yours: Stone, Parker, Droll, Hobble-Frank, and so on."

"Women and children, too?"

"Unfortunately!"

"Then listen carefully to what I tell you! First, get the children up to us, but they are not to make a sound. Then have the women follow; they, I hope, will also be quiet. After that come those who don't know the West and are inexperienced. You should get them all up so that they are outside if we should be discovered. We overpowered the three guards up here. Above us are three more who can easily surprise us. Should that happen, I will climb up and take care of them. If I succeed, I will open the entrance and lower a ladder on which those still inside can quickly climb up to help me. Did you understand everything?"

"Everything," said the little man.

"Then let's start! I'll wait here to receive the children."

Right after that a boy's head appeared in the opening. Old Shatterhand pulled him out, handing him to Winnetou, who stood him close to the wall. This is how it was done with all the children and the women. It was heavy work for which Old Shatterhand, standing on the ladder, had to use all his strength. When this was done and Sam Hawkens reported that the men would now follow, with the German immigrants first, Old Shatterhand answered, "They do not need my help. I will go to keep an eye on the three guards above."

He climbed down to Winnetou, explained a few things, and moved quickly along the wall to the left side, to the ladder by which they had reached this platform. He pulled it up, leaned it against the next floor, and climbed up.

There he examined the platform illuminated by the fire and saw the large rocks that had been rolled onto the cover to keep it down and prevent the captives from escaping. Beside it lay the ladder that the Indians had withdrawn before they had thrown on the cover. A second ladder led up to the next platform. Two of the guards sat with their backs toward him.

Old Shatterhand had climbed onto this roof to be on hand quickly should they be discovered. In case all the captives were able to get out, he had no intention of letting himself be seen by the Indians. He therefore lay still and waited. He started figuring the time it would take a person to creep through the hole and how many might be outside already. He had just told himself that it should be about the turn of the sixth when a shrill woman's voice sounded through the night, "Good Lord, Mr. Cantor, do not fall on me!"

Immediately the three guards jumped up, stepped to the edge of the platform, and peered down.

They saw the Apache standing by the fire. Recognizing him, one of the guards shouted so loudly so that it rang across the entire pueblo, "Akhane, akhane. Arku Winnetou, nonton schis inteh!" These words meant, "Come, come! Winnetou, the Apache chief, is here!"

Barely had this call sounded when another, just as loud, rang out behind them, "And here is Old Shatterhand to free the captives. Winnetou, take care of these fellows!"

The white hunter leaped up and onto them as they were shouting. While shouting, he felled one of them and pushed the other two over the platform's edge. They were caught by those standing below. He next toppled the ladder leading up to the next platform so that none of the warriors could climb down. Then he rolled the hundredweight rocks from the cover and removed it. Lowering the ladder into the hole, he called down, "Come up quickly! We may have a fight!"

Then he jumped with both feet into the fire to stomp it out. It got dark because Winnetou had also extinguished the fire below. Old Shatterhand had acted with such speed that from the moment the careless woman's voice had sounded hardly a minute had elapsed. The last captives had already come out through the hole.

On the platforms above them things became lively. Loud, questioning voices arose. Lights appeared, and you could see dark figures descending ladders. Then Old Shatterhand's mighty voice arose, "The red men shall stay up there if they do not want to die! Here stand Old Shatterhand and Winnetou with their people. Whoever dares to approach us will be shot!"

Although he had no intention of killing any of the Indians, he had to demonstrate to them that it was truly he. He could best prove this with the multishot carbine they all knew and feared. He leveled it and aimed at the hand of an Indian who was in the process of quickly clambering down while holding a torch.

"Hahi, Latah-Schi—ow, my hand!" the man who had been hit cried, dropping the torch.

Three more shots, one quickly after the other, and just as many lights disappeared. A voice sounded, "That is Old Shatterhand's magic rifle. Up, up again, quickly!"

It got dark up there and suddenly very quiet, as if there were no longer any people.

"Are you all here?" Old Shatterhand asked the people standing around him. "No one is down there anymore?"

"No one," answered Sam Hawkens.

"Then put the two ladders in place and climb down to the others! I think the redskins will leave us in peace for a while."

They followed his request. Old Shatterhand came down last.

When he reached the next lower platform, he saw that the thoughtful Apache had already provided what was to be required next. The freed prisoners were in the process of descending the ladders.

Winnetou did not think of hurrying them. On the contrary, he exhorted the women and children to proceed carefully, nice and slow, since he knew that, at least for a while, the Indians were not to be feared. They were spellbound by the names of Old Shatterhand and Winnetou.

The descent, therefore, went ahead at a rather leisurely pace, where-upon all ladders were brought down to make any pursuit by the Indians more difficult.

When all stood in the open at the foot of the pueblo, Old Shatterhand said, "It succeeded and much more easily than I thought possible. Now, there—"

He was interrupted by several people wanting to express their gratitude, but he quickly interrupted them, "Quiet! Not now! First things first. Later, when we are away from here, you can talk as much as you want. Where are your horses?"

"There in the corral, to the right, behind the wall!" Sam Hawkens answered.

"Do you have all your weapons?"

"Yes!"

"And your belongings?"

"What we had on our bodies they could not take from us. Whatever was in the saddlebags the red rascals will probably have taken."

"Did you also have packhorses?"

"Yes. They carried the immigrants' belongings."

"Are these belongings around here?"

"Don't know, but I don't believe so. The storm started so rapidly that we had no time to unload and take the saddles off the animals."

"Hmm! If all your belongings were nearby, we could leave right away. In this case, though, we must force the redskins to release the spoils. Sam Hawkens may accompany me to the corral. The rest of you remain here and watch the lowest platforms. As soon as a redskin lets himself be heard or even seen, shoot at him, but don't hit him! Understood? It is enough for the enemy to hear the bullet strike beside him. All the redskins need to learn is that we will not let them come down. Meanwhile, my brother Winnetou will go to fetch our two stallions."

The Apache left quietly, as was his custom, and Old Shatterhand, together with Sam Hawkens, went to the enclosure the horses were being kept in.

After the three left, the cantor said, in German, of course, "Then these are the two great heroes whose sight I so eagerly longed to behold. One cannot see them properly because it is so dark, but already their bearing appeals to me hugely. They will receive most prominent positions in my opera."

"Well, have a look at the two in daylight first!" answered Hobble-Frank. "Is it not just as I prophesied? No sooner do these two famous people appear than we are free!"

"Very true!" Droll agreed. "It is a truly heroic feat to get us out without even a hair of our heads being hurt. It would have gone even better had Mrs. Ebersbach kept her mouth shut."

"I?" Mrs. Rosalie quickly interjected. "Do you consider it my fault that I let out the scream?"

"Of course! Who else?"

"The cantor, not I!"

"Please, most humbly!" the accused defended himself. "You know very well that I am retired! If only you would not forget this all the time! You have no right to insist that I broke the requested deep silence. No sound crossed my lips, none whatsoever, not even *pianissimo*. It was you, Mrs. Ebersbach, who screamed."

"I do not deny that at all. But why did I scream? Had you only held on more tightly, you emeritus! Should it please you once again to tumble from a ladder, please do not do it just when a lady stands below you! If you do not take your scales any firmer into your hands than you hold onto a ladder, I feel pity for your nice heroic opera. You understand me!"

"I do understand you, dear madam. But you are at a loss to understand how to deal politely with a son of the Muses. I promised you once to keep you in mind for a soprano aria. But with your talking of my art in such manner, I will desist from doing so. You will not have the honor of appearing in my opera!"

"No? You do not say! Do you think I am much interested in appearing on the stage of the world? I would not think of it. And I was to sing soprano? Listen, do not even talk to me about that! When I want to sing, no one is going to tell me, and I sing whatever I want, bassoon, clarinet, or bass, whatever I like. And with that we are done for life. Farewell for all time!"

Angrily, she turned away from him. He wanted to make one more remark, but Hobble-Frank quickly silenced him with "Psst! Be quiet! I think I saw something darting around up there on the first platform. There it goes again! Now it is stopping and bending its head down. It is an Indian looking for where we might be. He is going to find out soon enough!"

He raised his rifle, aimed briefly, and pulled the trigger.

"Uff!" cried a frightened voice right after the shot rang out.

Just then Old Shatterhand and Sam Hawkens returned.

"What happened? Who fired?" Old Shatterhand asked.

"I did," answered Frank.

"Why?"

"That is a fateful question I will happily answer. On roof number one there stood a red man. He probably wanted to know the time, so I showed him the time the clock would strike if he did not hurry off. He withdrew rather quickly."

"Was he hit?"

"Naw. I aimed to his right, two feet, maybe," said Frank. "If he had four-foot-wide ears, the bullet would most likely have penetrated his right earlobe, which, I hope, served him as a warning."

"Then they've already dared to come down to the first platform! We need to watch out. Let's keep far enough away that they can't see us, since then they'll shoot at us. They must, however, be kept aware of our presence and that we will not let them come down. How about Frank and Droll slinking over there and lying down close to the wall. If you look up, you can see every head appearing over the edge. Then a quick bullet!"

"But without aiming to hit?" asked Hobble-Frank.

"Yes. I do not want to take any lives," said Old Shatterhand.

"Then I will be careful not to shoot my nice bullets into the air! I would rather not put any into the barrel."

Schi-So approached Old Shatterhand and asked him in German, "Sir, permit me to take part in guarding the pueblo! Six eyes are better than four."

"That's true," the hunter responded, looking at the young man inquiringly, whose face he could not recognize. "You seem to be very young yet. Do you have any experience?"

"I am my father's pupil," Schi-So answered modestly.

"Who is your father?"

"Nitsas-Ini, the chief of the Navajo."

"What? My friend Big Thunder? Then you would be Schi-So, who was in Germany for some time?"

"I am."

"Take my hand, young friend! I am glad to meet you here. Let's talk as soon as there is time. Had there been more light, I would surely have recognized you. Because you are who you are, I know I can agree to your request. Go with Frank and Droll and the three of you set yourselves up so that you can watch the entire width of the pueblo!"

The chief's son left, proud to have had his request granted. Just as he was leaving, Winnetou returned with the horses, which he staked at some distance from the pueblo. When this was done, he asked Old Shatterhand, "I heard a shot. Whose rifle did it come from?"

His friend told him and continued, "The captives' horses are over there in the corral. But all baggage and bridles have disappeared."

"Must be in the pueblo!" exclaimed Winnetou.

"Yes. We cannot leave until we get them back."

"That should not be difficult, since the chief is in our power."

"That's true," responded Old Shatterhand. "We must get him. Will my red brother take charge here? I'll ride with Sam Hawkens, Will Parker, and Dick Stone to bring Ka Maku here."

"My brother may go. Upon his return, everything will be in good order here."

The Shamrock was pleased to ride with Old Shatterhand. They went to the corral to obtain their mounts. The lack of bridles and saddles was of no concern whatsoever to these horsemen. They swung themselves onto the horses and rode off in a northerly direction. On the way, Old Shatterhand inquired about how they had met the immigrants and how they had fallen into captivity. They had time to recount everything and to describe the character of every member of the party. When the hunter had heard it all, he said, quietly shaking his head, "Peculiar people. Most careless, too! So you three have taken them under your protection and intend to accompany them?"

"Yes," answered Sam. "They need us, and it is all the same to us whether we ride here or there."

"Hmm! I wanted to cross the border with Winnetou, but I also think it my duty to take care of these folks, the more so since they intend to cross areas where they would perish without the aid of experienced people. It seems to me that you have to make allowances for the immigrants, yet you must be cautious, too. That retired cantor, for example, could even become dangerous."

"He already has. I would have preferred to run him off, but that's not possible. And what do you think about the story of the Oil Prince?"

"Fraud!"

"Well, that's my opinion, too. The bookkeeper is German. Can we allow him to perish?"

"No. We'll follow this Grinley, who, most likely, uses other names, and I think we'll catch up with him in time. I wonder how he has charmed the oil from the ground, or will do so!"

They had been riding very fast and were now not very far from the spot where the bound chief and his people had been left.

Old Shatterhand told them how Ka Maku had fallen into his and Winnetou's hands and added, "He denied everything and deserves punishment. Yet I am a friend of the red man and would like to see him make an admission after all. Seeing you will make him aware of the state of affairs. Let me ride ahead, therefore. Follow slowly! If you keep straight to the north, you will arrive at the rock behind which we left the prisoners."

It was very dark. Nevertheless, Old Shatterhand found his way remarkably well on the flat countryside. Though he was convinced he would find the four redskins just as he had left them, he knew he had to be cautious. They might have found the opportunity to free themselves and might now be waiting for him and Winnetou in order to exact revenge. Therefore, he dismounted at an appropriate distance, staked his horse, and on foot stole to the rock. When he was close enough to make it out, he crept along on his hands and knees. Soon he saw the rock ahead and to his left. He crawled around it in a small arc and saw the captives still lying there. But they could be free and cleverly have kept their positions. Hence he made sure he was not heard yet, but crept quietly behind the chief. Old Shatterhand felt for the rifle buried in the ground like a pole and to which Ka Maku had been tied. The thongs were still in the same position; they had not been loosened. Seeing this, he stood up in front of the startled captives, as if rising from the earth.

"Time must have grown long for Ka Maku," Old Shatterhand began. "Because he was gagged, he could not even talk to his companions. I shall give him back his voice."

Pulling the gag from Ka Maku's mouth, he continued, "The chief has had time to reflect. If he is ready to admit that the captives are in his pueblo, I will free him without anything happening to him."

From these words Ka Maku concluded that Old Shatterhand did not know any details yet; he was, therefore, determined to admit nothing. Knowing Old Shatterhand's ways and manner, he was convinced that his life was not in danger. He chose to admit nothing and to stay tied until his people came to free him. He assumed that they would do this soon after daybreak. He saw only Old Shatterhand. Where was Winnetou? "Why has the chief of the Apache not come to talk with me?"

The sound of his voice revealed that the gag had made breathing difficult for him.

"He had to stay close to the pueblo to observe it."

Ka Maku guessed from this answer that Winnetou and Old Shatter-hand's efforts had been in vain and that the hunter had come only to obtain further information by questioning him. Therefore, he sneered, "Winnetou will not hear and see anything different from what I said before: there are no prisoners with us. Why do the two brave warriors sneak around the pueblo in secret? Why do they not demand entry to convince themselves of my having spoken the truth, of my honesty?"

"Because we don't trust you and are convinced we would also be taken prisoner."

"Uff! Where did Old Shatterhand's wisdom go? The Great Spirit has taken his brain. I was his friend. Now, since he treats me as an enemy, the knife will decide between him and me!"

"I don't mind that. Then you truly do not keep any white men, women, and children imprisoned in the pueblo?"

"No."

"It would not be difficult for Winnetou and me to liberate them! Then you would be punished. But if you admit it, we shall remember that you were our friend and brother and shall treat you leniently."

"Old Shatterhand may think and do as he pleases. I have told the truth and shall take revenge!"

"Just as you like! But listen! Who is coming there?"

They could hear approaching hoofbeats. Ka Maku rose as far as his ties permitted and uttered a cry of joy. The approaching horsemen could only be his people looking for him. They came around the rock and remained standing there. Because he couldn't clearly distinguish their figures, he called to them, "I am Ka Maku, for whom you are looking. Dismount and untie me!"

That's when Sam Hawkens answered with a laugh, "That you are Ka Maku I gladly believe. But I don't think I will loosen your bonds. Old Shatterhand will decide what to do. Do you perhaps recognize my voice, old rascal?"

"Sam Hawkens!" the chief cried, literally from fright.

"Yes. Sam Hawkens and Dick Stone, Will Parker, too," confirmed Old Shatterhand. "You still think the Great Spirit has taken my brain? Or was it not true when I said it would not be difficult for us to free the prisoners? We have turned the tables against you now. Your captives are free and you are caught instead. None of your warriors are able to leave the pueblo, for we have it under siege and shall put a bullet into anyone trying to get out.

We will now tie you onto your horses, and I advise you not to fight it if you do not want to taste our knife blades!"

Sam Hawkens, Dick Stone, and Will Parker got off their horses and went to work on the four Indians, who were so dismayed they did not even think of offering resistance, which would, in any case, have been to no avail. They were tied onto their animals, which had been staked. Then they left on their silent return. Arriving at the pueblo, the four Indians were taken off their mounts and put under heavy guard. Despite the darkness, they could make out that all their captives had been freed. It was easy to imagine how enraged they were.

The whites, particularly the more lively among them, wanted to talk through the night. But Old Shatterhand would not permit this. He reminded them of the hard, long ride awaiting them the next day and got them to turn in, except, of course, for those on guard duty.

The night passed without the Indians attempting an attack. When dawn broke, they noticed that the Indians had withdrawn to the upper platforms. Most of them were asleep, but were awakened by the guards they had posted. Assembling up there, they shouted threats at the whites, who by now had also awakened. The redskins could not tell that their chief was a prisoner of the whites.

Winnetou and Old Shatterhand were determined not to enter into long negotiations. No time was to be lost if they were to catch up with the Oil Prince. Both of them, therefore, went to talk with Ka Maku. The others formed a circle around them to listen, or, if they could not follow the conversation, then at least to watch. Since Winnetou spoke only when absolutely necessary, Old Shatterhand took the lead, "Ka Maku sees that all his captives are free?"

The chief did not respond. The frontiersman therefore admonished him menacingly, "I do not like to talk to the wind. You will be treated as gently as possible. If you do not answer, you are to blame if we speak only of revenge. Answer my question!"

"I see that they are free," Ka Maku growled angrily.

"And that your warriors are now our prisoners?"

"That I do not see."

"No? Can even one of them leave the pueblo without our permission? We need not even permit them to stand on the roofs. Our rifles carry to the uppermost platform, and we can force them all to take cover inside the dwelling. Where do they get food and drink? They cannot get to where the well is and the provisions are stored. Besides, we hold you and your three companions. What do you think we will do with you?"

"Nothing! None of my prisoners were hurt."

"For that my friends can thank only Winnetou and myself. You had other plans for them. I shall be brief with you. They are still missing many of their belongings, which are kept inside the pueblo. If everything they are missing is returned, we will set you free and ride off. But if you refuse, you will be shot, and we will burn your bun so that you will arrive without it at the eternal hunting grounds. The same shall happen to your three fellows. Decide! Look, the sun is just rising. When it is a hand's width above the horizon, I want your answer. I will wait no longer. I have spoken!"

He rose and, together with Winnetou, left, indicating that he would speak no more. Ka Maku stared broodingly ahead. He knew his victors' humanity and did not believe they would make good their threat. To return all the spoils seemed too great a price to him. When the sun had risen to the point indicated, the two returned and Old Shatterhand asked, "What has Ka Maku decided? Will the missing belongings be returned?"

"No!" he exclaimed.

"Well! I told you: I have spoken. We are done. Take the fellows away, over to that rock, cut off their buns, and put a bullet through their heads."

Sam, Dick and Will, Frank and Droll dragged the four redskins to the designated rock. An Indian buried without his bun will not encounter the pleasures of the eternal hunting grounds. Therefore, when Hawkens grabbed his hair with his left hand and swung his knife with the right, the chief cried, "Hold, hold it! You get everything!"

"Well!" Old Shatterhand nodded. "High time. Don't renege, for then there will be no mercy! I demand that everything down to the least item be returned. Your squaws may bring us everything. If men appear, we will shoot them down. Do you agree?"

"Yes," Ka Maku ground out.

"This man shall be the messenger to your people. But if the delivery is not made within five minutes, your life is forfeit!"

He pointed to one of the captives. He was relieved of his bonds and got a ladder to climb into the pueblo. Only from him did the Indians learn that their chief had been captured. This caused a great uproar as they ran back and forth and made threatening gestures. The messenger talked to them urgently, and the first squaws started to climb down with their loads within the five minutes allowed to deliver the captives' belongings. Every person took what belonged to him and indicated what was still missing.

The Indians were forced to return even the smallest items. This required some effort, but finally everything was distributed. That's when the chief called, "It is done as you demanded. Now untie me and leave!"

"You are mistaken," answered Old Shatterhand quietly. "You have not yet replaced everything."

"What else do you want?"

"The time we have lost."

"Can I give you time, make you a gift of hours?" responded Ka Maku.

"Yes. Because of you we all have lost valuable time we must regain. This is impossible with the bad horses some of us have. I saw some very nice animals you keep in the corral. We will trade our bad ones for your good ones."

"You dare not!" cried Ka Maku, his eyes throwing darts.

"Pshaw! What is there to dare? Do you believe I am afraid of you! Who can keep us from making this trade? You are in our power, and your warriors cannot risk coming down to prevent us. Our rifles carry farther than theirs. We would hit them, but they couldn't hit us. They are well aware of this  and will not risk coming too close."

"That would be theft."

"Only retribution!" declared Old Shatterhand. "You are thieves. But we will punish you. Are all these people to have been taken prisoner and robbed for nothing? You need to be shown that the dishonest will always succumb to the honest. Resistance will not help you. Winnetou, Sam Hawkens, and Droll shall come to select the horses with me!"

He went to the corral with the three he had named. The chief fell into a rage. He reared up under his ties and acted as if he had lost his mind. At that, Mrs. Rosalie stepped up to him and bellowed at him angrily, "Be quiet now, you screaming weakling you! What are you really? You want to be a chief? If you think I believe that, you are crazy! You are a scoundrel, a long-fingered ragamuffin! You understand me? You should get smacks, a spanking, a good thrashing! Lock us up, we poor souls! And now, since righteous judgment is spoken over you, like pepper into the soup, you act as if you were sweet innocence personified. Watch out that you do not fall into my hands someday. I shall tear your hair out strand by strand! So, now you know who you are and who you are dealing with. Be good! There is still time. Later you will get to deal with the law."

She gave him a withering look and turned away. Her words left their mark, although he had not understood a single one. Clearer had been the tone. His gaze followed her in silent surprise. He kept quiet even when the horses were taken from the corral and saddled. Some of his best animals were among them. Even without saying anything, his looks spoke eloquently.

When the redskins on the upper levels saw the whites getting ready to depart, they started climbing down. They thought they could risk it because the palefaces no longer appeared threatening. Had the frontiersmen permitted this, the departure would not have been peaceful. Old Shatterhand leveled his carbine on them and shouted threateningly, "Stay up there, or we will shoot!"

Because they did not comply, he fired two warning shots. With a great howl, they once again retreated upward. Considering everything, they had actually gotten off very lightly. Except for the torch bearer hit in the hand by Old Shatterhand, no one had been injured. There were no dead. Yet the chief said to Old Shatterhand, once he put down his rifle, "Why do you shoot at my people? Do you not see that they no longer have any hostile intentions?"

"And did you not see that my intent was peaceful as well?" the hunter responded. "Or do you think I missed? If I want it to, my bullet will always hit. I only intended to scare your people with my shots."

"But do you not see some standing up there with their hands bandaged? They raise them to tell me that they have been injured."

"They should be grateful that I aimed only for their hands, not for their heads."

"Do you also call it kindness to have taken our horses?"

"Certainly. It is a punishment you can be satisfied with. You actually deserved a much more serious one."

"You say that. But do you know what I will say in the future?"

Old Shatterhand made a disparaging gesture with his hand, turned and mounted his horse. The others were already mounted. Indignant because of the contempt shown him, Ka Maku angrily shouted after him, "I will tell everyone who comes here: Winnetou and Old Shatterhand, so proud of their names, have become horse thieves, and horse thieves need to be hanged!"

The hunter made as if he had not heard the insult. But little Hobble-Frank was so incensed about it that he rode over to the chief and told him angrily, "Shut up, you bandit! A rascal like you should consider himself lucky that he was not himself hanged by a nice rope himself. For you it would even be better to have you drowned in the deepest part of the

Indian Ocean, with a millstone around your neck. There you have my opinion, now farewell!"

Hobble-Frank rode off, unaware that Ka Maku had not understood a word of this lecture, because it had been delivered in German.

The two Navajo crept slowly along the Nijora tracks toward the rock.

# 9

## SCOUTS

HEN TWO INDIAN TRIBES have gone on the warpath, they will fight each other to the death. First, scouts will be sent out from both sides to try to find out where the enemy tribe is and how many adult warriors it can put in the field. Reconnoitering the enemy's location is necessary simply because the so-called wild tribes are not settled, but move across the land to set up their campsites within certain boundaries according to their needs and purposes.

Even when the enemy is located, the scouts' work is not complete. Their most difficult task is to attempt to discover by what means the enemy intends to wage war, whether he is well provisioned, when he is to start, which direction he means to take, and where he plans to meet his foe. This takes experienced men who, aside from valor, which is absolutely required, also possess the requisite wariness, caution, and cunning.

In less-important cases, with no great danger expected, younger warriors are employed to give them an opportunity to display their courage and skills and to make a name for themselves. With more at stake, however, older, proven men are chosen. It may even happen that the chief himself will go on a scouting mission should he consider the affair important enough.

Because both sides send out scouts, they may encounter each other. This situation calls for every effort to neutralize the enemy scouts to keep information from the enemy. The enemy can then be surprised by an attack and more easily defeated.

During such encounters, the scouts will often exhibit more cunning, agility, and daring than they expend during an actual battle. Feats are often accomplished that become the subject of tales that are recounted for years.

As mentioned earlier, very serious hostilities had broken out recently between the Nijora and the Navajo, who at that time lived north of them. The Chelly arm of the Colorado River formed the border between these two tribes. The area it crossed was, therefore, dangerous territory where the adversaries would most likely clash, and which had to be scouted.

This area was dangerous not only for Indians, but also for whites, because experience had taught that, once redskins were fighting each other, both sides considered palefaces their enemy. Whites in this situation find themselves as if between open scissor blades ready to snap closed at any moment.

Gloomy Water, the Oil Prince's destination, was close to the Chelly River. Grinley knew of the potential danger, especially now, yet he believed he could risk the ride there, because he had never been treated with enmity by either tribe.

He could not delay if he were to accomplish his purpose. Neither could he permit the banker to gather his thoughts, nor let anything transpire that would alarm him.

Duncan and his bookkeeper, although they had heard about a split between the Nijora and the Navajo, did not possess the necessary experience and knowledge to understand how they were threatened by it. And the Oil Prince was careful not to enlighten them.

The five men were perhaps a day's ride from the Chelly when, riding across an open grassy stretch broken here and there by bushes, they suddenly met a horseman they had not noticed because bushes had been between him and them. He was a white man with a satchel strapped behind him. He was riding a sturdy Indian pony that, one could see, had been pushed hard. Surprised, both parties stopped and faced each other.

"Hello!" the stranger called. "You could have been redskins!"

"Then your scalp would be gone," answered the Oil Prince with a forced laugh to cover his embarrassment, because he, too, had been startled by the unexpected encounter.

"Or it would have cost you yours," responded the other man. "I'm not the man to have his head skin easily pulled over his ears."

"Even with five against one?"

"Not then, either, if they're redskins. I've had other encounters and kept my scalp."

"My high regard for you then, sir. May I ask who you are?"

"Why not? Don't need to be ashamed to tell." And pointing to the satchel behind him he explained, "I'm actually surprised by your question.

You don't seem to be real frontiersmen. You ought to see from this thing here that I am a courier."

He was, therefore, one of these bold men who, on their fast horses, fearlessly rode across the prairies and the Rocky Mountains, their satchels filled with letters and similar items. These days, though, such couriers would no longer be encountered.

"Whether we are frontiersmen or not is no concern of yours," the Oil Prince retorted. "I certainly did see your satchel, but also know that no courier has ever crossed this area. They usually take the route from Albuquerque to San Francisco. Why did you deviate from it?"

At Grinley's prying question, the man gave a somewhat disparaging look from his intelligent eyes and answered, "I'm not obligated to give you any information. But because I see you running unsuspectingly to your ruin, I'll tell you that I deviated from my route because of the Navajo and the Nijora. The regular route would have taken me right through the area a smart man would be better to leave to the redskins at the moment, that is, the environs of the Chelly River. Don't you know that the redskins are at loggerheads right now?"

"Do you think you're the only smart man in the entire Wild West?"

The Oil Prince would have done better being polite, but the courier's words had enraged him. Against a lone man he did not find it necessary to hide his essentially inconsiderate nature. The courier looked searchingly from one to the other and, without responding to the rudeness in like manner, nodded quietly and said, pointing at the banker and his bookkeeper, "I'd say that these two men, at least, have not seen much blood spilled. If you're so smart as not to need advice, I'd at least invite them to be cautious. Maybe they don't know what they're risking. No reasonable person sticks his head into a press that's being screwed tight!"

These serious words led the banker to inquire, "What do you mean to say, sir? What kind of press are you referring to?"

"The one behind me at the Chelly. You apparently want to ride straight into it. Turn around, sirs, or you'll get between the scalping knives of two tribes who are out to butcher each other, and what is left of you the vultures and prairie wolves will eat! Listen to me. I mean you well!"

One look at his open face and his honest eyes was sufficient to recognize that he was speaking the truth. Duncan therefore asked, "Do you really think the danger is so great?"

"Yes, that's my opinion. I've seen tracks this morning telling me that their scouts are already sneaking up on each other. A wise man will take

202 The Oil Prince

that as a warning. Do you absolutely need to get into this area, especially right now? Can't you put off this incautious ride until better, more peaceful times?"

"Hmm, that we could," voiced Duncan. "If you're sure that the danger is so great, I indeed think it'd be better—"

"No such thing!" the Oil Prince interrupted him. "Do you know this man? Do you trust him more than us? If he is afraid of tracks in the grass, then that is his concern, not ours."

"But couriers are usually experienced people," protested the banker. "He seems to speak the truth. And speaking of one's life, as it is all we have, it is not advisable to be foolhardy. Whether our business is concluded today or a few days hence doesn't make any difference."

"But it does! I don't care to hang around here forever, sir."

"Ah, we are dealing with a business proposition, then!" the courier smiled. "Well, that's none of my business. I've done my duty by warning you. You can't ask more from me."

With these words he took the reins of his pony to leave.

"We aren't doing that at all," the Oil Prince thundered. "We didn't demand anything from you. You can keep your opinion to yourself. Get away from us!"

This behavior didn't cause the courier to lose his composure, either. He answered in the voice of a teacher admonishing a student, "I've never come across a boor like you before. Very peculiar people ride around in the Wild West at times!" And turning to the banker he continued, "Before I follow the order of this high and mighty gentleman and 'get away from you,' I must tell you one more thing. Speaking of business in this kind of country, such dealings are dangerous any time, even during peace. But if a business deal can't afford any delay, even under the current conditions, then it's not just dangerous, but also downright suspicious. Beware, sir, that you don't lose your shirt!"

He was about to leave when the Oil Prince pulled his knife and shouted at him, "That was an insult, man! Do you want this pointed steel between your ribs? Say another word and I'll let you have it!"

In an instant two revolvers had appeared in the courier's hands, his eyes asparkle. With a contemptuous laugh he answered, "Try it, my boy! Put your knife away at once, or I shoot! There are twelve bullets, sirs. If any of your hands move even slightly, I'll shoot a hole in the poor soul. Once more, put away the knife, man! I'll count to three! One— two —"

Obviously, he was serious about his threat. Therefore, Grinley did not let him get to three, but prudently put his knife away.

"That's good!" the courier laughed. "I wouldn't have advised you to let it come to a head. Enough for today. But should we perhaps meet again, you'll learn a lot more from me!"

He rode off without looking back even once. Grinley reached for his rifle to level it at him, but the bookkeeper put his hand on his arm and told him in an almost stern voice, "No further foolishness, sir! Do you want to shoot the man?"

"No further foolishness!" repeated the Oil Prince. "Have I committed any?"

"Indeed! Your rudeness, your entire conduct, was foolish. The man obviously meant well, and I really saw no reason to address him in such manner!"

Grinley was ready with an angry response, but reconsidered and answered, "If I was rude to him, it's now you who are rude to me. Let's call it a wash. The fellow was a coward."

"But when you threatened him with the knife, he didn't act like one. You were the one who had to eat humble pie."

"That's no disgrace. Only the devil may look on quietly with two six-shooters pointed at him! But enough of that. Let's ride!"

During the entire scene, Buttler and Poller had remained quiet, but it was obvious that they were upset about the appearance of the courier and his warnings.

The party's mood had changed. No one spoke and everyone seemed to be occupied with his own thoughts. After a while the sun disappeared. They soon found a suitable place for the night's camp. They did not have to worry about an evening meal, as the Oil Prince had been sufficiently provisioned at the pueblo. They ate their meal in silence, and only after dark did anyone speak. Baumgarten asked, "Will we light a fire?"

"No," answered Grinley.

"Then you are also concerned about the Indians?"

"Concerned? No! I know this area and the redskins around here much better than the courier, who was probably passing through here for the first time. No, there's no reason for concern or fear. If the man saw tracks, that doesn't mean that they were produced by Indian scouts. Nevertheless, caution should not be cast to the wind. Let's not light a fire. I don't want you to accuse me later of having failed to provide for our safety."

"Hmm!" the banker murmured thoughtfully. "You are convinced, then, that the danger the courier talked about doesn't exist?"

"Not for us. Rest assured. Although it is totally unnecessary, but to convince you and to ease your mind, I shall go beyond what's required and send Poller and Buttler ahead tomorrow."

Poller and Buttler had expected this. They made no comment.

"What for? What will they do?" asked the banker.

"Be our scouts, make sure you don't get into any danger."

"Then all of us will not leave tomorrow morning?"

"No. I'll stay here with you and Mr. Baumgarten. Only Buttler and Poller will ride ahead. They'll be on the lookout and, should they encounter any danger, return to us immediately to warn us."

"That eases my mind, Mr. Grinley. This courier did make me rather anxious."

Mr. Duncan had no idea that the precaution promised to quiet his concerns was designed exactly for the opposite purpose, that is, to prepare for the fraud of which he was to be the victim.

Since Buttler and Poller were to set out early, everybody went to sleep. They took turns standing guard. Baumgarten had the first watch and Duncan, the second. After Duncan awakened the Oil Prince, who was to relieve him, and then lay down to sleep, the latter remained sitting motionlessly for close to half an hour. Then he bent down to Duncan and the bookkeeper to ascertain that they were asleep. When he had satisfied himself that this was the case, he quietly awakened Poller and Buttler. The three moved far enough from the campsite that they could neither be seen nor overheard. They had to talk in secret.

"Thought you'd wake us up," said Buttler. "The devil with the courier. He could easily have spoiled the entire game. By the way, you should have conducted yourself differently!"

"Are you criticizing me?" grumbled his brother.

"Are you surprised? The fellow had hair on his chest and beat you handily."

"Oho!"

"Pshaw! Admit it. It's true! The more excited you got, the quieter he remained. So he already had you there. Duncan and Baumgarten, too, probably got this impression. And then the thing with the knife! That was a gigantic mistake, because we weren't able to respond! One against five! What will Duncan and Baumgarten think!"

"Let them think what they want! They've recovered their confidence in us. Let's talk about something else! I've described to you the exact location of the oil. Do you think you can find it?"

"Absolutely."

"If you take off early and aren't delayed, you'll be there by afternoon. You'll find the cave just as easily as Gloomy Water. You'll find everything you need there: the forty barrels of oil, the tools, and everything else. Now, listen up! Start to work as soon as you arrive, because it'll take some time to erase all traces of what you've done. Roll the barrels one by one to the water's edge. After the oil has run into the lake, return the barrels to the cave. Close it up and leave it like you found it. It mustn't be discovered, even by the sharpest eye. Then wipe out all traces of the barrels. I expect you to be finished with everything by evening."

"Then what, once work is finished at the lake?" Buttler asked.

"Then you rest up and ride back to us next morning to tell us that you found the lake and that the trail is not dangerous. The main thing is that you express great enthusiasm about the petroleum find."

"There'll be no lack of enthusiasm. We'll infect them with our enthusiasm! I trust you will then fulfill your obligation!"

"By all means. You two get fifty thousand dollars to share."

With these words, Grinley gave his brother a stealthy wink as a sign that this promise was only bait for Poller. It was not money, but a knife or a bullet that was planned for him. Poller had no inkling whatsoever. He trusted the two cheats and happily but quietly exclaimed, "Fifty thousand we're going to share! That means twenty-five thousand for me?"

"Yes," Grinley nodded.

"That's wonderful! I'm all yours! If only we could cash it in right away!"

"Unfortunately, that's impossible. The banker will pay with a draft payable in Frisco."

"Then the three of us will ride to San Francisco together?"

"All three."

"Shucks. I'll happily travel that distance. For twenty-five thousand dollars I'd gladly ride even farther."

"Well! One more warning. I'm not nearly as relaxed about the Indians as I let on. Be careful. Don't let yourselves be seen so you'll get to Gloomy Water without mishap and can make the preparations! It would be unthinkable if I were to arrive there with the two and no oil were in the lake."

"That won't happen," Buttler said. "If something should happen to us, we wouldn't return, and you'd know that something was wrong."

"You're right. I wouldn't take them to the lake in that case."

"What would you do?"

"Look for you, of course, to help you."

"That's how it needs to be. We must help each other. Neither one of us must let the other down. But now let's get back to the camp. They might become suspicious if one of them woke up and missed us."

When they returned to Duncan and Baumgarten, they found the two still fast asleep and settled down beside them. The night passed without any disturbance and, when morning broke, Buttler and Poller set out.

Duncan and Baumgarten thought the two were going to ride ahead only for a short distance and they would follow. But the Oil Prince set them straight: "This would be unwise and unsatisfactory. They're scouts and must ride slowly. We would, therefore, soon catch up with them and would be forced to remain behind again and again. It's decidedly better to allow them time to scout the entire distance in one uninterrupted ride."

"And when will we follow?"

"Tomorrow morning."

"That late?"

"That's not so late. You yourself requested that I not fail to take precautions. Should the two encounter any enemies, they will return to report. If they don't return by this evening, we can take this as a sure sign of not having to worry about anything. Tomorrow, after the horses are well rested, we can cover the distance at twice the speed."

The day passed and evening came without Buttler and Poller's returning, which put the waiting men in a cheerful, confident mood. Possessed by a feverish excitement, the banker was unable to sleep for nearly the entire night. Tomorrow was the day when he would conclude the biggest and most important deal of his life, the likes of which he would not ever have dreamed of! He was to become an oil prince, owner of a rich oil well! His name would be listed among the greatest millionaires. Yes, in a short while he would even be among the famous "Four Hundred" of New York! Peace would not come; when dawn arrived, he had hardly closed his eyes and woke Grinley and Baumgarten to urge them to get ready for departure.

They were glad to oblige, and by the time the sun rose they had covered several miles already on their rested mounts.

The area they crossed was mountainous. The higher elevations were covered by dense woods and the valleys were dressed in fresh grasses. From time to time in the grass they discovered the tracks of their advance party. By noon the horses were requiring an hour's rest.

"We'll soon find a suitable place," the Oil Prince told them, "a deep valley whose floor cannot be reached by the sun on its southern side. It'll be cool there. We'll reach it in a quarter of an hour."

They found themselves on a rather steep incline. As they put it behind them, the ground, covered by conifers, dropped so steeply that they had to dismount and lead their horses.

"Only another two hundred paces," Grinley promised, "then you'll see the valley directly in front of you. It isn't large, and in its center lies a massive rock. Beside it grows a many-centuries-old beech tree."

They covered the distance, and his companions stopped in surprise at the view presenting itself. Close to their feet the rock dropped off almost vertically. They stood at the western edge of the valley basin, which was enclosed by high rock faces that showed only two narrow exits, one in the north, another one in the south. They stood on a balcony of rock that jutted from the western cliff. The rock overhang extended far into the valley, so that the stone slab the Oil Prince had talked about earlier did not lie far from them. The beech tree beside it was so beautifully shaped that it would have delighted an artist.

"What a magnificent tree!" Baumgarten exclaimed. "Such a—"

"Psst!" Grinley warned, grabbing him by the arm. "Quiet! We're not alone here. Do you see the two Indians there at the north face of the stone slab? Their horses are grazing just beyond it."

Two Indians sat by the rock, which afforded them some protection from the sun's hot rays. They were decorated in war paint, so their features could not be distinguished. One of them wore two white eagle feathers in his hair. And only now did the three observers notice the dark stripe in the grass starting at the southern entrance and leading straight to the rock slab.

"This line is the redskins' track," Grinley explained to his companions. "They entered the valley from the south and will ride off to the north after they have rested."

"Then we cannot continue, cannot go down!" the banker noted worriedly. "I do not trust any Indian since our captivity at the pueblo. Who might these two be?"

"I know them, even know the name of one of them. It is Mokaschi, the chief of the Nijora."

"What is the meaning of this name?" inquired Baumgarten.

"Mokaschi means 'bison.' The chief was a famous buffalo hunter when large herds still roamed the prairies and crossed the passes. That's how he got his name. Years ago I visited with his tribe several times."

"How does he feel about you?"

"Friendly, at least he was, and that would not change as long as times are peaceful. Now, however, they are on the warpath, and you can't trust anyone."

"Hmm, what can we do?"

"I truly don't know. If we ride down, he may receive us in a friendly way, but maybe not. But, in any case, he would learn of our presence, which better remains a secret."

"Can't we bypass him?"

"We can, but a detour would be so great that we would not reach our oil lake today. And we wouldn't meet up with Buttler and Poller, who would probably come riding toward us. It is really quite awkward to come across these two Nijora here—Wait a minute," he interrupted himself, "what's that?"

His observation put the three observers on maximum alert. Two more Indians, following the tracks of the Nijora on foot, had appeared at the southern entrance. Their faces, too, were covered in war paint. One of them wore an eagle feather in his hair and, while not necessarily a chief, must have distinguished himself by martial exploits. They were armed with rifles.

"Are they also Nijora?" asked Duncan.

"No, Navajo," the Oil Prince answered as quietly as if the redskins could overhear him.

"Do you know them?"

"No. The one with the feather is still young. He must have distinguished himself after I was last with the Navajo."

"There! Look! They are lying down in the grass. Why are they doing this?"

"Can't you guess? They are enemies of the Nijora. Scouts of the two tribes are encountering each other here. That means blood. The Navajo came on the Nijora tracks and followed them secretly into the valley. Watch what happens now!"

He shook from excitement, as did his two partners. They could observe the events below without being seen.

The two Navajo crept slowly along the Nijora tracks toward the rock.

"By the devil!" remarked the Oil Prince. "Mokaschi and his companion are lost if they sit even a minute longer!"

"Good Lord!" exclaimed the excited bookkeeper. "Can we not prevent the butchery?"

"No, no—and—yes, sure," answered Grinley breathlessly, "we must use this opportunity to our advantage!"

The two Navajo were still about ten paces from the rock. If they reached it, the two Nijora would be in trouble.

"Use the opportunity? How?" inquired the banker, barely daring to breathe.

"You'll see."

Quickly taking his double-barreled rifle from his saddle, Grinley leveled it.

Baumgarten exclaimed, "For God's sake, you do not want to shoot!" But the first shot had already rung out, followed a second later by the second. The Navajo wearing the feather was hit in the head by the first shot and killed immediately. The other received the second bullet. He leaped into the air, leaped again, and then collapsed.

"My God! You've killed them!" Duncan shouted, shocked.

"To our advantage," explained the Oil Prince while putting his rifle down and stepping to the rock's edge so he could be seen from below.

The effect of the two shots on the Nijora was remarkable. At the first shot, they leaped from their sitting position and immediately threw themselves into the grass so as to offer the smallest target. They believed the two shots to have been directed at them, because they could not see the two dead Navajo. The Oil Prince called from the rock ledge, "Mokaschi, the chief of the Nijora, may rise safely. He does not need to hide. His enemies are dead."

Mokaschi looked up at him, uttered a shout of surprise, and asked, "Uff! Who fired?"

"I did."

"At whom?"

"At the two Navajo behind your rock. Go look! They are dead."

The cautious redskin did not accept the invitation right away, but crawled to the nearest corner of the rock and peered cautiously around it. Then, raising his head higher and higher, he pulled his knife to be prepared for anything and in two or three quick leaps jumped over to the Navajo. When he saw they were no longer alive, he stood erect and called to the Oil Prince, "You are right. They are dead. Come down!"

"I am not alone. Two other men are with me."

"Palefaces?"

"Yes."

"Bring them!"

"Shall we do it?" Duncan asked the Oil Prince.

"Of course," he answered.

"Is there no danger?"

"Not the least. I saved the lives of the two Nijora. They are in our debt."

"But, sir, this was cold-blooded murder, a double murder!"

"Pshaw! Don't let that bother you. Two Indians had to die, in any case. My not saying or doing anything would have meant the Nijora. Had I shouted a warning, there would have been a fight to the death. They would have butchered each other. So I tossed the black bean to the Navajo and thus earned Mokaschi's gratitude and friendship. We don't have to worry anymore. Come now, you can safely follow me!"

Duncan and Baumgarten did so, but could not quell a horror for this man who, to gain an advantage, had, without any compunction, taken the lives of two human beings who had not done a thing to him. Their route led them outside the valley to the southern entrance. They reached the bottom of the valley without being aware that behind some bushes the glittering eyes of an Indian fell on them.

"Uff!" muttered the redskin. "The skinny one is the murderer! I could not help my brothers, but I shall avenge them."

Ducking down again, he disappeared into the bushes. He was a Navajo. He had been left behind as a precaution while his unfortunate companions entered the valley.

Together with Duncan and Baumgarten, the Oil Prince confidently approached the chief awaiting them at the rock. Earlier, Mokaschi had been unable to properly recognize Grinley due to the distance. Now, seeing him close up, his forehead, under the markings of his war paint, wrinkled into a frown.

"Where do the three palefaces come from?" he asked. The Oil Prince had expected a much friendlier reception. Disappointedly, he answered while he and his companions dismounted, "Our trail started at the Gila River."

"Where will it end?"

"At the waters of the Chelly."

"Are you alone?"

"Yes."

"Will more palefaces be following you?"

"No. And should more come, they are not friends of ours."

"You know that we have broken the peace pipe?"

"Yes."

"And you nevertheless risk coming up here?"

"Your hostility is directed against the Navajo only, not toward the whites!"

"The palefaces are worse than the dogs of the Navajo. When there were no whites, there was peace among all red men. We have only the palefaces to thank that the warpath destroys our lives. They will not be spared."

"Are you saying we are your enemies?"

"Yes. Enemies to the death."

"And yet both of you owe your lives to my two bullets! You want to put us on the stake for that?"

A contemptuous smile flickered across the chief's face as he answered, "You speak of the stake as if you were already in our power, although we are only two against you three. You seem to have the courage of a frog jumping into the maw of a snake while the snake is still just observing it."

These insults were not a result just of the current hostile conditions. It appeared that Grinley's reputation among the Nijora was not as shining as he had described it to his companions. Desiring to sway the latter in a more favorable direction, he said, "Does Mokaschi, the brave chief, not know me anymore?"

"Never have my eyes forgotten a face, even if I have seen it only once."

"I've never done the warriors of the Nijora any harm."

"Uff! Why are you even saying this? Had you insulted one of my warriors even with just your fingertips, you would no longer be alive."

"Why are you so hostile toward me? Is your life worth so little that you do not even welcome your rescuer?"

"Tell me first why you killed the Navajo and how long you pursued them! demanded the chief.

"I saw them only two minutes before I killed them to save you."

"What had they done to you?"

"Nothing."

"You were not trying to avenge yourself?"

"No."

"And yet you killed them!"

"Only to save you!" exclaimed Grinley.

"Dog!" Mokaschi thundered at the white man, his eyes glittering. "Many hunters and warriors have me to thank for their lives, but I have not mentioned it even once throughout the years. You, however, stand before me for only a few moments and already have called yourself my rescuer four times. If you pay yourself in this manner, you should not expect any reward from me. Did I ask to be rescued by you?"

Grinley felt intimidated, yet risked an objection. "No, but without me you would be dead now."

"What tells you that? Do you see our horses standing here beside the rock. They would tell us of the approach of any stranger. We had just heard them snort and reached for our knives when the shots rang out. The Navajo had not done anything to you. You did not fight them; you killed them from ambush. You are not a warrior, but a murderer. There lie their corpses. Can I take their scalps? No, for they were felled by your insidious bullets. Had you not interfered, I would, warned by the snorting of our horses, have greeted them with a knife and could now adorn myself with their scalps. Do you know the one with the feather in his hair? His name is Khasti-tine [Old Man], although his lifetime counts only twenty summers and winters. He received this title of honor because of his cleverness and bravery. And you murdered such a warrior! And deprived me of the glory of having defeated him! And you still ask for a reward from me."

The Oil Prince became greatly alarmed and his companions were no less anxious. The chief continued, "All palefaces are like you. How many upright men are among them? For one Old Shatterhand there are a hundred times a hundred others bringing us nothing but ruin. Stay right here until I return. If you dare leave, you are lost!"

With a nod to the other Nijora, they walked back beside the tracks, carefully checking them, to the entrance of the valley, where both Indians disappeared.

"Woe to us! That's not what we expected!" lamented the banker. "You got us into a soup so thick we'll choke on it if we have to eat it!"

"A murderer!" agreed the bookkeeper. "The chief is right. Why did you have to shoot? This Khasti-tine, so young and yet so famous already! Do you not shudder at your infamous deed?"

"Shut up!" the Oil Prince spat at him. "It's as I said: I saved the chief. The horses' snorting is an excuse, a lie!"

"I doubt it. The man looks to me as if he knew what he was saying. Did we not stand like schoolchildren before him? It will be best for us to disappear before he returns!"

"Don't try it, Mr. Baumgarten! He seems to have more warriors close by. If we left, he'd keep on our heels and we'd be lost. If we stay, he may let us go. Let's wait!"

After more than a quarter of an hour, the Nijora returned. When they arrived, Mokaschi said, "An avenger is following you already, and you will perish without my laying a hand on you. Not two but three Navajo have been here. The third kept guard at the valley entrance and probably saw everything without being able to prevent the murderous deed. He will put his moccasins to your tracks and follow you until his knife has entered your heart. Your scalp is no more firm on your head than a drop of rain the wind shakes off a branch. I will have nothing to do with you, either for good or bad. What is your purpose at the Chelly River? What do you want there?"

"A piece of land," came dejectedly from the Oil Prince's mouth.

"Does it belong to you?"

"Yes."

"Who gave it to you?"

"No one."

"And yet you claim it belongs to you!"

"Yes. It is a tomahawk improvement."

"That is a phrase used by robbers and thieves! A piece of land at the Chelly River! It is yours. And here stands Mokaschi, the chief of the Nijora, who are the legitimate lords and owners of the entire Chelly territory! You mangy dogs! What would the palefaces beyond the Great Sea say if we came and claimed that their land was ours? Yet we are to accept their setting upon us and taking everything! A piece of land at the Chelly River belongs to you, although you neither bought it from nor had it granted by us! My fist should fell you. But it is too proud to touch you. Get away from here, away to the scrap of land you hunger for! Sit on it and you will not have to wait long to collect a bloody harvest!"

Imperiously, his hand pointed to the northern exit.

The whites quickly mounted their horses and hastily trotted away, glad in their deepest hearts to leave this place, which had become so dangerous to them, with their skins intact.

To understand the words and behavior of the chief, one needs to know how the whites gained possession of land in the Wild West. According to the so-called Homestead Law, every head of family and every man at least twenty-one years of age who either was a citizen or who had declared the intention of becoming one, could acquire an unoccupied parcel of 160 acres without payment. The only requirement was to occupy and cultivate it for five years. In addition, millions of acres were sold dirt-cheap, especially to the railroads.

Concerning the so-called tomahawk improvements, anyone could call himself owner of a desirable piece of land by striking a few trees with an axe, building a cottage, and sowing some grain. No one asked what the owners of these lands, the Indians, had to say about it!

After leaving the valley, the three whites rode silently alongside each other for quite some time through the open forest. The Oil Prince was angry about the treatment he had received from the chief of the Nijora and pondered how to regain the respect of the banker and the bookkeeper. Finally breaking the long silence, he said, "That's how the red rascals are! Ungrateful to the highest degree! One can have lived with them in peace for the longest time and have done them many a kindness, and yet on some beautiful day they will breach the faith and simply forget the gratitude they owe."

"Yes," Duncan nodded. "That was a bad situation we were in. We can be glad to have escaped it without a black eye. I thought our lives were forfeit."

"Of course, our lives would have been lost had the chief not secretly agreed with me, since he had to realize that I had saved him. But I will never again do a good deed for an Indian."

"Right! These red fellows are not worth a care."

Obviously, the banker had little inclination to condemn the Oil Prince for his conduct. Duncan was the type of individual to whom another person's life counted little. The dangerous situation had passed and likewise the momentary impression the murder of the two Navajo had made on him. Not Baumgarten, though. He thought Grinley's behavior criminal and asked the Oil Prince in a serious and reproachful voice, "Have you ever done anything good for an Indian, sir?"

"I? What a question! These very Nijora have me to thank for numerous favors!"

"Yet the chief did not act as if that were the case!"

"Because he is an ungrateful fellow. By the way, it seems you are reproaching me, instead of remembering that it was I who rescued you from captivity in the pueblo."

"Hmm! To be honest, the more I think about this event, the more questions arise for which I have no answers."

Grinley gave him a sharply inquisitive sideways look. He started to address him angrily, but reconsidered and asked quietly, "What questions could there be? May I hear them?"

"I do not think it necessary."

"No? Most likely I can answer them for you."

"It is not only likely, but certain that you could. But I doubt you would."

"If I can, I will, sir. Rest assured."

"Maybe. Nevertheless, let us not talk further about it! But since you stress that we have to be so very grateful to you, I want to tell you that not every day's evening has yet come."

"What do you mean?"

"Quite likely we will reach a point at which you cannot demand further gratitude from us."

"I would like to know how this is going to happen!" exclaimed Grinley.

"Very simple," explained Baumgarten. "With regard to the business to be concluded, you cannot ask for gratitude, for you will be paid. And we have credited you with freeing us from the pueblo; however, we may soon have to cancel this debt because of your shooting of the two Navajo."

"What bearing does this have on our account?"

"Do not ask this! When we encounter Navajo, they will take revenge on us for the death of their two scouts."

"Pshaw! How are they to know what happened?"

"What? Didn't you hear what Mokaschi said? There were three Navajo, not just two. The third will follow us."

At first the Oil Prince's face seemed to turn serious and reflective, but then he forced a mocking laugh and responded, "This shows what a smart chap you are! Do you believe that Mokaschi spoke the truth?"

"Yes."

"Really? Then I must tell you that you will never make a true frontiersman. Mokaschi is out scouting against the Navajo. That he is doing this himself and did not send ordinary warriors is a sign that he considers this a matter of the greatest importance. He met up with three enemies, also scouts, and now must do everything to eliminate them. Two I shot; the third is still alive and has seen the Nijora. He will not pursue us, but will quickly return to his tribe to report on Mokaschi's whereabouts. The latter must prevent this at all costs. He will, therefore, follow the Navajo's tracks to catch up with and kill him. Do you understand?"

"Hmm!" Baumgarten mumbled. "Maybe it is as you say and maybe not."

"It is so, I assure you, and—"

Grinley stopped his horse and looked attentively into the distance. The three presently found themselves on a small open prairie. The edge of a forest could be seen in the distance. Two horsemen stood out against its dark background. They, too, stopped when they say the three.

"Two men," Grinley said. "It appears they're whites. I bet a hundred to one that it's Buttler and Poller. Let's go!"

They began to ride toward the others. When the other two realized this, they also spurred their horses on. Soon they recognized each other. It was indeed Buttler and Poller. When they were within earshot, the Oil Prince shouted, "It is you! A good sign. Did you find the way?"

"Yes," answered Buttler, "as easy as pie. We didn't see the tracks of even a single Indian."

"And you found Gloomy Water?"

"Yes, easily."

"And the oil?"

"Grand, simply splendid!" answered Buttler, his face beaming with delight. Turning to the banker, he continued, "Be so kind as to smell us! What do you think of our scent? Could that be essence of rose, sir?"

Indeed, because of the work they had performed, the two smelled heavily of petroleum. Duncan's features quickly took on an expression of clearest delight. He answered, "Not rose oil, of course, but just as dear to me! How long does it take to gather a pound of rose oil, sirs? Petroleum, though, springs so readily from the ground that one can fill hundreds of barrels daily. Don't you think so, Mr. Baumgarten?"

"Yes," the bookkeeper nodded, now also looking happy and confident.

"Well! Until now you still weren't quite ready to believe in all this. I've often noted that in you."

"I don't deny it, sir."

"But now? Is your mistrust turning to belief?"

At that point the Oil Prince interjected, "I too noticed, of course, that Mr. Baumgarten trusted me very little. But I was too proud to be insulted. He now realizes that he faces an honorable man deserving the trust he claims. But let's not stay here on the open prairie! There are Indians about who could easily see us."

"Indians?" Buttler asked as they were again riding toward the forest he and Poller had come from. "Have you met redskins by chance?"

"Unfortunately!"

"Darn! When, where, and how?"

Grinley recounted the event, and in true character both Buttler and Poller expressed their agreement with his action. By then they had reached the forest. Their conversation came to a halt, since the trees grew so densely that they had to ride in single file. This annoyed the banker, who had a burning interest to learn more about the petroleum lake.

The woods soon ended and a large prairie opened up before them once more. Now the horsemen could ride alongside each other, and Duncan asked about Gloomy Water in all its details. Buttler and Poller satisfied his curiosity in a manner that only increased his expectations and raised his excitement to even greater levels. When he insisted that he could hardly wait to get there, Buttler calmed him, "Your patience will not be taxed much longer, for we have at most one and a half hours to ride."

"One and a half? And half an hour ago we met up with you. That means that you left the petroleum lake only two hours ago?"

"Just about."

"Why not sooner? We couldn't learn soon enough of a your message!"

This question was rather inconvenient. The banker was not to suspect the lengthy work they had had to perform at Gloomy Water. Buttler extricated himself from the predicament by explaining, "It was our task to provide for your safety. This included searching the environs of the lake. That was not easy, since in places the land is very rugged and difficult to cross and was slowing us down. We also had to be very cautious. This is why we finished only a few hours ago."

"And did you find anything indicative of danger?"

"Nothing, nothing at all. You need not have the least worry, sir."

Duncan not only felt calmed, but as cheerful and confident as he had ever been in his life. A treasure worth many millions awaited him in only an hour and a half!

He would have liked to embrace all of his companions, but settled for pressing his bookkeeper's hand and saying, "Finally, we are at our destination! And finally, finally freed from the uncertainties! Aren't you happy, too?"

"Of course, sir," came the simple response.

"Of course, sir," repeated Duncan, shaking his head repeatedly. "That sounds so indifferent, as if the entire matter did not concern you!"

"Do not think that!" protested Baumgarten. "You know that I always take care of your business as if it were my own. I am happy, too, but I am not used to expressing these feelings openly."

"Well, I know you, Mr. Baumgarten. Here, however, you can be a bit louder. I haven't told you yet, but you probably realize that I have plans for you, since I brought you along. You are to take a greater part in this new enterprise than you might have thought. Do you really believe I'd leave Arkansas with my family to settle permanently here in the Wild West? Wouldn't think of it! But first I'll do everything required here. My firm and actual residence will remain at Brownsville. I'll hire engineers and above them put a managing director I can rely on. Who do you suppose this man is going to be?"

He gave the bookkeeper a significant sideways glance, and when the latter did not respond at once, he continued, "Or do you, too, intend to spend the rest of your life in Brownsville?"

"I have not yet had any reason to ponder this question, Mr. Duncan."

"Well, then, be so kind as to think about it now! What about if the director's name I was talking about were Mr. Baumgarten?"

The German rose up in his saddle and asked, "Are you serious, sir?"

"Yes. You know I don't joke about important matters like this. The position calls for responsibility and is difficult. That's why I would, in addition to a salary, have a profit-sharing arrangement with you. Do you accept the position?"

"With all my heart!"

"Then shake on it! Here's my hand."

Baumgarten extended his hand and said, "I don't want to waste any words, Mr. Duncan. You know me and are aware that I am not ungrateful. My greatest wish is to measure up to the position I am to hold."

"You will, I know."

"But I do not wish to assert this so confidently. What Mr. Grinley has so often expressed is true: I am not familiar with the West, and it takes men with hair on their chests."

"I'll get you such fellows for the enterprise."

"There will be fights. Or do you think the Indians will peacefully put up with our settling in with such a grand oil operation?"

"They can do little about it."

"Hmm! They will insist that the place is theirs, and—"

"Don't entertain such useless ideas!" the Oil Prince interrupted. "Didn't you hear what Mokaschi said? Namely, that I can go confidently to my parcel of land to take possession of it."

"He was hardly serious," replied Baumgarten.

"Oh, yes."

"Fine! But does the place really belong to the Nijora? Is it not possible that other redskins, Navajo, for example, will lay claim to it?"

"What these fellows say and claim is irrelevant," announced Grinley. "I will assign my tomahawk improvement to you. The document for it is here in my pocket. You had it verified in Brownsville. It was found to be good and true and will be yours as soon as you hand me the San Francisco draft. With that done, and according to the laws of the United States, Mr. Duncan is the legal owner of Gloomy Water, and no redskin can drive him off."

"And if the redskins do not follow the law?" queried the bookkeeper.

"Then they'll be forced to obey it. Of course, you will hire only people who know how to handle rifle and knife. That'll make the Indians cooperate with us. And beyond that, you can rest assured that your operation will soon attract a white population numerous enough not only to repel any attack victoriously, but also to entirely displace the redskins from the area. First set up your machines! You know the machine is the Indian's most overwhelming enemy."

He was right about that. Wherever the white arrives with his machines, the red man must leave. The machine is an invincible adversary. Yet it is not as cruel as the rifle, firewater, or smallpox and other illnesses to which numerous Indians have fallen, and are still falling, victim.

Duncan checked the water at various places, not saying a word.

# 10

# AT THE PETROLEUM LAKE

N UNDER AN HOUR AND A HALF, the five riders found themselves in an
area of caves and rock overhangs densely overgrown with dark conifers. Here and there, leafy trees lessened the country's gloomy aspect
with their bright green color. When Duncan commented on this, the Oil
Prince remarked, "Wait till you get to Gloomy Water! It'll be even darker
there."

"Is it still far?"

"No. The next canyon is our destination."

Soon they entered the canyon. Dark cliffs rose on both sides, their
slopes and tops bearing dark conifers. Along the canyon floor flowed a
shallow, narrow brook with drops of oil floating on its surface. Seeing this,
Grinley sent a satisfied glance toward Buttler and Poller. He had been unable to talk with them in secret and had silently worried about whether
they had completed their work to his expectations. Now he felt at ease and,
pointing at the water, said to Duncan, "Look there, Mr. Duncan! That is
the outlet of Gloomy Water. What do you think is floating on it?"

"Petroleum?" the latter answered, looking it over.

"Yes, petroleum."

"Indeed, indeed! A pity, a real pity it floats away like this!"

"Let it run. It's little enough. The best thing I discovered is that the lake
has only this one discharge, scarcely worth mentioning. Later you can
make certain that even this small quantity won't get away."

"Certainly, certainly! But, Mr. Grinley, don't you notice the smell? It
becomes stronger the closer we get to the lake."

"Of course! Wait until we arrive at the lake! You will be surprised!"

And the petroleum smell did become stronger with every step. The canyon walls suddenly opened up and an elongated valley appeared before Duncan's and his bookkeeper's surprised eyes, its basin occupied so fully by the "petroleum lake" that only a small strip of land remained between the shore and the canyon walls around it. From the strip's dense brush gigantic black firs stretched upward. The same kind of trees rose up the rock walls to the forest at the top, like guards refusing to allow a single sunbeam down.

On the valley floor, dusk ruled, despite its being a clear, bright day. No breeze moved the branches. No bird could be seen. No butterfly fluttered across flowers. All life seemed to have departed. Seemed? Oh, no, it not only appeared so, but everything had truly died, for on the lake floated numerous dead fish, whose shiny bodies contrasted peculiarly with the dark, oily surface. And then there was the strong odor of the oil. This unmoving, sunless lake, staring at the visitors like an eye arrested by death, rightfully carried the name Gloomy Water. Its sight cast such a spell on Duncan and Baumgarten that for some time the two remained frozen on the shore without uttering a word.

"Now, then, this is Gloomy Water," the Oil Prince broke the silence. "What do you think of it, Mr. Duncan? How do you like it?"

Rousing himself from his amazement as from a dream, the banker took a deep breath and answered, "How do I like it? What a question! I believe the ancient Greeks knew of a body of water across which the dead were ferried to the nether world. That water must have looked like this lake."

"Don't know anything of these Greek waters, but I bet they can't be compared with our Gloomy Water, for I doubt they had petroleum there. Dismount, sir, and check the oil. Let's make a round of the lake!"

The riders dismounted. They had to tie up their horses, since they snorted and pounded the ground in an attempt to get away. The penetrating smell of the petroleum was repugnant to them. Grinley stepped close to the water, scooped up a handful, smelled and looked at it, then said triumphantly to the banker, "There float millions of dollars, sir. Convince yourself!"

Duncan, too, took a scoop, moved on a few paces and took another one. He checked the water at various places, not saying a word. Again and again he shook his head. He looked as if he had lost the power to speak. But his eyes shone and on his features worked the excitement that had taken control of him. His movements were hasty and insecure, almost giddy. His hands shook and he appeared to gather all his strength to finally shout in an almost squeaky voice, "Who would have thought! Who! Mr. Grinley, my expectations have been exceeded!"

"Truly? I'm glad, sir, I'm immensely happy!" the Oil Prince laughed. "Are you finally convinced that I am an honest man, who is being truthful with you?"

Duncan stretched both his hands toward him and answered, "Give me your hands. I must shake them. You are an honorable gentleman. Forgive us if our trust was shaken several times! It was not our fault!"

"I know, I know, sir," Grinley nodded in an upright manner. "Those strangers made you doubt me. You shouldn't have listened to them. But now everything is in order, everything! Check the oil, sir!"

"I have already."

"Well, then—"

"It's the best, the sweetest oil one can find. Where does it come from? Where's the lake's inflow?

"It has only the small outlet. There must be two subterranean springs, one for the water and another one for the oil. You see, one needs only to scoop the oil off to fill the barrels."

Duncan was so enchanted he did not know where to turn. Baumgarten was more level-headed and commented on Grinley's last words, "Yes, one needs only to scoop it off. But what happens after it has been scooped off? What is the rate of replenishment?"

"Fast, of course, so fast that work will not be interrupted."

"I do not want to accept that without verification. There can be only as much supply as there is runoff. Look at the scant discharge at the valley entrance! I think the brook is not carrying off more than a quart of oil an hour. That, then, is the entire yield we can expect."

"You think so? No more? No more than a quart per hour?" the banker asked in a voice filled with bitter disappointment.

Duncan's mouth hung open in dismay. His face had turned as pale as a corpse.

"Yes, Mr. Duncan, that is how it is," the bookkeeper answered. "You must admit that the supply cannot exceed the outflow? And even if it were greater, ten times, a hundred times! What are a hundred quarts of oil per hour! Nothing, nothing at all. Figure the size of the investment and operating expense, the remoteness of the area, the dangers lurking here, the difficulties in distribution! And that with only a hundred quarts an hour!"

"Can't it be more after all? Isn't it possible you are mistaken?"

"No. How old is this lake? Hundreds if not thousands of years have certainly passed since its formation. And for this entire time only this little has seeped out and run off. If more oil flowed, would it not be deeper on the water? No, there is nothing, nothing at all to obtain here!"

"Nothing, nothing at all!" the banker repeated, with both hands reaching for his head. "Then all hope, all joy was for naught! The long, long trip was for nothing! Who can endure this? Who can bear it!"

The Oil Prince, too, had been scared by the bookkeeper's words. With what effort and danger had he transported the petroleum barrel by barrel here and hidden it away! What had it cost him! And now, so close to success, everything was to be in vain! He saw sparks in front of his eyes. Feeling helpless, Grinley could not utter a single word, and turned his eyes to his brother in a plea for help.

Once again the cunning leader of the Finders showed that his composure could not easily be shaken. Loosing a brief, superior laugh, he told the banker, "What are you whining about, Mr. Duncan? I don't understand you! If you're right about what you're now thinking and saying, Grinley would never have put such great hope in Gloomy Water."

"You think so?" Duncan asked hastily, gaining renewed confidence.

"Yes, I do, and more. If the oil here could be easily scooped into barrels, he'd not have offered you the place, but would have kept it to himself. It's just that oil production requires expensive preparations for which he does not have the means."

"Preparations? How so?"

"Hmm! I'll try to explain it to you. Assume your horse is lying here in the grass and you get into the saddle. Can it get up with you astride it?"

"Yes."

"Fine. But let's assume a lapdog lying here instead of the horse. Would it be able to get up?"

"No."

"Why not?"

"Because I am too heavy."

"Now then, apply this to the petroleum! Do you know which is heavier, petroleum or water?"

"Water," the bookkeeper answered.

"Very well! Now think about how heavy the mass of water is in the lake!"

"Thousands of hundredweights."

"And on the bottom of the lake is a petroleum seep, that is, a small hole from which the oil comes. But thousands of hundredweights of water press on this hole. Can the oil escape?"

"No."

Baumgarten fell into the trap. He possessed a merchant's background. He understood little of the laws of physics. He did not realize that oil, because it is lighter than water, has to rise. Grinley started to breathe easier. Buttler's face sported a victorious smile. He continued, "Then the oil, which wants to rise, cannot. What we see here is only the small quantity seeping through a small crack down there. But if we install a pump here and pump the water out of the lake, or drain it in some other way, then you'll see oil gushing high into the air and filling several hundred barrels a day. If Grinley had the money for such a pumping station, he wouldn't have thought of turning this over to you."

This argument worked. The banker rejoiced once again and Baumgarten dropped his objections. Oil was present; one could see that. It only needed an exit. Talk skipped back and forth in such a way as to generate excitement in the two buyers. Duncan decided to enter into the deal, but first he wanted to inspect the lake's entire circumference.

"Do that, Mr. Duncan," Grinley said. "Poller will show you around!"

The immigrants' unfaithful scout left with Duncan and Baumgarten. When they were gone, the Oil Prince breathed a sigh of relief. "Hell's bells! That was an awkward situation! They might have backed out at the very last moment! Your idea was excellent."

"Yes," Buttler laughed. "If not for me, you could have kept your petroleum lake to yourself. Now, though, I'm convinced they'll fall for it."

"Who would have thought they'd accept your explanation of the laws of physics so readily!"

"Pshaw! Duncan is too stupid and Baumgarten too honest."

"They'll pass by the cave. Nothing is visible there?"

"No. But the work cost us more than sweat. Make sure to wrap up the deal today. We shouldn't lose any time, since we can't trust the Indians. Let's get out of here no later than tomorrow morning. How should we finish off the two blockheads, with a knife or a bullet?"

"Hmm, I'd like to avoid both."

"Let them live? Are you crazy?"

"Don't misunderstand me! I just don't want them to die before my eyes. The memory would be unpleasant. What do you say about imprisoning them in the cave?"

"Not a bad idea. We tie them up and lock them in there. They'll perish without our having to watch. I'm agreed. But when?"

"As soon as we have the money, each of them gets a rifle butt against the head."

"Poller, too?"

"Not yet. We probably still need him. Until we've left this dangerous area behind, it's better to be three than only two. After that, we can do away with him any time."

The area certainly was dangerous. They were not aware that they were already being observed. Not very far away, where the canyon met the lake, an Indian lay in the brush watching the two. It was the Navajo who had been unable to prevent the murder of his two companions.

Grinley and Buttler lay down in the grass. When the Indian saw that, he said to himself, "They will stay here. They will not leave the area now. There is time for me to go get our warriors."

He crept from the bushes and disappeared in the canyon without the least trace.

After a while, the three whites had rounded the lake and returned to Buttler and Grinley.

"Well, sirs," the Oil Prince asked, "did you see everything? What's your intention now?"

"To buy," the banker answered, "even if the deal isn't as big as you figure it to be."

"Quit saying that, sir! I will not reduce my asking price by even a dollar. And I have no desire to lose any more time here. I think it's possible that redskins are following us, and I have no intention of letting them have my scalp."

"Then we should leave as soon as possible," Duncan said anxiously.

"Yes, but not before the purchase contract has been signed. We agreed to conclude it here at the lake. As soon as we have signed and exchanged the papers, we will depart."

"It's all right by me. Mr. Baumgarten, do you still have any objections?"

Before Baumgarten could respond, Grinley interrupted in a sharp tone, "If even now you are still talking about objections, I must consider this truly an insult, Mr. Duncan. Tell me quickly: Do you want to buy or not?"

Intimidated, the banker declared, "I do. That's understood."

"Well, then, we can move toward the conclusion. The documents have been prepared and need only be signed. Bring out your ink and quill!"

Duncan fetched the articles from his saddlebag and, after the signatures had been executed, received the title from Grinley and then signed the prepared draft on the bank in San Francisco. Grinley studied the paper in his hands greedily and said, with a peculiar chuckle, "So, Mr. Duncan, now you are master and owner of this grand petroleum site. I wish you much luck! And since everything here now belongs to you and it is of no use to me any longer, I will reveal a secret to you."

"What kind of secret?"

"A hidden cave. At the start, it can serve you or your people as a storage place and, in an emergency, as a hiding place from Indian attacks. It may even connect with the subterranean petroleum deposit certainly present here."

"With the petroleum deposit? Tell me quickly where the cave is! I must see it. I will have it explored later."

"Come! I'll show it to you."

They walked a short distance along the shore to where the rocks came close to the water. At the foot of these rocks lay a rather high pile of boulders whose top Buttler and Poller began to remove. Soon a hole leading into the rock appeared.

"That's the cave, that's it!" the banker cried. "Let's open the entrance further. Quickly! Help me with it, Mr. Baumgarten!"

The two bent down to help. Buttler rose and looked at Grinley questioningly. The latter nodded. They reached for their rifles. Each of them executed a blow with his rifle butt—the banker and Baumgarten, struck on their heads, toppled over. They were tied up, hands and feet, and, once the entry had been widened enough, were carried into the cave and put down at the far end. Had they been conscious, they would have seen the many barrels with which the cave was almost entirely filled.

It goes without saying that the three murderers took everything they thought usable from their victims. Then the rubble was piled back up so the hole could no longer be seen and they returned to the horses.

"Finally!" the Oil Prince said. "No deal has ever cost me so much effort and as many problems as this one. And it's still not completed! Now we have to get the draft to San Francisco. I hope we arrive there unharmed! Should we leave immediately?"

"Yes," answered Poller. "But first we must share."

"What?"

"The stuff we took."

Grinley would have loved to knock him down right then and there, but told himself that everything Poller got could later be taken from him. Therefore, he said, in seemingly good spirits, "All right! For the time being, the two horses remain common property, and we'll not fight about the other things. We are friends and brothers who won't fall out for trifles."

They sat down and spread out the stolen weapons, watches, rings, moneybags, and other items to estimate their value and to divide them equally.

While this was happening, eight Indians came stealing through the canyon leading to the lake. They were Navajo. At their head prowled the scout. They stopped at the valley entrance to listen from behind the bushes. They saw the three whites sitting there.

"Uff!" whispered the eldest, turning to the scout, "it is truly as my brother reported: the lake is full of oil. Where did it come from?"

"The palefaces will know," he answered.

"Did my brother not count five whites? I see only three."

"Earlier there were five. Two are missing."

"Which one murdered our brother Khasti-tine?"

"The man who is holding the two rifles." He meant the Oil Prince

"He will die a terrible death. But the two others will also be tied to the stake. Uff! They are sharing the things lying in front of them. The fourth and fifth have disappeared. Those things belonged to them. Might they have been killed?"

"We will find out. Follow me quickly, my brothers."

He, together with the seven others, rushed the three whites. This attack happened so suddenly and was executed so quickly that the three were tied up before they could move a limb in their defense.

At first the redskins did not say a word. Five of them sat down by the captives. The other three left to search the valley. When they returned, one of them reported, "The two palefaces have disappeared. We did not see either of them."

"They did not climb up the rocks?" asked the eldest.

"No. We would have seen their tracks."

"We will find out where to look for them."

The redskin pulled his knife, pressed it against the Oil Prince's chest, and threatened him, "You are the scoundrel who killed Khasti-tine, our brother. If you do not tell me at once where the two palefaces who were with you earlier have disappeared to, I will plunge this knife into your heart!"

These words struck an unholy terror into Grinley. If he obeyed, the Indians would pull the banker and his bookkeeper from the cave. That must not happen. If he did not obey, the redskin would make good his threat and stab him to death. What to do? Once more the cunning Buttler rescued him. He called to the Indian, "You are mistaken. The man you want to knife is not Khasti-tine's murderer. We are innocent of his death."

The Indian let the Oil Prince go and turned to Buttler, "Shut up! We know very well who the murderer is."

"No. You do not!"

"Our brother here saw it!"

He pointed to the scout.

"He is mistaken," Buttler insisted. "He saw us with the chief of the Nijora. But when the two shots struck we were standing in a place that he could not have seen."

"Then you deny you were present at the murder of our two brothers?"

"No. I have never spoken a lie. The two white men you asked for are the murderers."

"Uff!" the redskin exclaimed. "We do not see them. They must be gone. You want to save yourself by charging them with the crime!"

"They are gone, you say? Where might they have gone? You are scouts, warriors with sharp eyes. Have you seen their tracks? You would surely find them if they had left."

"No. Are you saying that they are still here?"

"Yes."

"Where?"

"There!" said Buttler, pointing at the water.

"Uff! They are in this lake?"

"Yes."

"They drowned?"

"Yes."

"Do not lie! No one would willingly enter this oily water."

"Not of one's own will, that's true. They did not want to."

"Who forced them?"

"We did. We drowned them."

"You—drowned—them?" the Indian asked. Although he was a savage, he was, nevertheless, so perplexed that he was able only to stutter. "Drowned? Why?"

"As punishment. They were our mortal enemies."

"And yet you entertained their company! No one rides with his mortal enemies."

"We did not know they were our enemies. We found out only after arriving here. They wanted to own this lake of oil all by themselves and intended to murder us for it. When we became aware of this, we threw them in the water."

"They did not fight?"

"No. We knocked them down by hitting them with our rifle butts."

"Why can we not see them?"

"We tied rocks to their feet to make them sink to the bottom."

The redskin fell silent. Then he said, "I believe you speak the truth. But I have a horror of you. You have drowned sons of your own kind as if they were mangy dogs. You killed them furtively without fighting them. You are bad people!"

"Could we have acted otherwise? Were we to wait until they executed their plan and shot us from behind? That's what they were ready to do. We spied on them."

"What you think is no concern of mine. No red man, though, kills another from behind without fighting him, even if he is his greatest enemy. Have you been at this lake before?"

"Yes, I have," the Oil Prince answered.

"When?"

"Several months ago."

"Was the oil there already?"

"Yes. That's why I went to get some other whites to show it to them. I wanted to start a company with them for the extraction of the oil. The other two, though, intended to murder us to become the sole owners."

"Uff! Never before was there oil here. It must only recently have sprung from the earth. But how could you think yourself the owner of the lake! It belongs to the red man. The palefaces are robbers who wish to take everything belonging to us. Our tomahawks are on the warpath. By coming here you have ridden to your death."

"To our death? Are you warriors or are you murderers? We did not do anything to you!"

"Silence! Have not Khasti-tine and his companion been murdered?"

"Unfortunately, but it wasn't us who killed them," lied Grinley.

"You were along. You could have prevented it."

"That was impossible. The two fellows shot so quickly that we did not have time to say a single word to stop it."

"That will not save you. You were in the company of the murderers. You will die. We will bring you to our chief. Then the Old Ones will sit in council and decide your death."

"But we punished the two murderers!" protested the Oil Prince. "You should be grateful to us."

"Grateful?" the Indian laughed disdainfully. "Do you think you have done us a service? We would rather have them alive. Then we could get their scalps and see them die at the stake. You deprived us of this pleasure. Your fate has been decided. Death is awaiting you. I have spoken!"

He turned to signal that he would speak no further. The whites had their pockets emptied. The Indians took everything they found there. When the leader saw the draft, however, he handled it very carefully with his fingertips only, returned it to Grinley's pocket, and said, "This is magic, a talking paper. No red warrior takes such a paper into his hands, for it would later tell of all his thoughts, words, and deeds."

By this time, it had started to get dark at the lake. The Indians would have stayed overnight, but the strong smell of the oil drove them away. The captives were bound onto their horses, then the party took off, back through the canyon, and a distance into the forest, where water was to be found. There the Indians dismounted, bound the three captives to three trees, and prepared their camp. They appeared to feel entirely safe at this place; however, they were in error. Had they known what was happening behind them, they would have ridden as far as possible.

Mokaschi, the chief of the Nijora, had been cautious enough to check the tracks of the Navajo scouts more closely after the whites left. He knew that, besides the two murdered men, a third had been there. He wanted to know where that man had gone.

After a search he found the track, which led to the palefaces' tracks. "This Navajo wants to take revenge on the murderers. He is following them. I therefore conclude that the war party he belongs to will be moving in the same direction. I will follow him and catch these Navajo."

The chief rode first in the opposite direction, where, in a hidden clearing deep in the woods, he met up with approximately thirty Nijora warriors. These were the scouts riding ahead of the much larger war party. They all returned to cautiously follow the tracks of the whites and the Navajo. Along the way, Mokaschi noticed that two others, that is Buttler and Poller, had met up with the three whites.

The chief and his scouts approached the canyon leading to the lake of oil and hid. They soon saw the Navajo scout exit the canyon and run off quickly. One of the Nijora reached for his rifle to shoot him. The chief stopped him and whispered, "Let him go! He will soon return and bring other Navajo. Then we will catch them."

It soon became apparent that he had guessed right. The scout returned with seven others, all of whom entered the canyon. Their plan was to ride to the end of the canyon, dismount, and then attack the whites.

The Nijora waited. Mokaschi was quite puzzled when he saw the Navajo coming from the canyon with only three white captives. He had intended to attack them as soon as they appeared, but instead he gave his people a signal to remain hidden. He first wanted to find out why two whites were missing. He therefore let his foes leave, then went through the canyon to Gloomy Water. Very quickly and as carefully as possible, they searched the entire lakeshore without finding a trace of the missing palefaces.

"They cannot be gone," Mokaschi said. "They are no longer alive. And since we do not see their corpses, they were probably thrown into the water."

Together with his troop he left the lake to return to where the others were hiding. Mokaschi followed the Navajo with the remaining twenty-eight men on foot. The horses were left under the watch of two guards. The Navajo could not be far away, for, with night closing in, they would set up camp.

There was just enough light to see their tracks, which led into the woods, where they could no longer be made out. This did not bother Mokaschi. To find the party, he had only to keep going in the same direction.

It was not long before they noticed smoke and then the light from a small Indian campfire. Mokaschi whispered to his people, "These Navajo are not warriors, but young boys without brains. What scout would light a fire at night! My brothers shall surround them and, when I sound the war cry, throw themselves onto them. We must take them alive to put them to the stake."

Inaudibly, the Nijora scurried under the trees. Mokaschi crept as close as possible to the fire to get a fix on a Navajo he wanted to capture. When he felt sure his people were ready, his well-known war cry sounded shrilly through the forest. Then he leapt into the midst of the Navajo to grab his target. His warriors sounded the war cry and, from all sides, threw themselves onto the enemy, who had not thought an attack possible and were so surprised they did not even think of offering resistance. They were overpowered before any of them could reach for knife, rifle, or tomahawk.

"Thank God!" the Oil Prince whispered to his two companions. "We are safe now!"

"Or not!" answered Poller.

"Oh, sure. Mokaschi let us ride off once before. Why should he keep us now?"

"These red scoundrels don't ask for reasons."

"Wait! You'll see I'm right."

No one had paid any attention to this short, quiet conversation. The Navajo lay bound on the ground. The Nijora divided the captured weapons among themselves. Mokaschi, standing very upright by the fire, commanded, "The sons of the Navajo shall tell me who their leader is!"

"I am," the eldest answered.

"What is your name?"

"I am called 'Fast Steed.'"

"Maybe this name fits you. As you flee from the enemy, you are probably faster than the mustang of the prairies."

"Mokaschi, the Chief of the Nijora, is mistaken. Never before has an enemy seen my back!"

"You know my name. You therefore know me?"

"Yes, I have seen you. You are a wise and brave warrior. It would please me greatly to fight you. Your scalp would then hang from my belt."

"No enemy, especially one like you, will ever possess my scalp. Did the Great Manitou create you without brains? Do you not know that the scouts of the Nijora are out working against you just as you are working against us? What scout walks through the forest and across the grass without being on the lookout for enemy tracks? Above all, a smart scout tries to remain concealed; you, though, light a fire as if you wanted to attract us! Of course, you will never again have the opportunity to commit such errors, for you will die at the stake, and before that you will be tortured, so that your voices will echo in pain across the mountains."

To that Fast Steed answered, "Torture us! We will die as warriors without making a sound or blinking an eye. The warriors of the Navajo have learned to deal with even the greatest pain. What will you do with the whites?"

When the Oil Prince heard this question, he said, "Mokaschi, the noble and famous chief, will set us free."

But this noble and famous chief bellowed at him, "Dog! Who was asked, you or I? How dare you to speak before I have opened my mouth!"

"Because I know you will do what I have said."

"What I shall do you will find out soon enough. I let you go once to show you how I despised you. But it will not happen twice. You were five. Where are the two missing palefaces?"

"Dead," responded Grinley, substantially more subdued than before.

"Dead? Who killed them?"

"We did."

"Why?"

"Because we found out that they sought to kill us. They planned secretly to murder us."

"Mokaschi raised his eyebrows in surprise and shouted, "Uff! To murder you in secret? I closely observed the eyes, the faces of these two men; they were good and honest people. You, however, are murderers and thieves who need to be exterminated like wild, venomous animals. Where are the corpses? I did not see them."

"In the water."

"There was no trace of blood. You did not kill them before you threw them into the water?"

"No."

"Then you drowned them?"

"Yes."

It took quite an effort for the Oil Prince to utter this "yes." The effect was immediately evident. The chief kicked him, spit in his face, and said, "You are not human, but rather a beast of prey and shall die the death you deserve. You fell upon your companions from behind, just as you maliciously murdered Khasti-tine!"

When Fast Steed heard this, he rose as far as his fetters would permit and said, "What has Mokaschi just said? Who murdered Khasti-tine?"

"This paleface here."

"Uff! This miserable creature claimed the two drowned men were the murderers."

"Lies! He bragged to me that he killed the two Navajo scouts. Now this cowardly scoundrel shakes from fright and puts the blame on the two honest men he murdered. The two scouts he shot and the two murdered palefaces shall be horribly avenged, though none of them belonged to my tribe. Look at these three men lying in front of you, you red warriors. They shall suffer before they die and then shall be drowned, just as they drowned their victims! Howgh! I have spoken!"

Once more Mokaschi spit into the Oil Prince's face, gave Buttler and Poller a vigorous kick, then turned away from them.

A warrior was sent to fetch the horses. When they were brought to the campsite, dried meat was taken from the saddlebags for a meal. The captured Navajo were also given food; the three whites did not get even a bite.

"A devilish story!" Buttler whispered to his half brother. "This supposed drowning is breaking our neck. It might have been better to tell the truth."

"No," answered the Oil Prince. "The redskins would have freed the banker and the German without improving our position at all. And we would have lost the draft."

"Pshaw! What use is it to us when we're going to burn at the stake!"

"We're not there yet!"

"You still have hope?"

"Naturally! It's not the first time I've found myself in such a dilemma; I have always escaped with only a black eye," boasted Grinley. "And even if I am tied to the stake, I will maintain hope until they give me the death blow. As you know, many a man has hanged on such a stake but was rescued at the last minute."

"Those men had friends who freed them. Who do we have?"

"Hmm!"

"There isn't anyone who would risk tackling the redskins for our sake. If we can't free ourselves, we'll be lost."

He was only too right. Had they been worthy of friends, they would now have had help much closer at hand than they could have guessed. There were rescuers nearby, that is, Old Shatterhand and Winnetou.

The latter had quickly decided, after spying on the Oil Prince and his company, to follow the five men to Gloomy Water. But since they had to go first to the pueblo to free Ka-Maku's captives, Grinley had acquired a lead of two days. He lost one of those days, however, when he sent Buttler and Poller ahead to the lake while he waited behind with Duncan and Baumgarten an entire day. The second day's travel was almost made up by Winnetou and Old Shatterhand because they took the pueblo Indians' best horses and they did not follow the Oil Prince's tracks at all. The Apache knew of a trail that, by detouring around various difficult areas, led them more quickly to their destination. Thus it came about that their party of riders, shortly before evening, had at the most only a two-hour ride to reach the lake. This was a commendable accomplishment, particularly as they had women and children in the party.

They had not seen a single track since leaving the pueblo. Now, however, Winnetou's trail rejoined that of the Oil Prince at a clearing that was more a forest meadow than a prairie. The tracks of those being pursued could be seen as a rather broad and straight line.

The party stopped. Winnetou and Old Shatterhand dismounted to inspect the tracks. The others remained mounted; by now they were used to giving precedence to the two famous men. Even Sam Hawkens, experienced and cunning as he was, joined in only after being invited by the other two.

The tracks seemed to be difficult to read, for Old Shatterhand followed them ahead while Winnetou followed them backward. The two men met again where the others were waiting, so they were able to overhear what was reported.

"What does my red brother say about these tracks?" Old Shatterhand asked his friend. "I have rarely seen tracks as difficult to interpret as these."

Winnetou stared straight ahead, as if an explanation would be forthcoming from there. Then he responded with the certainty customary to him, "Tomorrow we will see three groups of people: palefaces and the warriors of two red nations."

"Yes, I think so, too. The redskins will be Navajo and Nijora. The three groups are at Gloomy Water to spy on each other."

"My white brother has read the tracks correctly. First, five horses passed by here—those of the palefaces we are following. Then came a single horseman, an Indian, later followed by a party most likely consisting of three times ten red men."

He looked west to study the sun's position and continued, "It would be advantageous to reach Gloomy Water today. But day is drawing to a close, increasing the danger. What does Old Shatterhand say?"

"I agree with you. Night will fall before we get there, and it will be too late to accomplish anything. We would not be able to see anything, but we could be seen by our enemies. Finally, we must consider that our party is not made up of warriors only."

"Very true!" agreed Winnetou. "At daylight we shall arrive at the lake. We should set up camp soon."

"Where?"

"Winnetou knows a suitable place an hour from Gloomy Water. There we can even light a fire without its being seen or the smoke being smelled. My brothers should follow me there."

As far as he was concerned, the issue had been decided. He rode on without glancing back to determine whether the others were following him. Old Shatterhand, though, with a little smile, stayed put. The frontiersmen dismounted to investigate the tracks.

They seemed unable to agree. Finally, Old Shatterhand urged them, "Finish up, sirs! Winnetou is far ahead already. He's disappearing into the woods.

The frontiersmen remounted and caught up with the Apache. Before the sun had completely disappeared, Winnetou left the track and moved into the forest, where the group soon arrived at a depression in the ground that looked as if a pit or a tunnel had collapsed. It might once have been a cave whose roof had long ago fallen in. The Apache pointed into it: "We will camp down there. If we post a guard up here, we can light a fire without an enemy spotting us."

The horses were led down the descent without difficulty. The men found enough forage for the night from the twigs of trees growing in the depression. A guard took up his post, and down below a fire was lit to prepare the evening's meal.

Conversation naturally revolved around the next day; however, the talking did not last long because everybody was so tired from the long ride. Soon almost everyone turned in. Before Old Shatterhand and Winnetou did the same, they held a brief discussion. The white hunter said, "We may get into a fight tomorrow during which we should not endanger the women and children. I would rather not have the immigrants with us. They are inexperienced and only a hindrance. Shouldn't we leave them here? It's safe and makes a good hiding place."

"Should it come to a fight, my brother is right. But what if we have to leave Gloomy Water quickly? There may not be time to return here to pick these people up."

"Hmm, yes! We probably will have to leave in a hurry. I am afraid of the redskins capturing the five whites."

"I think this has happened already," said Winnetou.

"Then we must follow right away to free them. If we were forced to return here, we would lose precious time. On the other hand, it is dangerous to head straight for the lake with the women and children."

"There is a way to avoid this danger and yet not lose precious time."

"I know. One of us two must ride ahead early to reconnoiter the area."

"You are right," the Apache agreed, nodding. "And it is Winnetou who shall do this. My brother Scharlih will remain here, because he can deal with these people better than Winnetou can. Winnetou will protect the white squaws and their children, because he has promised to do so, but he lacks the skill to entertain them with words. Winnetou will depart before the break of day. My brother may follow slowly with the others. He needs only to follow my tracks. Should I encounter danger, you will find my warning signs, or I shall return myself."

That's how it was left. When Old Shatterhand awoke the next morning, the Apache was already gone. After approximately an hour the group departed. The frontiersmen did not tell the immigrants that the day's ride might become dangerous. They did admonish them to maintain a deep silence.

Winnetou had taken care to leave an easily recognizable trail. They followed it slowly to allow him time for scouting. After about two hours they reached the lake area. There they saw Winnetou riding toward them.

"Shucks. That's not a good sign!" said Dick Stone.

"On the contrary," declared Hobble-Frank. "He will tell us how things stand. After that we will know what to do. We would be stuck in a quagmire of uncertainty if he did not return."

"No. If everything were all right, he would wait for us at the lake."

"Do not be so quarrelsome, old fellow! We shall soon know which of us is correct!"

The party stopped and Winnetou explained, "I am not returning because of danger; it is past. I am coming only because there is nothing more for me to do. My brothers may follow me!"

Some of them asked him questions, but he said, "Winnetou will speak at the place, but not before."

They rode on. The tracks of those who had passed here yesterday were still clearly visible in places. Only on rocky ground did it take eyes like the Apache's to make them out. They reached the canyon entrance leading to the lake. There Winnetou stopped and reported, "This short canyon must be crossed to reach Gloomy Water. Winnetou has investigated what took place here yesterday."

Pointing to the top of the mountain, he continued, "Up there seven Navajo scouts were camped. The eighth, also part of their group, is the single horseman whose tracks we saw yesterday. He was following the whites, and while they were at the lake he brought in his seven warriors to take them prisoner."

"And did this really happen?" asked Sam Hawkens.

"Yes. The whites were overpowered. But in the meantime, the thirty Nijora arrived and hid behind the trees. My brothers can still see their tracks very clearly. They waited until the Navajo left the lake with their white captives, then followed to attack them."

"Why didn't they do this right here? This spot is made for an attack."

"Winnetou has thought about this, but cannot explain it. We may discover the reason why the Nijora waited. The Navajo and their prisoners turned left over there into the woods to a place where there is water. There they camped, and there they were attacked by the Nijora."

"Then there was a battle and blood flowed?"

"My eyes have not seen a drop of blood, nor did a real fight take place. The Navajo were taken by surprise and were probably bound before they could think of resisting. The Nijora remained there with their red and their white prisoners and then rode off in the morning."

"Where to?" Sam Hawkens asked.

"That I do not know. I could not follow their tracks because I had to wait for you."

"We must follow them!" cried Sam. "It's not that I care about the Oil Prince and the two fellows with him. I don't care whether they get scalped. But the banker and his bookkeeper must be freed. One thing, though, I don't understand: there is enough water and food for the horses at the lake. Why didn't the redskins stay there? Why did they camp in the woods?"

Until now Old Shatterhand had not said anything, but had kept his attention trained on the shallow brook spilling from the canyon. Now he pointed to the water and answered, "It appears to me that the explanation is flowing here."

"How so?"

"Don't you smell anything? Look at the water! There are oil drops floating on it."

All of them looked at the brook, breathed in the air, and realized it smelled of petroleum.

"Did my brother see oil on the lake?" Old Shatterhand asked the Apache.

"Yes," nodded Winnetou.

"Then the Oil Prince succeeded in executing his plan. Let's ride! I must find out where we stand."

"But we lose time with that plan," Sam Hawkens interjected. "Don't we want to follow the Nijora?"

"They won't get away. They'll be slowed down by their prisoners."

Old Shatterhand directed his horse to the canyon, and the others followed him. As they drew closer, the odor of petroleum increased, until they saw the lake ahead of them. It drew their eyes to its dark, sinister surface. Only Mrs. Rosalie Ebersbach, upon seeing the lake, let out a shout of surprise, slid off her horse, rushed to the shore, stuck a finger into the water, looked at and smelled it, and then exclaimed, "Holy Saxony, this is a magnificent discovery! Mr. Hobble-Frank, smell my finger! Do you realize what this is?"

She pushed the finger under his nose. He pulled his head back and answered, "Leave my nose in peace! I do not need it to know where I am. If I want to smell the lake, I shall stick my nose into it. That will give me the pleasure of the petroleum firsthand."

"Then you admit that it is oil?"

"Of course! Or do you think I believe it is raspberry juice? You do not know my nose, in that case, which is often finer than I am."

"But such a lot, such a lot!" she shouted, still very disconcerted. "I have heard that in America petroleum flows from the ground, but I did not believe it. Now I have seen it with my very own eyes. I will stay here. No one gets me away from this spot! No ten oxen can pull me away from here, not even if you help it, Mr. Hobble-Frank!"

"What do you want here?"

"I will start a petroleum trade. A business bigger than any other. Here the oil does not cost even a penny, but in Saxony one has to pay almost twenty cents a quart. That is it; I shall settle here and trade in petroleum!"

She clapped her hands enthusiastically as a sign that her decision was irrevocable. But Frank answered laughingly, "All right! Settle down in this beautiful area! But the very first day Indians will come to tear your hairs out one by one. Do you think you can comfortably settle down here, as if you were at home in an armchair or on a bench by the stove? You want to trade? Who will buy from you here? What will you live on? And what will you smell like? After sitting here for just three days, your kind personality will acquire a scent you cannot wash off, even using the entire Atlantic Ocean."

This warning turned Mrs. Rosalie's face doubtful, and she turned to her husband for his opinion. By now the others had recovered from their surprise. They knelt at the shore, checked the oil, and exchanged opinions in loud exclamations. Winnetou and Old Shatterhand left the others so they could walk around the lake and investigate its shore more closely than the Apache had earlier been able to do by himself.

The petroleum lake made the strongest impression on the cantor. Long after the others had recovered from their surprise, he stood there staring at the water with wide-open eyes and mouth. When Hobble-Frank noticed, he stepped over to him, gave him a pat on the back, and said, "Looks like you have lost your wits. Really, you seem to have lost your mother tongue! If you cannot speak, at least try to sing a few notes, Mr. Cantor!"

That's when language returned to the musical gent. He took a deep breath and answered, "Cantor Emeritus, if you please, Mr. Frank! I feel wonderfully touched. It is an indescribable sight. I am overcome by a thought, a thought just as wonderful and indescribable as this lake is, I tell you."

"What thought, Mr. Cantor Emeritus? May I ask?"

"Yes, I shall tell you, provided you not give it away."

"Rest assured of my discretion. Is your thought such a great secret?"

"Indeed! If another composer should hear of it, he would at once use it for his own devices. You know about my heroic opera, right?"

"Yes—twelve acts," said Frank.

"So it is. And you know what I will present in this opera?"

"Certainly I do."

"What?"

"Music," Frank said simply.

"Of course! That is understood. I mean the music's contents, the scenery, the setting."

"I must admit to have occupied myself with the sciences; musical settings are yet to come. Go on, then! What do you intend to present?"

The cantor brought his mouth close to Frank's ear, held his hands to it like a megaphone, and whispered, "I shall present a petroleum lake like this one."

Frank backed off and asked, "On the stage?"

"Yes! You are surprised?" the emeritus asked triumphantly. "Even Akiba ben Joseph would be proved wrong by claiming that there is nothing new under the sun. There's never been a petroleum lake on the stage."

"You may be correct about that. But you are wrong about Akiba ben Joseph. You know who said that there is nothing new under the sun?"

"Akiba ben Joseph."

"Naw. If you think that, you believe that two and two equals five. Ben Franklin said there is nothing new under the sun after he invented the lightning rod, then found a barn that had had one for a long time. Akiba ben Joseph was another man altogether, a Persian general who defeated the Greek emperor Granikus at the naval battle of Gideon and Ajalon."

"But, my dear Mr. Frank, Gideon and Ajalon is from the Bible, the Book of Judges, where Joshua—"

"Be silent!" the insulted Frank interrupted him. "Where this happened is my business, not yours. Do not tell me about my specialty, and I will not tell you about yours! I shall let you have your own way. Whether you have a petroleum lake in your opera or whether you have your opera in a petroleum lake is all the same to me!"

He turned away in indignation and joined Droll, Sam Hawkens, Dick Stone, and Will Parker, who, like Winnetou and Old Shatterhand, also began searching. The famous hunter noticed this, approached them quickly, and requested, "Take care, sirs, that you don't ruin the tracks for me! What do you expect to find?"

"We want to find the place where the five whites were taken," Sam Hawkens answered.

"You will not find that. Those tracks have been trampled by our horses. They were close to the entrance. But we want to find something else, something much more important."

"What, sir?"

"The cave where the petroleum barrels were hidden. These fellows wiped those tracks out extremely well."

"Odd! A cave that could hold that many barrels must be large and have a wide entrance. The barrels were taken out, rolled to the water, and, once emptied, were rolled back into the cave. That must have left tracks! Let us help you, sir! That will speed things up."

"All right. But don't ruin anything for me."

The frontiersmen, usually so shrewd, explored the entire lake valley. An hour passed without their having accomplished their purpose. Winnetou, an unsurpassed tracker, finally gave up all hope and said to Old Shatterhand, "My brother shall try no longer. The cave can be discovered only by chance."

But Old Shatterhand was determined. He was angry. Who was to say that he could not find a place whose existence was clearly proven? He now considered it a point of honor and said, "What is 'by chance' supposed to mean? Why did we learn to reason?"

He closed his eyes to eliminate all distractions and stood immovable for a while. Winnetou, observing him and seeing a peculiar movement stir his face, asked, "My brother has found the way?"

"Yes," Old Shatterhand responded and, opening his eyes again, said, "at least, I hope so. The full barrels must have been heavy and there were many of them. Where heavy barrels are rolled back and forth, the grass will be so compressed that it would be impossible to straighten it up again by hand. It would remain flattened for several days. The work was performed only yesterday, however, or, at the outside, the day before yesterday. The grass should, therefore, still be flattened. Does my red brother agree?"

"Old Shatterhand is right," the Apache concurred.

"They must have rolled the barrels to the water where there is no grass between the shore and the rock cliffs where the cave is."

"Uff, uff!" Winnetou exclaimed, his bronze face aglow, maybe from joy, but maybe also from shame, because he had not hit on the idea himself.

"Furthermore," Old Shatterhand continued, "oil must certainly have been spilled as they emptied the barrels. The shoreline must also have been damaged. Both should be visible, if the shoreline is grassy. If, however, it consists of soil or rock, it could easily be covered up. If my red brother searches the entire shoreline, he will find grass everywhere except in two places. We will check them immediately."

One of these places was not far from the valley entrance. The two went there first, followed by the frontiersmen, who were eager to find out whether Old Shatterhand's shrewdness had once again hit the mark.

An approximately ten-foot-wide strip of land extended from the rocks to the water, grassless and covered with mud, sand, and pebbles.

Close to the shore, the hunter knelt down and smelled the ground.

"Found it!" he shouted. "It smells of oil here. Some has been spilled."

He scraped the ground with his hands; the layer underneath was soaked with oil. To hide it, soil and rocks had been thrown on top of it.

"The barrels were emptied here," he stated. "If the shoreline was damaged by it, it was easily and quickly repaired, since it is pebbles. Over there, where this bare strip meets the rock, the cave will be! Let's see!"

Old Shatterhand crossed the bare area that ended at the rock cliff in a great pile of boulders and rubble. The others followed him. He stopped in front of the pile of rocks, looked it over for a moment, and then declared, "Yes, this is the place. The cave is behind this pile of rocks."

Hobble-Frank, too, wanted to flaunt himself as an experienced frontiersman. He asked, "You see that with one look, Mr. Shatterhand?"

"Yes," the hunter answered.

"I should also be able to work that out. May I have a look?"

"Go ahead!"

Frank looked at the pile from all sides, but did not find anything.

"Well?" asked Old Shatterhand. "What do you see, my dear Frank?"

"A pile like any old pile. That is a rock pile consisting of a pile of rocks."

"Do you see only the rocks? Consider that even the smallest item may be of the utmost importance!"

"So, then, I am to look for a small object. I still do not find anything."

The others explored just as fruitlessly. Only the Apache sounded a quiet, satisfied "Uff." His eyes had seen a dead beetle laying halfway beneath a rock.

"Odd!" Old Shatterhand smiled. "Only Winnetou found what I was talking about. Frank, don't you see the dead black beetle with half its body peeking out from under this rock?"

"Yes, the beetle, I saw it. What about it? It is just a beetle, nothing else."

"Nothing else? It is certainly something, for it tells me we are in front of the cave."

"What? The beetle? What can it tell you? Even if it had spoken while it was alive, it is now dead."

"Yes, it is dead. What might it have died of?"

"How should I know? Maybe of liver shrinkage or eardrum infection."

"Pick it up and look at it!"

Frank had to lift the rock in order to remove the beetle.

"It was crushed by the rock," he stated.

"Correct! But how did this happen? Did the little beast perhaps push itself underneath the rock, so that it could be crushed by it?"

"Naw, the little bugger would not have had the strength. The rock was dropped on it—"

Frank stopped, thought for a moment, then hit his forehead with his hand and exclaimed, "I get it now! I would not think that a smart fellow like me could be so colossally stupid! The rocks were piled any which way and in the process the beetle lost its earthly life. This rock pile consisting of a pile of rocks was first removed and was later piled up again. Why and what for? It forms the locked gate to the cave and—"

Hobble-Frank fell silent and listened.

"What's the matter?" Old Shatterhand asked.

"I heard something," Frank answered.

"Where? From the cave?"

"Yes. A sound like a subterranean voice. It sounded so hollow. My soul, there cannot be a bear in there!"

"Hardly."

"But it almost sounded like it! Listen! I heard it again."

Old Shatterhand knelt down to listen. He quickly jumped up and shouted, "Good Lord, there are people in there! They are calling for help. Remove the rocks, quickly, quickly!"

Immediately ten or more arms were at the ready to follow his command.

After only a few moments a hole became visible.

"Is anybody in there?" Old Shatterhand asked in English.

"Yes," two voices answered in unison.

"Who are you?"

"My name is Duncan."

"And I am Baumgarten."

"Duncan and Baumgarten!" sounded from everyone's mouth. What a great surprise. They had thought the two captured by the Nijora after they'd been taken prisoner by the Navajo. The two men were only too happy to hear people and to see the light of day penetrating the ever-widening hole. Was it possible, though, that the Oil Prince, Buttler, and Poller might be standing out there? The banker therefore asked their rescuers to identify themselves. Always the helpful little fellow, Hobble-Frank answered, "We are your saviors in time of need: Old Shatterhand, Winnetou, Droll, Sam, Dick, and Will. And who I am you shall soon see. I am coming in!"

He forced himself through the hole, from which sounded a shout of joy. It did not take much longer to remove the entire pile. The entry was as high as a medium-sized man and was wide enough to roll an oil barrel in and out. The rescuers wanted to enter, but Frank called, "Stay there! We are coming out. But first I have to cut the poor devils' bonds."

When Duncan and Baumgarten emerged, they were as drawn and pale as corpses as a result their harrowing experience, and from the oil fumes in the cave. They shook hands with those they knew from Forner's rancho and looked respectfully at Winnetou and Old Shatterhand.

"You escaped alive, sirs," the great hunter said. "We searched long and in vain for this cave and had almost decided to leave the lake. Had we done so, slow death from hunger and thirst would have been your fate. You must certainly be thirsty and hungry?"

"Neither," Baumgarten answered. "Thank you, sir! We did not think of food and drink, only of death."

"Didn't you hope that your friends here would come after you?"

"How could we be? We thought they were still imprisoned in the pueblo. May I assure you of our gratitude—"

"Don't mention it!" Old Shatterhand interrupted him. "Save your thanks for later! First, we want to know a few things! I hope you aren't feeling too bad to answer some questions?"

"Oh, no. Now that we are in the open air again, all is well."

"Good! By the way, you are not entirely unknown to me. Winnetou and I have seen you before."

"Ah! When and where?" the banker asked.

"A day's ride from the pueblo, in the evening, when you were sitting by the creek. We sneaked up so close to you under the trees that we could follow your conversation."

"Lucky us! Then you heard the talk about the oil lake?"

"Yes."

"And that we were going to Gloomy Water?"

"Where there is no petroleum, yes, that we heard."

"You thought that there was none to be found? Why did you not make yourselves known? Why did you not warn us?"

"Why? Because it is doubtful that you would have believed us. You had been warned before by others without those warnings having any effect. Besides, we did not have time to deal right away with your noble Oil Prince. We first had to go to the pueblo to free the captives."

"You two did that all by yourselves?"

"As you can see, yes."

"But that is impossible!" Duncan cried, his eyes wide open in wonder. "Two men! No one else! How did you do it?"

"I'll tell you later, Mr. Duncan. Now I would like to hear from you how you got away from the pueblo and what has happened to this point. Sit down and tell us!"

The entire company sat down in the grass, and the banker reported his experiences of the past few days. It's easy to imagine what he said about Grinley, Buttler, and Poller. At that point, Old Shatterhand interrupted him, "Do not be angry only with them, but also at yourself, sir! I cannot understand the trust you extended to these fellows. And the—may I call it 'innocence'—with which you entered the trap set for you is totally incomprehensible to me!"

"I thought Grinley to be an honest person," Duncan defended himself dejectedly.

"Pshaw! A scoundrel's character peers from his eyes! And when talking of such a large amount of money, of an enterprise of such magnitude, one should make very different preparations."

"He didn't want to. Everything was to be secret."

"Aha! Is Mr. Baumgarten a petroleum expert?"

"No."

"What kind of people are you! You should at least have taken an expert with you!"

"Grinley claimed this was not necessary. Since the petroleum was floating openly on the water, it would take me just a look to prove that the deal would be truly splendid."

"And when you arrived and saw the beautiful oil floating so nicely on the surface, you were enchanted?"

"Of course! Won't you admit an exceptional well of oil here?"

Old Shatterhand gave him an almost perplexed look before answering, "It seems, even now, that you don't know where you are. You think this lake to be a natural oil catchment?"

"Indeed! Grinley told the truth about that. But once he had my draft, they knocked us down and locked us up to let us perish. He probably intends to sell the lake a second time."

"Did you not look around in the cave?"

"How could we? When we regained consciousness, it was dark around us. But it smelled so heavily from petroleum that the actual source is probably to be found in the cave."

"That is correct. Only it isn't just one source, but many, all made of wooden staves."

"Staves? I don't understand."

"Well, then, why don't you go back in and see what you find? Although I haven't been in the cave yet, I believe I know its content well. But let me ask you beforehand whether you looked closely at the petroleum once you arrived here?"

"I did indeed."

"And how did you find it?"

"Excellent!"

"Yes, I did, too," Old Shatterhand laughed. "It doesn't even have the properties of raw petroleum, which needs cracking for use as lamp oil, lubricating oil, and naphtha; it is already refined. Didn't you notice that?"

"No. You mean to say that it isn't raw petroleum? What is it, then?"

"That question you shall answer yourself once you have gone in the cave again. How long do you figure the oil has been on the lake?"

"Who knows? Probably for centuries, or even longer."

"I shall tell you: since the day before yesterday!"

"The d-d-day bef-fore y-yesterd-day?" the banker stuttered. "Once again, I don't follow you, sir."

"No? Well, then, I must be more straightforward. You have eyes. Do you see the large number of dead fish floating there? What do you suppose was the cause of their death?"

"The oil. No fish can live in petroleum."

"Very well! And for how long do you think these fish have been dead?"

"Two days, maybe, no longer, otherwise they would be further decayed."

"And where did they spend their time while alive? Did they maybe walk under the trees here? The fish have been dead for two days; therefore, they lived here in the lake until two days ago. They cannot live in petroleum. Since when, therefore, has the oil on the water?"

Only then did the banker see the light. He jumped from his sitting position, stared down at Old Shatterhand, looked over all the others, moved his lips as if wanting to speak, but was unable to utter a single word.

"Well, sir, don't you want to answer my question? Since yesterday there has been a type of oil here that was artificially cleansed at a refinery. How can this incomprehensible event be explained? You will find the answer in the cave there. Go on in, Mr. Duncan!"

"I shall, I shall!" the banker exclaimed. "I am beginning to think something that I don't dare follow to its logical conclusion. Come along, Mr. Baumgarten!"

He pulled the bookkeeper from his sitting position and disappeared with him into the cave. The others listened. A few shouts could be heard. Then they heard the banging and rolling of barrels. The banker came rushing out, shouting with great excitement, "What a fraud! What an audacious fraud! The oil was transported to this area to coax the money from me!"

"So it was, sir," confirmed Old Shatterhand. "As soon as I heard the fellows talk about the oil found here, I was convinced this was a fraud. Buttler and Poller were not sent ahead to scout the trail to assure your safety, but to empty the barrels and then to hide them again in the cave. The fraud was planned at great effort and over a long time, for it really requires some energy to transport nearly forty heavy barrels of oil one by one to this place."

"But it was very well paid for, *heeheeheehee*," Sam Hawkens laughed. "You want to scoop the oil back in or take only the empty barrels, Mr. Duncan?"

"Don't make fun of me now!" he cried. "My money, my good money. You must help me, Mr. Shatterhand!"

"We are not yet dealing with cash, but with the draft only," the hunter answered. "Do you think it can readily be cashed in San Francisco?"

"Certainly. If the fellows succeed in escaping from the Indians and in reaching Frisco. Didn't you remark earlier, during my story, that they were captured by the Nijora?"

"Yes. They were first attacked by the Navajo, then together with their attackers, captured by the Nijora."

"The reds probably robbed the whites. Don't you think so, sir?"

"Surely."

"Then they would also have taken the draft from the Oil Prince? In that case, it probably wouldn't be presented in Frisco."

"I don't think so. I think they won't even take the slip of paper from him. There are Indian tribes who have become civilized to the extent that they can read and even write. The local tribes, though, are not among them. In general, the Indian holds all writing to be magic with which he does not want to deal. It is, therefore, likely that the Nijora will let the Oil Prince keep the draft. Should he be able to escape, he will go to San Francisco to cash it."

"Then it would be best to stay ahead of him. What do you think, sir, if Mr. Baumgarten and I at once get under way to San Francisco to inform the bank? Should the scoundrel appear later, he would be arrested."

"I wouldn't advise it. You wouldn't get very far. And in any case is it unnecessary to make the long trip to San Francisco. It will be sufficient to go to Prescott, inform the local authorities, and have them inform the bank through the mails."

"Right, very right! Let's go to Prescott, then."

"Don't be in such a hurry, Mr. Duncan. From here to Prescott is at least ten days' ride, as the crow flies. It's approximately fifty geographic miles. Besides, do you know the way?"

"No. Maybe one of you could take us there for good pay."

"There is probably none among us who would be your guide. You must also consider that the route to Prescott leads through areas that, under current conditions, are not just unsafe, but might even be called dangerous. Even if your guide were capable, you could not be expected to reach your destination alive."

"Am I then to do nothing but lose my money?"

At that Schi-So, the young Navajo, stepped up to Old Shatterhand and said, "Sir, permit me to answer the question Mr. Duncan just asked."

"Go ahead!" the hunter nodded. Schi-So turned to the banker and said with assurance, "You do not need to worry, sir. You will have the draft returned, through me, that is. I am a Navajo. The Nijora are now our enemies. They have captured eight Navajo warriors whose brother I am. It is my duty to do everything I can to free these captives. Once I do that, the Oil Prince will fall into my hands. I will take the draft from him and return it to you."

The banker looked in surprise at the young Indian, who spoke with such assurance and certainty, and asked him, "You want to free the Navajo, my young man. Do you know how many Nijora there are?"

"There are only thirty."

"Only? And you, you alone, want to tackle them?"

"I am not afraid of them. And I will not be alone. I will seek out the warriors of my tribe. They must be close by. The presence of the eight Navajo scouts tells me that."

"But before you find them, much time will be lost and the Nijora will escape!"

"They will not escape," Old Shatterhand said. "We are still here. What does my brother Winnetou say about my decision?"

He had not yet explained his decision; however, the Apache guessed what he planned at once and declared, "It is good. We will follow the Nijora, free the Navajo, and take the bank draft from the Oil Prince."

"Thank you, thanks!" Duncan cried jubilantly. "If you say it will happen, then surely I will have the draft returned and my money saved. But when will we leave? Immediately, gentlemen?"

"As soon as possible," answered Old Shatterhand. "First we want to have another close look at the cave, and then Winnetou will take me to the place in the forest where the Nijora camped with their captives."

They inspected the cave. It had not been artificially created, but had been washed out by seepage penetrating the rock crevices from the forest above. From there the water had found its way to the lake. This was the origin of the strip of sand and pebbles leading from the cave to Gloomy Water. They found forty empty petroleum barrels, some hoes and an ax, nothing else. Two of the barrels were smashed to be taken along as fuel should they get into an area where wood was scarce.

Then Winnetou and Old Shatterhand left to look over the Nijora campsite. The others settled down on the grass to await their return. They randomly formed small groups. For all of them, the subject of conversation was the same: the experience of the past days and the fact that their rescue was due solely to Old Shatterhand and Winnetou. Praise for these two men came from all sides.

Hobble-Frank, especially, knew how to tell what had happened. Sitting with the German immigrants, he reported in his dramatic way several events that occurred when he was with Old Shatterhand and Winnetou. The cantor listened attentively and used a pause to remark, "That is what I need! Such deeds are what I want to introduce to the stage. They will create the effect I intend! But there is a difficulty you may be able to help me overcome, Mr. Hobble-Frank."

"What is it? I love problems. I cannot warm up to easy things. But things that are difficult, that require effort and exertion, have always been my favorite kind of activity. You may turn to me with the greatest assurance, Mr. Cantor Emeriticus! What kind of difficulty are you talking about?"

"Hmm! Have you perhaps heard Old Shatterhand or Winnetou sing?"

"Them, sing? Naw!"

"But these two men can sing? Do you not think so?"

"Can they sing? What a question! Are you not ashamed to think otherwise, much less say it? I tell you, both these men can do anything, even sing."

"Do not get so upset, Mr. Hobble-Frank! I did not mean anything. Do you think Old Shatterhand might sing once if I asked him?"

"Hmm!" mumbled Hobble-Frank with a doubtful face.

"And Winnetou?"

"There is no way he would. He is great in all things, which makes me certain he is also a most accomplished singer. But if I may speak openly: I cannot imagine him singing."

"Truly not?"

"No. Imagine this famous chief standing in a concert hall with legs apart and mouth agape singing the wonderful song 'Shiny moon, you drift so quietly past the neighbor's pear tree forth!' Can you picture him like this?"

"What you say is not without merit. But do the Indians not sing, too?"

"Of course. I have heard quite a few sing."

"How did it sound?" asked the musician. "What did they sing? Was it a solo or in harmony? It is very important to me to find out about this."

"This is another odd question! If someone sings, is it not always a solo? Or do you think a single man can sing in eight voices? And if twelve sing, it is in twelve voices; every schoolchild can see this. Do you want to know how it would sound?

"Well, not quite like the great composers, such as Mozart, Galvani, and Correggio," continued Frank. "It is not easy to describe. Think of a huge smithy's bellows with a polar bear, a turkey, and three young pigs in it! Once you start pulling and pushing the bellows, you will probably hear something that sounds very much like a true Indian operetta! Did you understand that?"

"Oh, yes. Your example is clear enough."

"Well, what do you want with Old Shatterhand and Winnetou? Why should they sing?"

"Because I want to know what kind of voices they have."

"Good voices, of course, very nice voices, even. To think differently would be an insult to them."

"I did not mean good or not good. I wanted to know whether they sing tenor, baritone, or bass."

"Is it really so important that you know?"

"Yes. They will be the heroes of my opera. Therefore, I need to know where their register lies."

"Nonsense!" snorted Frank. "Their register! The register always lies in the throat. Where else is it to lie? I have not seen a single person singing with the stomach or with the elbows. You should know that if you want to compose an opera in twelve acts. And I must reprimand you also for inquiring beforehand into that thing about the tenor and the bass. That is not necessary at all. Old Shatterhand and Winnetou are to appear and sing. Fine! Just wait and you will hear whether they sing tenor, bass, or baritone! It is not really necessary to worry about it beforehand."

"You are in error," protested the cantor emeritus. "I must compose everything to be sung beforehand! Therefore, I need to know whether to put the song in bass or tenor."

"Put it in the score. That is where it belongs! The conductor will later find it if he understands something of music, which I should hope is the case."

"But," the cantor declared eagerly, "it is before I work on the score that I need to know the register—"

"Oh, leave me be with your register!" Frank interrupted him, becoming angry. "I have told you that it is to be found in the throat! You possess some kind of human power of reason; it is not really necessary for me to tell you the same thing twice! Remember that true wisdom need never be repeated!"

The cantor opened his mouth to retort, but Hobble-Frank quickly continued, "Be quiet! Let me finish! The advice I am giving you is excellent and will save you lots of time, sorrow, and labor. Go ahead and compose your heroic opera. You need not bother about bass and tenor, for when the curtain rises and the actors begin to sing, it will turn out all by itself, whether they were born for tenor or counterbass! It can be only the singers' affair whether they want to sing high or low. I, at least, would not have it dictated to me to be a tenor if I had a bass viola in my throat. You can believe that. I am the right man to judge that, for when I worked as a forestry helper in Moritzburg, I was a member of the local singing club and even held the responsible position of locking up the scores and the conductor's baton after rehearsals, which surely must mean something!"

Hobble-Frank would have continued with his speech, but Winnetou and Old Shatterhand returned and the white hunter asked everyone to get ready to leave. He told the frontiersmen, "We followed the tracks of the Nijora for a distance. They seem to be heading for the Chelly River, which is fine by us, since it's on our way, anyway."

That very moment he was beside Mokaschi, lifted his hands, bound though they were, and with a blow of both fists smashed Mokaschi to the ground.

# 11

# IN THE HANDS OF THE NIJORA

HE GROUP STARTED TO MOVE. It made no sense to close off the entrance to the cave, so it was left open.

As they left the canyon behind, Winnetou, riding at the head, led them to the forest where the Nijora had spent the night. They came upon tracks leading higher and beyond the ridge into a long valley, which opened onto a flat, endlessly broad savannah. The Indians' tracks cut straight across these plains.

They did not need to worry about unexpectedly meeting enemies here, since they would notice any approach from afar. Hence the two leaders tolerated their companions' moving at their own pace and engaging in loud conversation.

The cantor had not been satisfied with the information he had requested from Hobble-Frank, so he rode to Frank's side and asked, "Mr. Hobble-Frank, would you do me a favor?"

"Why not? The question is only what kind?"

"I have noticed that you are on good terms with Old Shatterhand. He may grant you a wish he would probably refuse me. Would you ask him to sing a song, if only a single verse! Would you?"

"No, dear friend, I will not! I cannot ask that of him. He would tell me off, mind you! Try asking nicely yourself! I do not want to get burned. By the way, you always talk about the music for your opera, but not of the text. Do you have that already?

"No."

"Well, then, do not lose any more time. As soon as possible, contact a poet with the requisite talent!"

"I intend to write the text myself. By the by, I would look in vain for a poet here."

"A pity! You think there are none around?"

"Yes."

"Listen. You have succumbed to an optical illusion I must disabuse you of. There is a poet among us."

"Truly? Whom do you mean?"

That's when Hobble-Frank pointed his index finger at himself and, with tremendous emphasis, voiced the little word, "Me."

"Ah, you? You can write poetry?"

"And how!"

"Unbelievable!"

"Nonsense—unbelievable! I can do anything! Have you not figured that out by now! Give me a word and I will compose twenty verses on it! In at most two or three hours I will write you an opera text that will hold its own. If you doubt me, you have my permission to test me."

"To test you? You would take offense."

"Would not think of it! How can the lion or the eagle take offense from a sparrow! Go ahead, then, set me a task! Tell me what I am to write!"

"Well, then, let us give it a try! Imagine the first act! The curtain opens. A great jungle is seen. In its midst Winnetou lies on the ground crawling quietly to sneak up on an enemy. What would you have him sing while doing that?"

"Sing? Nothing, of course!"

"Nothing? Why? He must sing something. Once the curtain rises, the public wants to hear something!"

"Such a public would be rather stupid! Winnetou—creeping up on an enemy—and singing! Do you not see that the enemy would hear this and run away?"

"Yes, here in the Wild West. But we are talking about the stage. He must sing, he absolutely must sing!"

"Well, if he absolutely must, if it is positively required for him to raise his voice, let him do so."

"But using what words? The public does not know him. His singing must tell who he is."

"Fine! I am already done. He creeps along the ground and sings:

'I am magnificent Winnetou
was born in America's West,

have good eyes and what's more,
two sharp ears left and right,
and while I'm on my belly with grass so close
I smell every foe with my excellent nose.'"

Frank cast a triumphant look at the cantor as if expecting the greatest appreciation. But when the emeritus remained quiet, he asked, "Well, what do you say! Are you enthused or not?"

"I am not enthused," the cantor admitted.

"No? I certainly hope you sincerely appreciate what you just heard? Give me your opinion!"

"I would offend you!"

"Do not worry. There is no inferior who could offend me. I soar high-spiritedly above!"

"Fine. You made up a doggerel. That Winnetou was born in America, that he has eyes, that he smells everything with his nose, not with his ears, and that the latter are to be found on the left and right sides of his head, that he does not creep on his back, but on his belly—that is so obvious that one need not say it, much less sing it. Please, put together another verse!"

When Hobble-Frank heard this judgment, his eyes became large and then larger and his eyebrows rose. He cleared his throat as if not believing he had heard correctly and then broke out, "What are you saying? What do you mean? What kind of verse did I make? A doggerel, you think?"

"Yes. That is what such rhymes are called, Mr. Hobble-Frank," the cantor responded without embarrassment.

"Doggerel. Doggerel! I have never heard the like! I, the famous prairie hunter, frontiersman, and Hobble-Frank, have composed a doggerel! That does it! No one has ever told me that, no one! First you ask me to say who Winnetou is and what he intends to do, and when I do, you tell me it was unnecessary to do so! Let me tell you, then, that you are superfluous. Why are you no longer employed? Because you are superfluous, a retired and defunct emeriticus. I, however, am still employed as a prairie hunter, and from now on will dwell in the spheres of the happy spirits and Olympic fellowship you are unable to ascend to!"

On these last words, Frank gave his horse the spur and galloped off into the savannah.

"Stop, Frank, where are you going?" Aunt Droll called after him.

"Beyond your mental horizon!" Frank shouted back.

"Then hold on tightly and do not fall off the horizon over there!"

The angry little man would have ridden even farther had Old Shatterhand not called to him to return immediately. He obeyed and went to Droll's side.

"What happened?" Droll asked. "Why such an angry face? What made you mad again?"

"Be quiet! Do not be shocked by my indulgence and stubborn tolerance! I have been misjudged in a way that has caused all of my hair to stand on end."

"By whom?"

"By the former cantor and organ player."

"He offended you?"

"To the highest degree of Celsius!"

"How?"

"You do not need to know that, you old, big, nosy Aunt!"

Droll, laughing quietly, remained silent. He knew it would be best to leave Hobble-Frank be and that, as usual, his anger would blow away.

Soon the savannah lay behind them. The grass disappeared and with it all plant growth. The ground consisted mostly of hard rock on which no plant could grow. They were now on the plateau of the Colorado River, which dropped off in steep canyons to the Colorado itself and its tributaries.

Here very sharp eyes were required if the tracks of the Nijora were not to be lost.

At midday they stopped for the sake of the women and children and allowed two hours' rest. Toward evening the Apache stopped and dismounted, Old Shatterhand following suit.

"Why stop here?" Sam Hawkens asked. "Are we going to spend the night at this barren, unsuitable place?"

"No," responded the Apache. "Caution dictates that we wait here for darkness. We have only half an hour's ride to the Chelly, where there are woods. The Nijora are probably camped there. Since the area is flat, they would see our approach and hide. That is why we must wait for nightfall so they will not notice us."

"But then we cannot see them!"

"We shall find them, if not today, then certainly tomorrow."

The others dismounted and settled down. A few vultures, turning in tight circles, swooped above the northern horizon. Old Shatterhand drew everyone's attention to the birds and said, "Where there are vultures, there is either carrion or other food. They are not flying away, but are staying in the same spot. There must be something for them. I figure the Nijora have their camp there."

"My white brother has figured correctly," Winnetou agreed. "These birds show us the way. Today we shall creep up on their camp. But we need to be very cautious. These thirty Nijora have covered the distance from Gloomy Water to the Chelly without stopping. When scouts do this, they have returned to where they set out from. I assume, therefore, that at the Chelly all the Nijora warriors have assembled for their move against the Navajo."

"Then the captives must have been turned over to them," said Hawkens, "and it will now be twice as difficult and dangerous to free them."

"They will be freed," Winnetou stated in his certain way. "But we must not be careless."

A quarter of an hour before dusk, they rode on. Before the sky began to darken, they saw to the north something like a dark line at the horizon.

"That is the forest at the Chelly River," explained Old Shatterhand. "Wait here! I will ride ahead to search it with my telescope. A single horseman is not as easily visible as an entire party."

He trotted off, then halted. They saw him pointing his telescope toward the woods. He returned to tell them, "You need to know that the Chelly River is flowing in a deep valley whose steep slopes are wooded. But since the humidity generated by the river affects only the vegetation within the valley, the woods reach only to its top, but not onto the plateau beyond. I searched the narrow strip of vegetation at the top with my telescope. Were the Nijora camped up there I should have seen them. They must be down at the bottom, at the river. Let's ride!"

Dusk is brief at this latitude. Dark fell rapidly, and they could now be sure that they could not be seen from the edge of the river valley. Barely a quarter of an hour later they could tell from the sound of the hoofbeats that the ground had become grassy. They soon reached the edge of the forest, where they dismounted.

They couldn't light a fire because of the Indians' proximity. They had to camp in the dark and at a distance from the Nijora, in case one of the horses should neigh. Old Shatterhand and Winnetou were satisfied that the Nijora were not far from the area above which the vultures had circled. The two hunters left to spy on them. They entered the woods, and after more than half an hour Old Shatterhand returned.

"We're at just the right spot. The Apache's skill in getting us here is truly commendable. The woods bordering the top of the valley are barely thirty paces deep here. Then they descend into the valley. We climbed quite a way down, which wasn't easy in this darkness, but then saw fires. We counted three, but it is quite possible others are burning that we were unable to see. From the number of fires we conclude that all the Nijora warriors are down there. It will be difficult to free the captives."

"And where is Winnetou?" asked Dick Stone.

"I returned to report to you. Had we stayed away longer, you might have become concerned. The Apache went to look around more closely. I don't think we can expect him before an hour. The ground is very difficult to traverse, and to spy on a camp with that many fires requires great care and much time."

Almost two full hours passed before the Apache returned. He sat down with Old Shatterhand and said, "Winnetou has seen two more fires in addition to the three. That makes a total of five fires, by which we may assume that well over three hundred Nijora are camped."

"Just as we thought. Who is their leader? Could you make him out?"

"Yes. It is Mokaschi, whom you also know."

"The 'Bison,' a warrior I respect," said Old Shatterhand. "If we came in peacetime, he would surely receive us without enmity."

"Since we want to free his captives, we are his enemy and must hide from him and his people. My eyes have seen the captives."

"All of them?"

"Yes. Eight Navajo and three palefaces. They lie by a fire and are surrounded by a double ring of warriors."

"Too bad! That makes it well nigh impossible to get them out!"

"It is not just difficult, but truly impossible," agreed Winnetou. "We cannot attempt anything today."

"I agree with my red brother. It would be foolhardy to risk our lives if success is so extraordinarily improbable."

"Permit me to observe that I don't understand this decision," Sam Hawkens remarked. "Do you think we can achieve more tomorrow? The prospect will be no better than today."

"Oh, yes it will!" responded Old Shatterhand. "Don't you agree that the Nijora intend to move against the Navajo?"

"Of course!"

"Do you believe that they'll take eleven prisoners with them? Certainly not! They'll keep them here under guard. If we wait them out, we will have it much easier."

"That makes sense," admitted Hawkens. "Didn't think of that, if I'm not mistaken. If we only knew when they would ride!"

"I figure tomorrow."

"That'd be good. If they stay, though, we run the danger of being discovered."

"We must take that into account."

"Of course," agreed Hawkens. "But it's easier said than done. There's no water up here. The horses suffer little, since they find grass. But it's different for us! At Gloomy Water we couldn't drink because of the oil. Today there was none for the entire ride. If we can't drink tomorrow, either, I fear for the women and children, not to mention us."

"Oh, let's talk also about us," Hobble-Frank interjected. "For the moment, we are not yet immortal, but human beings whose mortality is a proven factotum. Every mortal being requires water, and I admit fully that I have such a thirst I would happily pay three marks for a few sips of water or a glass of lager."

At that the cantor could not restrain from assuring him of his concern, "I am extremely sorry, Mr. Hobble-Frank. Had I water, I would gladly share it with you." Being a very good natured fellow, he had felt repentant for some time for having angered Hobble-Frank earlier. The latter, who was no less good natured, felt the same way. He had admitted to himself that he had been too harsh with the cantor. Although he was in a conciliatory mood, however, he found it beneath his dignity to let on, and thus responded to the emeritus's assurance, "Are you so sure, then, that I would accept it from you?"

"I hope so!"

"Do not be too sure! As great as my thirst is, my character is even greater. And if you brought the entire world ocean here, I would not touch a drop. You know, by calling my rhymes doggerel, you have dogged your best friend. That is a very great loss for you. It is sad for you but true, and I cannot help you, as much as I would like to."

This so affected the cantor that he could not abandon the idea. Even after the meal, when everyone had settled down to sleep, he could not. He wondered how he could reconcile with Frank and hit upon an idea he thought to be excellent, although no man lacking experience of the Wild

West could have come up with a more imprudent one. Frank had complained about thirst and had been prepared to pay three marks for a few sips of water. If the cantor, then, were to quench Hobble-Frank's thirst? This surely would touch the angry Frank, the more so since getting water was not only difficult, but dangerous. Down in the valley the river flowed, and he, the cantor, had a leather drinking cup. But going down there had been prohibited. If he wanted to do it anyway, it had to be in secret. He raised himself up halfway and listened. All slept except Dick Stone, who had the watch. But at the moment Dick was with the horses.

The emeritus used his saddle as a pillow. Its saddlebag held the cup. He took it out and slowly crept away through the trees. He snaked through the forest until he thought he was safe from being heard or seen by Dick Stone. Then he stood up and groped on.

Soon the flat ground came to an end. The woods descended into the valley. Now the difficulties began. He turned around and began to crawl down, his feet cautiously testing the ground. It went extremely slowly. He was able to place a foot only after first testing the ground with the other. Sharp rocks and thorny vines injured his hands. He did not notice. The farther he got, the more his desire to complete his task grew. At times, he lost his hold and slid for some distance. This did not happen quietly, but because of his eagerness, the cantor did not hear the dislodged rocks and the cracking and breaking of twigs.

Then the emeritus saw the light of the campfires. Thinking he had won the game, he hurried on. He was unaware that he had been noticed. Five or six Indians who had heard the noise jumped up and scurried after him. Then they stopped and waited. He was breathing so heavily that they could hear him clearly.

"Uff!" whispered one of them. "This is not an animal, but a person!"

"Maybe several?" asked another.

"No, only one. Let us capture him alive!"

The cantor was very close to them. They bent down to see his outline clearly against the fires. Once they had him in sight, they convinced themselves that he was alone and reached out to grab him. He became very frightened, but not a sound escaped him. He did not understand the few words spoken to him, but he did understand the language of the knives whose points pressed against his chest. He did not even think of fighting back. When he was led away, he went without resistance.

The sensation his appearance generated in the camp can only be imagined. Yet this stir did not trigger any noise. A white had been seized. He could not be alone in the area; he had to have companions close by. Therefore, all noise had to be avoided.

Immediately, a circle of redskins formed around the cantor. None of them spoke a word. Mokaschi, the chief, approached the emeritus. First, though, Mokaschi did what every wary leader must do: he sent out several scouts to check the surrounding area. Then he asked the prisoner his name and what he wanted. The cantor, not understanding a word, said in German whatever he thought he should say.

The chief said, "He does not know our language and we do not understand his. Let us show him to the three captured palefaces. Maybe they know him."

The circle opened up and the emeritus was taken to the captives' campfire . When they saw him, Poller exclaimed in surprise, "The German cantor! The crazy guy! This brainless fellow must have escaped from the pueblo where he was imprisoned!"

He said this in a mix of English and Nijora; the cantor did not understand. He did realize, however, that the words referred to him. He recognized the erstwhile scout of the immigrants' party and said in German to Poller, who was fluent in the language, "Hello! There is our guide! Tied up, even! Mr. Poller, how did you get into this miserable position? I am glad to see you again."

"These scoundrels have taken us prisoner," the other answered.

The chief interrupted quickly and threateningly, "You are not to say anything I do not understand! Or do you want to have our knives in your bellies? Do you know this man?"

"Yes. He is from Germany."

"Germany? Is this where Old Shatterhand was born?"

"Yes."

"Then he is a famous hunter?"

"No. He does not know how to handle weapons. He wants to make music and sing. He is mad."

The chief looked at the cantor with much less enmity. There are many wild peoples who not only do not despise the insane, but who instead accord them shy reverence. They are of the opinion that a spirit, an unearthly being, has taken possession of the deranged person. The Indians, too, adhere to this belief and do not dare lay hands on such a one, even if he belongs to a hostile nation. Therefore, the chief inquired further, "Do you know for sure that this man is not in his right mind?"

"I am very sure," Poller answered, thinking that he might gain an advantage from what he replied. "For a long time, I rode with him and his companions."

"Who were they?"

"Germans, too, who came over here to buy land belonging to the red man."

"An evil spirit must have suggested this, for any land they buy will have been stolen from us, and it is not us, but the land thieves, who will get the money. Everybody coming to this country to buy land is our enemy. Does this man want land?"

"No. He wants to get to know the red men and western heroes, then return to his home country to sing songs about them."

"Then he is not dangerous to us. I will permit him to sing as much as he wants to. But where are his companions?"

"I don't know."

"Then ask him!" commanded the chief.

"I can't," replied Poller. "You have forbidden us to say anything you don't understand. He speaks only the language of his home country. I would have to talk with him in his language and would then get your knives in my belly, as you threatened earlier."

"You must talk with him in his language, of course. I will permit it."

"A wise decision, for you will learn very important things through me."

"Important things? How so?"

"The immigrants he is with are not alone. Famous hunters are with them, and are perhaps close by. They must be, since I do not understand how he, who does not know anything and is mad, could have come here all by himself."

"Uff! Famous hunters! Do you mean palefaces?"

"Yes! Sam Hawkens, Dick Stone, Will Parker, Aunt Droll, Hobble-Frank, and some others perhaps."

"Uff, uff, uff! These are all famous names. These men have never been our enemies, but now, because we are on the warpath, we must be ten times as cautious. I want to know where they are. But beware of telling me a lie! If an untruth crosses your lips, you are dead."

"Don't worry! You treated us as enemies, but I will prove to you that we are your friends after all. I can give you this proof right now by telling you that we sought to render these white warriors harmless to you."

"How could you do this?"

"We lured them into Ka Maku's pueblo."

"Uff! Ka Maku is our brother. They were with him?"

"Yes. He had taken them all captive, the white hunters and the immigrants with their women and children."

"This deranged man, too?"

"Yes."

"And now he is here! He could not have come this great distance all by himself. I must know who is with him and where they are now."

"Shall I ask him?"

"Yes. But beware of trying to deceive me! Whatever you tell me, I will not believe a word until I have convinced myself of its truthfulness."

Poller turned to the cantor and asked him to tell his story.

After some resistance, the emeritus talked openly without considering the treacherous Poller an enemy. With surprise, the immigrants' former guide learned about Old Shatterhand and Winnetou. The emeritus's account was interrupted once by the suspicious chief, who was intolerant of a long dialogue he did not understand. Poller, however, reassured him, "I am learning things of great importance to you. I must question this mad one, which requires much time, since his mind is not working well anymore. Let me speak. You will see that I am acting as your friend."

Finally the cantor finished his story. Poller now knew everything and turned to the chief, "I will tell you the most important thing first: out there on the plateau Winnetou and Old Shatterhand are camped!"

"Uff, uff! You are telling the truth?"

"It is as I say. They have come to attack you."

"Then they must die. Where do they come from? Where are they camped, and how many people are with them?"

Poller gave him the information. He did not even consider lying to the chief or misleading him. He counted on Mokaschi's gratitude. His most prominent warriors stood nearby and heard Poller's words. When the man finished his report, the chief pondered the situation quietly for a while, then said, turning to the Indians, "My brothers heard what the paleface has said. But the whites' tongues are forked, one point speaking deceit, the other, falsehood. We must convince ourselves that our ears have heard the truth or a lie. I shall select some scouts to climb to the plateau."

Going from campfire to campfire, he designated the warriors he thought capable of spying on men like Winnetou and Old Shatterhand. The warriors left, armed only with knives. The chief returned to Poller and told him, pointing at the cantor, "Since this paleface is possessed by a spirit demanding only to sing, we will do nothing bad to him. He may wander about unfettered and as he pleases. But should he think of escaping, he will get a bullet. Tell him!"

Poller obeyed. When the emeritus heard this, he said exultantly, "You see, I was right. There is no danger to a disciple of the arts. The Muses protect me. Remember, we composers are no ordinary human beings!"

Poller was annoyed at this display of self-confidence and responded, "No one's talking about your Muses. Yes, you are under a special protection, but a rather different one."

"So? Which one then?"

"The one of madness."

"Ma—d—ness," the great musician expanded. "May I ask what you mean by that?"

"Why not? No Indian will harm a crazy person. For this reason, you may walk around freely."

"Crazy? You do not mean to say that—" He stared straight at Poller.

"Yes. That's exactly what I'm saying," nodded the latter. "The redskins believe you to be mad!"

"But why?"

"Because they do not understand why a reasonable person would cross the ocean and come to the Wild West only to make music about the people he was going to meet there."

"To 'make' music? Please, Mr. Poller, you are employing a totally inappropriate term. Music is made by an organ grinder or at a beer garden; I am a composer. I shall compose a heroic opera in twelve acts, and you will have the honor of appearing in it."

"Thank you. But, please, leave me out of it! By the way, the Indians don't seem to be that far off the mark, for, to be honest, I must tell you that you do seem to be touched, and not just a little."

"What? You really mean this? Then I prefer to lie bound on the ground like you and to be considered a rational person. Tell the chief this!"

"No. Your being able to move about freely may be of great value to us. But don't abuse the privilege and don't entertain the idea of leaving! You would be killed on the spot."

"Pah! No one would do this. I am under the protection of the arts."

"Hell's bells, forget your art! Think what you want, but think also of those you can be useful to! Look how the chief is looking, how he is watching us! We should not talk too much together, or he will suspect something. Keep an eye on me! When I signal you, I will need to tell you something. Approach me as unobtrusively as possible. Don't look at me, but stand close by until you've heard what I want to convey to you. It will certainly be of great use to your friends. Will you do this?"

"Happy to, Mr. Poller. Although we disciples of the arts live on a higher sphere, I am not proud, and if, in ordinary life, I can be helpful to someone, I do not refuse to descend from my lofty heights."

Poller felt like replying rudely, but thought it better to keep his composure. "You have been disarmed. Try to obtain a knife secretly! I hope you are clever enough to accomplish that?"

"Clever? Well, sure! A composer without artfulness is unthinkable. But why do you want the knife?"

This question obviously provided no evidence of artfulness, and Poller would have loved to tell him. But he was afraid the statement would insult him and so he answered, "To free myself and your companions."

"But they have not been captured!"

"That's true. But we don't know what may yet happen. I told the chief the wrong direction, yet the smallest coincidence may put his scouts on the right track, in which case, your friends will be captured, at best. They can be saved only if you get me a knife. We can't talk any longer with each other now. The chief watches us all the time. Are you willing?"

"Yes. If I can be of use to my friends, I don't mind playing a thief by stealing a knife from the redskins."

Poller had been correct, for the chief now stood up, came over, and separated the two. His attention, however, was diverted by the return of his scouts.

They reported to him that everything was as Poller had said.

"He is lucky!" Mokaschi said. "Had he lied to me, he would have died this very night. He has betrayed the palefaces and thinks I will be merciful in exchange. In that he is mistaken, for a traitor is worse than the worst enemy."

After he had heard the scouts' observations, he decided, "We will surprise them in their sleep so as not to have to fight them. Two warriors of ours against one of theirs, but four each for Winnetou and Old Shatterhand. Also three for the guard on watch to quickly and safely overpower him. We take only knives and tomahawks and the necessary thongs to tie them up. Such great and famous warriors are not to be killed, for it is of great glory to us to bring them as captives to our people and an even greater disgrace for them to have fallen into our hands without a fight or having been wounded."

He selected the most reliable and strongest from among his people and took off with them. The moon stood above the valley. Its pale, feeble light did not penetrate the crowns of the trees among which the troop of hand-picked redskins now disappeared to cautiously and noiselessly climb the mountain slope.

Deepest quiet ruled. Schi-So had stood guard until only recently and had been spelled by Droll. To remain awake after the taxing day's ride, Droll quietly and slowly walked back and forth. Everyone else was fast asleep, except for Hobble-Frank. He had had an upsetting dream in which he had quarreled with the cantor and rushed at him to grab him. As a result, he had awakened. He saw the pale moon above him and was glad the quarrel was only a dream. He turned to the other side to look for the emeritus, who had lain down not far from him.

The cantor had disappeared. Might he have transferred his resting place somewhere else? That was unlikely. Frank sat up and looked around. He did not see him. He counted the sleeping bodies. One was missing, and that was the cantor. Hobble then woke his neighbor, Sam Hawkens, and whispered to him, "I am sorry to awaken you, Sam, but I do not see the cantor. Where might he be? Shall I awaken the others?"

Sam yawned a bit, then answered just as quietly, "Wake them? No, they all need their sleep. Let's do this by ourselves. The careless man probably walked off once again to torment himself with his famous opera in silence."

"In which direction?"

"I don't suppose he'll have ventured into the woods and down the mountain to where the redskins are camped."

"No, he surely waltzed out to the left there, onto the plains to sing of the moonlight. Let's go that way. Shall we take the rifles? We'll probably not need them."

"Need them or not, a frontiersman never leaves his rifle. I'll take my Liddy in any case."

Before they left, they checked with Droll, who had also noticed the emeritus's absence and said to them, "He must have run off before I took up watch. Hurry and find him, or something bad may easily happen!"

"We shall get him back, if I'm not mistaken," Sam nodded. "If we walk in a semicircle, we'll come across his tracks for sure. Although the moon isn't very bright, I think we'll find them. We'll fix the emeritus this time, once we have him!"

Hawkens and Frank walked west along the edge of the woods, then cut back eastward in an arc with the camp at its center. They were forced to stoop low in order to recognize any tracks. Since they did not see the man they were after, they assumed that he'd wandered far afield.

Droll followed them with his eyes until he could no longer make them out. Concerned as he was about the careless cantor, he involuntarily directed his attention toward the plateau. Thus he did not notice the three Indians who appeared at the forest's edge and approached him with inaudible steps. Suddenly he felt two hands on his throat. He wanted to shout, but produced only a brief rattle before a blow with the flat side of a tomahawk struck him unconscious.

Sam Hawkens and Hobble-Frank had covered maybe two-thirds of the distance without having found the cantor's tracks when they suddenly heard Winnetou's loud war cry. A moment later the voice of Old Shatterhand boomed, "Wake up, the enemy is—" The words ended in a rattle even they were able to hear.

"Lord God. We've been attacked! Back, quickly!" cried Frank and turned to rush back to the camp. Sam grabbed him and held him back.

"Are you mad!" Sam whispered to him. "Listen! It's all over. Nothing we can do."

A many-voiced Indian victory howl arose.

"Do you hear that?" whispered Sam. "Our friends have been taken by surprise. If we play it smart, we may be able to save them."

"Save them? I'll give my life to free them!"

"I hope that won't be necessary. Now I'm glad you woke me up to look for the cantor, or we would now be lying bound with our companions. But we are free, and knowing Old Sam Hawkens, he will not rest until they, too, are free again, if I'm not mistaken, *heeheeheehee!*"

Hobble-Frank was in great turmoil and leaned forward, listening for sounds from the camp as if ready to run off at any moment. Sam kept hold of him and drew him slowly and quietly away. At the woods, they sneaked through the shadows at its periphery. They soon had to stop, for a loud call sounded, "*Ustah arku etente*—Come up, men!"

"Stop, we must wait," whispered Hawkens. "The people the chief is calling will come up this slope. We'll encounter them if we continue. Listen!"

The leader's voice rang out into the valley. Soon they heard the rolling of rocks, the cracking and breaking of branches, and the sound of many footsteps. The captives, with their belongings and horses, were to be transported down to the valley, which required more Indians than were present.

A confusion of commands, questions, and responses arose. The two listeners heard hoofbeats and footsteps draw closer and saw a long line of people and horses pass by. The moon allowed them to clearly differentiate the individual figures. Their friends were all bound hand and foot in such a way as to allow them only short steps. No one was missing, except the cantor. Like Old Shatterhand, Winnetou walked between four burly Indians.

When the line had passed, Hobble-Frank shook his fist threateningly after them and grated, "If I could only do what I would like, I would tear those red rascals to pieces so they'd fly like sawdust through the air! But I will make them see yet what it means when Hobble-Frank's fury has become furiously angry! There they go and we stand here like two broken umbrellas as if our felt boots were rooted to our feet! Are we not going to follow them?"

"No."

"Why not?"

"This would take us out of our way because the prisoners will force them to take the more comfortable route. They will travel alongside the plateau and descend at a suitable place. We'll sneak down the slope here, where they climbed up."

"And after that?"

"Later we shall see what we can do."

"Fine, go ahead then, Sam! All my fingers itch to deal the red scoundrels a blow!"

Slowly and cautiously they descended straight into the valley. At the bottom, their stealthy approach was facilitated by the fires they could use as guides. They moved uphill from the Indian camp until they reached a spot where two high, flat, thin rocks came together to form a kind of tent-shaped roof below which two people could stand. In front of it stood some small firs whose low branches almost covered the entrance. They crawled in and lay down so their heads were below the branches and they could peer from between the trunks.

When they had made themselves as comfortable as possible, Hobble-Frank nudged his companion and whispered to him, "You see, my grand prescience was not mistaken! The prize jerk is sitting over there by the fire. He was really the one who gave us away, this twelve-act emeriticus!"

"Yes, you were right."

"But he does not seem to be a prisoner. Why have they not tied him up?"

"I don't understand that either."

"And there! Who is lying there?"

"Ah, the Oil Prince! And the two others must be Buttler and Poller."

They counted approximately 150 Indians. As many more had attacked the whites and brought them back. At the river the horses slept or grazed. Their bridles had been removed and the saddles had been placed together in several piles. The camped redskins jumped up and expectantly looked upslope, then exchanged joyous howls with the party approaching the camp.

First a small group of redskins appeared, then came Old Shatterhand and Winnetou with their eight guards. Neither man looked humbled. Their bearing was proud, and with free and open looks they examined the place and the people standing or sitting by the fires. The other frontiersmen did not appear dejected, either. The German immigrants looked around anxiously, and their women looked even gloomier. They were trying with some difficulty to control their children's crying. However, Mrs. Rosalie Ebersbach, although bound, looked around with a downright challenging air.

It finally dawned on the cantor that he had committed a huge error. As soon as he realized what had happened, he walked up to Old Shatterhand and said, "Mr. Hobble-Frank complained about thirst. That is why I climbed down secretly to give him the pleasure—"

"Oh, shut up!" the hunter roared at him and turned away.

Several Indians surrounded the emeritus, as he was not to speak with his traveling companions. The Nijora formed a circle around the prisoners. Their chief, with his most important warriors standing in the middle, now took charge and turned to Winnetou. "Winnetou, Chief of the Apache, has come to kill us. For this he must die at the stake."

"Pshaw!" The Apache responded with this word only, then he sat down. He was too proud to defend himself. The chief raised his eyebrows in anger and directed his speech at Old Shatterhand, "The white men will all have to die with the Apache. We are on the warpath, and they were out to kill us."

"Who said this?" Old Shatterhand asked.

"This man."

With that, Mokaschi pointed at the cantor.

"He speaks a language you do not understand. How could you talk with him?"

The chief pointed at Poller and answered, "Through him! He was the interpreter."

"This liar? You know who I am. Can anyone call Old Shatterhand an enemy of the red man?"

"No. But now fighting has broken out and every paleface is our enemy."

"Also without having harmed you?"

"Yes."

"Fine. Then we know where we stand! Look at these three palefaces you captured before you captured us. They are liars, cheats, thieves, and murderers. We came here only to apprehend them, not to bother you or even to fight you!"

"Uff! Has Old Shatterhand suddenly become so naïve that he makes such a demand of us? We are to hand these palefaces over to him? They are ours; they will adorn our victory march and then die at the stake. The same will happen to Old Shatterhand and all the others we took prisoner with him. What chief of the red men would release such captives! And if I were to do so, would Old Shatterhand ask even more of us?"

"What?"

"We have captured your horses and everything you had with you. It belongs to us now. The most precious thing we obtained, though, is Winnetou's silver rifle, your famous Bear Killer, and the magic rifle, with which you can shoot as many times as you want without having to reload. Would you not demand all that if we let you go?"

"Indeed."

"Then you see I was right. We shall not release the booty and we shall hold onto you, too, for your death at the stake will make our tribe more famous than any other tribe the red man has ever known. After our deaths, we shall be among the most blessed in the eternal hunting grounds, since your departed souls shall have to serve us there."

Despite his hands being bound, Old Shatterhand made an undeniably proud movement of his arm and asked, "Pshaw! Is that your final decision?"

"Yes."

"Then you have spoken and I too shall speak my last word: You cannot keep us, and you will also return what you have looted. Our souls will not serve yours for, if it pleases us, we will send you now, at this very moment, into the eternal hunting grounds, where you then must serve us, instead of us, you. I have spoken."

He started to turn away, but the chief stepped several paces closer and shouted at him, "You dare to speak like this to the greatest chief of the Nijora! Are you our prisoners, or are we yours? Count your people! They are bound and number only a few men. We are free, armed, and count over three times ten times ten brave warriors!"

"Pshaw! Old Shatterhand and Winnetou do not count our enemies, whether we are bound or not. It is all the same to us. We are not your enemies; we wanted to leave you peacefully. But you have forced hostility upon us. All right, we accept. The tomahawk of war now exists between you and me, between your people and mine. Not the number of heads or bound hands shall decide, but the superiority of the weapons and the power of the spirit!"

He gave Winnetou a quick look, and he nodded a consent that was barely noticeable to the others.

The two understood each other without words.

In his anger, the chief of the Nijora did not pay attention to this accord. He shouted, enraged, "Where are your weapons, and where is the spirit you are talking about? Your three famous rifles hang here from my shoulder—"

"The spirit I was talking about will take them from you!" Old Shatterhand interrupted him.

That very moment he was beside Mokaschi, lifted his hands, bound though they were, and with a blow of both fists smashed Mokaschi to the ground. Winnetou was beside him immediately. With his bound hands he tore the knife from the belt of the unconscious chief and cut the straps tying Old Shatterhand's hands, after which the white hunter cut his. Two more cuts and their feet were free, too. This happened so fast that the redskins had no time to prevent it. They were frozen in surprise at the two men's daring to act like this amidst three hundred of their enemies. It was critical to seize the moment. Old Shatterhand with his left hand lifted the chief from the ground, drew the knife, and shouted, "Get back! If a single Nijora dares to move so much as a foot toward us, my knife will instantly pierce the heart of your chief! And look at Winnetou, the chief of the Apache! Shall he send the bullets of my magic rifle into your heads?"

Winnetou had grabbed the Henry carbine and held it at the ready. The power of such personalities is extraordinary, the more so on wild, superstitious people. Nevertheless, it was a very dangerous moment. If only a single Nijora had had the courage to attack, Winnetou would have had to shoot him, and then the need to avenge the death would have resulted in the slaughter of the captives. As yet, however, all faces were perplexed and frozen, and no one risked a move. But this could have changed in a moment.

Help, the bold hunter had hardly thought possible, suddenly appeared, however. From under the trees a loud voice rang out, "Get back, you Nijora! Here stand more palefaces. If you do not yield at once, our bullets will eat you. As a warning, we shall clip the secondary chief's feather! After that we shall hit heads. Fire!"

The secondary chief so named stood close by Old Shatterhand. As a sign of his status, he wore an eagle feather in his hair. His scowling, pugnacious look said clearly that he was unwilling to be intimidated. But then a shot rang out from the dark of the woods where the two flat rocks formed the previously mentioned tentlike shelter, and the bullet tore the feather off the redskin's head. This immediately convinced him that the threat would be made good within the next second. So far it had cost him only his feather; the next time it might cost his life. He could not know that only two people were hiding in the dark. He imagined many more, since they had acted so boldly. He, therefore, uttered a cry of terror and leapt away from the fire.

The other Nijora followed his example, removing themselves just as quickly.

"Thank God!" whispered Old Shatterhand to the Apache. "We have won. That was Sam Hawkens we heard. Hobble-Frank will be with him. You aim at the chief while I cut the others' restraints and set them free."

He dropped the chief, on whom Winnetou now held the rifle, and proceeded to cut his companions' bindings. This happened so quickly that the Indians could not prevent it. The loot they had taken from the captives they had brought down to the valley and thrown in a heap beside the fire. The whites had only to bend down to retake possession of their knives and rifles. They stood free and armed after barely two minutes.

"To the horses, then follow me into the woods!" commanded Old Shatterhand.

He took his own and Winnetou's animals by the reins while the Apache lifted the chief of the Nijora onto his shoulders to disappear with him into the darkness from which they had heard Sam Hawkens's voice. The area around the campfires had emptied. The redskins stared at it, barely able to comprehend that they had been taken so quickly.

The two heroes were not aware of an occurrence whose consequences were to become very exasperating later. The cantor emeritus had suddenly remembered that he carried a penknife in his upper vest pocket, which had not been emptied. Desiring to make up for the mistake he had made, he went, while all eyes were on Old Shatterhand and Winnetou, to Poller, sat down beside him, and said, "I just remembered my penknife. You wanted to help my comrades. Here it is."

"Good, good!" answered Poller in delight. "Lie down beside me and cut the straps on my hands so no one sees you do it. Then give me the knife and I will do the rest myself."

"But you must also free my companions!"

"Of course, of course! Now hurry up, hurry up!"

The cantor transferred the knife just as Old Shatterhand cut the thongs with which the whites were tied. The emeritus said, "Look there! Now your help is no longer required. Old Shatterhand will cut you loose, too. You may return my knife."

"No!" responded Poller. "Return to your people. Quickly! We will follow right away!"

The cantor got up and was jumping for his horse when he saw the others responding to Old Shatterhand's command. Now only Buttler, Poller, and the Oil Prince were lying by the fire. The Indians had withdrawn into the dark toward the river to avoid making good targets; the whites had taken cover among the trees at the base of the valley slope. From this hiding place, Old Shatterhand shouted to the redskins, "The warriors of the Nijora shall remain very still! At the least sign of hostility, or if even one of you should dare to creep up on us, we will kill your chief. When daylight comes, we shall negotiate with you. We are friends of all red men and will harm Mokaschi only if we are forced to defend ourselves."

The Indians took this threat seriously. In reality, Old Shatterhand would never have committed a murder. And murder the white hunter considered it to take the life of a defenseless prisoner, the defenseless chief, who now was being bound hand and foot. Never did Old Shatterhand kill an enemy without dire need. Never did he treat even the keenest enemy cruelly or unjustly, but rather, magnanimously and considerately.

Sam Hawkens and Hobble-Frank had crept out from beneath the rocks. In his peculiar way, Sam said, "The red gentlemen didn't expect this!

Three hundred of these fellows let themselves be taken by two men. That's a first! But even had we not succeeded, the result would have been the same, if a bit later, for we lay here to free you, *heeheeheehee!*"

"Yes," Hobble-Frank chimed in, "we would have gotten you out, that was plumb-certain. Whether it was ten or three hundred Indians, it would have been one and the same to us."

"Yes, you are great heroes," Old Shatterhand told them, half angrily, half amused. "Where were you? You went on a stroll when you should have been sleeping?"

"We were not just walking around. I had had a dream that upset my poor soul. I woke up and noticed, to my surprise, that our Mr. Cantor was missing. That was when I woke my good friend Sam and we left to return the missing gent to our fold. In the meantime, the attack took place, which we could not do anything about. We hid and watched as you were led past us. Then we descended into the valley and hid to free you at the opportune moment. Lucky for us, Mr. Emeritus had taken himself away from camp, for had that not been the case, we would not have looked for him and would also have been taken captive."

"That is probably not the case," noted Old Shatterhand. "I am convinced the attack would not have taken place had this bad-luck fellow stayed put. Where is he now?"

"Here I am," answered the cantor from behind a tree.

"Fine! Now tell me how in all the world it could have occurred to you to leave our campsite?"

"I wanted to get water, Mr. Shatterhand."

"Water! Down here at the river?"

"Yes."

"How is this possible! Was your thirst so great that you could not control it until tomorrow morning?"

"I did not want the water for myself, but for my good friend Mr. Hobble-Frank. He complained of thirst, and I had fallen out with him in a quarrel. I wanted to make up for it by helping him quench his thirst."

"What nonsense! For a silly quarrel you endangered all our lives! Truly, if we were not in the middle of the wilderness, I would chase you away on the spot. Unfortunately, I cannot do this, since you would perish for sure."

"I? Do not even think this! Someone with as great an artistic mission as mine cannot perish."

"That's laughable! In the future I will have to tie you up in the evening so that you cannot commit any further stupidities. And at the first civilized place we reach, I shall leave you behind. Then for all I care, you can collect whatever material you need for your famous opera from whomever. Did you succeed in reaching the river?"

The emeritus answered in the negative and recounted his capture and what happened to him, including the detail of having lent Poller his knife.

"Drat!—Hol's der Kuckuck!" Old Shatterhand exclaimed. "This man is surely bad luck. We must quickly make sure that they don't get away. I will risk going back to the campsite to tie them up again. I just hope the Nijora will not get it into their heads to—"

He was interrupted by the loud shouting of the Nijora. When he looked toward the campfire, he saw its cause: Poller, Buttler, and the Oil Prince had suddenly risen from their places and were running to where the Indians' horses were tethered.

"They are escaping! They are escaping!" screamed Hobble-Frank. "Quickly, get on the horses and follow them, or—"

He did not complete the sentence as he moved to turn his words into action. But Old Shatterhand held him back and ordered, "Stay here! And be quiet! Listen!"

They saw and heard the Indians running for their horses. But the three escapees were faster. Despite their howls of fury, the frontiersmen could clearly hear hoofbeats as the escapees galloped away.

"There they go, kaput, lost to us for all eternity!" lamented Hobble-Frank. "I wanted to follow. Why was I not allowed to do so?"

"Because it would have been of no use and would have been very dangerous," answered Old Shatterhand.

"Dangerous? Do you think I am afraid of those three rascals? If so, you still do not know me!"

"I am thinking of the redskins. We have not yet negotiated with them and must, therefore, be very cautious. If we were to pursue the escapees now, we would probably fall into the hands of the Nijora. We must stay hidden here until we have made our arrangements with them."

"And the three scoundrels are to escape?"

"Do we have a chance of catching them at night? If there is a possibility, let's leave it to the redskins. Listen! They are following the escapees. We don't need to make the effort ourselves."

"Oh, no! A man does such things himself! These Indians will not try hard enough."

"Which would only confirm their intelligence. If we wait until daylight, we can see the tracks and follow them."

"But the lead these fellows will have then!"

"We will catch up with them. It will then be very easy to capture them, since they have nothing with which to defend themselves, only the pen-knife our clever Mr. Cantor has lent them, and that doesn't appear to be a dangerous weapon to me."

Everyone saw that Old Shatterhand was right, and even Hobble-Frank agreed. After a while, hoofbeats could again be heard, then it was quiet. The Indians had returned without success from the chase; had they apprehended the escapees, they would have been celebrating.

Because they assumed that the coming day would be strenuous, the party had to get to sleep again. Winnetou and Old Shatterhand remained awake to watch the Nijora, however, since an attempt to free their captive chief could not be written off. Things remained quiet for the rest of the night, though, and dawn saw the guards sitting by the river's edge, where they had stayed awake all night.

No one had yet spoken with Mokaschi, and he, too, had not opened his mouth. In fact, he had lain as still and unmoving as if Old Shatterhand's blow had killed him. But he was alive and looked around keenly. It was time to tell him what was expected of him. Old Shatterhand wanted to start the conversation. Winnetou guessed his intention, but asked him with a wink to remain silent. In a manner unlike his usual self, he spoke to Mokaschi himself, "The chief of the Nijora is a strong man, a great hunter, and a brave warrior. He has killed the strongest buffalo with a single arrow. That is why he is called Mokaschi. I would like to speak to him as his friend and brother and ask him to tell me who I am!"

This seemed a peculiar request, but Winnetou had a good reason for it. Mokaschi appeared to agree and answered willingly enough, "You are Winnetou, the chief of the Apache."

"You have spoken correctly. Why did you not name a particular tribe of the Apache?"

"Because all tribes of this great nation recognize you as their chief."

"It is so. Do you know to which nation the tribe of the Navajo belong?"

"They are Apache."

"And what are the Nijora, who call you their chief?"

"Apache also."

"Your mouth speaks the truth. But if the Nijora, like the Navajo, belong to the great nation of the Apache, then we are brothers. If a father has several children, they are to love each other and assist each other in all sorrows, difficulties, and dangers, but not to quarrel or even fight with each other. In the southeast live the Comanche, deadly enemies of the Apache. This is why our tribes should stand by each other against these thieves and murderers. But they do not. Instead, they fall out with each other, they wear each other down and are then too weak when the time comes to repel the enemy. When my soul contemplates this, my heart gets heavy with sorrow, like a rock that cannot be rolled from its place. The Nijora and the Navajo call me the Chief of All the Apache. Both are Apache. This is why you should lend your ears to the words of my mouth. You captured me and my white brothers, although we had done nothing to you, and although we are of one tribe and one nation. Can you name a reason I would have to account for your action?"

"Yes. Winnetou's heart beats more for the Navajo than for my tribe."

"Mokaschi errs. Winnetou is brother to you all!"

"But his soul belongs to the palefaces, who are our enemies."

"That, too, is in error. Winnetou loves all people equally, whether they are redskins or palefaces—provided they do good. And he is the enemy of all bad people without regard to whether they are Indians or whites. The tomahawk of war has been raised and now brother moves against brother to spill his blood. That is not good, but bad, and that is why Winnetou is not your friend today. But do not think that he is your enemy. He helps neither you nor the Navajo, but urges you to bury the tomahawk of war and let peace ensue."

"That is not possible. The tomahawk, once held in the hand of the warrior, cannot rest until it has tasted blood. We will not listen to any mouth speaking of peace."

"Mine included?"

"No."

"Then I see and hear that each of my words has been for naught. Yet Winnetou is not used to speaking in vain. He will keep silent. Fight your fight with the Navajo. But do not dare to drag Winnetou and his white brothers into it! You treated us as enemies. We shall forget that. Now you are in our hands. Your life is in our power. Shall the gossip in the tepees of your enemies be 'Old Shatterhand and Winnetou, these two men alone, took Mokaschi prisoner while he was surrounded by three hundred of his warriors?'"

Winnetou asked this question for good reason. It was by any measure a disgrace for Mokaschi to have been taken prisoner under such circumstances and despite his large band of warriors. He was to let his erstwhile prisoners leave unhindered and in return be set free himself. If he did not agree to this, Winnetou's promise to keep his disgrace quiet might yet make him compliant.

Mokaschi stared gloomily into space and did not respond. Winnetou continued, "Your warriors have heard that you will be killed at once if they attack us. Did you also hear those words when my brother Old Shatterhand shouted them?"

"I am a warrior and do not fear death. My people will avenge me!"

"You are mistaken. We are protected here by the rocks and trees. And we, too, have never been afraid of the number of our enemies."

"Then my people shall die with me! Like me, they carry the disgrace you have spoken of."

"If you are smart and they obey you, this disgrace will not remain fixed upon you. We promise you not to talk about it."

At that Mokaschi's eyes flashed happily and he cried, "You promise that?"

"Yes. And has Winnetou ever broken his word?"

"No. But tell me how you will conduct yourselves against us if we let you leave?"

"Just as you conduct yourselves toward us. If you follow us to fight us anew, we shall defend ourselves."

"Where will you go? To the Navajo, probably?"

"We must follow the three escaped prisoners. Where they ride, we shall, too. If they go to the Navajo, so shall we."

"And aid them against us?"

"We shall urge them to make peace, just as I did you. I have already told you that we are not your enemies, but neither are we theirs. Decide quickly! We must leave soon, or the three palefaces will gain too much of a lead."

Mokaschi closed his eyes to weigh all the options.

When he opened them he declared, "You shall have everything returned that belongs to you and then may ride away."

"Without your pursuing us?"

"We shall no longer think of you. In return, you shall not talk about how I fell into your hands here!"

"Agreed! Is my brother Mokaschi willing to smoke the pipe of peace with us?"

"Yes. Untie me!"

His bonds were removed and everyone sat down in the open, where yesterday the campfires had burned. Winnetou filled his peace pipe, lighted it, and had Mokaschi take the first draws. It was passed from hand to hand. Even the women and children had to at least take it into their mouths, because otherwise, as the Indians perceived it, the agreement would not include them, and they could have been ambushed or even killed without those who had smoked having the right to accuse the redskins of perfidy.

When the solemn ceremony was over, Mokaschi shook hands with everyone, even the children, then went to his people to tell them of the agreement.

"I would have liked to have freed the eight Navajo," Old Shatterhand said. "Now we must leave them in the hands of the Nijora!"

"My brother need not worry about them. Nothing will happen to them," Winnetou assured him. "The Nijora will be forced to release these prisoners also."

"Who will force them? The Navajo?"

"Yes."

"Then you think we will have to go straight to the Navajo?"

"We will, since the Oil Prince has fled to them."

"Hmm! There are reasons to believe this. The three fellows have no weapons; Therefore, they cannot kill any game. They have no means of lighting a fire. They will go hungry and will be forced to seek out people. But where they are headed, there are no other people but Navajo. Their reception by the Navajo is questionable, though."

"Well."

"That I doubt, yet it is possible," said Old Shatterhand. "If they say that they are enemies of the Nijora, having been their captives but escaped, they may be received passably well."

"It depends on what they say. But Nitsas-Ini, the great chief of the Navajo, is a wise man. He will examine every word he hears from them before he believes it. But look over there at the Nijora! They are mounting their horses."

It was as Winnetou said. Mokaschi had told his people that peace had been agreed upon. Although they were not in accord, they had to go along, since the calumet had been smoked over it. Because of their vexation about the inglorious outcome of the adventure to them, they preferred to see the last of this place. They mounted their horses and rode off. Several remained behind and returned a number of items the whites were still missing. Although a few minor items remained missing, they were of such small value that not a word was said about them. Why mention such trifles when they had just dealt with such larger matters, even life and death!

# 12

## THE CHIEF OF THE NAVAJO

IT WAS TWO DAYS LATER. Where the Chelly flows into the San Juan River, a major Indian camp was located on a spit of land between the two rivers. Close to six hundred Navajo were assembled there, not for hunting, but for a war campaign, for all faces were daubed with war paint.

The place was well suited for a camp. It formed a triangle protected on two sides by the rivers and could be attacked only from the third. There was enough grass; there were trees and bushes, too, and no shortage of water.

Long, thinly cut strips of meat were strung on long thongs stretched from tree to tree for drying to provision the war party. The redskins either lay idly in the grass or bathed in one of the rivers. Some trained their horses while others practiced the use of their weapons.

In the middle of the camp stood a hut made of brush. A long spear stuck into the ground beside the entrance was decorated with three eagle feathers. This was the dwelling of Nitsas-Ini, the greatest chief of the Navajo. He sat in front of the entrance.

The chief was not quite fifty years old. He was well and sturdily built and, most remarkable, his face was not painted. For this reason, his features were clearly distinguishable. His features could be described in one word: *noble*. His demeanor exhibited reason, calm, and a clarity not usually found in Indians. He in no way gave the impression of being a wild or half-wild human being. And if one were looking for the reason, one had only to glance at the person sitting by his side, talking with him—a squaw.

This was unheard of! A squaw in a war camp and by the side of the chief! As is known, even the most-beloved Indian woman does not dare sit

publicly by the side of her husband once he occupies a somewhat prominent position. And here it was a question of the highest chief of a tribe who
in this day was still able to gather five thousand warriors. This woman was
no Indian squaw, but, rather, a white. She was, in short, Schi-So's mother,
who had taken the chief of the Navajo as her husband and who had earned
a providential, instructive influence over him, as has been mentioned.

Leaning on the saddle of his horse, a tall, lean, but very strong-looking
man, whose full beard was a shiny ice-gray, stood in front of them. It was
easy to see that he was not used to keeping his hands folded in his lap and
that he probably had much wider experience and had gone through much
more than many others. The three conversed in German, even the chief,
whose wife was German.

"I, too, have started to worry now," the ice-gray man had just said.
"Our scouts have been gone long enough that we should have had some
news from them by now."

"Some misfortune must have befallen them," the woman nodded.

"I do not fear this," the chief threw in. "Khasti-tine is the tribe's best
scout and was given nine other experienced scouts to take along. I am thus
not concerned for them. They probably did not come across Nijora and
had to search extensively to find their tracks. They have had to split up to
cover different areas, after which it is not easy to find each other again.
That will cause some time to pass."

"Let us hope so! I shall leave, then. May I take some warriors with me?"

"As many as you like. He who wants to hunt the antelope must not
ride by himself, but must have enough people to drive them until they are
tired."

"Then farewell, Nitsas-Ini!"

"Farewell, Maitso!"

The ice-gray man mounted his horse. As he rode away, he asked several Indians he passed to join him. They were happy to comply, since
hunting antelope is a pleasure the Indians living in this area pursued with
a passion. The chief had called the ice-gray man Maitso. This word in the
Navajo language means "wolf." Thus the man's German name was Wolf.
Schi-So's young friend and comrade's name was Adolf Wolf, so this Maitso
was the uncle Adolf was to look up.

Together with his Indian companions the gray one rode far out onto
the plains, and they succeeded in killing several antelope. On the way
home, long before they reached the camp, they noticed three horsemen
slowly approaching from an easterly direction. Their three horses must

have covered a long and strenuous distance, since it was easy to see, even from afar, that they were very tired.

When they noticed the hunting party, the three riders brought their animals to a stop to confer. Then they came closer; it was Poller, Buttler, and the Oil Prince.

"Good evening, sir!" the Oil Prince greeted them as the sun set. "You are white and I presume that you will therefore give us truthful information. To which tribe do the redskins who are with you belong?"

"They are Navajo," answered Wolf, looking the strangers over with a not-quite-friendly countenance.

"Who leads them?"

"Nitsas-Ini, the supreme chief."

"And you? Who are you? You cannot possibly belong to the Navajo?"

"Pshaw! There can also be white Navajo. For many years, I have lived near them and count myself to be one of them."

"Where are they now?"

"Hmm? Why do you ask?"

"We want to see Nitsas-Ini to convey an important message."

"From whom?"

"From his scouts."

If he had thought to trick the old one, he was mistaken. The latter looked at him even more suspiciously than before and said, "Scouts? I would not know where we have scouts!"

"Don't play games with us! You can trust us," said Grinley. "We truly have an important message from them."

"Well, now, assuming that we really had sent out several scouts for whatever reason and that they would have something to report, do you think they would convey this through three palefaces? They would more likely send one of their own."

"Yes, if they could!"

"Why should they not be able to?"

"Because they have been captured."

"Captured! By Jove! By whom?"

"By the Nijora."

"Where?"

"Two days' ride from here, up the Chelly Valley."

"How many are there?"

"Eight men."

"Unfortunately incorrect, really not correct!"

"By the devil, don't be so distrustful!" exclaimed the Oil Prince. "I know there were ten originally. But two were killed by the Nijora."

"Killed? Listen, mister, be careful! None of you three has a face I could learn to like. If you tell us something, make sure that it's the truth, or something bad may befall you!"

"Keep shrugging your shoulders! You will be grateful yet to have met us. Do you perhaps know of Gloomy Water beyond the Chelly?"

"Yes."

"Well, not very far from there your Khasti-tine and another scout were shot by Mokaschi, and the other eight were captured at Gloomy Water and taken to the Chelly. There the three of us, who had also fallen into the hands of the Nijora, managed to escape."

Now that Wolf had heard the name Khasti-tine, he could no longer doubt their story. Alarmed, he exclaimed, "Khasti-tine shot dead? Can it be true? And the others captured? By God, that is bad for them!"

"Oh, there are others in the same bind!"

"Others? Who?"

"Winnetou, Old Shatterhand, Sam Hawkens, and some other frontiersmen; in addition, a whole company of German immigrants."

"Are you crazy?" Wolf spit out. "Old Shatterhand and Winnetou captured, too?"

At that point, Poller joined the conversation by saying, "More, many more. Schi-So, too. He's on his way from Germany with another young man by the name of Adolf Wolf."

"Good heavens! I am the uncle of this Adolf Wolf. He is coming to see me. And he has been captured? And Schi-So, too! Quickly, quickly, then, come along to the chief! You must tell us everything. Then we will take off at once to help them."

He spurred his horse and galloped toward the camp. The three whites followed him, all the while exchanging furtive but satisfied looks. The Indians brought up the rear.

Poller, Buttler, and the Oil Prince's interest lay only in obtaining weapons and munitions from the Navajo. They wanted to ride on as quickly as possible. They expected to be pursued and had not the least intention of being caught. Their main concern was to find the best opportunity for their escape. From the Navajo they could escape unhindered only if a meeting between the Navajo and Old Shatterhand and his people could be prevented.

These thoughts occupied the Oil Prince during the ride to the camp. At first nothing occurred to him, but at last he had a suitable idea: Old Shatterhand and Winnetou and their company were on the left side of the Chelly River. If they could induce the Navajo to keep to the right bank, a meeting could be delayed by several days. They could then expect an opportunity to ride away during the delay. To prevent Wolf from hearing him, the Oil Prince urged his two friends in a low voice, "Let me talk when they question us, and remember one thing absolutely: we were not on the left, but the right, bank of the river, and Old Shatterhand with his people are on the same side."

"Why?" inquired Buttler.

"I'll explain later. There's no time now."

He was right, for they were approaching the camp. The assembled Indians looked wonderingly at the three strange whites. They had not expected any palefaces in this remote area, particularly now that they were on the warpath. The three whites and Wolf rode to the chief's hut. The latter, as before, sat at the entrance. They dismounted and Wolf reported, "I met these men and brought them to you, since they have an important message for you."

Nitsas-Ini wrinkled his forehead and answered, "An experienced eye can tell from the tree's bark whether it is rotten inside. You did not have your eyes open."

The three whites had not made a good impression on him, either. They would have had to be deaf not to understand the meaning of his words. The Oil Prince approached him and said in a half-courteous, half-reproachful tone, "There are trees that are healthy inside, although their bark seems to be sick. May Big Thunder judge us only after he gets to know us!"

The wrinkles on the chief's forehead increased and his voice carried a sternly rejecting tone as he answered, "Several hundred summers have passed since the palefaces came to our land. We have had time enough to get to know them. There were few among them who could be called friends of the red men."

At these words, the three men became anxious. The Oil Prince, however, did not let on, but continued in a confident voice, "I have heard that Big Thunder is a just and wise leader. Will he treat with hostility warriors who have come to him to save him and his people?"

"You, save us?" asked the chief, all the while letting his eyes slide disparagingly over them. "What kind of danger is it that you want to keep us from?"

"The danger from the Nijora."

"Pshaw!" the chief exclaimed with a flip of his hand. "The Nijora are dwarves we will crush! And you want to help us, you, who do not have any weapons? Only a coward lets his rifle be taken."

Had the Oil Prince ignored this insult, he would certainly have been seen as a coward. He had to show that he was aware of it, which is why he feigned anger, "We have come with good intentions, and you repay us with insults? We shall leave you right away."

He went to his horse, seemingly to get into the saddle. The chief jumped up, stretched his hand out imperiously, and shouted, "Navajo warriors! Keep these palefaces right here!"

This order was obeyed immediately. When the three whites had been completely encircled by the redskins, Nitsas-Ini continued, "Do you think you can come to us and leave us like a prairie dog moving in and out of his burrow? You are in our hands and will not leave this place until I permit it! If you take a single step without my permission, my people's bullets will strike you."

His words sounded threatening and the situation looked no less menacing, for several rifles were aimed at the three. Still the Oil Prince did not let on that he was concerned. Taking his foot from the stirrup and his hand from the saddle horn, he stated quietly, "Just as you like! We realize that our fate is in your hands and must comply. But all your rifles shall not force us to convey to you the message we had intended for you."

"Pshaw! You wanted to tell me that the Nijora dogs have gone on the warpath and have set out against us from their tents. For that I do not need you, since I have sent out scouts, who will inform me in good time."

"There you are mistaken. Your scouts cannot bring you information because they have been captured by the Nijora!"

"That is a lie! I have selected the most experienced, the smartest, men, who would not think of letting themselves be caught!"

"And I tell you that the leader of your scouts, Khasti-tine, is dead!"

"Uff, uff, uff!"

"Together with another of your warriors he was shot by Mokaschi, the Nijora chief himself. The other eight were taken prisoner, just like us."

"Just like you? You had fallen into the hands of the Nijora?"

"Yes. We managed to escape, but without the weapons they had taken from us. That's why we arrived here weaponless. This is why you think us to be cowards. What do you call your scouts, who also had to surrender their weapons and were not clever enough nor had energy enough to manage to escape?"

"Uff, uff, uff!" the chief exclaimed. "My scouts captured and Khasti-tine killed! That calls for revenge! We must leave at once to attack these Nijora dogs. We—"

He was very excited, quite unlike his usual manner, and wanted to go into his hut to get his weapons. At that, Wolf, who had been silent, took his arm and said, "Hold it, wait! You need to find out where the Nijora are if you want to attack them. That is what these men will tell you. They also know even more important things."

"More important?" asked the chief, turning back again. "What can be more important than Khasti-tine's being dead and our scouts captured?"

"Schi-So has also been captured!"

"Sch—Schi—Schi—." Horror prevented him from saying his son's name completely. Then he stood stiffly, as if turned to stone, and only his rolling eyes showed that there was still life in him. His warriors pressed closer, yet none made a sound. The Oil Prince thought he might use the moment to his advantage. In a far-reaching voice he called, "Yes, it is so. Schi-So has also been captured. He is to die at the stake!"

"And my nephew Adolf, who came with him from Germany, is also in the hands of the Nijora," Wolf added. Composure returned to the chief, and he remembered that it was beneath his dignity to show how hard the news had hit him. He forced himself to the utmost quiet and asked, "Schi-So captured? You are sure of that?"

"Very sure," the Oil Prince assured him. "We not only lay bound close to him, but talked with him and his companions."

"Who was with him?"

"A young friend of his by the name of Wolf, several German families, emigrated from over there, and a whole band of famous frontiersmen whom you certainly won't believe allowed themselves to be captured that easily."

"Who are these men?"

"Old Shatterhand—"

"Uff, uff!"

"—and Winnetou."

"The great chief of the Apache? Uff, uff, uff!"

"Sam Hawkens, Dick Stone, Will Parker, Aunt Droll, and Hobble-Frank, surely all people you would not call cowards."

All around shouts of surprise, even of alarm, rang out. During all this the chief found time to gather his thoughts, for his self-control once more had waned. Pushing the people standing in his way aside, he hurried into his hut. From inside one could hear his voice and that of his white wife. Then both came out, and the woman turned to the three palefaces, "Is it possible? Is it true? My son, Schi-So, is in the hands of the enemy Nijora?"

"Yes," the Oil Prince answered.

"Then he must be rescued! Tell us what you know about it and where the enemy is! We must hurry. Come on then, talk, speak up!"

Being a woman, she could show her excitement more openly. She had taken hold of Grinley's arm and shook it as if this would speed up his delivery of the desired information. The Oil Prince, though, responded quietly, "Yes, we did come to tell you what happened. But the chief has received us like enemies, and if this is the case, we would much rather keep our knowledge to ourselves."

"Dog!" Big Thunder roared at him. "You do not want to talk? There are ways of opening your mouth!"

At that, the woman placed her hands on the shoulder and arm of her red husband and asked him, "Be kind to them! They wanted to give us information and do not deserve to be treated like enemies."

"Their faces are not the faces of good people. I do not trust them," he grumbled gloomily.

The woman, though, continued to beg, and Wolf added his pleas to hers, since he was afraid for his nephew. He, too, liked the three whites less the more he looked at them. But they had not done him ill, and most likely he could save his nephew by using their information. This was reason enough for him to intercede also. The chief, who would much rather have acted more severely, was unable to resist this twofold pressure and finally declared, "So be it, as you wish: the palefaces may say in peace what they have to say. Speak!"

This invitation was directed to the Oil Prince. If the chief thought that the latter would comply right away, he was mistaken, for Grinley answered, "Before I follow your command, I must know first whether you will fulfill our request."

"What are your wishes?"

"We need weapons. Will you give us some if we do you the service you are asking of us?"

"Yes."

"For each of us a rifle, a knife, powder, and lead, as well as a supply of meat, since we cannot be sure we'll come across game soon?"

"Meat, too, although it will not be necessary, for, as long as you are our guests, you will not go hungry."

"We believe that, but, unfortunately, we cannot stay long."

"When do you want to leave?"

"Right after we have told you what happened."

"That is impossible. You must stay with us until we have satisfied ourselves that what you have told us is true."

"Your mistrust is insulting. Either we are your friends or your enemies. If we are the former, we wouldn't think of lying to you, and if we are the latter, we would not have risked visiting your camp."

The chief wanted to resist further; however, his white squaw urged him, "Believe them, believe them, please; precious time will pass and we may be too late to save our son!"

Wolf joined in this request, so Big Thunder declared, "The wind wants to blow in its own direction, but if it is held up by high mountains, it must turn in a different one. The wind is my will and you are the mountains. It shall be as you wish."

"Then we may go as we please?" the Oil Prince asked.

"Yes."

"Then our agreement is made and we shall smoke the peace pipe over it."

At that the chief's face grew dark again and he shouted, "You do not believe me? Do you think me a liar?"

"No, but in times of war one cannot trust any promise given without the smoking of the calumet. You can confidently light the peace pipe, for we are dealing fairly. We are speaking the truth and can prove it to you if you demand it."

"Prove it? How?"

"When you have heard our report, you will be convinced that each word is the truth. Furthermore, I can show you a piece of paper whose content will confirm it."

"A piece of paper? I do not care to know of any paper, for it can contain more lies than a mouth can speak. I have also not learned to speak with the symbols on your papers."

"Mr. Wolf can surely read. He will tell you that we are open and honest. Are you going to smoke the peace pipe with us?"

"Yes," answered the chief, seeing his wife's pleading look.

"For you and all your people?"

"Yes, for me and for them."

"Then take your calumet. We must not lose any time."

Nitsas-Ini had the peace pipe hanging from his neck. He took it off, filled the beautifully cut head with tobacco, and lighted it. He took the prescribed six draws and passed it to the Oil Prince, who handed it to Buttler, after which it was Poller's turn. When this was done, the Oil Prince thought himself safe. He had not noticed that Wolf had not received the calumet and was therefore not bound by the agreement.

# 13

## THE FATAL DOCUMENT

VERYONE SAT ON THE GROUND, and Grinley began his account. He told of the petroleum find, but without naming the place or its sale to the banker and his trip into the mountains. He reported that he had met with Buttler, Poller, the immigrants, Winnetou, Old Shatterhand, and the other hunters at Forner's rancho. He claimed that they all fell into the hands of the Nijora and that during their capture they met the captured Navajo scouts and had learned from them that Khasti-tine had been shot by Mokaschi.

The Navajo listened silently up to this point, but neither the chief nor his squaw was as calm as they appeared. They knew their son was in danger. Wolf, too, remained glued to the narrator's story. The Oil Prince paused in his audacious lies, and the chief used the opportunity to ask, "How did you succeed in escaping?"

"With the aid of a small penknife the Nijora did not notice. Despite our hands being tied, one of my companions was able to reach into my pocket, pull the knife out, open it, and, once he had cut my ties, I could do the same for the others."

Big Thunder stared quietly ahead for a moment. Then he quickly raised his head and asked, "And then?"

"Then we jumped up and ran for the horses. We mounted the best three and got out of there."

"Were you pursued?"

"Yes, but they did not catch up with us."

"Why did you free only yourselves and not the others, too?"

294 The Oil Prince

This was a captious question, and the chief kept his eyes closely on the Oil Prince. The latter was aware that he really had to keep his wits about him and answered, "Because we had no time. One of the guards had seen us move and came to check. We didn't have time for anything but to flee at once."

He thought he had sufficiently explained the situation and did not expect a trap when the chief inquired further, "You still have the small knife?"

"Yes."

"You lay beside the other captives?"

"Yes."

The Oil Prince realized that a negative reply would have been better, but this was no longer possible, since he had earlier confirmed the opposite. He began to see the trap Big Thunder had set for him and at this moment the latter bellowed at him, his eyes flashing angrily, "Had I not smoked the peace pipe with you, I would now tie you up!"

"Why?" Grinley asked, frightened.

"Because you are either liars or cowardly scoundrels."

"We are neither!"

"Shut up! Either you are lying to us now or you acted like cowards with regard to your fellow captives!"

"We could not save them!"

"Oh, yes, you could have! You could have given the small knife to the person lying next to you."

"There was no time."

"Do not lie! If you are telling the truth, you could have outwitted the Nijora. You should have returned covertly to free the captives."

"That was impossible. If only 20 or 30 were following us, the other 270 remained behind."

He regretted these words the moment he uttered them. It was obvious immediately that he had made an unforgivable mistake, for the chief asked, "Then there were 300?"

"Yes."

"There are many more of us, but you said earlier that there are far more Nijora than there are of us. You speak with two tongues. Beware!"

"I had not counted your warriors properly," Grinley excused himself.

"Then open your eyes! If you were able see at night how many Nijora there were, you should be able by day to tell even more easily how many warriors are gathered here. On which bank did the Nijora camp?"

"The right."

"When did they intend to break camp?"

"After only a few days," the Oil Prince lied, "since they expected more warriors to arrive."

"Describe the place to us exactly!"

He did as well as he could, then added, "Now I have told you all I can and hope that you will keep your word. Give us the weapons and let us go!"

Big Thunder shook his head doubtfully and after a while declared, "I am Nitsas-Ini, the highest chief of he Navajo, and have never broken my word. But have you proved that your words are true?"

"I will present you with incontrovertible proof, which will eliminate your mistrust totally."

The Oil Prince either did not observe or did not care to take notice of the warning looks Buttler and Poller gave him. He reached into his pocket and pulled out the bank draft that he had received from the banker. He handed it to Wolf and said, "Here, take a look at this document! Under the conditions described, such a sum could be assigned only to an honest person. Don't you agree?"

Wolf examined the document carefully, then read it to the chief. Nitsas-Ini once more stared contemplatively at the ground, then said, "So your name is Grinley?"

"Yes."

"What are the names of your two companions?"

"This here is Buttler, the other, Poller."

Wolf started to hand the draft back to the Oil Prince, but the chief took it quickly from him, folded it up, stuck it into his belt, and continued as if he had not done anything odd, "Where is the oil well you sold?"

"At Gloomy Water."

"That is not true. There is not a drop of oil there."

"Oh, yes!"

"Do not contradict me! There is not a place as large as my hand upon which I have not set foot. There is no oil in this area. You are a cheat!"

"Hell's bells!" the Oil Prince started. "Am I to—"

"Be quiet!" the chief interrupted him. "I saw right away that you are not honest men and smoked the calumet only because I was urged to do so."

"Then you are looking for an excuse to break your word?"

Big Thunder made a proud, dismissive move with his hand and responded with a disdainful smile, "No man shall say of me that I do not keep my word because of people such as you."

"Then provide us with weapons, ammunition, and meat and let us leave! And return my paper! Why did you pocket it?"

"I shall not return it to you, but to the one it belongs to! You have cheated the paleface who bought the oil well, which does not contain oil. Maitso will know what he has to do."

He pulled the paper from his belt and gave it to Wolf with a pointed wink. The latter quickly pocketed it.

"Hold it!" Grinley cried with flashing eyes. "The paper is mine!"

"Certainly," Wolf nodded with an easy smile.

"Then return it!"

"No," declared Wolf with the same pleasant smile.

"Why not? Do you intend to steal it?"

"No, but be careful what you say!"

"Then return the document!"

"No."

"Why are you keeping this draft, which belongs to me?"

"Because many things in your story do not make sense to us, and because you want to leave here so quickly. People who have escaped from captivity and death require quiet and care. You can have both here. You, however, want to get away. Also, anyone else in your place would want to join our campaign against the Nijora to avenge himself. You do not want this, either. You want only to leave, to get away, and that very fast. That looks very much as if you were mighty scared of someone following you."

"What we think and what we want is no concern of yours," the Oil Prince claimed defiantly. "I have smoked the pipe of peace with the chief and, through him, with all his people. He must keep his promise that nothing is to be taken from me."

"Very true, sir! Big Thunder will certainly keep his word."

"Then return the paper!"

"Would not think of it! I do not want to steal it by any means, just to keep it safe."

"Damnation! For whom?"

"For those coming after you."

Before the Oil Prince could fly into an angry roar, Wolf cut him off with the peremptory command, "Keep your mouth shut! Do not think you are man enough to intimidate me! If you are honest people, you can easily stay with us. It will not put you in the poorhouse if you get the money four days later. I shall tell you what I think. When I first met you, I trusted you, despite your suspicious faces. But that is over, now that I have heard your peculiar story."

"It's true!"

"Nonsense! You say Old Shatterhand, Winnetou, Sam Hawkens, and others were captives together with you? And you alone escaped! Mr. Grinley, that is more than remarkable. You have named men who are much more likely than you to have gotten away. You may even have played them into the hands of the Nijora. Be that as it may, Winnetou and Old Shatterhand can take care of themselves. What matters most to me now is the draft. We shall free the captives, or they will free themselves and follow you. In either case, we shall meet them. Then we shall, of course, show the draft to this banker, Duncan. If your deal is on the up and up, you can confidently stay with us. If you are frauds, however, this time your effort was for naught."

At that the Oil Prince leapt from the ground and screamed, "This is how you intend to treat me? It is no business of yours why I must get on my way quickly! Do I need to tell you my reasons? I remind you that the peace pipe has been smoked and no one may keep me here!"

"No one will do so," answered Wolf quietly.

"And I must receive what I have been promised."

"Weapons, powder, lead, and meat? Yes, that you shall get."

"And the return of my document! It is my property!"

"Once that has been proven, it will, of course, be returned."

"No, now, at once! Nothing may be taken from us, since the chief has smoked the calumet for himself and his people."

"That is true. But, Mr. Grinley, do you consider me an Indian, a Navajo? Did I smoke the calumet with you?"

Grinley stared at him speechlessly.

"Yes," Wolf nodded with a superior smile. "You may usually be smart as a fox; today, though, you were not. It is clear to me that the document does not belong to you. You have heard what I have to say to you; we are finished."

Wolf stood up to leave. The Oil Prince grabbed him by the arm and screamed at him, "Return the document or I'll throttle you!"

With a vigorous jerk, Wolf shook him off, pulled his revolver, pointed it at him, and told him threateningly, "Dare come a single step closer and my bullet will enter your head! Stay with us or leave, it is the same to me.

But I shall not relinquish this document until I have freed my nephew and have spoken with the banker, Duncan. Enough now!"

He walked away. Grinding his teeth, the Oil Prince could not stop him. In a rage he turned to the chief. Smiling, Nitsas-Ini listened to Grinley, then answered with great calmness, "Maitso is a free man. He can do as he pleases. If you stay with us, you will get your draft back."

"But I must leave!"

"Then the banker can forward it to you. You did bring us information, and I shall give you weapons, ammunition, and meat in exchange, although your report is probably not true. Do not ask more from me! Do you want to stay with us?"

"No."

"You shall immediately receive what you stipulated, then you may ride away."

He left to issue the necessary orders, and the Navajo moved away from the three whites like doves leaving the field to crows. The cheats stood alone. No one was listening to them. They could, therefore, air their feelings about each other.

"Damn this fellow Wolf!" Grinley grated. "He really isn't returning the draft!"

"I thought something like this would happen when I realized you intended to show it to them," Buttler said. "You are such a blockhead!"

"Oh, shut up, you ass! There was no other way. They didn't believe me, so I had to prove I was telling the truth!"

"Prove it? With a document obtained by trickery? You see how well you succeeded in proving it!"

"I couldn't know that beforehand!"

"But I knew it! Now what will we get for all our work, for all the danger we have lived through? A single moment took everything away!"

It continued like this for quite a while. When Poller too started to reproach him, Grinley quieted him with a rude response and continued, "I may have been careless, but not everything is lost yet. We'll get the draft back."

"From this Wolf?" Buttler asked with a doubtful laugh.

"Yes."

"Do you by chance plan to stay here until the Nijora come, or maybe even Old Shatterhand and Winnetou?"

"No way! We will leave."

"But then we leave the bank draft behind!"

"No. We shall ride away, but not before I have forced Wolf to return it. Remember that we will get weapons."

"Then you want to fight him?"

"Yes, if he compels us to."

"And the redskins? What will they do?"

"They won't get involved. We've smoked the peace pipe with them; therefore, they cannot take sides against us and with him. He has stated that he is not one of them. It would be different if we left the camp and returned as enemies; the calumet would then lose its power. See there, they're bringing us meat! The rifles and knives will soon follow, and then I'll look up this Wolf. Are you with me?"

"Of course! That kind of money is worth the risk. Let's see how it goes. If it gets too dangerous, we'll avoid a fight. Look, several redskins are mounting up. Where do you think they're going?"

"I couldn't care less. It doesn't concern us."

In this assumption Grinley was mistaken. The chief approached them with a helper carrying long, thin strips of meat.

"When do the palefaces want to leave us?" he asked.

"As soon as we get what we were promised."

"And in which direction do you intend to lead your horses?"

"Down here into the bed of the San Juan River. We want to go down the Colorado."

"Then you may depart at once. Here is meat."

"And the other items?"

"You shall receive those, too. See the horsemen over there?"

"Yes."

"They have three rifles, three knives, powder, and lead for you. They will accompany you for an hour. Then they will hand over these items to you and return to us."

The three glanced at each other in disappointment. The chief noted this, but didn't let on that he had.

"Why can't we get the weapons and ammunition now?" Buttler asked.

An impish smile crossed Big Thunder's face, "I have learned that the palefaces are in the habit of extending an honorary escort to their guests. We shall do likewise."

"We gladly accept it, but we can carry the weapons ourselves."

"Why should you trouble yourselves with that? You do not need them yet. Look, my people are already leaving. Hurry and follow them, or they will reach the place for the transfer of the weapons before you. If you are not there, you will not get them."

Nitsas-Ini waved farewell and turned away, his face truly shining with mischievous joy. He had kept his promise and had thwarted the whites' plans at the same time.

"Smart fox, this redskin!" Grinley ground out. "He seems to have guessed our intentions."

"Yes," Buttler agreed. "Now we have no hope."

"Pshaw! I shan't give up hope for a long time yet."

"Really? You think there's still a possibility of accomplishing something?"

"Yes. We wait until the six Indians have left, then turn around."

"To tackle Wolf?"

"Yes."

"That wouldn't be smart," asserted Buttler, "since the redskins will help him. You said so yourself, that once we leave the camp, the calumet will lose its power."

"True, it would certainly be stupid to assault him openly."

"Covertly then?"

"Yes. They will soon set out to free the supposed captives. We know they'll move up the right bank. We'll follow them until we get to where they're going to camp for the night. We'll spy on them, and I'd be surprised if we didn't get a chance to grab this Wolf."

"You may be right. It gives me hope again!"

They mounted their horses and rode off without a farewell. It appeared that no one took any notice of them; but that only appeared to be the case. In reality, all eyes were secretly on them.

When the Oil Prince and his two partners disappeared behind the slope of the riverbank, Wolf reappeared. He had withdrawn behind a group of trees, but walked now toward the chief's hut, in front of which the chief had assembled his best warriors for a council. The white squaw was greatly agitated for her son and urged her husband to leave quickly to attack the Nijora. He consoled her with the thought that Schi-So was in the company of famous, brave, and experienced warriors.

"And," Wolf added to comfort her, "the prisoners will be killed only after the war has ended and after the war parties return to their camps. The war has not even begun, however, so you need not worry for your son, just as I am not concerned for my nephew yet. We need first to think about our next step. A spy must be sent down to the river."

"Why?" the chief asked.

"I do not want to kid myself, but I assume the three whites will turn around to follow us once they get the weapons. You do not give up a large sum like this without trying just about anything to get it back."

"You think they want to take the draft from you by force?" the chief asked.

"Yes."

"Let them come! They have left our camp. The smoke of the calumet will not protect them upon their return. They shall taste our bullets."

"If we see them, yes. They'll be careful not to be seen, but will follow us covertly to attack me once a suitable opportunity offers itself. For my own safety, I need to know if they turn around. For this reason, I am asking you to leave a scout on horseback down at the river."

"Why on horseback?"

"We shall be departing soon, and he couldn't easily catch up with us on foot."

The chief followed this advice, then the council of warriors, because of the changed circumstances, moved quickly to plan the campaign against the Nijora.

There was not much to be discussed. It could be assumed that Grinley, Buttler, and Poller had not told the truth about their experiences and intentions. That they had been prisoners had to be the truth, however, since they did not have any weapons. They could also assume that the Navajo scouts, together with Old Shatterhand and Winnetou and their companions, had fallen into the hands of the Nijora. In any case, the Nijora had also sent out scouts, who certainly had spied on the Navajo camp, since the Navajo scouts could not have prevented it. In any event, the Nijora had decided to attack, and this intention had probably been strengthened by the escape of the three palefaces. The Nijora could not know whether they would seek out the protection of the Navajo. The Nijora's only course of action was a quick attack. For this reason, they had surely already set out against the Navajo.

The Navajo, for their part, didn't want to wait for the Nijora attack, but wanted to prevent it. They were ready to depart as soon as the six riders returned from transferring the weapons and ammunition to Grinley, Buttler, and Poller. When they were asked how the latter had behaved, they stated that the three whites had quietly ridden on after receiving the weapons and ammunition, without letting any hint drop that they had any intention of turning around. Nevertheless, a scout was placed at the river and received instructions to let them pass, observe them for a while, then to bypass them in a wide arc and to follow his comrades.

The party moved upstream on the right bank of the river, since they believed the Oil Prince's statement that the Nijora were on this side. In reality, though, the Nijora were coming down the left bank. As the day came to a close, the Navajo scout caught up with them and reported that the three whites had indeed turned around and were following the Navajo's tracks. Because the Navajo knew this and could take precautions, the Oil Prince and his fellows were not to be feared.

They rode on through the evening and did not stop until midnight, since they mistakenly expected to encounter the Nijora at any moment. They set up camp but did not light any fires.

The moon stood above the trees, smiling at its image shining back from the narrow but rather deep waters of the river. Deep silence reigned. Once in a while a horse snorted or swished its tail at one of the biting flies common by the river. Nothing else could be heard. Suddenly from the other bank sounded a measure in six-eight time, "*Fitifitifiti, fititi, fititi, fititi, fititi, fitifitifiti, fititi, fititi, ti!*"

Startled, the Indians awoke from sleep and listened in surprise. Had that been a human voice? The chief moved silently to his wife's side and asked her, "Did you hear that? I have never heard anything like it. What could it have been?"

"Someone imitated a violin and trilled a waltz," she answered.

"Violin? Waltz? What is that?"

She was prevented from answering him, for a sound again came from across the stream, "*Clilililili, lilili, lilili, clilililili, lilili, lilili, lilili, lilili, li!*"

"That is different!" whispered the chief.

"That was the imitation of a clarinet."

"Clarinet? I do not know what that is. I think over there—"

"*Trarara—ta—ta—trarara ta—ta—ta—!*" he was interrupted from across the stream.

"That was the trumpet," explained the squaw, who also did not know what to think. Before the chief could respond, it resounded again, "*Tschingtschingtsching, tschingbumbum, tschingbumbum, tschingtschingtsching, tschingbumbum, tschingbumbum bum—!*"

"That was the big kettledrum together with the cymbals," said the squaw, whose surprise increased from minute to minute.

"Trumpet? Kettledrum? Cymbal?" asked Big Thunder. "These are all words I do not understand. Perhaps an evil spirit is over there?"

"No, it is no spirit, but a human being. He's imitating the sound of different musical instruments with his voice."

"But this is not the music of red men!"

"No, but that of palefaces."

"Is a paleface over there, then?"

"Possibly."

"But they are still captives! I shall send some scouts over there to spy on this strange being."

Shortly thereafter, downstream, where they would not be noticed by the strange musician, four Navajo swam across the river, climbed up the bank, and then sneaked upstream. A suppressed cry was heard soon afterward, and the four came swimming back holding a body halfway above the water's surface. After they stood the body on its feet, one of them reported to the chief, "It was this paleface. He was leaning against a tree and was drumming on his belly with his fingers."

Big Thunder stepped closer to the strange figure, looked it over, and asked, "What are you doing here in the middle of the night? Who are you, and whom are you with?"

He had spoken half in English, half in the Navajo dialect. Although the man he was questioning did not understand him, he guessed what Big Thunder wanted to know and answered in German, "Good evening, gentlemen! I am Mr. Cantor Emeritus Matthäus Aurelius Hampel from Klotzsche near Dresden. Why have you interfered with my studies? I am sopping wet!"

Only Nitsas-Ini of the redskins understood a word. But one can imagine the happy surprise of the white squaw upon hearing the familiar sounds of her mother tongue. She quickly approached the emeritus and cried, "You speak German? You are German, a cantor from the Dresden area? How in the world did you get to the Chelly River?"

Now the cantor was surprised. He backed up a few paces and clapped his hands, "An Indian woman, a real Indian woman speaking German!"

"You are mistaken. While I am now the wife of an Indian who is the chief of the Navajo, I am German by birth."

"And you have taken an Indian for a husband? What is the name of your consort?"

"Nitsas-Ini, Big Thunder."

"Big Thunder? But he is the one we want to see!"

"Really? You are saying 'we.' Then you must not be alone?"

"Beware! We are a whole company of excellent frontiersmen and heroes: Winnetou, Old Shatterhand, Sam—"

"May I ask where your companions are now?" she interrupted.

"They followed the Nijora."

"They do not plan to attack us?"

"Yes. If I am not mistaken, I overheard this."

"You have told me something very important. We are moving toward the Nijora to head off their attack."

"What? Toward them? I believe you to be on the wrong track, most honored Mrs. Chief."

"Why so?"

"Because they are over there on the left bank only."

"Not here on the right? You know this for sure? It is very important to us."

"I cannot be wrong. Once we disciples of the arts know something, we know it right and proper. We were only recently attacked by the Nijora."

"That I know. Three of you escaped."

"Three? You are probably thinking of Buttler, Poller, and the Oil Prince. Unfortunately, they got away from us."

"Got away from you? Escaped?"

"Yes. Did you come across these three?"

"I have even talked with them."

"Then I hope you watched out for yourself!"

"Why?"

"Because they are people one probably should not trust farther than one can see. They are rogues, yes, yes, very roguish. They even succeeded in deceiving me, me, a son of the Muses. That means something, a great deal! I shall tell you all about it, Mrs. Chief."

"Yes, later. For now, I would first like to know where Old Shatterhand and Winnetou are."

"That I do not know."

"No? But from your earlier statement, it seems apparent that you must know!"

"Perhaps so, but, on the one hand, I do not bother a great deal with such things, since my heroic opera claims my entire attention; on the other, my companions are not as communicative with me as they think they are. Their consideration is sweet, and for it I must really be grateful. They do not wish to burden me with these trivial events, since I have greater things to accomplish."

"When did they leave you?"

"Before noon today. They took only Schi-So along."

"Schi-So?" she asked in surprise. "What? My son?"

"Your son? What? He is your son?"

"Yes. You did not know?"

"No. I knew him only as Nitsas-Ini's son, but that he was also yours was unknown to me until this moment."

"But I told you that I am the chief's wife!"

"That is true. But, you know, it is not easy for a disciple of the arts to properly understand a family in which the mother is white, but the father is of a coppery color. I shall consider it very carefully, however, and then you will likely find a place in my opera, probably as a heroic red mother, for I already have a white one in the person of Mrs. Rosalie Ebersbach."

The woman thought the cantor somewhat odd. She shook her head, then inquired, "What were you really doing over there earlier?"

"I was composing the heroic entrance march for my opera."

"But so loud! This could easily have cost you your life! What if there had been enemies in the area?"

"Sam Hawkens told me that none were around. That is why he did not watch me and I was able to get away. I went far enough that they could not hear me and rehearsed the individual voices of the orchestra. Unfortunately, I was suddenly interrupted. I was grabbed from behind, I was throttled so that I could no longer compose, and I was dragged over here. I hope I will be returned there!"

"That will be done. How far is it to your camp?"

"A good quarter of an hour's walk, since I had to go that far in order not be heard."

"Then let it be. I shall speak with my husband now."

With Maitso's support, the chief's wife translated what she had learned from the cantor. They then decided that Wolf would swim across the river with two of the Navajo to find the whites' camp.

The three were good swimmers. They crossed easily and then turned left to slink along the stream toward the camp. Before progressing very far, they heard steps approaching. Quickly, they hid behind some bushes. Two people approached and spoke with each other in a subdued tone.

"He is truly a terrible person," one of them said. "He really does not have even the tiniest bit of sense. When we find him, we should put him on a leash. Do you not think so, Droll, old fellow?"

"Yes," Droll agreed. "The opera he wants to put together is crazy, and he himself is even loonier. He will get us into big trouble yet if we don't put him on a leash!"

Wolf heard that he was dealing with Germans and called from behind the bushes, "Good evening, gentlemen. I am very pleased to meet fellow countrymen here."

In an instant, he could see nothing of the two; he heard only their rifles being cocked. As soon as he spoke, the two disappeared as if swallowed up by the earth.

"Where did you go?" Wolf continued. "From your behavior and your quickness, I take you to be experienced frontiersmen. But your caution is not necessary now. You can hear that I, too, speak German."

"That does not mean a thing to us," came the answer from behind some bushes. "There are all kinds of rascals who at times also speak German."

"But I am a real German, that is, Adolf Wolf's uncle. I presume you know him."

"Shucks. It is good that we did not shoot at each other! Do not crawl around in the bushes; come on out, you old dog!"

"Pleased to do so. But another word first. There are two Navajo warriors with me. How will you act toward them?"

"As friendly as if they were my only two godchildren. The Navajo are our friends, are they not?"

"Fine, here we come!" Wolf and the two redskins stepped out of their hiding place. A few words were exchanged, then they quickly proceeded toward camp.

When they arrived, they found only the immigrants with their wives and children. The others had also gone in search of the cantor. "How do we get word to them now?" asked Frank. "We cannot fetch them, since we do not know their whereabouts."

"Fire a rifle," Wolf advised. "That will draw them in. Don't worry about shooting, since now that I know where your camp is, we don't have to be concerned about anything."

Frank discharged his rifle, which brought the searchers back one by one in no time. It can only be imagined how happy Adolf Wolf was when his uncle introduced himself. Everyone partook gladly in these moments of joy and good feeling.

There was not enough time for a longer talk between uncle and nephew. After he was introduced to all those present, Wolf turned to the banker and asked, "You were introduced to me as Mr. Duncan from Arkansas. Did you purchase an oil well?"

"Unfortunately, yes; however, it isn't an oil well."

"I thought so. You were defrauded."

"And how! The three fellows escaped us. I hope, though, that we will catch up with them."

"Hmm. Care to have a look at this?"

He pulled something from his pocket and handed it to Duncan.

After Duncan glanced at it, he exclaimed happily, "Sir, what is this I see! This is my signature, the draft I thought was in Grinley's hands!"

Wolf told him briefly how he happened to gain possession of the document. When he then reported that Grinley, Buttler, and Poller had turned back on their tracks, Sam Hawkens asked, "Are the fellows by chance following you, Mr. Wolf?"

"Yes. They will be holding out for an opportunity to attack me to take the draft away."

"I think you're right. But they won't succeed. They'll deliver themselves into our hands this way. Where are you camped?"

"A quarter of an hour downstream from here, on the other bank."

"Do you think they are close?"

"No. They were able to follow our tracks only during daylight. Then they had to wait. We have a good lead on them."

"Fine," said Sam. "Then we catch them tomorrow morning. Come to think of it, we have not spoken of Khasti-tine yet. Do you know where your scout is?"

"Yes. Ten scouts were sent out. Eight have been captured. The two others were killed by the Nijora."

"You think so?"

"We learned this from the Oil Prince."

"Ah! He is the one who told you? And you believed him?"

Wolf searched Sam's face, then said, "Why do you ask so oddly?"

"I'll tell you: the Nijora did not kill your scouts; the Oil Prince did."

"The—Oil Prince?" Wolf repeated in disbelief. "What makes you say that?"

"Listen, Mr. Wolf, Sam Hawkens isn't one to be fooled easily! I speak the truth!"

"Hell's bells! Tell me!"

"Khasti-tine had crept up so expertly on the chief of the Nijora that the chief would surely have fallen into his hands. But along came someone else, an outsider, and shot him and his companion dead from behind."

"And this murderer is—is—is supposed to be the Oil Prince? Prove it to me; prove it!"

"Nothing easier. There were witnesses, two men who attempted to prevent it, but they could not because it happened too fast. And these witnesses are sitting here among us. They are Mr. Duncan and Mr. Baumgarten. Ask them. Let them tell you!"

Wolf still did not want to believe it. But after the banker reported the event in detail, he could no longer doubt it and cried angrily, "Then it really was that scoundrel! And we had him and did not know anything, nothing, nothing at all!"

"Yes, you even armed them, *heeheeheehee!*" Sam laughed in his peculiar way. "You did very well, extremely well!"

"Be quiet, Mr. Hawkens! How could one imagine anything like this? Is such audacity possible? To murder our scouts, then dare come to us and ask for support! We shall pursue him and will not rest until we have caught him! The Oil Prince is the murderer of Khasti-tine! The chief needs to learn this at once!"

He quickly exchanged a few words with his two red companions, who quickly left the campfire.

To this point, the conversation had been in English. Because the German immigrants had not mastered it, however, Mrs. Rosalie asked Hobble-Frank to explain the gist. He did so in German. When Wolf heard him, he, too, switched from English to German and commented now and again on Frank's explanations. Frank closed his explanation with these words, "And now we shall demonstrate to these Nijora that they are nothing but Mustard Indians."

"Mustard Indians?" Wolf asked, surprised. "What is that? How so?"

"You do not know this expression?"

"No, Mr. Frank, I have never heard of a Mustard Indian."

"Really? I cannot believe it! There is not just one; there are two Mustard Indians. And you really do not know either one?"

"No."

"Neither the old nor the young one?"

"No. Where do these Mustard Indians live?"

"That does not really matter. It is sufficient to know that they visited with the 'Great White Father' in Washington. Maybe you know who is meant by this epithet?"

"Yes. This is what the Indians customarily call the President of the United States."

"Right! I see that you are not without talent for the sciences. Well, then, these two Indians were sent to Washington by their tribe to present some of the tribe's demands to the Great White Father. As envoys they had to be treated with honor and consideration, and so they were invited to dinner with the president. They sat next to each other at the end of the dinner table, which almost collapsed from the bottles, dishes, and plates on it. There were foods they had never seen in their life, much less eaten. Then there were the knives, forks, and spoons, and they had to observe how to behave themselves, that is, how to use the utensils. The older one cunningly whispered to the younger, 'My brother may watch with me which of the foods the whites take least of. Those will be the richest and tastiest foods. We will dig in.'

"So they watched and observed that the smallest quantity was taken of a brown food presented in small, fine glasses on little silver platters. In each little glass was a little spoon made of tortoise shell. The old one told the young one, 'In these glasses is the richest and tastiest food. A glass is within my young brother's reach. He may partake first of this food.'

"The young Indian pulled the glass closer, took a heaping spoon of it, and quickly took a second one. He looked around to see whether anyone had noticed him taking two spoonfuls at a time. No one had seen. He began to move the tasty food around with his tongue while the old one watched his face attentively. Little by little, his face turned yellow, red, blue, even green, but it remained stiff and unmoving, for an Indian may not lift his eyebrow even if he is in the worst pain. His look turned ever more rigid and his eyes started to tear until water ran down his cheeks profusely. Then the young Indian took a terrible, death-defying swallow and—down went the mustard. He felt better once again, except that the tears were still spilling from his eyes. The old Indian asked curiously, 'Why does my young red brother cry?'

"For nothing in the world would the latter have admitted that this tasty food had affected his nerves, even his life, and he therefore answered, 'I have just remembered that my father drowned in the Mississippi five years ago. That is why I cried.'

"With these words he pushed the glass toward the old one. The latter had observed how smart his younger brother had been by taking the tasty food and followed his example. He quickly put two heaping spoonfuls into his mouth and closed it rapidly. All at once, his lips parted, then opened and closed like those of a carp that cannot get any air, or as happens when one has put a terribly hot bite of something into his mouth but cannot get it out again. The skin on the old one's forehead stretched higher and higher, and suspicious sounds emanated from his throat. His face changed color like a chameleon. Sweat trickled from all his pores. His eyes turned red and filled with a lake of tears, which soon ran over and poured down his cheeks. The young one saw this and asked him compassionately, 'Why does my old red brother cry?'

"With the entire force of his will, the latter swallowed the mustard, took a deep, moaning breath, and answered, 'I cry because you did not drown, too, five years ago!'

"So, Mr. Wolf, that is the famous story of the two Mustard Indians you did not seem to know yet."

General laughter followed this story, a laughter in which Frank partook heartily and which probably could be heard a quarter of an hour distant in the night silence. Then a voice sounded from the water, "Why do the palefaces laugh so loud? Every tree can hide an enemy if one is not safely at home in his tent."

It was Nitsas-Ini with several of his best warriors and the cantor. He had also brought his white squaw along, since the messengers had reported the apparent presence of women. The group rose to welcome him. His probing looks covered the circle of people. When he saw Sam Hawkens, his serious face assumed a friendly mien and, shaking his hand, he said, "My white brother Sam is here. I know now that this loud merriment cannot mean harm, for Sam Hawkens will not let his voice be heard with an enemy nearby."

Stone, Parker, Droll, and Frank were also greeted by the chief, then the others were introduced. He did not take notice of the women. He put his hand on the head of young Wolf and said, "You are my son's friend and the nephew of my white brother. Be welcome in the tents of the Navajo! You shall be a child of our tribe."

Everyone sat down again and, after a short pause, as Indian courtesy demands in such situations, Nitsas-Ini turned to Sam Hawkens, "My white brother may tell me what happened!"

Hawkens covered everything, sparing few words. When he finished, Nitsas-Ini stared quietly ahead , then said, "Tomorrow punishment will be meted out. Are my white brothers prepared to help?"

"Yes," responded Sam, "your enemies are our enemies, and our friends shall also be yours!"

"They are. Let us smoke the calumet on it."

Nitsas-Ini took the peace pipe from its string, opened the tobacco pouch, and filled it. After he lighted it, he rose, blew the smoke toward the sky and the earth, then toward the four compass points, and said, "All palefaces assembled here are to be our brothers and sisters. I speak in the name of the entire tribe of the Navajo. Howgh!"

Then he gave the pipe to Sam Hawkens and sat down. Sam got up, also took six puffs, and affirmed, "I smoke and speak in the name of my white brothers and sisters present here. We want to be like sons and daughters of the Navajo and stand by your side in peace and war. I have spoken. Howgh!"

He returned the pipe to the chief, who finished smoking the tobacco. When the pipe was extinguished, he hung it back on its string and said, "Tomorrow the blood of the murderer and his two companions will be spilled."

"Do you think they are coming?" Sam asked.

"Yes."

"But they will not come riding in openly; they will sneak up. We shall have to be on the lookout."

"I shall send two men who have eyes like eagles to look for them. They will report their arrival."

"Hmm. Obviously, the three will follow your tracks and arrive where you are camped now. You need only to hide in the vicinity, and they will fall into your hands."

"My brother speaks correctly. But I shall nevertheless send the two scouts out, so that the murderers are really mine."

"But if you don't have time?"

"Who will prevent me?"

"The Nijora."

"They will not hinder me. On the contrary, they will help us seize the murderers. They are near our camp. They will find it abandoned and will follow us. The murderers, who are behind us, will be ahead of them. They will drive them toward us."

"Old Shatterhand seemed to be of a different opinion."

"Yet he left to warn us?"

"He may have pretended to do so in order not to have to tell the truth."

The chief thought about this for a few moments, then asked in a lowered voice, shrewdly guessing the truth, "Does he perhaps think that the Nijora have not gone directly to our camp?"

"Looks like it," Sam answered just as quietly.

"Then they can only have had intentions on someone else. On you, maybe?"

"Guess so. Old Shatterhand did not say. He may not have wanted to frighten the immigrants."

Just then they heard the shout of a guard. Shortly thereafter two men emerged from the semidarkness. One of them was Old Shatterhand, who approached quickly. Without commenting on the Navajo's presence, he cordially greeted the chief, Wolf, and the white squaw. The woman jumped up and, in a loud, jubilant voice, shouted, "Schi-So, my son!" She rushed toward the second of the arrivals and pulled him with tender insistence into the darkness of the woods. She did not want to welcome her son in front of so many eyes.

Everyone waited in silence. The chief sat, his face unmoving. After perhaps ten minutes they heard soft steps coming from the dark—the squaw hand in hand with her son. As she entered the circle, she let go of his hand and returned quietly to her place. Her heart had been satisfied, silently, without loud words and shouts, but with tenderness. Now Indian pride had to be allowed for.

Schi-So went to his father and offered him his hand. The chief saw his son approach, noted the youthful, vigorous figure, the fresh face, the intelligent features, and the adroit movements. For a moment, but only a single one, his eyes lit up in proud joy. Then his face was as unmoving as ever. He did not take the offered hand of his son, but pretended that he did not see him. Schi-So turned and sat down beside Adolf Wolf. He did not feel insulted. He knew how much his father loved him. He remembered the Indian code of behavior and regretted having offered his hand to his father. He had done so because of his stay in Europe. According to the customs of his people, it was not permitted. He was a boy and not allowed to do anything that was not absolutely required in the presence of men.

Old Shatterhand watched this scene with a contented smile. He knew that more love and happiness dwelt in this red family than in many a distinguished white one whose members expressed attention and tenderness in the presence of others but, when unobserved, related to one another like cats and dogs. He was asked by the chief, "My brother Old Shatterhand has been to our previous camp?"

"No, I did not get to it. But the Oil Prince with Buttler and Poller visited you?"

"Yes."

"You gave them weapons and ammunition?"

"Yes."

"They said how they rode with us, were captured with us by the Nijora, but had been lucky enough to escape?"

"So it is. From whom does my brother know all this?"

"I guessed," Old Shatterhand smiled. "Those murderers needed weapons. They had to get to you, because there was no one else to get any from. They had to lie to you and tell you they had been companions and protectors of Schi-So. Even had I had time, it would not have occurred to me to ride to your previous campsite, since by evening I had learned that you had left there."

"From whom?"

"From my eyes. I sat in a tall tree on this side of the river and saw you moving up the opposite bank."

"Perhaps the Nijora have also seen us?"

"No. I am sure of this, since I spied on them. Schi-So was with us. He held the horses while Winnetou and I crept up on the enemy. I then returned with Schi-So to report to my white brothers and to meet my red brothers. Winnetou stayed back to continue observing the enemy."

"Tomorrow they will be ours."

"That is my opinion, too, although I am aware that my brother's hope is based on a wrong assumption."

"Old Shatterhand errs. I think the same as he. The Nijora will find our camp abandoned and will follow our tracks."

"First of all, the Nijora will not ride to your campsite, but will attack us whites. They are not aware that the Navajo warriors have left their camp."

"Uff!"

"They think we are following them to seek out the Navajo and have established themselves at the Winter Water to encircle us there."

"At the Winter Water? This plan is very smartly devised, because there is no other place so well suited to an ambush as that. My brothers shall avoid it?"

"On the contrary; we shall go there."

"And fight?" asked the chieftain.

"Maybe no fight will be necessary. Quite possibly, the Nijora will have to surrender without a fight. Will the warriors of the Navajo help us?"

"We shall. But how are we to catch the Oil Prince and his two murderous companions?"

"You want to catch him?" asked Old Shatterhand, his face expressing some astonishment. "You want to go after them to avenge the death of the scouts?"

"I shall and must avenge them, but I do not need to follow them, since they are following us."

"Following you? Odd! They should be glad to have escaped you and us!"

At that Wolf, displaying a highly satisfied and self-confident expression, interrupted, "Yes, if they still had the signature, the draft!"

"Don't they have it anymore?"

"No, I took it from them and kept it."

"Ah! How did that happen?"

Wolf told them, then added, "We then had them watched and learned that they are following us. To be quite safe, we wanted to wait until tomorrow, then send out two scouts."

"Hmm! That course is not without danger, but cannot be avoided, for we must depart early tomorrow morning for the Winter Water," said Old Shatterhand. "But before we discuss plans, let me report first what we learned on our scouting trip!"

# 14

## OVERHEARD

THE WHITES HAD FREED THEMSELVES from captivity and the redskins had pulled out. The whites followed them. Winnetou and Old Shatterhand noticed that the Nijora, whose tracks they were following, were little by little slowing their pace. What reason could they have?

It was not the habit of the two famous men to ask the opinion of others on subjects they could explore themselves. Therefore, they had not told their companions, not even Sam Hawkens, anything about their observation. They began to watch more closely and soon understood the reason.

"What does my brother Scharlih think?" asked Winnetou.

"That they are in no hurry to get to the Navajo," answered Old Shatterhand.

"My brother thinks the same as I do. They appear to want to delay their attack on the Navajo. That leaves only one other possibility: they are out for us."

"I think so, too!"

"But why do they want to attack us? The smartest thing would be to quickly strike against the Navajo, who are poorly informed, since some of their scouts have been captured, others killed."

"My brother Winnetou should consider that we are hard behind them and have good horses. In a forced ride, at least a few of us could circle around them and warn the Navajo."

"Uff!" the Apache nodded. "That is probably it."

"Yes, most likely. They want to prevent this and protect their rear at the same time. We can certainly credit Mokaschi, their chief, with coming up with such an idea. That's why they are riding more slowly now—to keep us near so that, when a suitable area offers itself for an attack, they do not have to wait for us long. If this assumption is correct, we need only consider which place on our route would be the best suited to them."

"Uff!" Winnetou exclaimed after a moment. "There is one they can reach before this evening: the Winter Water."

"Yes, it is quite possible that they will wait for us there. Shall we run into their rifles and knives?"

"No. We must observe them. But which of the two of us?"

"Hmm. The Winter Water is a difficult place for a single scout."

"Then both of us will go!"

"Yes. Actually we need to have someone else along."

"Why?"

"If they want to attack us, the two of us are enough. But if this is not their intention, that is, if contrary to our expectations, they want to move against the Navajo right away, we must inform them. Neither one of us can be spared for that. Therefore, we must take a third person."

"Winnetou suggests Schi-So," said the Apache. "He is a good horseman and knows the area as no other. There remains the question of whether the others are to know the purpose of our ride?"

"Does my brother Winnetou think it better to keep it secret from them?"

"Yes. There are men among them who are no heroes, also squaws and children who should not be told of danger until absolutely necessary."

No sooner said than it was begun. Only a short while later, the three galloped off, with the others following at a slower pace.

The area was level. To the left was the flat, barren savannah, to the right, the river, whose banks were bordered by woods and bushes, then by a strip of grass. The ever-present clear air here afforded visibility into the distance, except when the river made a bend to the left. They were not concerned that they suddenly and unexpectedly might come face to face with the Nijora.

They continued until late afternoon, reading the tracks closely from time to time. It was obvious that they were nearing the Indians—now no more than an hour ahead of them.

From the south, to their left, a very straight, dark streak extended at a right angle toward the river. It consisted of individual, lean mesquite bushes. The bushes became ever more dense, greener and more succulent, while in the south they were more of a gray, hungry color. The closer the river, the denser and more luxuriant the brush became. Eventually, even trees grew, combining finally with the narrow growth along the river. This strip of green marked the bed of the Winter Water, if one could speak of a watercourse at all.

During the wet season, a span of a few days only, water collected in this riverbedlike depression, but, even then, running water was rarely generated. For a few weeks, the minimal amount of water gave the plant growth a fresh look, after which it reverted to its lean, poor, and sad appearance. The closer the plants stood to the water puddles, however, the longer their verdure lasted.

The three horsemen could almost be seen from this depression. They were thus forced to move to the protection of the brush bordering the watercourse. They dismounted and looked for a good hiding place for the horses, with which Schi-So was to remain. He also held the rifles for safekeeping, since they would only be a hindrance to scouts creeping through the brush or along the ground. Winnetou and Old Shatterhand slowly proceeded under the trees along the riverbank, their eyes keenly watching for any Nijora.

"Yes," said Winnetou. "These trees are tall enough."

"And are also densely foliated, so that if we climb into their crowns, we cannot be seen, even from afar."

They looked for two trees of the requisite height that also stood close enough together that two people sitting in their branches could hear each other without speaking too loudly. Both were excellent climbers and were up in a flash. The overlook afforded them from the treetops was more than sufficient: they could comfortably look over the trees standing along the Winter Water onto the plain extending beyond them. The plain was totally empty.

"They are at the Winter Water," Old Shatterhand said to Winnetou.

"Yes. They did not ride farther, otherwise, we would see them out there on the savannah," answered the Apache. "My brother may want to use his telescope."

Old Shatterhand pointed his telescope toward the brush surrounding the Winter Water and for some time sat motionlessly on his branch. When he lowered it, he quietly said to the Apache, "They are camped opposite the brush hard by the bank of the Winter Water. Many of them are returning with their horses from having watered them at the Chelly River."

"Then let us wait until dark to creep up on them and try to overhear them."

"Yes, but let's not wait up here. It's more comfortable on the ground."
Old Shatterhand was about to climb from the tree when he heard the
Apache's surprised "Uff!"

"Has my brother seen something?" he inquired.

"Yes, on the other bank. It is a long line of horsemen moving closely
along the tree line. My brother should wait for them to reappear. They
shall soon cross the small clearing opposite us."

The two peered across the river. First there appeared two Indian riders.
At a gallop they crossed the clearing and started to search the bushes there.
Then one of them returned and signaled. They had found nothing suspi-
cious.

"My brother may use his telescope; maybe he can recognize faces," offered Winnetou.

Old Shatterhand followed this suggestion and pointed his telescope at
the clearing. On the scout's signal, his people emerged from the bushes, a
long line of riders, all in war paint. Old Shatterhand was unable to recognize any faces. At the end of the procession, though, came two whom he
recognized immediately—Nitsas-Ini and his white squaw. When they had
all disappeared behind the bushes on the other side of the clearing, the
Apache said, "These must be Navajo warriors. Did you recognize anyone?"

"Yes. Nitsas-Ini and his squaw rode in the rear."

"They must have been camped at the mouth of the river. Why did they
leave that place?"

"And why do they stay on the right-hand side of the river?"

"Yes, that is odd. They must know that they need to look for the
Nijora on this side of the river, since their territory is here."

"I can think of only one reason: they have been misled by the Oil
Prince."

"Uff! He must have met up with them to have himself and his two
companions outfitted because they were unarmed. To gain time, they directed the Navajo to the wrong bank."

They climbed down from the trees. As soon as dusk fell the two men
set off on their dangerous mission. They could still see about six to eight
paces, but once they reached the vicinity of the Winter Water, it had become so dark that they could no longer rely solely on their eyes, but also
needed their sense of touch.

Here the Chelly flowed almost exactly from east to west. The Winter
Water entered it at a right angle, that is, from north to south. At this point,
the banks of both rivers were rather high and covered by woods and

bushes. From the top of the bank to the waters of the Chelly was easily sixty-five feet. Only a few puddles remained in the Winter Water, however, offering not the least hindrance to crossing. At the mouth of the Winter Water, the ground was very rocky and the banks dropped off so steeply that one could not descend on horseback. To cross one needed to go upstream to a spot where both banks inclined gently toward each other. This was the only place suited for a crossing, but it was just as well suited to an attack, since there was no other place to ford. Thus an enemy needed only to wait to close the trap at the right moment.

The Nijora had not camped at this ford. They had crossed, ridden downstream on the opposite—the left—bank, at the river's mouth, and had set up camp there. Anyone who wanted to water his horse had to return to this ford, ride down into the bed of the now-dry Winter Water, and follow it downstream to its mouth at the Chelly. It would have been easier had the Nijora camped at the mouth itself, but that was impossible without leaving tracks that could not be entirely covered.

Since the Nijora were camped on the other side, Winnetou and Old Shatterhand had to cross, too. When they reached the high bank of the Winter Water, they could see the campfires shining between large rocks on the opposite side.

"How careless!" Winnetou said.

"Yes," Old Shatterhand agreed. "They seem to feel very safe."

They walked on their side of the Winter Water until they reached the ford, walked down and up the other side. Then they sneaked downstream again on the left side of the Winter Water, more cautiously the closer they got to the camp. Moving quickly from tree to tree, from bush to bush, they avoided every spot illuminated by the light of the campfires.

When they were close enough to the enemy to make out the individual figures, Winnetou whispered, "My brother may stay here. I want to leave the woods and sneak around the camp to the open side, where the horses are, and find out whether they have posted guards."

He hurried away. In about a half hour, he returned and reported, "The horses are on the other side of the camp. They cannot give us away by their snorting. Guards have been posted facing the open plain."

"My red brother was able to see the camp from out there. Did he see Chief Mokaschi?"

"Yes. Together with three old warriors he sits by a big, broad rock."

"Can we get to it?"

"We can, if we are very careful. It is located on the riverbank, and thus there are no Nijora behind them. I shall move in first and my brother may follow me!"

They could not accomplish this in an upright position, since it would have been very dangerous. They lay down, therefore, and continued creeping on their bellies, all the while using, with great shrewdness and skill, every tree and bush, every plant and rock for cover. Their goal was the big rock Winnetou had spoken of. It was nearly twice the height of a man and was covered by moss. Leaves had been caught in the moss and had turned to soil over the years. This soil now lay in a rather thick layer on top of the rock and in its cracks and crevices. Several bushes had grown on the rock and their branches hung over the edge.

Between this rock and the steeply dropping riverbank there was only a narrow space, but it sufficed for the purpose the two spies had in mind. They reached the rock without being noticed and hid behind it. The space they lay in was only as wide as a man's body, so they were hard on the bank's edge. They carefully checked the ground and found to their relief that it was hard, firm rock, which would keep them from tumbling down the riverbank. They rose to climb the rock, from the top of which they would have the chief sitting just below them on the other side.

Old Shatterhand took a firm handhold, stepped on the Apache's back, and swung himself up onto the rock. This was a daring deed, since he could plummet as the result of the least misstep or bad handhold. Old Shatterhand had to make the climb very cautiously to avoid being seen by the Nijora on the other side. When he got to the top, he lay down flat and lowered his lasso to the Apache in order to pull him up. Behind them was the drop-off and in front of them the camp occupied by three hundred warriors. If they were seen, they would have no choice but to surrender.

Crouching close to the rock's surface, they warily pushed forward to the bushes, where they were able to overlook the entire camp. No less than eight fires were burning and the Nijora were preparing their evening meal. Below the two spies, and leaning against the rock, sat Mokaschi with the three older warriors, apart from the ordinary warriors. They spoke with each other in short sentences interspersed with pauses of varying lengths. As the two spies soon found out, these four redskins were not quite in agreement with each other. One of them, an old but still very vigorous man with gray hair, said, "Mokaschi will regret having acted as he has today. We should have attacked the Navajo dogs quickly and killed them."

"My venerable brother forgets that we have lost only a day. Once we have seized the palefaces tomorrow, we shall move against the Navajo immediately."

"We have lost more than a day because we rode more slowly to let the palefaces catch up with us."

"That does not matter. These Navajo jackals will not come out of their caves until we come to get them. They cannot leave their camp until the scouts they sent out have returned. My venerable brother must also consider this!"

"I have. But the year has a summer and a winter and all things on earth have two sides. So it is here, too. Mokaschi thinks the Navajo are waiting because they have sent out scouts. But I believe they will send out new scouts because the others failed to return. These new scouts will discover us and report to their chief. Instead of our attacking the Navajo, they will attack us!"

He spoke in a somewhat biting tone not customarily used with a chief. Mokaschi answered, "My brother carries the snow of age on his head. He has seen more winters than I and lived to experience more than I have. That is why he can speak boldly if he at times thinks differently from me. Yet he is not the leader; I am. Although I listen to the opinions of my experienced men, it is I alone who has to decide, and all others must comply!"

The old one lowered his head and said, "You are right. Your will shall be done!"

"Yes, it will be done, and you shall realize that I was correct. Or did you think we would succeed in surprising the Navajo?"

"Indeed I did."

"That is an error. They will post advance guards, as we do. Our scouts must find out where they are hiding first. These scouts can easily be spotted, captured, or even killed, just as we caught the Navajo scouts. And this is not even the most important consideration. There is something my venerable brother does not seem to have thought of: the Navajo know we are coming."

"Uff!" the old one cried. "Who has told them?"

"The three palefaces who escaped."

"Uff, uff! That is true! If they rode to the Navajo!"

"They certainly did so. Maybe they have already found them and told them about us. The Navajo will break camp right away to catch up with us and to attack unexpectedly. And that is what I am waiting for."

"Uff, uff! My brother Mokaschi knows the old rule of battle that he who arrives first wins more easily!"

"I do, and it is a very good axiom, but it does not fit all cases. The Navajo will come and attack us, but at a place that will prove fatal to them. We shall await them here at the Winter Water!"

"But that was not the original plan!" exclaimed the old warrior.

"No. I wanted to surprise the Navajo, which is no longer possible, since they have been warned by the three escaped palefaces. It was therefore necessary to change my plan. We shall hide here at the Winter Water. When the Navajo come, we will let them descend from the high banks into the deeper riverbed, where we will attack them. They will be stuck down there and will have difficulty defending themselves, squeezed as they will be in the narrow space between the rocks.

"There is but one snag: the palefaces behind us!" mused Mokaschi. "They are following us. If we let them pass, they will tell the enemy that we are waiting for him here. That must not happen. We shall, therefore, seize Winnetou and Old Shatterhand with all their people."

"Are they to be killed?"

"Yes, if they resist."

"And if they do not resist?"

"Then we shall capture them only and take them with us. We shall not bind them to the stake, since we have smoked the calumet with them, but we shall let them fight with our warriors for life or death."

"Uff, uff!" The old one's eyes literally shone with delight, and both the others broke out in enthusiastic "Uffs!"

Mokaschi, glad to have agreement, explained further, "The Winter Water, like no other place, is suited for ambushing an enemy and capturing or destroying him without much effort or even danger. Tomorrow my brothers shall see how easily we shall get the palefaces into our hands, although they are being led by the most famous men of the West."

At that the old one once more made a doubtful face and said, "It is precisely because these two men are leading the group that the task could easily fail."

"No. I know them to be very clever and know that they can divine the thoughts of other people, but they will not guess our plan. They think we are moving against the Navajo and will not bother with them."

"I hope very much that this will prove true. But I think about what we have experienced lately. No eagle has eyes as sharp, no mustang ears as acute, and no fox as much cunning as Old Shatterhand and Winnetou. We have already had them in our power. Were they not bound? Yet they freed themselves nevertheless!"

"This time we shall be smarter. We have done everything prudence demands. We have made camp up here instead of down at the water, where we would have left tracks. Tomorrow, when the palefaces come, they will not see a single track down there and will enter the riverbed unsuspectingly while we lie hidden here waiting for them. They will ride to the Chelly to water their horses and there we will attack them."

"You expect them not to ford quickly, but to stay for a while?"

"Yes. This is the only place for some distance where they can easily get to the water from the high banks. For this reason, they will not fail to quench their thirst and water the horses. They will have to take into consideration their squaws and children. As soon as they are down at the water, we will all rush down—"

"All of us? We must leave several warriors up here with the horses and the captives!"

"No," said Mokaschi. "We will tie the captives to trees and the animals we will stake down. We are not to be short a single man. When the whites become aware of our superior numbers, they will forget about resistance. My venerable brother should think about the situation they will find themselves in! To the left and the right they have the vertical rock walls of the riverbed, which cannot be climbed. In front of them, the waters of the Chelly, and behind them three hundred hostile warriors. They would be insane to entertain any thoughts of defending themselves."

"But if they attempt escape!"

"That is impossible! Where are they to turn?"

"To the Chelly."

"Into the water? They know as well as we do that a swimmer makes an easy target. And what shame it would be for them later to have stories told about how they risked the lives of the women and children whose safety had been entrusted to them!"

"Mokaschi is right. Your explanation has erased all my objections. Without fear we can expect the palefaces, for they will be forced to surrender without a fight. And then we shall deal with the Navajo dogs in a like manner!"

"Yes, we shall lure them down into the deep bed of the Winter Water and shall not let them come up again," said the chief.

"Uff! This will be satisfying, since we shall enjoy the cover of the rocks, trees, and bushes and can shoot them from up here one after another without fear of their bullets reaching us. Uff, uff, uff!"

The four Indians talked themselves into ever-greater enthusiasm. Had they but known who was lying above them, almost in reach of their hands, hearing all their words! Winnetou pushed back a bit and then tugged on Old Shatterhand's arm.

"Shall we leave?" the hunter asked softly.

"Yes. We have heard enough."

They crept to the back of the rock and Old Shatterhand lowered the Apache again by means of the rope. Old Shatterhand's descent was quite dangerous, but, with Winnetou's help, successful.

They had to leave as unobtrusively as they had come. Creeping low along the ground, they took exactly the same path by which they had arrived and made it without incident far enough from the camp to allow them to continue their retreat upright. They went to the ford and, after crossing it, were safe again.

There they stopped and Winnetou said, "They intend to set a trap for us and catch us."

"Yes, the trap is a good one!" agreed his companion. "And we shall enter it!"

"My brother and I think alike. We get the Navajo here, and they shall close the open trap behind us so that the Nijora will find themselves caught in it. Let us return to Schi-So! It is no longer necessary to send this young, brave warrior to the Navajo, for we shall visit them ourselves."

Old Shatterhand put his hand on Winnetou's arm and said, "Let my brother wait for a moment! If we are to enter the trap tomorrow without danger, we must reassure ourselves that our enemies' plan will be executed as intended."

"My brother thinks the Nijora may change their minds?"

"Yes. Then we might enter the noose without being able to release it."

"Right. I shall remain and watch the Nijora. My brother Old Shatterhand knows better how to interact with the white men and women. He may ride off and inform them."

"Very good! But it is not necessary that you stay at the Winter Water for the entire night. It will be sufficient if you go there again tomorrow morning."

"Yes. I need to get back to my horse, where I shall spend the night."

"Let's go!"

They turned in the direction they had come from. It was no longer necessary to hide, since darkness had fallen. They kept to the open savannah and thus made rapid progress. During their walk, they discussed the approach to their plan.

Despite the darkness, the two friends readily found their way. Soon they neared the riverbank and called Schi-So's name. He answered and with the horses came out from his hiding place.

"Good night!" Winnetou said and took his horse Iltschi by the reins and led it back into the brush.

"Good night!" responded Old Shatterhand, mounting Hatatitla.

The young Navajo might have been surprised by the brief farewell, but he did not dare remark on it or ask a question. He, too, mounted his horse and followed Old Shatterhand.

The white hunter put his horse into a trot and remained silent for a while. Then he asked the youngster kindly, "Schi-So probably does not know what is going on?"

"I will learn it," he answered.

"Yes, you shall. If I were to tell you everything now, I would need to tell it twice, which I like to avoid. But one thing I want to say: I have seen your parents."

"Really? Where?" asked Schi-So, happily surprised.

"On the opposite bank. They were riding with a large number of warriors looking for the Nijora."

"They will camp for the night! May I go see them?"

"You may. I need to get to them anyway, and you shall accompany me. I think you shall greet your father and mother this evening. We must hurry!"

A brief command urged Hatatitla to a gallop, with Schi-So following silently, delighted to be seeing his parents again soon.

They easily found the campsite their white companions had agreed on with Sam Hawkens. After a brief, fast ride, they arrived, where they found to their great surprise and delight the chief of the Navajo and his wife. What followed was the meeting already described.

They saw the cantor, hands tied behind his back, bound to a tree trunk.

# 15

# AT THE WINTER WATER

HE NECESSARY DISCUSSIONS with Nitsas-Ini were soon completed. He was in full agreement with the plan. Old Shatterhand then advised all those present to get some rest, since tomorrow would be a taxing day.

The chief of the Navajo and his white wife did not return to his camp, but stayed. In his place, he sent his warriors to transmit his commands to the camp. Guards were posted. The fires were extinguished and quiet settled in.

Dawn had barely broken when Old Shatterhand awakened the sleepers. While they were at the river to wash, they saw the Navajo warriors come riding upstream in a long line on the opposite bank. As the redskins arrived at a point just opposite their allies, they drove their horses into the water to cross. The whites readied themselves quickly for departure, and the entire party headed downstream. Old Shatterhand and Nitsas-Ini rode in the lead. Nitsas-Ini had given the messengers he had sent to his camp the previous night the names of two Indians he wanted to scout the whereabouts of the Oil Prince and his companions. They had orders to kill the three rather than to let them get away.

The scouts, two of the most cunning and craftiest of the tribe, first backtracked on the Navajo's tracks for a distance, then hid where they could spot the three whites from a good distance.

At perhaps half an hour's ride from the campsite, the brush on the bank jutted out into the open savannah to form a long, narrow point. The scouts proceeded to this point, led their horses into the bushes, tied them there, and hid close by. The plain stretched in front of them, and they thought they could spot the Oil Prince and his companions from a good distance. They felt that they had made a good choice and were sure to be successful.

Unfortunately, that was not to be the case!

As mentioned earlier, Grinley, Buttler, and Poller had not been able to pursue the Navajo to their camp because night had fallen and they were unable to follow the tracks in the dark. They finally dismounted for the night. With dawn barely broken, they had saddled up again and ridden on. In the open area they kept to the Navajo's tracks. Wherever there was brush, they detoured around it. Soon they saw the brushy point ahead of them.

Buttler stopped his horse and examined the point, his eyes pinched reflectively. Then he remarked, "There's a wide open plain on this side and, if I'm not mistaken, another one on the opposite side. That's the most advantageous place to spot us from afar. If, by chance, an ambush has been laid for us, then the fellows are right there and nowhere else. We'll be careful, therefore, not to approach this place from the outside or to ride around it. No, we'll sneak up on it, and woe to the dogs we discover there! Come!"

He dismounted and led his horse to the river. The others followed him. At the river, they went upstream below the trees, always under cover of the bushes, so that they could not be seen from the outlying brushy point. Obviously, it took them a long time to reach the point at the river from where the long, narrow point of brush extended into the open plain. There they tied up their horses and at a right angle turned from the water to search the brush for hidden Indians. They did this a few minutes before the two Navajo scouts approached from the other side.

The three whites proceeded with caution without discovering a single human being or any tracks. They had almost reached the outermost point and the Oil Prince was about to propose a return to the horses when Buttler pointed toward the plain and said, "Hello! There are two redskins coming! They're probably the ones we're looking for. Shall we let them pass?"

"Let them pass?" answered Poller. "They don't want to go past here. It looks like they're headed straight for us."

"Indeed. Come back! We must observe them."

They carefully crouched down. The two Navajo came up, pulled their horses into the brush, and took cover, too. The two parties were no more

than ten paces apart. The Indians, convinced they were alone, did not find
it necessary to speak quietly. Their words were thus clearly heard by the
whites.

"Will the palefaces come?" one of them asked.

"They will," said the other. "They want to get the paper."

"Then they shall meet death. If they follow our warriors, they will be
captured and tortured, and if they become suspicious and do not, we will
shoot them."

"Do you hear that?" whispered the Oil Prince to Buttler and Poller.
"We don't need to hear any more."

"Right! We know enough," Buttler agreed. "What now?"

"To hell with them!"

"Well, I'm in. Aim your rifle at the one on the left! Poller can keep his
gun ready for an emergency!"

He aimed his rifle at the one on the right and counted, "One—two—
three!"

Shots rang out. The bushes where the redskins were hidden rustled. A
brief rattle from the throat and some moans, then it was still. The whites
left their hiding place and walked over. The redskins lay dead in the brush,
both shot through the head.

"That's it!" the Oil Prince laughed. "They aren't going to follow us
anymore, nor will they shoot us. Let them rot here for the vultures and
wolves. Let's take what we can use."

The three bandits plundered the dead, whose ammunition and food
were particularly welcome. They also took the Indians' horses, which
might come in very handy if they needed to escape.

The three murderers moved on, now equipped with five horses. They
no longer needed to be as cautious, since they didn't expect any more am-
bushes. They spurred their animals to a good pace until they reached the
Navajo campsite of the night before. There they dismounted to examine
it, but did not discover anything special except tracks showing them that
this morning the redskins had continued their ride upstream on this side
of the river.

They followed these tracks for a quarter of an hour until they reached
the place where the Navajo had crossed the river. They did the same and,
once on the other side, found the distinct signs of the whites' camp. Once
again they dismounted to give the place their close attention.

"There was another camp here," the Oil Prince said. "Do you know whose it was?"

"Of course—Old Shatterhand's and his people," answered Buttler. "It cannot have been anyone else. Look over there at the bushes! Their tracks lead west along the high bank."

"Yes! The Navajo crossed the river to join them. They have united and are now all going after the Nijora. That means—" He stopped in the middle of his speech. They could see he was upset.

"What is it?" Buttler asked.

"The devil take it! I had a thought, a pitiful, miserable thought!"

"What?"

"If it's what I think, we can only pack up and ride away like beaten, starving dogs! The money is gone, simply gone. We shall not get a single dollar, not a cent!"

"By Jove, why not?"

"Because the draft has gone to the devil! The Navajo will have told Old Shatterhand and Winnetou everything as soon as they met!"

"Yes. They probably told them that we had seen them and had led them so nicely by the nose."

"Don't feel too proud of that, for now we are the ones who were duped. Wolf, who had the draft, is with them. He has, of course, seen the banker and talked with him."

"Hell's bells! Now I know what you mean! They told them everything and afterwards—after that Wolf handed the draft back to the banker!"

"Of course!" hissed the Oil Prince.

"Then we have no hope," grumbled Buttler. "Everything was for nothing, and you must admit what an childish joke it was to show Wolf the draft!"

The Oil Prince sputtered excuses in order to disguise his mistake, resulting in a dispute that became so heated that the two were close to exchanging blows. Poller finally pushed them apart and said, "You don't want to break each other's necks, do you? That won't change anything. I don't see why we should assume the worst and give up hope. Nothing is really lost yet."

"Nothing!" the Oil Prince cried angrily. "The draft is gone!"

"No, it isn't," replied Poller. "First Wolf had it, now Duncan does. What's the difference? Whoever has it, it's the same, as long as it still exists."

"I know that, but it no longer exists! Don't you think that Duncan would've destroyed it immediately?"

"Destroyed it? I'll believe that only when I have proof. 'Destroyed,' I suppose, means 'torn up.' If you tear something up, you don't put it carefully back in your pocket to keep it safe; you throw it away. Do you see a single scrap of paper around here? Since last night there's been no wind at all. There wasn't a breath of air that could have blown the bits of paper away. They'd still be lying around here. Let's check very carefully, not just here, but also in the vicinity."

They did so eagerly, but did not find anything. Taking a deep breath, his face clearing up, the Oil Prince said, "I feel better about this. What Poller says is true. You don't pocket torn-up paper; you throw it away. The banker hasn't torn up the draft, but kept it."

"I think so," Poller nodded. "He may not have destroyed it, if only to keep it as a memento of his experiences in the Wild West."

"Yes, that's possible. In any case, I'm hopeful again. And I'd rather see him have it than Wolf. From Wolf's pocket we could recover it only at great cost to our life and by murder; Duncan is a greenhorn who doesn't even have the stomach to really defend himself."

"That's true," Buttler agreed. "We don't need to make any bones about our intentions with this Duncan. We can deal more easily with him than with any of the others. Let's decide! What are we going to do?"

"Let's continue to follow the whites and redskins."

"But with twice the caution!"

"That's probably not necessary. They sent scouts out and don't suspect us of having shot them. They believe we're under surveillance and will expect to hear from the scouts before we arrive."

The three mounted again, took the two captured horses by the reins, and rode out, following the tracks of the Navajo and the whites.

Things evolved as they thought they would: their ride went smoothly and no one stopped them. They rode along the high bank of the river close to the edge of the trees and bushes, following the same track until they came to a place where it broadened substantially and showed indications of increased activity. The three stopped and dismounted to check the tracks. They had arrived where the previous evening Schi-So had waited with the horses in the bushes for Old Shatterhand and Winnetou, and where the Apache had earlier today met the united whites and redskins.

"They stopped here for some time," said Buttler. "You can see that clearly. The horses pawed the ground. Why, I wonder?"

"Who knows!" the Oil Prince threw in. "We'll probably find out soon enough."

"But I want to know right now. Look, there are tracks leading directly into the bushes! Let's have a look at what happened there!"

They left their horses and were headed toward the bushes when they heard a voice calling in German, "Help, help! Come here, come in here!"

They stopped and listened.

"That wasn't English," said Buttler. "It sounds like German, but I don't understand it."

"I do," explained Poller, the former scout of the immigrants. "Somebody's calling for help and is asking us to come to him."

"We can do that," said Buttler. "We don't need to worry about some-one calling for help."

"But what if it's only a ruse! What if we're being lured into a trap!"

"I don't believe that. Come on!"

They followed the footsteps and horse tracks leading into the brush and soon saw two saddled horses tied to some bushes. The men were so close to the one crying for help that he could see them, for now he cried, "Over here, over here, Mr. Poller. Be so kind as to cut me loose!"

"Is it possible!" Poller cried. "That's that crazy cantor who wants to compose an opera in twelve acts and commits a bunch of blunders in the process! Come on! We don't need to be afraid of him."

"But," the Oil Prince offered cautiously, "he's now with Old Shatterhand and Winnetou, and who knows whether this isn't a noose into which we'll be sticking our necks."

"Hardly! I'm sure this crazy cantor has been left here because of fool-ish behavior. Come on!" Poller commanded confidently.

He pushed deeper into the brush, with the others following. Poller's hunch was confirmed. They saw the cantor, hands tied behind his back, bound to a tree trunk. It had, however, been done in such a way that he was very comfortable. He sat in the soft grass with his back resting against the tree.

"Is it you, Mr. Cantor?" asked Poller. "Isn't that odd!"

"Cantor Emeritus, if you please! Just to be accurate and also to make a distinction, because an emeritus is no longer active, Mr. Poller."

"Actually, your situation appears to be more passive than active. How did you get into this bind?"

"I was tied up here."

"That I can see. But by whom?"

"Stone and Parker. Mr. Old Shatterhand ordered them to do it."

"Why?"

"That I—actually—don't know at all," the cantor stammered, ashamed to communicate the real reason. "Don't ask me; just cut me loose!"

"Not so fast. In any case, Old Shatterhand had you tied up here to prevent you from doing something foolish. Nevertheless, I find it unfair of him to tie you up here and to leave you all by yourself in the wilderness without any protection."

"Alone? I'm not alone. There's someone else to watch over me."

"Who?"

"Mr. Duncan, the banker."

"Him?" Poller asked, a satisfied look crossing his face. "Only him, or someone else?"

"Only Duncan. He offered to do it. I begged him continuously to set me free, but he did not grant my wish. He's an insensitive, cruel man."

The cantor's view was highly pleasing to Poller. For this reason and to reinforce this opinion he said, "Yes, that was truly cruel of him and deserves punishment. We should in fact untie you and tie him up instead!"

"That would be all right with me! I would be very glad and would not untie him, either, even if he begged me to high heaven to do so. I would leave him hanging and follow the others down to the Winter Water."

"Ah, the others are at the Winter Water? What do they want there?"

"To attack and capture the Nijora. I was not allowed to come along because they thought I would—I would—hmm. That is why they tied me up and the banker offered to stay with me. He stayed here rather than endanger himself by being hurt or even killed by the savages during the fight."

"That was very smart of him. But I don't see him. Where is he?"

"Gone off. He was sitting over there at the edge of the bushes and saw you coming. He became afraid and hid."

"So he recognized us?"

"No. You were too far away. But since you came from this side of the river and therefore could not be friends, he thought you to be enemies. He preferred not to be seen at all."

"Then he left and you do not know where he is hiding?"

"Oh, I know!"

"Then tell us so that we can get him and show you that we mean well!"

"Mean well?" asked the cantor, trying to don a cunning, know-it-all expression. "You seem to believe I trust you, honored Mr. Poller. I would not dream of trusting you. We disciples of the sciences are not that easily fooled."

"That wasn't my intention at all. What I say is true: I mean well by him and by you."

"Maybe by me, but not by him! That thing with the oil well was not true. You wanted to take him for all that money."

"Nonsense! If he really checks the lake, he will find the well to be there. But he doesn't understand anything about it and let himself be influenced against us by other people. He should get a little lesson: we want him to be tied up a bit, too, and to set you up as the guard. Think of what a thrilling scene that will make for your opera! The man you implored in vain to free you must beg you to set him free! This is the compensating justice every theater piece most depends on."

"Yes, about that you are right!" the cantor exclaimed enthusiastically. "A scene for my opera, a magnificent, wonderful scene! First I implore him. This is done in a mercy aria for baritone. Then the baritone is freed and the second bass is tied up. That results in another mercy aria followed by a major duet for second bass and baritone. That will be effective, immensely effective! I am extremely grateful to you for having drawn my attention to it."

"Well, then, where's Duncan?"

"He said there was a small gap in the rock behind us overgrown by bushes. He wanted to hide in there."

Poller roughly translated the conversation for his companions. They laughed about the prank they were going to play and quickly found the crevice in which Duncan's tightly coiled body was stuck. With a knife in his hand, the Oil Prince asked sneeringly, "Hello, Mr. Duncan, what are you doing in this crevice? Are you perhaps looking for an oil well?

The banker was terribly frightened when he recognized Grinley. He was no hero, and in front of him stood three dangerous scoundrels.

"Be so kind as to come on out!" the Oil Prince invited him. "You are remiss in the duty you have been assigned!"

"Duty?" he answered as he exited, scared and embarrassed, from the crevice.

"Yes, sir. You were to guard your good friend, the cantor. Why did you run away?"

"I saw three riders approach, but did not know it was you."

"So, then, had you recognized us, you would not have hidden?"

"No."

"I'm glad you place such great trust in us! Be so kind as to return to the cantor with us!"

They led him to the tree. There the Oil Prince relieved him of his two revolvers and the ammunition and said, "You are covered by a mighty protector and need no weapons, whereas we are armed devilishly poorly. You are surely glad to help us out. And now I must tell you something funny. For all the cantor's begging, you didn't do him the favor of releasing him—"

"I was strongly forbidden to do so!" Duncan quickly responded.

"Doesn't matter to us! Naturally, he is very aggravated about it and wants you to also feel how it is to be tied to a tree. We are more good-natured than you and shall grant him this modest wish."

"What do you mean?" the banker stammered, frightened. "You don't by chance intend to—?"

"Tie you up? Yes."

"Listen, I am not going to tolerate this, sirs!"

Straightening up as much as possible, he made an effort to appear manly. The Oil Prince patted his shoulder and said laughingly, "Don't puff up unnecessarily, sir! We know you very well! We want to do the cantor the pleasure of tying you up, nothing more. Once we're gone, he can release you. Well, what do you say?"

Grinley assumed a threatening pose, playing with his knife. Buttler and Poller followed his example. The banker fell into a blue funk. He forced down his anger and answered as if he had no difficulty accepting the prank, "What do I say? Nothing. If it gives you pleasure to grant this crazy person's even crazier wish, then go ahead. I've no intention of scuffling with you because of it."

"That's very sensible, most sensible of you," grinned the Oil Prince. "Then let's have some fun!"

He untied the cantor. Duncan stepped to the tree, offered his hands, and said, "Here, give yourselves the cheap pleasure, sirs!"

He had thought he would be tied as loosely as the cantor, but he realized immediately that this was a misconception. Poller took him by the right arm, Buttler by the left. They pulled him to the ground with such a ruthless jerk that he cried aloud, then they pulled his arms backwards around the trunk. While they held his arms, the Oil Prince tied his hands together and told him, "Yes, Mr. Duncan, the cheap pleasure begins. But it can easily become expensive to you. If I remember correctly, you carry a wallet, very dear to you, in your coat. I would love to take a little memento from it." With these words, he eyed the banker's face with a sneering smile.

Duncan paled.

The Oil Prince brutally reached inside the banker's coat, tore out the wallet, and, with little effort, found the draft he sought. He pocketed it with a triumphant sigh. Then he threw the wallet at the banker's feet.

Duncan groaned from powerless rage. He wanted to tear himself off the tree, but his efforts caused the bindings to cut into his flesh. He cried out in a piercing yell.

"Be quiet. Calm down!" the Oil Prince sneered. "I take back only what has been unlawfully withheld from me."

The cantor, not understanding English, and always overly occupied with his opera, stood harmlessly aside without comprehending the connection and seemed not quite able to suppress a certain satisfaction at the banker's anger. Poller, calling out to him, wished him success with his planned mercy aria. The cantor responded with a bow. Then the three bandits walked to their horses, mounted, and rode away.

The composer now seated himself opposite the banker and examined him with a very satisfied expression. Duncan was unable to comprehend such behavior. It made him furious, which is why he angrily shouted at the cantor in English and in the most threatening terms to untie him at once. Unfortunately, the cantor did not understand. Earlier, when he was still tied to the tree, the emeritus had voiced the same plea probably a hundred times and with the same lack of success, but in German, which was unintelligible to the banker.

While Duncan swore at him in a variety of English curses, the composer studied him, all the while whistling through his teeth a melody from which a mercy aria was to evolve. The banker was boiling with anger. His rage reached a peak and a sudden, great exhaustion took hold of him. He became quieter and began to deliberate. From his bookkeeper, Baumgarten, he had picked up a few German terms, just as he knew the cantor had also learned a number of English phrases. Even though his knowledge was meager, he thought it should, nevertheless, be possible to come to an understanding. He began, "Mr. Cantor, unbind, unbind!"

"Cantor Emeritus, please!" was the response.

"Unbind, unbind!"

"Anbinden?" asked the cantor. "But you are tied up! What is it you want?"

Unfortunately for the banker, the German "anbinden," while pronounced similarly to the English "unbind," means exactly the opposite.

Thus it went back and forth between the two for maybe a quarter of an hour. First, the cantor did not understand the banker; and second, he did not see why the one who had earlier kept him tied up to the tree should not now also dangle a bit. But eventually his good nature got the upper hand. When Duncan renewed his painful attempts to tear himself loose, the cantor went to him and with great effort loosened the intentionally tight knots. He thought he would now hear words of thanks, but in this he was badly mistaken. Duncan stretched his limbs, then hit the emeritus in the head with his fist. The latter fell, staggering, into the bushes. Then Duncan untied his horse and rode to the west, where he knew his companions to be.

The cantor gathered himself slowly, felt the spot on his head where he had been hit, and said, "Gratitude is a rare virtue." Because he was afraid to remain alone, he, too, got his horse from the bushes, mounted, and rode away westward, where the tracks of the whites and the Navajo led.

But why had the good cantor been left behind and why had he even been tied up?

That very morning, the unlucky fellow had approached Hobble-Frank shortly after departure and had asked him, "Mr. Frank, if I am informed correctly, we are now moving against the Nijora, right? It appears they will be attacked by us?"

"Yes," Hobble-Frank confirmed.

"I am very glad; I am very glad indeed!"

"Why?"

"Why, you ask. You know very well that I want to compose a heroic opera in twelve acts!"

"Yes, it occurs to me that you have mentioned it once before."

"I am sure I told you. Whereas I have found the heroes I need for it here, I have not yet seen them in the execution of their activity."

"No? Well, I would have thought that enough had been accomplished already, things other people would not be able to do. Did we not skip from one adventure to the other?"

"I admit this readily. But heroism demonstrated in its fullest glory has not yet happened. You know, I need a battle for my opera, where man stands against man and the hero downs one enemy after another. I would like to experience a truly bloody fight."

"Why? Something like this is dangerous and I would not wish for it. If you want to bring this to the stage, you do not need to wish for a real fight, a real bloodletting."

"Oh, yes! If one has really seen and experienced something like this, one can compose much more effectively. The din of battle, the screaming and howling, the crack and ringing of gunshots, all that can be represented properly only if one has heard it oneself."

"But that can cost you your life, and then your entire nice opera is kaput!"

"Do not believe it! We composers are under the special protection of the Muses. Nothing can happen to us. Have you ever heard of a famous composer being stabbed to death or shot by the Indians?"

"No."

"Well, then! I am not in the least danger. Do you think it will come to a fight today?"

"Hmm! If everything falls into place as Old Shatterhand and Winnetou plan, the enemy will fall into our hands without a shot being fired. But if it turns out differently, then we may certainly see a fight."

"Different how?"

"Well, different situations may arise. One never knows ahead of time how everything will turn out. For example, the Nijora need only to notice that the Navajo lie in ambush for the trouble to start."

"How are they to find out?"

"Somehow or another. A fool always asks more than a smart man can answer! As I said before, one can never know what will happen. For example, when we get to the ford, your horse may get it into its head to turn left instead of right and everything may be given away."

Hobble-Frank was only half-serious, half in jest. The cantor's face, however, expressed satisfaction and he asked, "To the left instead of the right? Did I understand this correctly?"

He nodded in delight, which did not go unnoticed by the crafty Hobble-Frank. He intended to inform Old Shatterhand and thus to render the cantor's lust for battle harmless. But since, in his enthusiasm, the good composer also talked to Mrs. Rosalie about his intentions, Frank took it upon himself to thwart his plans.

Soon thereafter the party stopped, for Winnetou had appeared from the bushes. He approached Old Shatterhand and the chief of the Navajo and reported, "The Nijora stuck to their plan and have not changed their position. My brothers can thus execute the plan I discussed yesterday with Old Shatterhand. But I think a small change to be in order."

"And that would be?" asked Old Shatterhand.

"We had decided to ride into the ford and then to turn right in the dry Winter Water wash until we reach the river. The Nijora would then attack us, then, in turn, would be attacked by the Navajo from the rear. It is important, though, that the enemy not use their guns, to prevent any of us from being wounded or even killed. We achieve this by demonstrating to them immediately that they would lose if they entered into a fight."

"Winnetou is right. We must have Navajo with us up front to show the Nijora right away that they have fallen into their own trap."

"That is what I meant," the chief of the Apache nodded.

"The Navajo must not come with us, but should be in place before our arrival without being seen by the Nijora."

"My white brother has read my thoughts."

"It is easy to guess my red brother's meaning. The Nijora number three hundred warriors, while we have six hundred. It will be sufficient to send five hundred to their rear. The remaining one hundred must climb from the high bank here down into the wash and, once down there, sneak to the mouth of the Winter Water. There they will hide in the brush and wait until we come. As soon as we arrive and the Nijora are ready to throw themselves on us, the hundred warriors will come out of hiding and join us. That will have the intended effect. The enemy will be surprised, which will give our five hundred men time to gather at the enemy's rear."

"So it shall be. I agree with Old Shatterhand. Nitsas-Ini, the brave chief of the Navajo, may select the hundred warriors, and they may leave now to get to the mouth of the Winter Water under cover. Then the five hundred will leave, too, and, as soon as we think they are in their ambush position, we shall depart also."

One hundred Navajo were counted off to hide in the bushes along the bank, then to climb into the wash to sneak down to the river. They could not take their horses, but left them with the others. Soon thereafter the remaining five hundred got under way.

When the Navajo had all left, Old Shatterhand explained the plan to the German immigrants in their mother tongue, since it had been detailed in English before. He asked them not to worry because everything would work out and implored them to be very careful and to do nothing to compromise the plan. Mrs. Rosalie said to him, "We shall certainly not make any mistake. But I know of one person who is determined to commit a great foolishness."

"Who is that?"

"Who is that? You have to ask? When I am talking about foolishness, you should know immediately whom I mean. The cantor, naturally. He tried to talk me into the same folly, that is, to turn left at the Winter Water."

"That is unbelievable. That would ruin our plan! Has what Mrs. Ebersbach just said about you true?" This question was directed to the cantor.

"Yes," he admitted dejectedly.

"Without asking me, you wanted to take a different direction? Why?"

"My opera," he responded.

"Your opera? Once again you want to endanger us just because of your crazy fantasy? How is this famous opera responsible for what you want to do?"

The cantor did not want to answer. Hobble-Frank entered the discussion by saying, "I know what his unrealistic mind wants to do. He earlier told me that he needs a battle scene for his opera. He wants to turn left so that the Nijora learn of our ambush and a battle ensues."

Everyone was scandalized.

"What a terrible person!" Old Shatterhand said angrily. "But we shall take measures so that he can do us no harm. He may not come with us, but must remain here."

This outraged the future composer. Regaining his speech, he answered, "I will not stand for that, Mr. Shatterhand. I am not a soldier or recruit who must let himself be thundered at and who must obey!"

"You will obey. You will remain here, and I shall have someone stay with you to guard you."

"Then I shall run away!"

"Fine! In that case, we will tie you up."

This happened, despite all his objections. Now there remained the question of who was to stay with him. The banker offered, since the thought of being attacked by the Nijora frightened him. Old Shatterhand agreed, but implored him not to untie the cantor, even if he should seem rational. A messenger would be sent to pick the two up later.

The five hundred Navajo who had ridden south disappeared below the horizon. Because they likely reached their destination shortly thereafter, Old Shatterhand gave the command to continue the ride.

The Germans extended great trust in him and Winnetou, for they knew that these leaders were not men in whose presence fear would arise. Old Shatterhand admonished everyone to appear calm and not to look toward the area where the enemy was hidden.

Riding parallel to the river, they approached the Winter Water at a right angle. Sam Hawkens cracked all kinds of jokes. He laughed aloud and asked the others to join him to lull the Nijora into a sense of security. At the ford, they slowly rode down into the dry wash. Winnetou and Old Shatterhand rode ahead. Their sharp eyes missed nothing, although they appeared not to be watching out at all.

To the left of them lay several rocks that in the rainy season were covered by high water. From behind one of these rocks Nitsas-Ini peered carefully. "Altso-ti—We are here," he whispered to his friends in his language. Then he disappeared.

The party turned right and rode downstream in the wash toward the confluence with the Chelly. To the right and left rose high, steep rocks and ahead, at the mouth, the bank of the Chelly was densely bordered by trees and bushes. They stopped there.

To the left the precipitous, rocky bank formed a bluff. Old Shatterhand pointed to it and said, "The women and children may withdraw behind this corner; there they will be safe."

The people concerned obeyed his order. Only one took exception— Mrs. Rosalie. "What? I am to hide?" she exclaimed. "What will those

Indians think of me?" With these words, she took her husband's rifle from his hands, grasped it by the barrel, and swung the butt threateningly above her head.

"Psst! Don't do that!" warned Old Shatterhand. "The Nijora are watching us and might figure out what is about to happen. Soon they will come running, howling and screaming. Then all of you will aim your rifles at them, but without firing. If this does not stop them, only then will we shoot. In this case, I shall give the command to fire, but I ask you to shoot them in the legs only. Now sit down and act as if you have no idea of their presence!"

They also followed this request. They sat down with their backs turned toward the Chelly and looking up the wash of the Winter Water, so they could see the Nijora coming. Old Shatterhand and Winnetou stood together and appeared to be conversing casually.

During heavy rains, the Winter Water had deposited many big rocks near its mouth. Behind these rocks one could take cover. The Nijora could be expected to sneak up under cover of these rocks.

And that was how it happened. Winnetou noticed a movement behind one of them, looked more closely for an instant, then said to Old Shatterhand, "Behind the large triangular block is an enemy. Has my brother seen him?"

"Yes. I saw him creeping forward from the rock behind that one. It is Mokaschi, the chief."

"Then the moment has come," said Winnetou. "Does my brother not think it better not to wait for them to advance?"

"Yes. They will be much more confused. Do you want to talk to him?"

"No. My brother may do this. You carry the carbine he believes to be a magic rifle. Your voice will therefore be more effective than mine."

"Well, then, let it begin!" said Old Shatterhand.

In an undertone he called a few words toward the bushes in which the hundred Navajo hid and told the whites, "The Nijora have arrived. Stand up and aim your rifles!"

He stepped forward a few paces, the carbine ready in his hand, and called toward the triangular rock, "Why does Mokaschi, the chief of the Nijora, hide when he wants to visit us? He may come openly. We know he is here with his three hundred warriors."

"Uff, uff!" was heard from behind the rock, and Mokaschi stood up. "The white dogs know we are here? And they came anyway? Has the Great Spirit seared their brains that so few dare fight us here?"

"We are not risking anything, for the chief of the Nijora is victim of a great error. Does he not see my people standing here to welcome the enemy with their rifles? And does he not recognize the magic rifle in my hand?"

"We shall rush Old Shatterhand so quickly that he will be able to shoot only two or three times. Then he will be pulled down by the sheer numbers of my warriors. The palefaces' only choice will be to surrender or to be driven into the water and killed. They should be able to see that they are surrounded."

He lifted his hand and upon this signal Nijora surfaced behind all the rocks. Others, who had not found room there and had therefore remained farther back, drew closer; all raised a bone-chilling war cry. Yet they did not attack, but stood behind their chief, since he had not advanced, either. He once more raised his arm; at once the howling fell silent and he called to Old Shatterhand, "The palefaces can see that they are lost if they fight. If they are wise, they will surrender to us."

"We few palefaces are not afraid of three hundred Nijora. But we did not come alone. When Mokaschi lifted his hand, his warriors revealed themselves. Now I will raise my hand."

He raised his arm. The one hundred Navajo immediately sprang from the bushes and, lightning-fast, formed a double row and aimed their rifles at the Nijora, who loosed a howl of surprise. None of them had dared to aim a rifle at the whites, who had aimed their rifles first and had, therefore, the advantage. Old Shatterhand gave a signal indicating his wish to continue speaking, and the howling subsided. "Why does the chief of the Nijora stare only toward us? He might also want to look to the rear!"

Mokaschi turned, his warriors doing the same. They saw, barely twenty paces distant, the five hundred Navajo filling the entire width of the dry bed of the Winter Water, standing in eight to ten rows one behind the other. In front of them stood Nitsas-Ini, who called to Mokaschi, "Here stand five hundred warriors of the Navajo and in front of you another hundred besides the palefaces. Does the chief of the Nijora wish us to begin the fight?"

Alarmed, the Nijora howled like wild animals. The Navajo, outnumbering their enemies two to one, whooped much louder with joy. Then Old Shatterhand gave a signal for silence and immediately it turned quiet. He spoke in a raised voice, "I am asking Mokaschi, just as Nitsas-Ini has asked him, whether we are to start the battle. More than six hundred bullets will fly into the mass of Nijora. How many will survive? Not a single one."

Mokaschi did not answer right away. He looked gloomily ahead.

Grinding his teeth, he said, "We shall die. But each of us will kill at least one Navajo."

"You say this, but do not believe it yourself, because if even one of you raises his rifle, we will all fire. Have you become so blind and deaf that you neither heard nor saw me and Winnetou when we were in your camp to spy on you yesterday? With your older warriors you sat by a rock close to the edge of the high riverbank. We lay on top of this rock. There we heard what you talked about. Do you not know how careful one has to be when he has gone on the warpath?"

"Uff! Uff!" Mokaschi exclaimed, at a loss. "Old Shatterhand and Winnetou lay on the rock below which we sat?"

"Yes. We listened when you deliberated about how you wanted to attack us. Why do you pick fights with men whom you know are not afraid of you?"

At that Mokaschi laid his rifle on the ground and said, "The Great Manitou has worked against us. He did not want us to win. Old Shatterhand or Winnetou may fight me. Whichever of us kills the other shall win victory for his tribe."

"Do you believe you can defeat either Winnetou or me? Have you ever heard of either one of us losing to an enemy? Your proposition cannot change your fate. But we are no friends of bloodshed and would like to avoid a fight."

"How? Are we to put ourselves at your mercy?"

"No, for brave men do not surrender thus, and the Nijora are brave warriors. Are you so little acquainted with Old Shatterhand and Winnetou that you expect us to demand something whose implementation would bring everlasting shame to you and your descendants?

At that Mokaschi let out a deep sigh of relief and asked, "How can we avoid a fight without our women and children mocking us?"

"Let us discuss this. Mokaschi and Nitsas-Ini may approach me and Winnetou. Mokaschi may bring his weapons, for he has not yet surrendered and must come as a free man."

"I shall come."

The Nijora picked up his rifle from the ground and walked toward Old Shatterhand. Once there, he sat down in the dignified pose of a chief. The white hunter took his place beside him, as did Winnetou. Nitsas-Ini approached, too. The Nijora made room for him to pass, but many scowled at him. None of them dared touch him threateningly, or even say an unfriendly word.

The council could have begun right away, for those it depended on had come together; but, following Indian custom, they sat for maybe a quarter of an hour without a word. Each was occupied with his own thoughts. Old Shatterhand and Winnetou looked questioningly at the two others, as if wanting to divine their innermost thoughts. Then they traded a brief glance with each other. Winnetou was the first to speak, but he raised only a brief question, "Four warriors sit here for council. Who of them is to speak?"

Once more a period of deep silence ensued. Then Nitsas-Ini answered, "Our brother Old Shatterhand did not want to spill blood. He may speak!"

"Howgh!" the others said to express their agreement.

In order for his words to have greater impact, Old Shatterhand, too, waited. Then he began, "My brothers know that I honor all peoples, whether they are red or black, yellow or white. They know me to be a friend of the red man. All the land from one ocean to the other once belonged to the Indian. Then came the whites, who took it all from him and, in exchange, gave him their diseases. The Indian has become a poor, sick man who will soon die. The whites' greatest victory has been to sow discord among the red tribes and to incite one against the other. The red men were unwise enough to let it happen and have not become any wiser. They wear each other down, but could still achieve great things if they dropped their mutual hate and became that which they should be and to which they were born, namely, brothers. Am I right?"

"Howgh!" sounded from all around.

"Yes, I am right. The two tribes of the great Apache facing each other here in enmity prove it once again. May my brother Nitsas-Ini tell me why he set out against the Nijora!"

346 The Oil Prince

"Because they raised the tomahawk against us."

"Now Mokaschi may tell me why he has led his warriors against the Navajo!"

"Because they raised the tomahawk against us."

"Do you understand what I am saying? I wanted to hear the reasons for your quarrel, but you could not name one. Instead, you told me only that the tomahawk had been raised. Is this not like small children pulling each other by the hair without having the least cause?"

Old Shatterhand paused for effect and then continued, "My red brother Nitsas-Ini is not only a brave and famous warrior, but also a sensible and wise leader. He is convinced that the red man will ultimately die if he remains as he is now. He has, therefore, made prudent decisions and then carried them out. He has taken a white squaw he loves and to whom he owes much. He has sent his son across the ocean for him to learn how to convert a barren land to a fertile one. He knows that war brings only disaster, want, and misery and that happiness can be achieved solely through peace. Does he want to jeopardize the well-being of his tribe and pay for in blood what peace will give him for nothing or at twice the return? Has he suddenly changed? Is he asking today for the blood of his red brothers?"

"Uff, uff! I do not want that!" the Navajo exclaimed.

"I thought so. If it were otherwise, I would no longer want to be your friend and brother. But how is it with Mokaschi, the chief of the Nijora? He took off for battle, also without having a good reason, and he did not gain a single advantage over his enemies. He must even admit he is at present in a very dangerous position. Will he admit to this?"

"Howgh!" Mokaschi nodded, beginning to see Old Shatterhand's intention.

"And should a wise man amidst such dangers still desire the death of his adversaries, although they hold his life in their hands?"

"No."

"Well, then, we are of the same opinion. Neither Nitsas-Ini nor Mokaschi desires the continuation of hostilities. It is only a question, then, of determining how much blood has been shed so far and how to avenge it. Did Mokaschi lose any of his warriors, who must then be avenged?"

"No."

"Let me ask the same of my brother Nitsas-Ini."

"Khasti-tine and his companion have been killed," he said seriously.

"By the Nijora?"

"No, by the paleface calling himself the Oil Prince."

"Do you need to avenge the death of these two warriors on the Nijora?"

"No."

"Then here, too, you are in the same situation. The only inequality is that the Nijora are encircled in such a way that their blood would surely be spilled if it came to a fight. Yet Nitsas-Ini has declared that he does not want to shed blood. Another difference exists in that Mokaschi captured eight Navajo warriors. Can these circumstances not be balanced against each other? The Nijora will return the captives and the Navajo will open the grip in which the Nijora find themselves. The tomahawks will be buried. I hope my brothers will agree to this proposal and are ready for a peaceful compromise."

Following these conciliatory remarks, Old Shatterhand took the tobacco pouch from his belt and the peace pipe off the string around his neck, stuffed the pipe, and placed it in front of him. Then he asked Mokaschi, "Is the chief of the Nijora in agreement?"

"Yes," he answered, glad to have been rescued so inexpensively from certain ruin.

"And what does the chief of the Navajo say?"

Nitsas-Ini was not as quick to agree. "My brother Old Shatterhand has spoken more to the situation of the Nijora than that of the Navajo. The Nijora are in our power, and there is no advantage in holding these captives, who are as good as free anyway. I need only send some of my warriors to the camp of the Nijora to free the prisoners. Tell me the advantage of this proposal for us!"

"Let me ask you whom you have to thank for the advantageous position in which you find yourself?"

"You and Winnetou," Nitsas-Ini answered sincerely and truthfully.

"Yes, you owe it to us. I do not say this to flatter myself, but to move you to act humanely and nobly toward your red brothers. What does Winnetou say to my peace proposal?"

"It is as if I had spoken your words myself," the Apache answered.

"Then only Nitsas-Ini has to declare himself."

The latter examined the position of his people and that of the enemy with a long, questioning gaze. He was not eager to relinquish his great advantage, but the influence his white squaw had exerted over him little by little made itself felt here also. From a savage Indian he had changed to a peace-loving and judicious chief. He hesitated for a few moments, then declared, "My brother Old Shatterhand is right. The Nijora shall be freed from the trap."

"And you are ready to smoke the calumet with Mokaschi?"

"Yes."

At that Old Shatterhand stood up, turned to the Indians, and called in a loud voice, "Warriors of the Navajo and Nijora: direct your eyes here to see what your chiefs have decided!"

He lit the tobacco and gave Nitsas-Ini the pipe. The latter stood, took six puffs from the pipe, blew the smoke toward the sky, the earth, and the four compass directions, and proclaimed in a loud voice, "The tomahawks shall be buried; we smoke the pipe of peace. The Nijora will return the captives and then shall be brothers of the Navajo. This I promise for all my warriors and I have smoked the calumet on their behalf. I have spoken, howgh!"

The Navajo were likely not pleased by the result of the negotiations. They had such an advantage that they found it difficult to relinquish it. Yet obedience to the chief prevented them from refusing to comply, the more so because the smoking of the calumet was such a sacred rite that they would not have dared question their chief's decision.

Nitsas-Ini gave the peace pipe to Mokaschi, who also rose, took six puffs, and then pronounced just as loudly as Nitsas-Ini, "Hear me, you warriors of the Navajo and the Nijora, the tomahawk of war is buried again in the earth. The men of the Navajo shall open the circle with which they surround us and shall then be our brothers. I have confirmed this with the calumet, and it is as if my warriors had spoken so and had smoked the calumet to seal it. I have spoken, howgh!"

No one was happier than the Nijora, who had not thought such a fortunate ending possible in so dangerous a situation. As witnesses to the contract, Old Shatterhand and Winnetou also had to take the six puffs on the pipe, but made no further comment.

The council was now finished and the hostile picture changed to a peaceful one. The Navajo released the Nijora and, because of the lack of space by the river, friend and former foe went to the Nijora camp to celebrate the peace and to free the captives. Winnetou, Old Shatterhand, and Wolf also went there, as their presence was required. The other whites remained at the river, glad that the hostilities had had such a happy resolution.

Thanks to Old Shatterhand's strong desire for peace, an almost-certain fight had ended in a peace agreement. The conquered Nijora were treated with magnanimity. Old Shatterhand's humane and civil gesture had once more made friends of vengeful adversaries.

Before the terrified Oil Prince could defend himself,
the sharp knife circled his head.

# 16

# THE PUNISHMENT

SOON EVERYONE WAS ENGAGED in a lively conversation about the recent events. Hobble-Frank and Mrs. Rosalie particularly entered into a keen dialog in which Adolf Wolf also participated briefly. Soon, though, he left the two to look up his uncle, who was on the high bank in the camp. When he came to the ford, he passed the Navajo who had brought their horses from the hiding place to the camp. Their chief had organized this task; Winnetou and Old Shatterhand had joined him for company. A horseman appeared at the ford's entrance and, seeing them there, called down, "Mr. Shatterhand, it's good to have found you! May I come down?"

"Mr. Duncan!" the hunter called in astonishment. "What are you doing here? Weren't you to stay with the cantor until I sent a messenger? Why did you leave?"

"I will tell you." He slowly rode down, jumped off his horse, and told his story in an excited manner, "If only I had not stayed there, but had come with you! If you only knew what I have experienced!"

"What happened?"

"Something terrible! The Oil Prince took my draft once again!"

"The Oil Prince? Unbelievable! Tell us, quickly!"

The banker recounted what had happened.

"Sir," Old Shatterhand remarked sarcastically at the close of the report, "you handled that smartly, very smartly! Why hadn't you destroyed the scrap of paper?"

"I wanted to keep it as a memento. Now I regret it bitterly. Get me back this paper, sir! I ask you most urgently, please!"

"Yes, first you make the mistakes, and then I am to fix them! Did you see where the thieves rode off to?"

"Upstream from where they had come, and from where we came, too."

"Then they followed the Navajo's tracks to attack Wolf and to take the draft from him. A peculiar convergence of circumstances helped them accomplish their goal much more easily. How long ago did this happen?"

"Quite a while. This idiotic cantor did not untie me quickly."

"Then we must get going promptly."

"Upstream?" the Navajo chief asked.

"Yes! To start with, in any case. Later, they probably rode downstream."

"Then they would have had to pass here!" exclaimed Nitsas-Ini.

"No. They crossed to the other bank."

"Uff! Has my brother reason to think so?"

"Yes," explained Old Shatterhand. "They have the draft and want to get to San Francisco. Thus they must get down to the Colorado, the same way they took when they visited you. Having learned of our presence from the cantor, they could not pass here. Therefore, they rode upstream to where we camped yesterday and crossed the river there. My red brother may ride swiftly downstream with a party of his warriors to a place to cross the river. Once on the other side, he should look for their tracks and find out if they have already left this area."

"They must surely be gone!"

"No. They are probably hanging out somewhere on the other side to watch how the attack over here turned out. My brother must block their path over as wide an area as possible, so that they cannot pass."

"And what will Old Shatterhand do?" asked the chief.

"I shall ride upstream with Winnetou and follow their tracks. Since one set will be on top of the other, they will probably be hard to read, which is why we want to do this ourselves. We will not ride alone, but will take some companions along."

"I sent scouts against these dogs!" Nitsas-Ini interjected. "They must not have been seen by my warriors."

"Something else is possible. Either they tricked the scouts or killed them. My red brother may depart right away."

Another rider appeared at the ford. It was the cantor.

"Here I am again," he said innocently.

"Glad to see you," snapped Old Shatterhand, annoyed. "So that nothing happens to you and us, we shall tie you up again right away."

"I will not tolerate this. You have no authority over me!"

"I do, and I shall immediately prove it to you." Old Shatterhand said to several Navajo a few words the cantor did not understand, whereupon they surrounded him and his horse and took him to the camp. Despite his struggles, he was indeed tied up.

Shortly thereafter, Nitsas-Ini and twenty horsemen chased off downstream. Mokaschi, his new friend, accompanied him with twenty Nijora. Winnetou, Old Shatterhand, and Sam Hawkens, however, rode upstream in the company of ten Navajo. The other frontiersmen wanted to come along, but were asked by Old Shatterhand to remain behind to maintain order in camp.

The immigrants, together with Nitsas-Ini's wife, sat together by the water. They spoke of their future and their plans. Wolf came looking for them. The squaw who, when speaking German with Wolf, addressed him formally, but informally when speaking Navajo, beckoned him over and said, "We are talking about the plans of our countrymen. They came over here to forge a new life. They have no resources. Only the Ebersbachs have money and are willing to support the others. What do you say? I shall talk with my husband as soon as he has time."

"That is not necessary," smiled Wolf.

"Why?"

"Because I have done so already."

"And what did he say?"

"He wants to extend to these Germans the option of remaining here, in his territory."

"That makes me very happy! I know he would have granted my wish in any case, but that he has not waited for me to ask makes me twice as happy. How do you think this will work?"

"Very easily. These people will be given as much land as they need. There is more than enough—forest, arable land, and pasture. Then we'll arrange for a ride over to Guajolote or La Tinaja, where we shall purchase agricultural equipment and all necessary tools. We shall also provide for horses, cows, and other grazing animals, and all our men and squaws will assist the settlers in the construction of their houses, so that they shall very soon be established. But we do have a problem."

"A problem? Really?" she asked, a little worried.

"Yes, a bad, a terrible problem," he smiled. "What would be the use of all this if the settlers did not want it! How would it look?"

This question was directed to the Germans. Naturally, all of them responded with a happy "yes." Mrs. Rosalie, always ready to speak for the others, hugged the white squaw, offered a handshake to Wolf, and exclaimed, "No one should ever tell me again that the savages are bad people. No person in our homeland would be so kind as to make a gift like this to a poor schmuck, and such a big one at that. From now on, I am on the side of the Indians and no longer with the whites. Let us hope that the cantor does not want to remain here, too! If that were the case, the bottom could yet fall out of our barrel of good luck."

"No, we'll send him back," Wolf assured them. "That foolish bird would only bring us bad luck. You, though, will like it here with us. You've come at the right time, because we have big plans for cultivation. When you hear them, our generosity will make more sense. Later, Schi-So and my nephew will complete the project that we'll start. We shall prove that the red man can be the equal of the white— Wait!" Wolf paused suddenly. "What was that across the river? It sounded like a death cry! Were the Oil Prince and his compatriots hiding over there, and are they fighting with our people? How could that be possible!"

As Old Shatterhand had surmised, the Oil Prince and his two companions had ridden up the river to the Navajo's last campsite and there crossed the river. Their intention was to travel downstream on the opposite side to get to the Colorado. They thought that it might be better to know which of the two tribes had been victorious over the other; therefore, they stayed near the Chelly's bank. When they reached the opposite side of the confluence with the Winter Water, they looked for a place from which they could covertly observe the events on the other side.

But they had had to make a wide detour and so much time passed that they arrived too late. The reconciliation of the two tribes had already taken place. The redskins had withdrawn to the camp in the woods, where they could no longer be seen from the other side; thus the three bandits saw only the white women and men seated and chatting near the water. This led them to believe that no decision had been made yet, so they stayed on longer than was safe. They were unaware that Old Shatterhand was already tracking them and Nitsas-Ini and his forty warriors were blocking their way.

As mentioned earlier, the Oil Prince and Buttler had been using Poller for their own purposes, intending to get rid of him later by murdering him. Proper timing was the issue, however, and now they looked for an opportunity to discuss it. Poller was no poor observer, though, and felt the danger to himself in the air. It struck him as suspicious when the two removed themselves from him. He crept along through the bushes and saw them standing close together and speaking quietly. He succeeded in getting within two paces of them, but could not understand what they were saying until the Oil Prince said somewhat louder, "Now's the best opportunity. He gets the knife unexpectedly and we leave him lying here. If the whites find him, they'll think the redskins did it."

Poller, indignant at their insidious intent, forgot to be cautious and stood up suddenly in front of them. "What, you want to kill me, you scoundrels?" he bellowed at them. "Is that your reward for what I—"

He was unable to continue. With a single look, the two understood each other. Grinley quickly took hold of Poller, and Buttler rammed the knife into his chest. The blade hit so precisely that Poller could only shout his death cry, then collapse lifelessly. The two robbed him of his belongings and left his body, after which they continued watching the mouth of the Winter Water for close to an hour.

When still nothing happened over there, they decided it was too precarious to wait any longer. They mounted their horses, took the three riderless horses by the reins, turned toward the open plain, and rode off.

Five minutes later, Old Shatterhand arrived with Winnetou and the others. They had overcome the difficulties they had encountered in following the overlain tracks, and now they found the body.

"My God, it's Poller!" Old Shatterhand exclaimed, shocked. Right away he began to examine the dead man. "They murdered him to get rid of him. He has now received his reward! Here's where they hid to observe us—"

"My brother must delay no longer," Winnetou interrupted him. "They left barely five minutes ago. Their tracks lead into the open. Let us follow them quickly!"

Leading their horses, they mounted up once they left the brush and followed the two murderers at a gallop. Ten minutes later, they saw the two ahead of them on the open plain. At the same moment, Buttler turned and noticed the pursuers.

"My God! Old Shatterhand and Winnetou with some whites and redskins!" he exclaimed. "Let's go!"

They spurred their horses, yet the pursuers were catching up.

"It won't work; they're gaining on us!" cried the Oil Prince. "We can't get away in the open. We must get into the brush!"

They turned left toward a point of brush that extended from the river onto the plain like a green tongue. It was the same area where they had murdered the Navajo scouts.

In the meantime, Nitsas-Ini had placed a long line of redskins across the plain. Because the villains might also come down near the river, he took some of his warriors there and slowly walked upstream, leaving their horses behind. They, too, arrived at the brushy point and found the still-visible, older tracks. Following them, they came across the corpses of their two scouts.

A terrible anger took hold of the chief, then he heard hoofbeats. He headed for the edge of the brush and saw the villains approaching at full speed, followed by their pursuers. A few mighty leaps brought him close to them and he leapt up behind the Oil Prince's saddle.

"I avenge Khasti-tine," he yelled, tearing the hat off the Oil Prince's head. "Your scalp is mine!"

Before the terrified Oil Prince could defend himself, the sharp knife circled his head. Nitsas-Ini, throwing the weapon away, with his left fist grasping Grinley's neck tightly, tore the scalp off with the other hand.

The Oil Prince let out a desperate howl. Buttler, whose horse had briefly leaped ahead by a few steps, looked fearfully back and saw his brother's horse almost collapsing under the weight of both riders.

He brought his rifle to his cheek, aimed at Nitsas-Ini, and pulled the trigger.

At that very moment, the just-scalped Grinley suddenly reared up in pain, which brought him into the line of fire. The bullet hit him squarely in the throat and, with a choking rattle, he sank forward, dead.

"Get the other one!" the chief commanded. "We shall torture him at the stake!"

With horror, Buttler heard this terrible threat. With a last scream of fury and desperation, he tore his knife from his belt and rammed it to the hilt into his chest. Dying, he dropped from his horse.

When Old Shatterhand and Winnetou arrived, Nitsas-Ini stood cold-bloodedly beside the two bodies. "Pity," he said. "It went too fast!" Then he turned to his warriors and ordered, "Take our murdered brothers and tie them on the horses. They shall be buried where we are camped as brave sons of the Navajo. These white dogs, though, may lie here to be eaten by the vultures!"

At that Sam Hawkens whispered to Old Shatterhand, "We'll come secretly to bury them later, if I'm not mistaken. They were criminals, but also human beings."

A silent nod of agreement indicated the hunter's consent.

All the redskins were called together, then the party with the two bodies got under way, crossed the river at a suitable spot, and moved up to the camp. There the appearance of the dead changed the joyous reconciliation festivities into a time of grief. Hollow, plaintive sounds arose until that evening when two tall rock mounds rose above the murdered.

The Navajo and the Nijora remained together for two more days, then they separated. The whites moved on with the Navajo, eastward to the Chaco River, where the tribe had its huts and tents. And then what happened? Several books could still be written about that. Nitsas-Ini kept his word. The four families received everything Wolf had promised them at the mouth of the Winter Water. Never were their relations with the Navajo other than friendly.

The frontiersmen stayed on for some time to assist the four households with advice and help, then said farewell, but not forever, to their white and red friends. They crossed into California and on their ride experienced many an adventure. In San Francisco the others said their good-byes to Aunt Droll and Hobble-Frank, who felt an obligation to accompany the inexperienced and scatter-brained cantor home. At the leave-taking, Sam Hawkens asked, "When will we see you again, you two heroes of the Wild West, *heeheeheehee?*"

"When you have smartened up, you old joker, you," responded Hobble-Frank. "Write to me at my villa Bärenfett, once you smarten up. Then I shall return."

The End

# ABOUT THE TRANSLATOR

 Herbert Windolf was born in Wiesbaden, Germany, in 1936. In 1964, he emigrated to Canada with his wife and their three children to set up technical services for a German industrial company with branches in Canada and the United States. Six years later he moved to the United States and presently resides in Prescott, Arizona.

Before undertaking *The Oil Prince*, Windolf had already translated several German literary works into English. When he was approached by history professor Albert W. Bork to translate *Der Ölprinz*, Windolf was excited to accept the challenge, having read many of May's novels as a boy. He has found it to be a personally satisfying project.